Atlantic Warriors

Atlantic Warriors

Georgina Hunter-Jones

To keep you quiet as long as possible

[signature]

Goodwood 2012.

Fly Fizzi

Publishing
MMII

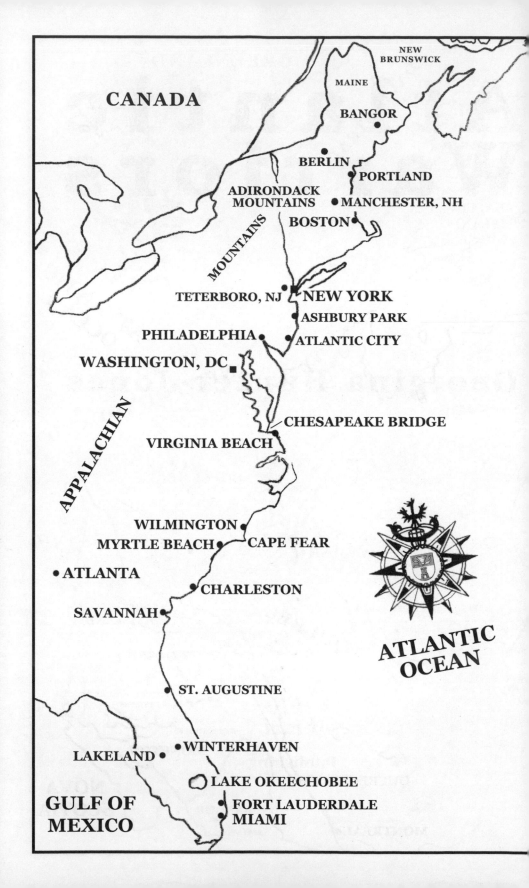

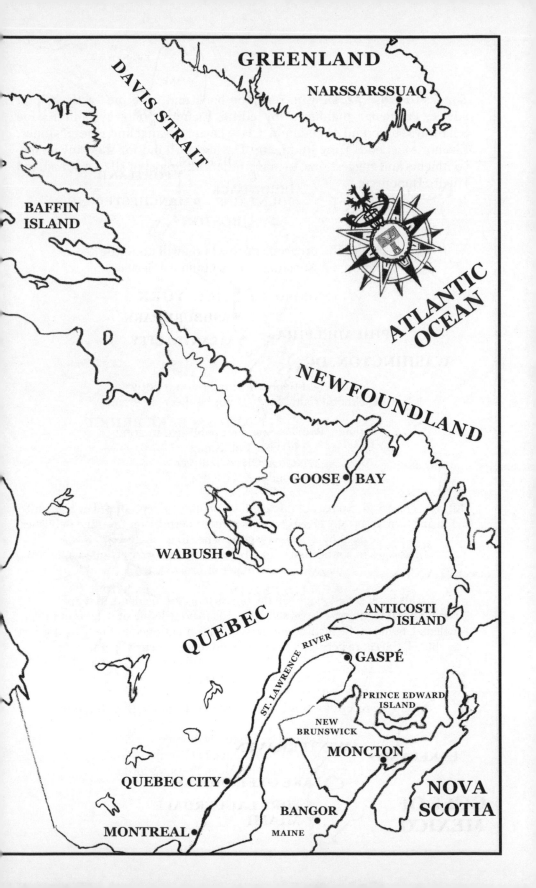

Thanks to those people who read the book and gave me vastly helpful advice. Particular thanks to my editor Richard Solloway, and Karine Solloway. To Berend Abendanon, Clare Hoare, Evangeline Hunter-Jones, Eleanor MacLeod, Tony Rudd, and David Shortland for their invaluable comments and suggestions, to many others and most of all to my husband Hilaire Dubourcq.

Part of the proceeds of this book will go to the
National Association Air Ambulance Services.

Atlantic Warriors was first published in 2002
FlyFizzi Publishing
59 Great Ormond Street
London WC1N-3HZ

ISBN 1-900721-15-5

A catalogue record for this book is available from the British Library.

Designed by Hilaire Dubourcq
Typeset in Bookman and Georgia
Printed and bound by Alden Press, Oxford

Table of Contents

Preflight Cheque	9
A Helicopter in the Hand	11
A Computer in the Bush	17
Unstable Pilots Steer a Leaking Ship	23
Love is a Cruel Pilot	25
Pilot on the Wine-Dark Sea	33
Flying even when his Canvas is Rent	47
Weather does more Business in Winter	49
Pilots gain Reputation from Tempests	53
The Lightning Pilot	57
Coffee Spells Disaster	59
Flying Boots and Spurs	61
If the Pilot Slumbers at the Helm	69
Stretching the Sainsbury's Bag	71
In a Calm Sea Every Man is a Pilot	77
A Kiss through a Veil	89
Fortunate in Fort Lauderdale	97
Charlee's Aeros	109
Heart of Fool's Gold	115
In Chapter Eleven	141
Committing Liberticide	147
The Importance of a Fan	153
Dropping Down with Costly Bales	157
Atlantic Dogs of War	177
Pilots' Pals	215
Hope Springs Eternal	219
Queen of the Scene	221
I Follow Roads	227
Slant Visibility	233
A Computer Game with Humans	239
Major Overhaul	245
British Banana Republic	247
Paling's Policy	253
Hangar Rats	259
A Warrior's Conquest	267
Graffiti Gouged Glass	271
Cooked Cheese	275
Life Enhancing Curve	281
Air-Mail Letters	291
The Wisdom of the Pilot	295
Glossary	*300*

This book is dedicated to my brother Mark,
who lived and died a warrior

Preflight Cheque

Heathrow was still dark. A pervading, misty early morning greyness slipped in through the terminal doors and contaminated the bones of summer-seeking passengers, making them even more irritable than security checks and delays would normally have done. Mothers dragged unwilling children and fathers shouted wantonly, while in their midst an aged-adolescent, with white-boy dreadlocks hanging from his head like a bundle of mop strands, glanced anxiously from his watch to the Arrivals screen. Early morning businessmen streamed importantly around him, bumping and cursing, as he looked up at the gleaming digits.

The boy pulled a scrumpled piece of paper out of his pocket. Anger and disillusionment mixed in his rheumy eyes, unobserved by the moving multitudes. He cursed. Pants! Wrong number. Idiot! Fool. The plane was in and he was late. Falling over his feet, he hastened towards the first class transit lounge, only the dignity of the area preventing him breaking into a headlong run. At the entrance his path was blocked by a security guard, whose body exuded contempt. Ben showed his pass and the sneering castellan, his eyes ostentatiously travelling down the young man's scruffy exterior, motioned him towards the electronic body checker. Sensitive to the patronising glance, Ben walked stiffly through, but the screamer remained indifferently silent.

He turned into the passage and pushed open the heavy door into the Upper Class lounge. Deep pile carpets and designer curtains cut down the noise of the plebeian travellers outside. There were not many people in the room yet, but over on the far side, drinking coffee, was a middle-aged man accompanied by a much younger woman. Ben would have walked straight over to him, winking at her (at least in his dreams), but one of the three girls behind the long, blue, exclusion desk noticed his entrance.

"Can I help you, Sir?" Did she hesitate before enunciating, 'Sir'?

Ben pulled out his pass, scratching himself in his haste. "Special courier service, Mam. I've come to fetch a package."

She looked on her list and saw that this was verified. She smiled at him; brittle he thought. The bitch!

"Your party's over by the window, drinking coffee. Wanted to give you instructions himself."

Fancy that, thought Ben, hearing contempt in her tone. He wanted to tell the bitch he knew well what the guy looked like; having seen a photograph. He wanted to scream at her insolence, did she know who he was!? But he remembered himself in time. "Thanks." His young-boy mutter contrasting with her clean, sharp speech.

As Ben approached the table the man looked up, automatically giving Ben's suit the once over, although he was wearing jeans and leather himself. The young blond didn't even give him a glance. "Hi, you the carrier?"

[9]

"Yup." Ben wanted to say more, something clever, something witty, but was bereft of words. "Yup, Sir, that's me."

"OK. Here's your package. You know what to do. Keep it until my sister picks it up, I don't know when that will be, but you ain't in a hurry are you?"

Ben shook his head obligingly. "Good. She'll deal with you when she picks it up, but this is for your trouble." A hundred dollar note slipped into Ben's top pocket. "Thanks buddy."

And that was it. All he had to do was keep this brown envelop until the pick up. So little for $100 plus. It must be nice not to give a toss about money. He realised he was still standing at the table; alone; man and girl having moved away to the bar. Looking over at the desk-girls, he could see his 'babe' already rising to show him out.

"All right!" he snapped as she approached (at least when he retold the story). "Hold your horses Sheila! I'm going." He felt the $100 in his pocket with surreptitious fingers. Yeah, this was OK. This kind of job, for this kind of money, was his thing. Far better than being a flipping pilot!

A Helicopter in the Hand

Although it was only 6 am the sun shone strongly onto the African veldt, reflective rays which promised throbbing, oppressive heat later in the day. Carrie heard the noise of the helicopter starting and realised she was late; the others were already out, getting ready for the day, while she was still in bed. She jumped up and grabbing a long, cotton dress pulled it straight on, with nothing underneath. She slipped quickly out of the French windows, past the barbecue area, to where the grass rolled away towards the lake. Here, between the sixties huts and the stout wooden post and rails separating the game-park from its more vulnerable occupants, Ignatius had parked the helicopter, ready for this morning's hunt.

As Carrie hastened over, Pierre, the vet, looked up from his medical box where he was prepared his darting gun, his hands white in their rubber gloves, his muscular, bare legs solid in his cropped shorts.

"Afternoon, Carrie," he joked, but his voice was kindly. Pierre was never harsh; always treated women fairly.

"Morning," she replied, moving past quickly, but now moderating her pace, knowing the helicopter could not lift without the vet.

Inside the helicopter Ignatius sat chatting to the journalist. Carrie approached the cockpit from an angle, as she'd been taught to do, and slipped her right hand through the weight-saving, cockpit-cooling, door-less space, putting it proprietorially onto his left leg.

"Just came to wish you a good flight, darling," she murmured.

Ignatius couldn't hear her over the drumming of the helicopter blades, which chorused with the throb of the engine, but he knew what she was saying. Her inability to get up in time to see him off had been legendary since the second year of their marriage. Momentarily checking it was securely in place, he took his right hand off the cyclic control and ruffled her hair, winking at her. "Have a good morning," he mouthed, before leaning forward to motion her away.

Defeated, Carrie stepped back, narrowly avoiding colliding with the vet and his gun, who were approaching the back seat of the helicopter. He caught her shoulder and spun her slightly. "Careful Carrie," he said, and she heard a half-understood presentiment of warning in his voice.

"Thanks," she murmured, backing away towards the huts.

Already she could feel the increasing breeze as Ignatius wound up the helicopter blades, ready to lift off and climb over the fence towards the barren, heat-baked veldt. Pierre strapped himself in tightly, gave her a wave and said something through his headset to the couple in the front. As he did so, Carrie saw Ignatius's left hand lift the collective lever and the helicopter start to rise. The downwash was terrific, and her thin cotton dress sucked away behind her, outlining her underlying nakedness. Carrie crossed her arms, embarrassed lest any of the game-wardens, now climbing into their bakkies preparatory to following Ignatius out onto the veldt, should look back and see her shape. However, all the men were too busy and ignored her.

Carrie waited until the men drove out of the yard, those in the back swaying over the open sides, before she returned to the hut. As she stepped through the elongated sliding windows she sighed, realising that in her haste she'd left them open and the helicopter-induced-whirlwinds had thrown her clothes into a tangled heap in a corner of the room. "Damn!" but it wasn't only the sight of her clothes that made her uneasy.

Outside, two widow birds, who had been feasting companionably on the remains of last night's barbecue, lifted their long tails nervously, ready to run. Carrie saw them and gratuitously threw a shoe towards the elegant splash of coloured feathers. Then felt guilty; on the one hand she didn't want the creatures upset, but on the other she remembered that her bush-born mother had warned her widow birds foretold a death in the household.

"Not," thought Carrie defensively, "that anyone'ud call this combination of bedroom and cockroaches' cooking area a house."

She yanked off her dress, chucking it onto the helicopter created pile and made her way through the cool, tiled-floor corridors to the shower-box, with its paint peeling walls and minute, leaf covered windows. Washing in ice-cold water, she wondered loudly how an arid, barren bushland could have a shower which smelt like an unventilated cave, but she knew the answer: money. When the huts had been built, they were cleverly situated to keep them cool and shady. But now lack of finance had turned cool into plant growth and shade into insect-supporting mould.

Out in the flat Free State shrubland, Ignatius, his right arm resting lightly on his knee, guided the JetRanger with the cyclic control; left, right, up, down; eyes and machine searching. Experience had taught him that the best height to look for sable was 800 feet; lower, they heard you before you saw them; higher, their tan hides melded invisibly with the surrounding scrub. Even at 800 feet, though, the heat was pounding back off the dirt, the scrubby bushes doing little to deflect the sun's angry rays. He felt the sweat rolling down his back and, glancing at the girl beside him he saw her face glistening too. But, he noticed, she was hunched forwards, entranced with the flight, excited by closeness of the ground, the vastness of the shimmering ochre brushland around them and the promise of the chase to come.

Pierre's voice broke into his thoughts over the intercom. "Keal's had a promotion to head office, so he'll be leaving us soon."

"Damn," replied Ignatius, his eyes checking the helicopter's instruments before returning to scour the treeless tracts below, "and he was the best chief we've had. Who's likely to come in his place?"

"The government's putting in an outsider; political appointment."

"Shit!"

"What's this?" asked the journalist, alerted, scenting scandal across the collective, "trouble?"

Ignatius glanced briefly at the young girl. "Oh! It's simply 'Affirmative Action' means we get town men; men who've never seen an animal before and sometimes they don't understand...sometimes I wonder where South Africa is going..."

"Over to your right, Ig, at 3 o'clock," broke in Pierre, "a group of sable, middle distance, grazing."

"Contact."

Ignatius descended until the helicopter was just above the level of the higher bushes, then accelerated towards the group, waiting for the vet to tell him which one. As the helicopter came closer the animals lifted their heads, paused a moment, then, as an item, dived into a headlong gallop away from the approaching noise. It seemed as though a giant mass of dark sand was plunging across the veldt. Then one sable broke away from the others and lunged to the left, destroying the illusion. Another animal followed him, only to change stride and twist right, aiming for some over-hanging bushes.

"That's ours," yelled Pierre his voice girlish with excitement, "the right one! Steady now."

Ignatius turned slightly, pulling the helicopter round and following the buck, trying to give the vet a clear shot out of the right-hand side of the helicopter. But the animal was cunning and ducked under the bushes, stopping immediately. The helicopter overshot with a burst of sensation; greens, browns and purples blurred into a haze beneath them; Ignatius lifting the collective only just in time to clear the bushes.

"Wow!" screamed the journalist, her face suffused with excited-red like a Christmas poinsettia, "that was trick! Something else."

Ignatius turned and brought the helicopter back to the trees, hovering above, trying to drive out the animal beneath with the noise of the rotors. But the old male was wary and although he looked up at the helicopter through the shivering leaves, he stayed under cover.

"Damn! They're getting too clever for us," said Ignatius, giving the girl beside him a conspiratorial smile. "OK. I'm going to climb. Once we're over a thousand the animals can't hear the helicopter, or not so it scares them. I'll get Thom on the radio."

Flipping the radio channel, Ignatius climbed to 1500 feet and stabilised the helicopter. "OK, Thom, bring in the bakkies." He automatically looked in their direction. "You'll have to flush him out."

"OK, Ig," came the reply, scratchy over the aged radio.

As the helicopter crew watched from above, the bakkies jolted their way across the rough, dipping ruts, dodging bushes and bouncing the balancing men in the back, their hands scrabbling to keep a secure finger-hold. The sable watched them, cowering under the protective branches.

"Does this hurt the animal?" asked the journalist nervously.

"Ag, no," replied Pierre, his eyes on the action below, "not as much as not having the jabs. The diseases..."

"I thought this was tagging. That's not really necessary, is it?" she urged, suddenly and unexpectedly provocative.

Ignatius ground his teeth a little. "I'll explain it all to you later," he said tersely, "and show you some other things. For the moment we need to concentrate." He looked at her, then smiled, taking away the rebuke.

She giggled, embarrassed. "Sorry," she put her hand lightly on his shoulder appeasingly.

With a swish of leaves, the sable decided the bakkies were worse than the helicopter and catapulted out through the thinnest bushes, into the clearing and away from the men. His body made a graceful arc as he leapt free and the journalist gave a grateful sigh as the shutter on her camera clicked.

"Wicked!"

The helicopter descended again, speeding after the sable, low across the sand, its downwash causing occasional flurries of dust as they brushed a wind-swept pile. Pierre positioned his gun and looked down the sights. The sable was running now, flat-out, muscles at full stretch, powerful haunches pushing the lithe body along. Ignatius increased his speed, came up close, parallel to the pulsing beige form; holding level, using his instincts to follow its twists and turns, watching the deer with the concentration of the born hunter.

Then, unexpectedly, the animal stopped. Feinted left. Darted in front of the helicopter, crossing close and slipping away behind. Ignatius swore.

"One caught the skid like that once, nearly brought us down."

He repositioned. Turning the helicopter unnecessarily sharply, he saw the sable trotting more slowly now, apparently aiming to return where he had last seen his tribe. Ignatius dipped the helicopter's nose and increased speed, quickly levelling with the tired deer. He felt his jaw tense with concentration, and instinctively stretched out his chin. He kept pace with the sable. For a moment helicopter and animal ran neck 'n neck. Then, with a dull hiss like a valve releasing steam, the dart shot out from Pierre's gun.

"Got 'im?"

"Yup. In the rump."

Looking down, the journalist could see a little red tuft hanging off the animal's skin, like a splash of paint on a child's duffel coat.

"Great!" Relaxing, letting his chin drop, Ignatius began to climb again, explaining to the journalist that they needed to wait until the drug took effect.

"How long will that be?"

"Ag. It depends," explained Pierre, "on various factors including the age and size of the animal, strength of the potion. I'm timing." He checked his watch. "You don't want them to take too long to collapse or they could do themselves some harm, or even wander into one of the lakes. On the other hand you don't want the potion too strong or you can hurt the animal. It's all a matter of compromise."

She nodded, panting slightly. She felt so happy and thrilled she could burst. This was living. This was why she had become a journalist, to explore different worlds, to feel the pulse of life away from her dull home. She took some photographs of the now slowing sable.

"Wow! This is just wild! Wicked. Intense."

A Computer in the Bush

In the hut Carrie was bored. Her shower finished, she had nothing to do until the hunters returned. She thought about going back to bed, but bed was so final: like the grave. She could have played computer games; she'd played 2,569 hours already, (the computer recorded it, she did not) or battled with the failing phone lines to try and surf the web, using its educative powers to supplement the small amount of knowledge she had gleaned from her erratic schooling. In Cape Town, with its greater sophistication, she had traversed from: 'A' Aviation: feats of fearless flyers, to 'Q' Quotations: after-dinner speaking, best; enabling her to know such life-stalling facts as Chaucer used 8,000 words, double the vocabulary of previous writers and the best known Shakespearian ciphers.

Brewing depression with her tea, Carrie flopped down on the sofa. Immediately the old Davenport enveloped her in a hole and her cup tipped out of her hand. Milky brown liquid flashed across her newly washed dress and onto the bedding, where it quickly soaked into the faded sofa cushions. A sweetly pungent scent drifted off the hot material, forecasting worse to come.

She half swore and jumped up, looking for something to wipe off the worst of the damage. Inside the Davenport's hole, partly torn by the springs, was a newspaper, a copy of USA Today. She pulled it out, surprised to see that it was relatively recent, dated co-incidentally with the day of her father's funeral, when she had been recalled to the UK by her step-sisters. She wondered idly where it had come from; not from Ignatius that was sure. The man had never been outside the country; unlike her or her previous husbands, all of whom were great travellers.

She tore the paper into long, thick strips, folded them into pads, and began rubbing the wet material. To her disgust, written words slipped off the pages and merged with the tea and milk into dark, inky stains.

"Oh, shit!" She suddenly wondered if her father was right when he had said that she drifted through life like a particle of air in a Sainsbury's bag, always believing itself in control. At least, she thought, there was romance in that. He was more like an angry accountant, noting every grinding detail and despairing of the world. Nonetheless she'd cried at his funeral. But whether for him, for herself or because she had lost any hope of finding that illusion of omnipotent goodness supposed to be a father, she did not know.

He hadn't spoken to her much anyway, after her mother left. Instead he had presented her with a continual stream of step-sisters, each younger and more forthright than the last. Then, after her marriage to "another fucking foreigner!" he threw out the cheese board.

While Carrie went to 'Kaas Kopia', her father's (and Hitler's) term, learning Dutch obsessively, her father burnt clogs in his yard shouting "pea-soup artists!" The neighbours called the police.

"Fuck," thought Carrie angrily, stuffing the remains of 2nd March's USA Today back into the hole, 'stupid bastard! We were both caught in the deceptive ecosystem of the Sainsbury's bag.'

"Bzz, bzz, bzz..." Carrie looked up. "Roger, wilco...." the radio by Carrie's side suddenly roared into action, "sable.. buzzz... bushes....bzz.... in sight.." and then trailed off leaving nothing but static.

She shrugged. Reception in the game park was terrible but Carrie was used to it. In the beginning, her heart full of love for her pilot husband, she had kept the radio by her side at all times, listening feverishly for the sound of his voice; excited by his excitements, pleased by his pleasures. Now, after five years of marriage, she only kept it on in case there was trouble.

Out in the scrub the sable had fallen, but Pierre was worried. The drug had taken too long to take effect. The animal was unhurt, but he had wandered a long way from the point of impact. Pierre decided to increase the strength of the drug for the following runs. But first an ear tag.

The helicopter landed about 20 meters from the staggering sable. He was still upright, sitting on his haunches, his head weaving slightly with impending sleep. Pierre jumped out, closely followed by the journalist, and ran towards the animal. Ignatius stayed at the helicopter's controls. If the deer did plunge towards the helicopter, it wouldn't be the first time. Once an angry rhinoceros had hit the tail boom, and Ignatius had been lucky to get away without injury. Those close calls made him question his on-edge way of making a living in this sweaty heat.

He fidgeted in his seat; his joints got stiff these days. The flying was still exciting but now you had to deal with the politics as well. When he started as a plane washer in Canada there had been an enormous freedom in the power of flight, as indeed when he returned to Africa after his jaunt abroad. All the thrill of the chase across the veldt, without the stress of the mother state. Then politics changed and he got married.

The journalist turned his way and waved; lips lifting he waved back. He watched the way the girl's buttocks swelled inside her shorts as she loped towards the vet, her camera held out in front like a boob extension. Why was fantastic, world-shaking sex never enough for women, he wondered idly.

The foot-rangers were out of the bakkies, closing carefully in on the animal. Scared, the sable made a last attempt to get away; staggered to his feet, took a few faltering steps, and collapsed again. Thom jumped in from behind and caught his horns. Immediately Pierre was there to support him, tag in hand. Ready with his quick, decisive movements. In moments the animal was blindfolded, tagged and Pierre was already administering the antidote.

A quick jet from the syringe, an instinctive shudder from the animal's sweaty skin and they stepped back, tensely poised, awaiting the effect. Silent. Only the gentle buzz of breath and insects in the hot air, and the reassuring smell of wet animal. Then the sable heaved his haunches. Heavily. At once there was a hasty, chaotic retreat to the vehicles. Only Pierre waiting calmly as ever.

As the sable clambered up, fazed but unhurt by his ordeal, Pierre too legged it back towards the helicopter. The journalist was ahead of him and already in the passenger seat, chatting to Ignatius; her hands waving in excitement as he leant towards her, clearly entranced.

Carrie walked out onto the patio and looked towards the park, hoping to hear the sound of the returning helicopter. There was only the sound of birds. She walked down to the lake and felt the heat of the sun on her back as she walked. Far, far above a plane crossed silently overhead, on its way to the Atlantic. Carrie watched it dreamily, caught by the romance of distant aircraft and their flights into the unknown. It was lovely here, there was no doubt about that. But dull. And too much meat. They chased it. Saved it. Medicated it. Tagged it. Culled it. Bred it. Lived with it. And even ate it. Meat. Flesh. Meat. She lent on a tree and stared into the water, slipping her painted feet out of her sandals. Everyone here laughed at her townish ways but she liked dressing up, got bored with jeans and a T-shirt. 'Let them laugh,' she said loudly, grinding her nails into the bark.

After the death of her first husband, she left Thailand for the UK. Rich enough for a 19 year old to avoid work, she quickly fell into a chardonnay and cappuccino set, drifting around from bar to bar, conversations inspired by the Daily Mail, laughing when unamused, waiting for people who didn't ring back. Others of her age were forging careers at university or actually working, but her group mocked them; calling them hacks and techies. Even so, unease remained. And, in an attempt to 'spit out the butt-ends of my days and ways,' she began travelling again.

With her facility for languages she found herself similar sets in Paris and Rome. Within a year she had become the vacant, gabbling Eurotrash her first husband despised. Then she met Kees van der Pick. Because of her youth she confused his passivity with profundity and saw his jokes as humour: she assumed that his apparent wealth would offer her something more substantial than her present wandering. They married three months later, in a romantic, fog-encrusted wedding on a Dutch beach.

Marriage, thought Carrie, is only for the unwed; others should know better. She put thoughts of her ex-husbands aside. The past so long ago and indisputably in different countries. Shaking her head Carrie walked back into the house, deciding to make it up with her third husband and try again.

Pierre had changed the strength of the mixture and the helicopter crew had downed another three sable. The first two animals worked well, falling easily and rising delightedly once the antidote was given; bounding away, glad not to be on the dinner table. However, the last one fell lethargically and, even after the antidote, seemed unwilling to get up.

"Is he dead?" asked the journalist nervously, "he will be OK won't he?"

"Ag sure," Pierre reassured her, "they get a form of shock though and sometimes they just want to decline. White muscle shock. Don't worry, the boys will get him up. But that's why we never leave them until they're on their feet. Ig can you call them?"

Ignatius called the bakkies on the crackling radio and, as the helicopter crew watched from above, the cars came in towards the kneeling sable. At first a couple of the game wardens jumped out and advanced with their arms outstretched, calling 'oy, oy, oy,' and clapping. The animal ignored them. More adventurous then, the wardens tapped the sable with a long stick but he merely flinched and rested his muzzle more firmly on the striated ground. The wardens looked back at the bakkies, shrugging. Thom nodded. He drove his bakkie in close, closer still, until finally the car tapped the sable's rump. He drew back, and came in again, gently shoving the animal. The game wardens 'oy oy'ed again. For a moment it seemed nothing would happen. Then slowly, lugubriously, the animal got to its feet; stood for a moment. Unwillingly it started walking away; stood again for a moment, its tail swishing; turned its head and watched the bakkies. Then, unexpectedly, jumped and cascaded away from the watching wardens. The men gave a cheer; so did the journalist. Ignatius laughed. He pushed down the helicopter's collective and made his approach towards the cracked earth. He turned to Pierre as they descended near the bakkies.

"Is that it for this morning?"

"Yup."

"OK, do you want to go back with the bakkies, while I show our young journo a bit of real flying!" He grinned measuringly at the journalist.

Pierre hiccoughed, understanding immediately. "Sure! I need to talk to Thom. Important things! See you later big boy! You too Mam."

"Oh, wow!" breathed the journalist, "I love this so much. Bye Pierre. Wicked to have seen you at work." She stuck her thumb up. "See you later. OK 'big boy' show me your worst!"

And then she screamed, because Ignatius had lifted them up into a towering take-off. Straight up to a thousand feet.

Pierre walked over to the bakkies shaking his head in amusement. The first couple of years after Ignatius had married Carrie he had seemed like a changed man; courteous, loving, spending time at home. But now he was back to all his wicked, womanising ways again. It was hard to see how the marriage could last. Privately he wondered how much longer the English girl would stay. There was no doubt she was bored here. Unhappy too. Pierre had worked all his life with animals and he recognised signs of distress hidden to others. It didn't pour off her like it did with some women, but it was there nonetheless.

A shaft of sunlight struck Carrie's eyes and she looked up at the clock. It was nearly nine, soon the happy hunters would be returning. The journalist giggling and excited as she had been all week, getting her wires wrapped around Carrie's feet and giggling more and more. Asking dull, blindingly obvious questions.

"Dreadful girl," thought Carrie. Her mind didn't want to speculate on why she disliked her so much. "Tiresome child. She even speaks too fast."

She got up and, digging into the damp-smelling formica and hardboard cupboard, looked for the plates. As she was stretching deep into the fridge for the yards of meat insisted on by Afrikaaner men, she heard the bakkies drawing in, out in the yard. That was slightly unusual in that her husband, in the quicker vehicle, tended to be already tucking into plates of blood sausages, kudu and venison by the time they turned up. But she knew him, knew that with a journalist, especially a nubile writhing woman like that one, he'd be showing off, taking her along the shore and driving a herd of poor hapless animals into the lake just to show he could.

Carrie heard a patter of little feet, somewhat uneven owing to the swaying of the rickety wooden steps. With a bang the door thrust open, hitting the wall behind with a dull thud, and one of the younger game wardens burst into the room, panting from the force of his running.

"Mrs Nordsuitlaan come now." He gasped at her.

Carrie stared at him. Bacon smoke from the greasy pan filled her eyes. She was making breakfast; couldn't go running around now. What did he want her to do, anyway? Look for game at this time? She waved him away impatiently, her heavy bracelets clinking with indignation.

"No time!" she said. She usually spoke in telegraphic style to the wardens. English was their third language and Carrie never thought they were up to a proper conversation. "Busy!"

"An accident!" he panted. "Come."

She had a vision of that half witted journalist and her wires. She could just imagine her having got into trouble somewhere. Perhaps she'd fallen out of the helicopter; they never used doors in this heat. There'd be hell to pay if she was hurt. In the old days journalists were just part of life's flotsam; now they were like gold dust and had to be cosseted like babies.

"They shouldn't let a journalist up here in my opinion," she muttered. "So! What's happened? What has she done...?"

The game warden shook his head and there were tears in his eyes. In spite of the 30 degree temperature, Carrie shivered as she heard him say very quietly. "The helicopter...the lake.....an accident....so sorry..."

Unstable Pilots Steer a Leaking Ship

The MD's office was large, the windows were one of English Heritage's finest pieces, and a deeply red leather finish improved an otherwise simple oak desk. Behind this, reading the Training Captain's report rather impatiently, was the new director, a short man whose spreading girth and greying beard made him look like an aging bumble bee. In front of him, relaxed as a mother's favourite son, was the latest of his pilots to be caught drunk on duty.

This time the Training Captain had included a list of the pilot's previous misadventures: flight under a low bridge (in a jet); forgetting to renew his mandatory licence stamp; unauthorised aerobatics (also in a jet); numerous indiscretions with cabin staff; and several occasions asleep on duty. How did they ever employ such a fool? The new director was tolerant. He knew he was admired for his fair-minded rationale. But this pilot had gone too far. Looped his last loop as the Top Banana liked to say. Unwillingly he looked up.

"So," he said, picking at something hard in the wing of his nose with his left thumb and forefinger. "You've been here before."

The tall moustachioed man in jeans opposite him swung backwards, balancing his chair on creaking hind legs. He'd put his leather hat on the desk, and was smoking in defiance of the prohibiting sign. "We have too, and a fine office it is."

The director ignored the levity. Pulling the hard bit from his nose, he slipped it into his mouth. "Why were you driving drunk to the airport? Look, I know you boys take risks, that the oxygen gets used for quick-fix hangover cures, but you were three times over the limit! Christ! Three times! Why didn't you take a taxi? Keep it internal! Now it's all over the papers. Look!"

He threw the middle section of one of the tabloids towards the pilot. It slithered over the shiny red leather and slipped onto the floor, where neither man was willing to retrieve it. Lying face up on the Turkish rug, large, bold letters proclaimed:

Safe Skies or Skinful?
Police Nab Legless Pilot on his way to work !!!

Below were pictures of an aircraft in the company livery and a long, imaginative report by the policeman in charge. The caption slapped across the photo read: Booze Airlines!

"Well," said the pilot rocking cheerfully, "it's a matter of the angle of the dangle. Oscar Wilde said all publicity is good publicity."

"Did he? I doubt he ran an airline then. And the policeman says you tried to bribe him. Why? You know what these Rozzers are, after any excuse to become celebrities; he'll be getting his own TV show next!"

With an effort he pulled himself back from anger and tried to be positive, as recommended by the company shrink. "Look, the airline doctor knows a good psychiatrist who specialises in drink related illness....."

"Drink and fly, you rule the sky. I find alcohol improves my flying. Have you tried it yourself?"

"I don't drink," the director snapped, fiddling with a pen on his desk.

"I wonder," asked the pilot swinging down the chair, "while you've got that pen in your hand, would you be after writing me a reference?"

"What?! Get out!"

The pilot didn't move. "Now," he said, "suppose that I couldn't do my fluid flying any more, but still had to make a living in this cold inhospitable world. I'd be using my motor mouth, perhaps about the time the undercart got stuck down and we had to fly like that all the way back from JFK; risking so much for so few. Then suppose I got delayed. One of our older captains purposely holding the flight to get into another duty period and more money. Ah, the joy of 'lateness pay'. On the other hand you know how keen the public are to travel fast and safely these days..."

The director's pen hovered like a student pilot over the helicopter pad. "Well," he began uncertainly, "well..."

Love is a Cruel Pilot

Carrie was a widow again, the following weeks passing in a daze.

After the accident the game-wardens had taken her down to the lake, where the helicopter lay half submerged in the water. Its tail cone, detached by the force of the accident, had fallen rotor-up in the mud of the bank, where it sat looking like a ship's mast above a sunken vessel. The major part of the helicopter was some distance away, out in the lake. The blades and engine had been knocked off, dangling alongside the main body by an orange thread, while the cockpit, half submerged in the water looked like a scalped fish.

The wardens had found three boats and these were clustered around the passenger side of the cockpit, where two men were attempting to drag out the girl's body. Watching them from the shore, Carrie realised she was expecting the girl to look up and say something, to giggle as she had been doing all week. Although this was the third dead body Carrie had seen close up, she still could not get used to the curious way the dead resemble the living; in all but spontaneous movement. Of Ignatius there was no sign.

Pierre came over to Carrie and took her arm, leading her away from the activity out in the lake to one of the bakkies. "Sit down, Carrie," he said, gently pushing her shoulders so that she plopped down on the worn seat. She hardly noticed the hardness, her mind absorbed by one thought.

"Ignatius?"

"We don't know. We are still hopeful. His seat belt was undone and that could mean he climbed out and went to get help before anyone arrived. Alternatively we have to accept it might be that he was thrown out of the machine, and to be honest, Carrie, knowing the man as you do, you must admit it would be very unlikely he'd leave his passenger without pulling her out too." He paused and squeezed her shoulder. "We're still looking, Carrie."

The next few days were a blur with sharp moments. Carrie woke up the following morning; realised Ignatius was not beside her; thought she was late, that his flight had already left. Then she remembered. And tears flooded her eyes, followed by a dull, dull ache in her heart. "Women," she thought sadly, "love all the time; men only when it suits them."

She remembered telling Pierre that it was unfair. She told him a story of her teens, when, at school, in what she called her purpled-out period, she had had an affair with the languages master, who was kept on while she was expelled. She remembered finding her first husband dead in bed.

The pain was always worse in the evening, when Pierre and the others had gone. She eased it in the only way she knew how: computer games, a multidimensional fight between green giants and an often failing super-hero. Carrie told herself she liked computer games because here, when all seemed lost to the green sharks in the boiling lake, when the future led only to destruction, the superhero could turn the game around and win: good practice for life. However, a creeping reality suggested that only when playing games did she feel like a winner.

The government sent divers to the park and the lake was trawled for Ignatius's body. Carrie asked Pierre if it was possible that Ignatius had been eaten by crocodiles. He gave her a strange look, before squeezing her shoulder again. "Don't think about it, Carrie."

At the end of the week someone escorted Carrie to the airport, and back to her house in Cape Town. Pierre promised to let her know if anything happened, but she could see that gradually everyone was accepting that Ignatius could not have survived. Pierre explained that even if Ignatius had been able to leave the helicopter and set off across the park to find help, the hot weather was against him. He didn't say 'so were the animals'. Somehow he didn't like the idea of telling Carrie that even if the crash and the water hadn't got him, one of those animals he looked after might have.

Then there was the funeral. Ignatius's family, with strangely caustic humour, had decided to bury the mangled helicopter rotor blades in the coffin in his place. They explained that the rest of the salvaged helicopter might be worth something.

As a mark of respect to the dead helicopter pilot his sister organised a wake in the traditional manner. She pointed out that, since Carrie knew little of her husband's traditions, or indeed his tastes at all, it would be better if his sister did everything. Sissy even arranged a fly-in by a local Orynx and it's crew; always glad to help in sending off a fellow pilot.

In the yard outside the church Sissy had made a barricade of barriers; favoured guests put their cars next to each metal fence, forming a little circle in which the helicopter could land. Carrie, understanding heli-copter-induced whirlwinds, tried to protest, but her sister-in-law merely smiled deafly.

Exactly on time, just as the funeral service ended, the helicopter arrived. All the guests flooded out of the church. They entered the church-yard as the large, impassive helicopter began its descent onto the make-shift pad. As the guests watched, the sand between the barriers churned up in little dust devils. As they admired the pilot's skill, grabbing their hats, they noticed the wind getting stronger. Slowly, undramatically, bushes began bowing, an open window in the church banged loudly back and forth, and the little trolley supporting the blade-filled pine coffin slipped away down the path towards the grave; hurrying as though chased by Ignatius's ghost. No one, however, noticed the trolley, entranced as they all were by the simultaneous lifting of the barriers.

In a great well orchestrated sweep, all Sissy's delicately placed fences rose in deadly unison and threw themselves against the guests' cars, including Sissy's. While the guests stared gormlessly at the devastation, Carrie's muttered, 'told you so' was drowned out by the phut phut of the helicopter's continued descent.

Then there was the reading of the will. Carrie felt weird about hearing the financial direction of a man who might not be dead, but subsequently realised that since all the credit-worthy bank accounts were in Ignatius' name, they'd better get on with it and zip up to probate or she wouldn't have any money to live on. The lawyer apparently didn't object, since he allowed her to make an appointment via his secretary.

Carrie's house was in a sheltered, jacaranda-filled area under the shelter of Table Mountain and she decided to walk down to the lawyer's office in Kloof. Not a long walk, but a good one for soothing an aching soul, with its warm scent of musky flowers, and the filtered patterns of leafy blue light. Although she knew she could never be happy again, the realisation that she was probably going to be left a considerable sum of money did help to lessen the pain. Besides, she had to admit to herself, Ignatius had not been as loving recently as he had when they married five years before.

Knowing Ignatius' preference for modern things, Carrie had vaguely expected the lawyer's office to be in a new block. So she was rather surprised to find herself arriving at an older, colonial, building with a small door and creaky stairs. Only the windows had been recently renovated, and that had clearly been done on the cheap as the rust was already beginning to show through the concealing plastic skin. There was, however, a large vase of jacaranda blooms on the table, giving a blue-wood scent to the reception and allowing Carrie to ignore the film of dust on the waiting room chair, which was already turning sticky. Having let Carrie in to the office, the receptionist said she was going out to lunch and left, although it was only 11.30.

The inner office was appropriately gloomy, with monstrous wooden, colonial furniture emphasising the smallness of the room. Not much imagination had gone into decoration, Carrie noticed, as slits of light shone through the modernised window onto her attractive black silk funeral outfit: a recent extravagance, which she felt sure Ignatius would have applauded.

Mr Barbar, the lawyer, was an absurdly over jolly man. Carrie found it hard to relax opposite his constant benign smile. A third generation South African of Scottish extraction, he had kept the infamous ruddy colouring and stocky frame of his ancestors but seemed to have lost most of their rugged bravery. Indeed like many of his non-genetic forebears, he suffered from Lawyer's Caution, which forced him to pepper his speech with muttered, often unintelligible, phraseology and to make light remarks at inappropriate moments, as men will do when they are embarrassed or have something to hide.

He glanced at his watch, smiling widely. "So, Mrs Nordsuitlaan, shall I cast the first stone? Not a heavy one I hope!"

"Please."

"Talking of stones....I assume your husband was insured?"

"Of course," Carrie nodded to emphasize the point, then found she couldn't stop, like a nodding dog in the face of his merriment. "I signed the cheque out of our joint account only a couple of months ago."

"Well done. Er...Do you know...did he have any..investments...or any pension policies..annuities?"

Carrie shrugged, stroking the silk of her dress. "How would I know? He did all the financial things, I just signed where he asked me to."

"Oh," Mr Barbar laughed, muttering some joke about blond women and ink pens, which Carrie couldn't follow.

"Well now, to the will. As you know, you and your husband made mutually compatible wills just after your marriage, leaving all your worldly goods to each other. Brave 'eh!" he laughed happily. "However, I think it is only fair that I should just remind you about South African law. I'm sure you know this already, but as a foreigner you may have had different ideas. Prejudices obscuring reality. You follow?"

He raised his eyebrows and Carrie, noticing a chill from the window, wondered if he wasn't waffling a little. She wanted to know how much.

"No, I don't! What do you mean?"

"I was simply referring to the marital law in South Africa, which is based on the old Dutch law...you follow my drift..clear as Rouke's snow 'eh?"

"No. You mean we weren't legally married?"

This time the smile was reassuring. "No, no, nothing like that. It was just...when you and your husband married you sold your flat in London and put the money into a house in Cape Town..."

"Yes?" Carrie wondered why her heart had started beating faster. "My beautiful, jacaranda bowered house. The best thing I ever did was buy that beauty.."

"Er no," said the lawyer, still smiling but moving slightly back in his large, colonial chair as though to avoid the drama, "you see under Old Dutch Law, everything a wife owns belongs to her husband...."

"Yes? So?"

"Well, the problem there is that, because, as I say, and as indeed you no doubt know, under our Old Dutch Law everything belongs to the husband, and you see, while your husband was alive he made use of this ability, to do what you might call a little investment."

"Investment?"

The price of the silk dress passed in front of her eyes like a death threat. It was cold in that office; even without air-conditioning.

"Umm... and so he sold the house, which under Old Dutch Law he was entitled to do, although one would have thought nowadays he might have informed you." He gave Carrie a peripheral look, tinged with a smile and hastened on. "But, of course, I know nothing of how you and your husband conducted your domestic affairs...and he put the money into a plane."

Carrie stared at him, noticing that his red hair had bald patches. She was confused, the plane coming rather too quickly after the domestic affairs. She trusted Ignatius but felt instinctively uneasy. Putting her hand on the arm of the old colonial chair she steadied herself, reassured by the wooden lion under her palm. "What do you mean? Where was the plane going?"

"Oh, nono," he said, shaking his head so his red hair waved at her like a warning. "Very funny, my dear. I meant he bought a plane with the money."

"Are you saying he sold my house and bought a plane!? No! I don't believe it. Why would he? Anyway we're ..that is ..I am still living there."

"Your husband was paying rent, but unfortunately the landlord wants you out now." The smile was sympathetic. "He thinks it isn't right for a woman to be living alone."

Carrie said nothing. Not right? Sure! And I'm a sable rug.

Confused by her silence, the lawyer started to explain again, his voice growing kinder by the word. But Carrie was floundering; she wanted to understand, not to be patronised.

"You're telling me I own a plane. God! It wasn't the helicopter he was flying...that wasn't his? I'm sure that was his family's."

"No," said the lawyer, pinching the end of his nose, "this is an aeroplane...that is with wings, not rotor blades"

"Well that is something! What sort of plane? An airliner? Commuter plane? Is it leased? How am I receiving income from it?"

The smile was one of those adult, concerned smiles that parents give to children. Carrie understood it and felt a deep urge to walk out of the door: to be reborn and start again like a computer game.

"Well, you aren't exactly." His voice dropped and he began muttering again, "income comes in and out....sometimes you buy, often you sell..."

Carrie focused on one comprehensible word. "Sell? Good. Where is it? Cape Town? Jo-burg? Stellenbosch?"

"No," said the lawyer, "it's in Florida."

It didn't make sense, of course. Florida is a suburb of Johannesburg and, as far as she knew, a built up area. But she kept plugging on. Clearly lawyers were nuts, bound up in the rules of indecipherable legislation.

"Florida!? Is there an airport there? Or is it in a museum?"

"Not Florida in Johannesburg. Sorry, I was thinking internationally."

"Internationally? What? You mean..Florida in the USA? How? He's never been there!"

"Your husband saw it as an investment opportunity," the lawyer said, neatly avoiding a direct answer.

He lent over his desk and passed a folder towards her. Lines of writing joggled in front of her eyes. Inside was a picture of tethered aeroplanes. One was circled with black marker. Minute. Tiny! Fifty of them would have fitted in a Jumbo, maybe a hundred. Carrie couldn't believe it. She felt sick.

"Is that..this..it?"

Off he went into export, the fall of the Rand, the strong dollar and so forth again but Carrie wasn't listening. Her loving, sensationalist husband had sold her beautiful, shadeful, scent-creating, elegant little house to buy a single engine, four seat, under-sized rust-bucket called a Piper Warrior. Unseen! A thing last used Heavens knows when for Heaven's knows what. A note said it was built in 1978, had a 160 hp Lycoming engine and a maximum speed of 145 miles per hour. It was worth $20,000. She stared at the lawyer, who had stopped talking and was looking at his desk drawer as though it concealed a fortune.

"$20,000 US! What else did he leave me?"

"Nothing."

"What!? What do you mean nothing? What nothing? How nothing?" screamed Carrie, feeling like King Lear, and comically wanting to add, 'mend your speech lest you mar my fortune.'

"There is nothing in his bank account. An overdraft in fact. Unless you know of any shares or other accounts, there is nothing. Everything went into the plane."

Carrie continued to stare at the lawyer, gob-smacked. "No, impossible," she said eventually. "Why would he do that?"

"Well," said Mr Barbar humorously, smiling as ever. "Perhaps he was thinking of starting a new business flying small passengers from America to South Africa. They might advertise it as 'the most individual attention you'll ever get on an international flight!'"

Carrie didn't laugh. She shut her eyes.

"Wait! I sold my flat in England for £250,000, put that into a house in Cape Town. There was another £200,000 in the bank.." She opened her eyes and looked up. The lawyer's red hair was waving at her again.

"...you're telling me the only thing I've got left out of around half a million pounds is this plane! A $20,000 plane? How can that be? Where did the rest go?"

"Ah," said the lawyer cheerfully, "that is the mystery. All we know for certain is the house is sold and the plane was purchased. I shall become a detective in your cause." He smiled busily, and checked his watch. "I shall examine the resale value of planes, but until then..." He rose, indicating, by tapping his papers smartly into a tight bundle and no longer smiling, that their interview had concluded.

Carrie had a headache; this was all she had left of three husbands. She slammed the office door to ease her pulsating emotions, nearly knocking the old hinges out of place.

"Ha! Three husbands down the drain and all I've got out of it is a lousy no-value plane the other side of the Atlantic. Thank God he was insured."

There was no news from the lawyer for a couple of weeks, and every day was a fight for Carrie. Her Indian landlord made it quite clear that he thought the whites had had their allotted sphere here in Africa and it was time to head towards the departure gates, especially for 'Moneyless Brits' who couldn't pay their rent on time. She rang the insurance company everyday, the operatives getting testier each time they told her; 'claims always take a minimum of 21 working days. You will be contacted in due course of time.'

Eventually the lawyer did get in contact. Beaming down the phone, he said that she could sell the plane where it stood in Florida for around $20,000, or take it to the UK where she could expect to get between $40,000 and $50,000 at present rate of exchange. He dis-advised trying to sell it in South Africa where the market was currently limited.

"Fine," she said, "no problem. I'll learn to fly and take it back to Britain from Florida myself. It can't be that hard, thousands of fools do it."

The lawyer laughed. "I was thinking of a container," he said. Giving her some good advice which later, as she hung poised over a bank of trees with a dead engine, she wished she had taken.

Carrie had to find somewhere to live until she had sorted out the plane. In her low financial state there were only two choices: Cape Town, where she could live with her sister-in-law; or London, where she could force herself upon a distant cousin. After a short conversation with Sissy it became obvious there was only one choice: London.

Her sister-in-law wept when Carrie left. Carrie had given her an ultimatum; a first class ticket to London, or a permanent guest. Cursing her brother, Sissy paid. The lawyer agreed to sell Carrie's furniture, unlikely to attain even the price of an economy ticket.

"Goodbye, Sissy," said Carrie, outside the airport, looking pointedly at the dents on the car.

"Goodbye! Darling! We won't come in with you. It will only excite the children. Have a great life. Personally I'd love you to stay, darling, but you'll be much happier elsewhere. Our ways always were too complicated for you. Darling." Air kisses followed.

"Bitch!" Carrie thought. Then laughed, remembering the perky spirit that had sent her travelling at nineteen, nearly ending up in a brothel: and that she had given her nephew the contents of her husband's work-shed, including a large packet of stink bombs.

On the flight to London she read a British newspaper, hoping to acclimatise herself to the country she was returning to after ten years. And wished she hadn't. The Britain ahead of her was, the paper said, entering a deep depression, full of race riots and animal diseases. Smoke from burnt cows hung over most of the country, creating equivalent human sicknesses. It had rained non-stop for the last six months. The government was using credit cards and emails for mass supervision. Airline pilots regularly arrived for work drunk. Human rage was so bad that supermarkets had been forced to make their aisles ONE WAY only. It was very cold. And Jerry Adams was standing for president.

"Oh, Africa!" Cried Carrie, as the plane dipped in and out of cloud on its descent into Heathrow. "Why did I ever leave you?"

Pilot on the Wine-Dark Sea

Carrie's cousin, Roberta, lived in an inner-city suburb, an investment which had failed to come up. A land of divided terraced houses and wash-ing-filled patios, with collapsing wooden fences and chicken wire rather than tall, selective walls. Roberta lived there alone, like a settler with siege-mentality, bombarding the council in-trays with anger-focused mis-siles about the state of the streets, the never emptied recycling bin and the groups of boys. Day and night children's voices filled the street; laughing, playing football, throwing bottles, and fag butts, onto the railway track. Older boys sat dropping pistachio shells from stationary cars, waiting for business contacts.

Here blood began to look more like tomato ketchup when Roberta asked. "You planning to stay long? I may have to charge you rent, you know. I'm not made of money."

When Carrie explained that she was going to bring her plane back from America and sell it, Roberta was characteristically succinct. "Impossible!"

"Thanks! What do..?"

"Do you know how far it is from America to England?"

"Of course I.."

They were sitting in the living room, a typical Victorian double room with separating doors. Roberta, who had a liking for coffee table books, pulled one towards her; a glossy bound Atlas of the World. She flipped it open on the World-Political. She pointed. "See this; America. See this tiny little pink spot; England. See this.."

She stamped her hand on half the page.

"...water! Water, water, everywhere and not a drop to drink....! How are you, who has never flown.."

"I had a helicopter lesson once!"

"Precisely! You, who have never flown, are going to bring some single-engine thing back across all that water. Ha ha! Ever counted the number of engines on a Jumbo? It sure ain't one. Ha."

"Yeah but.."

"Impossible! No wonder we lost the Empire. Do you even know how far that little thing can go without getting more petrol?"

"No, but.."

"Remember what happens when you run out of petrol 'eh? "

"Yes, but..."

"So! Where are the petrol stations in the Atlantic 'eh? Or will you be landing on ocean-going tankers?" Roberta laughed dryly.

"OK," said Carrie, finally able to stop her cousin, "I don't know now, but I will. I am going to learn to fly. I am going to fetch it from America, and sell it here and make a fortune. This plane is going to be my saviour."

"Yeah. And I'm the high priestess."

Ignoring Roberta's pessimism, Carrie ensconced herself in the spare room, got a generous loan from her cousin's bank, on the strength of the Warrior miles away in Florida, and began looking for flying lessons.

In flying magazines, imaginatively named Flyer, Pilot and Flight, she discovered a hoard of incredibly attractive sounding schools; so cheap Carrie imagined they must be giving away flying lessons with tea spoons. She booked with the 'École de Vol' at Biggin Hill Airport. The phone girl said there was a special discount for weekdays. Another price reduction! Wonderful. Everybody in South Africa had been complaining about the Rand to Pound value. Nonsense. London was cheap.

The following Monday Carrie hired a car to take her to Biggin Hill. Here, though, she saw Rand earner's complaints had a point; car hire was not cheap. Yet cars were everywhere, and, it seemed to her, used as she was to courteous African drivers, out to get her. Either they blocked the road or they sat on her tail hooting, under the cow-burnt sky.

As she turned into the Croydon Road, following the curves of the small, high banked lane, Carrie was suddenly struck by the strong colours of autumn. The deep orange glow shot with contrasting lemon-yellow leaves, which melded into the blackish red of the copper beech. The few remaining green stems leant towards the road, suggesting a long leafy bower would be re-formed in spring. This and the smoky wood smell of late autumn, polarised all that she had forgotten about England in her years abroad. Even the ferns, whose ranks bordered the road like soldiers on a war-plain, now had a burnt suntan colour, presaging winter. She marvelled at the happiness such strength of colour gave her. For the first time since Ignatius's death she started to hope again, instead of merely living on adrenaline.

At that moment she noticed that a rusty, purple Peugeot, which had been following her since West Wickham, had now crept up beside her on the narrow road. She saw a flash of something that looked like tangled twine and young, gesturing skin, before they met a car going in the opposite direction and, under a hail of horns and abuse, the Peugeot fell back. Minutes later he was at her side again, closer now, almost door to door, skin to skin. She fell back to allow him to overtake, but after a pause, he too fell back, his hands off the wheel, making inexplicable signs which Carrie read as deeply aggressive.

Scared, she floored the accelerator of her hired Ford Fiesta, which responded surprisingly well and shot away from the Peugeot. She screeched across the road into a sharp right hand lane, while the Peugeot thundered past on the main road. Relieved she slowed down, trying to shoot glances at the map on the suicide seat. In spite of shaking so much that she could hardly distinguish the lanes, she saw she had fortuitously taken a short cut.

However, as she was congratulating herself on a natural police-driving ability, the Peugeot reappeared in her mirror, the driver waving and hooting. Jesus! She'd heard of road rage but this was ridiculous. She hit the accelerator again and jumping the two Keston mini roundabouts, narrowly avoiding the flashing lights of a robot, screeched past the 40 mph sign at 60, and got clear. There, on the main road and in sight of a police car in an evergreen-hide, the Peugeot fell back, eventually getting lost in the pulse of A233 traffic.

"Git!" she thought. The time limit on her life ought to be set by herself or nature, not by some drunken idiot in a purple Peugeot.

Once at the airfield, finding the school was an initiative test. After trying three entrances, one of which got her to the Pilot's Chapel, she finally found the 'Ecole de Vol'. A curved metal bunker, with a permanently temporary look, it was surrounded by wartime hangars and scarcely more modern planes. Outside the school, three Ray-Bans-wearing boys were smoking roll-your-owns, an ashtray balanced on the lower wing of a biplane. The tallest boy rested his foot on a wooden table, placed there for eating but now a dilapidated green, collapsing from the force of British weather. As she passed them she overheard their discussion.

"...the flight was over-weight, and because it was 20 minutes late took off down-wind. Taxiing would have been another 15 minutes. Then an undercarriage spacer was missing, so one of the struts allowed the wheels to turn..I saw the skid marks in 4 lines..."

"Yeah pants!" said the tall boy. "I've heard these Concorde conspiracy theories before, but you only believe them because the World's favourite turned you down..."

"Fuck man! You sound like some BA bureaucrat. This is inside gen.."

"Morning," said Carrie, hoping to get some attention.

The boys ignored her and continued talking, moving seamlessly from Concorde to the poor state of engineering in light aircraft.

She walked inside the school. It was empty; all the inmates outside avoiding passive smoking.

Carrie waited.

For a while the boys outside continued arguing, aspects of aviation crashes growing gradually more gruesome. But eventually, as she stood there refusing to go away, one of them opened the door offhandedly, "can we help at all?"

"I certainly hope so."

Unimpressed, the boy smirked, glancing back at his friends. "Have you come for a trial lesson?"

"No!" she said. "Dancing classes!"

He looked blank. "Say again?"

"Oh, nothing! Yes, I've come for a lesson. The name is Mrs Nordsuitlaan."

"Oh. Mrs Noodsy..." He wandered over to a stack of lined sheets sitting on the desk, reluctantly took off his Ray Bans, looked at them, then back up at her.

"You're with Tony Carr, but you can call him Wang if you like, we do. Wang Carr!" The boy waited for a reaction but when Carrie said nothing he added, "he's out flying at the moment."

"And..."

"Excuse me?"

"And when is he expected back? My lesson is now!"

The pilot checked his watch. "Ten minutes light of the hour," he said.

Putting his glasses on, he walked back to his friends leaving the door open. "Mind you," he said to the group, "I wouldn't want to fly with Tony after last night. He must have one Hell of a head on him this morning!" The boys sniggered.

"Excuse me!" Carrie said dangerously.

"Yes?"

"Is there somewhere I can wait?"

The boy shrugged. He indicated the rows of chairs. "Sure. Take a seat. Oh and..." he made a vague gesture, "there's a coffee machine over there. Takes twenties."

He turned back to his friends and resumed his conversation. Carrie, sitting down, heard him say, "..so then the lady radar controller said, 'can I turn you on at seven miles?' I came back quick as a flash: 'as a babe magnet, babe....'"

Carrie went to the coffee machine.

She'd just sat down with her coffee and a well-thumbed copy of the accident reports from the reception table, when a young man in blue mechanic's overalls, and with what looked like moulting twine twists on his head, walked into the school. She examined him, surprised to see that although he looked over thirty, he had the slope-shouldered slouching vulnerability of an adolescent. This could be the awaited Tony. He was carrying a pilot's bag and he approached the boys by the door.

"Anyone buying today?"

The boys shook their heads. "Sorry Ben, no. No money. Try her." One nudged his head in Carrie's direction. Ben turned, apparently seeing her for the first time. He walked over and put the bag down beside her, flipping the brass clips to expose boxes of familiar brands in cellophane: at least the packaging looked recognizable, the names appearing vaguely smudged.

"I've got some good stuff, special rate, if you're interested." He spoke in such an offhand manner that Carrie could hardly believe he wanted to sell. "Channel. Arpegs. Even some Nina Ricce and other, non-scent stuff."

Carrie put her hand into the bag. For a moment she thought she could buy discount Nina Ricci for her cousin. Then the price list, written in pencil on the flap, made her look again.

"Five quid?" She shook her head, "good stuff huh!"

The young man shrugged. "It's cool," he said. "If you're interested I can bring more. Some say it's better than the real thing."

She imagined Roberta's response to such a present and almost bought it. "No, thanks. I'll leave it."

Tony turned up an hour late, also uniformed with Ray Bands, a mobile phone pressed to his ear. Immediately he walked into the office Carrie knew he was one of life's superior beings. In spite of an extra roll of fat around his stomach, Tony was clearly one of those fortunate few who didn't have to suffer the inferiorities and anxieties of the rest of the populace. His walk, his smile, his laugh everything about him radiated deep confidence. He knew he was OK. He knew others thought so and that his future was assured. When Tony said, "I am a pilot," it was clear a pilot was something higher than God, and mere Managing Directors knelt at his command.

"Hello girls," he joked, saluting the sauntering boys. "And Hello to you," he added seeing Carrie, winking at her and automatically covering the voice piece of the mobile with his other hand.

"...darling," he said to the mobile, "I'm in the office now...must fly..ha ha ..yeah..yeah..I know you do..yeah...yeah..me too."

He cancelled his phone, hooked it into his belt and took off his Ray Bans, rubbing them on his shirt. Then he addressed himself to Carrie. "Welcome to 'Bigamy' Hill. So. You a trial lesson?"

"No," she said stiffly, "patience on a monument."

"Say again." He stopped polishing his glasses and stared at her. "Oh, a joke." He glanced at the other boys with an element of complicity. "Yes, very funny. Have you flown before?"

"No. Well, I had a helicopter lesson once." She spoke proudly expecting him to be impressed.

"Oh, egg-beaters. OK. Have you done the parachute jump and the balloon ride too? Well, you'd better come into the briefing room then. "

He walked ahead of her, through a flimsy white painted door with a glass inset, into a small room. The door shuddered as he pushed it shut. Behind an MFI table was a white board; in front, two plastic chairs. On the table was a model plane, which Tony picked up, sweeping it grandly across his body like a warrior's assagai. She sat down on a plastic chair.

"Do you know what this is?"

"A giraffe?"

"Say again? Oh. Still funny," he murmured. "I meant this," he added speaking slowly and kindly, indicating some part of the plane with his hand, "not the whole thing. It is an ail-er-on, we use them to turn."

Then, strangely, he changed the subject. "Was this a present? Would you rather we just went flying and had a go and we can worry about the theory later?" He looked at his watch without giving her a chance to reply. "Actually let's do that, to be honest I'm running a bit late and it would help." He gave her a sudden mesmeric smile and she found they were walking out of the briefing room towards the entrance.

"If you wait a second, I've just got to sign out."

He left Carrie standing by the door while he disappeared down a thin corridor, reminding her strongly of men who, having taken you out to dinner, suddenly need to pee just as you are leaving the restaurant and leave you standing there, coat on, ready to travel but forced to wait. Carrie wondered if she had made a mistake making the male sex her life's work.

She walked in the direction Tony had gone. Behind an open door she heard him say. "Yeah, she's quite a babe, nice legs but...you know women..she didn't even know what an aileron was!"

"Bloody Hell!"

His companion laughed heartily. Carrie turned around and walked out of the door, towards her car. Thank God, she thought, she hadn't paid yet; there had to be better schools than this one. The last thing Carrie saw was Tony's surprised face at the window, watching her drive away.

Driving towards the exit, hating herself for not hitting Tony before she left, she realised there was more than one school here. She passed one and then another. With flying schools as with computer games it was clearly all about making the right (or in her case wrong) choice. Finally she stopped by a third: "Charlie's School of Flying." An ornately decorated double portacabin with a connecting outside staircase. In the lower cabin there was a girl behind a computer, brushing her hair.

"Hello," said Carrie, walking in and sniffing damp. She noticed mould patches on the walls and a computer game on the screen.

"Hi there." The girl continued brushing. She had blue nail polish on bitten nails which flashed with each stroke of the brush.

"I was passing. I'm interested in a flying lesson." Carrie stated, suppressing the urge to apologise for interrupting her toilette.

"Yeah. Now?"

"Yes."

"'ang on I'll just.." The girl put down her brush and started shuffling some papers, her blue nails skidding like little ants through the black and white. The telephone began to ring. "Just a tick my luv...Hello. Charlees at Bigamy Hill, can I help you? Aw it's you. Naw, I'm not doing nuffing. Yeah, yeah, I know..yeah I heard! It was well out of order that..."

Still holding the telephone to her ear, one shoulder raised stiffly to grip the ear-piece, she stood up. Put a piece of paper in front of Carrie on the desk, tapping a blue nail on the white form.

"'ang on gorgeous," she said into the phone. To Carrie she said, "'ere, can you fill this in..it's club membership, you 'ave to do it before you fly. Naw not you, silly. I'm afraid I've got a customer. 'ang on I've got a pen somewhere. Oh yeah, 'ere it is all the time."

Carrie looked at the form. Twiddled the pen. She looked at the girl now returning to her conversation. "Thanks," she said, "and since I see the telephone is more important than me, no thanks."

As Carrie walked out of the door for the second time that day, she heard the receptionist say. "Naw, just another one didn't like the price. Time-wasters! Never mind, 'eh!"

Carrie walked through the crisp English, November air, back to her hired Ford Fiesta, but as she approached the car something seemed wrong. She felt a tingling of instinctive signals. The car's outline was odd; different. At first it looked as though the boot was open, not fully but hanging disengaged and bouncing like a toy on a string. Then, as she got closer, the door too looked unhinged. A seat belt had slipped out of the edge and was hanging in the dirt. There was an indication of black rubber around the outline. She could have left the door open, but she hadn't even tried the boot yet. Tentatively she approached the car. As she touched the door, it swung wide revealing inside, dumped over the seats and sprawled onto the floor, the contents of her case, the glove compartment and the side pockets. Everything had been tossed about as though a small dust devil had whipped around the car.

"Shit!" She'd never had a single problem in Africa, but come back to the UK and straight away you get robbed. Ironic. At least they hadn't broken the windows, and the wiring was untouched; it still looked drivable.

She stared ineffectually at the mess. Depressed. Wishing Ignatius was here to sort this out. Then came anger: she felt a whole load of barbed wire fences entangling themselves in her mind. The little shits! How dare they violate her car. She smashed her hand impotently on the bonnet.

Forcing herself to check what was missing, she lent in and shuffled through the wreckage. As far as she could remember everything was there but just as no woman alive knows the exact contents of her handbag, Carrie could not have sworn on Ignatius's life what was in the car and what was elsewhere.

"You OK?" asked a voice behind her. "Trouble?"

Ben, the counterfeit seller, leant towards her, his eyes pin-points under his dreadlocks. In his hand he held a fizzy can decorated with a straw. Carrie thought she recognised the effects of a recent intake of drugs and shuddered. She indicated the inside of the car with an open hand. He looked inside and back at her, and shrugged.

"Yeah. Happens. Anything missing?"

"I don't think so."

"Probably they were looking for easy coinage. Anything I can do?"

Carrie shook her head, she just wanted to be left alone. "I don't think so. Thanks anyway."

"Yeah! You shouldn't leave the doors unlocked. Loads of kids here."

He wandered away, just as she was about to protest that she hadn't: then remembered she had. Damn! No need to lock them in the game park; animals do not steal.

As she stood there, wondering what to do, she noticed the aroma of warm fat. In front of the car was 'The Flying Pigs' cafe. Carrie felt a powerful passion for strong, black coffee.

The cafe was full. Outside the blue air twinkled encouragingly at pilots. Inside, in air redolent with grease, many young men in uniform were eating bacon sandwiches. Not forking chunks into their mouths like men on a mission, but savouring the flavour, men with time to spare and conversation to be had, talking between, and during, mouthfuls. Carrie ordered a coffee.

"Sure thing, mate," said an elderly, bald man behind the counter, his arms wafting bacon-odour towards her. "Eat here or take away?"

"Here. Can you recommend a good flying school?"

He shrugged. "Try next door. They're all much the same."

The coffee was ghastly. She left it and went next door, a blue building with steps down to a flying shop. The school entrance, she eventually discovered, was up some stairs, cleverly concealed behind a curtain.

As she climbed the stairs she heard Dire Straits. At the top of the stairs, behind a computer, a well-built lass with long ear-rings read accident reports to a girl whose skinny arms, sticking awkwardly out of her short sleeves, would have made her look like a grasshopper had they not been so muscular. A string of pearls dropped out of the girl's shirt as though she had dribbled on herself, and into these she had hung her Ray-Bans. Behind the girls a man lent against the radiator, his stomach stretching his pilot shirt like pregnancy.

"All right?" said the reader, breaking off from a particularly juicy accident as Carrie appeared at the top of the stairs. "Can we help at all?"

"Yes, please. I would like a lesson, now if possible. A ..a..tester."

The phone rang. The grasshopper picked it up, while the well-built girl said to the stretched-shirt, "here Dave, this lady'd like a flight."

Dave looked out of the window up at the cloudless sky and winced. His hands became suddenly verbose like a man practicing deaf men's Braille. "Well you see, Miss, it's a bit like this...a wind is blowing up and well, you know how changeable the weather can be. Better to be down here, wishing you were up there, than up there wishing you were down here! How about we pop down to the cafe and have a chat?"

"I've just come from there," said Carrie tartly.

"Bless," said the girl, taking a strand out of her long hair and dropping in on the floor. "Dave you're a fucking character! Wait until Mitch gets off the phone, lover, she'll help you: she needs the money."

Mitch put down the receiver and turned to Carrie saying briskly, "hi ya. I'm Mitch, one of the instructors. So, did you want to fly now?"

Wow. The grasshopper! A woman instructor. Carrie hadn't even considered there were such things.

Mitch took silence for acquiescence. She had never met anyone who dared to suggest there was anything other than androgyny in flying skills. Certainly not a young person. Mitch herself was a visionary, blessed and cursed by obsession with flight. From the moment she was old enough to turn a screwdriver she had wanted to be a pilot, and it never occurred to her to question her destiny. While she had a rare intellectual honesty and, faced by her own ignorance felt humbled and eager to learn, she lacked the imagination to understand the tolerant, get-by attitude of so many of her contemporaries. Mitch could no more have envisaged Carrie's passion for romantic failure, than have purposely crashed an aircraft.

"Let's go to the briefing room, shall we. Janie, if Patrick phones can you tell him I can fly with him at.." she looked at her watch and then at Carrie, "how long did you want to fly for..er..I'm sorry I don't know your name..."

"Mrs Nordsuitlaan..Carrie."

Quaint name, thought Mitch. Dutch maybe or Swedish. Perhaps that explained why she had arrived for a flying lesson wearing what looked like a cocktail dress; and those shoes!

"Great. I'm Mitch. Actually, how long did you want to fly for Mrs ...er...Carrie?"

"Um..I don't know...an hour maybe."

"Good." She turned to Janie. "OK tell him I can fly with him at three."

"All right," Janie replied, "and your five o'clock's cancelled."

"Again! Charge him £20. That's the third time. Three strikes and you're fined." To Carrie she said, "that gives us two hours, so you can ask questions and I can tell you a bit about flying first. Actually that's a bit presumptuous of me...have you ever flown before?"

"A helicopter, once."

"Hey, great. I fly both. I'll tell you the differences."

"If I stay will I always fly with you?" Carrie asked, unsure what answer she wished to hear but asking anyway.

"Absolutely," her instructor replied ingenuously, "we have a one instructor policy here."

After a briefing, which Carrie almost totally forgot, remembering only that Mitch, in an effort to amuse her, had said; "..flying is a computer game with wings," they walked through the school and onto the tarmac apron.

Mitch was saying: "..look, if you don't remember everything don't worry. Flying is really a skill. Intellectually I can explain things to you, but 90% of it is feel..." when Carrie saw the plane and gasped. It was smaller than a toy and looked like a long eared dog that some kid had dropped in front of the school. "We're not going in that are we?" she asked in dismay. Flying IS a computer game!

"Sure. Cessna 152. Sturdy trainers. Were you hoping for a low wing?"

Carrie ogled. " No..er..it's just. ..it's a bit small."

"For what?" asked Mitch puzzled, and began walking round the plane. She pulled things up and down, explaining every bit, what it did and why. As she wiggled the flaps (sort of airflow brakes) up and down, muttering that it was a shame bits didn't work but then you can't expect these small planes to have the engineering criteria of cars, the balding man from the cafe shuffled up to her, accompanied by cafe-scent.

"Hey Mitch, my posh totty."

"Paddy?"

"Look Mitch,..er.. I was wondering,..er.. could you just show me how the plane starts again?"

Mitch grinned at Carrie, raising her eyebrows, before following the old man over to his plane. She was back in a few minutes.

"Sorry. Paddy had forgotten how to start the Cessna."

Carrie goggled. "Is he a pilot then?"

"Absolutely. An examiner actually." Mitch smiled casually, rubbing the side of her nose, "he's doing a test today, some chap renewing his FAA licence. Unfortunately Paddy can't do British tests any more, but he's still valid in America."

"Ah!" Carrie felt a warm sense of esteem for the British licensing board.

Mitch returned to pulling and pushing and Carrie was soon bored. Every now and then Mitch would compare a bit of the aeroplane to a car until Carrie suddenly said. "Look I'm sorry I have no idea how my car works. I merely fill it with petrol and drive it. Anyway it's hired."

"That's OK."

They climbed into the tiny plane and the efficient instructor showed

Carrie how to strap in. Carrie slipped on the black headset, trying to ignore the dandruff on the ear cuffs and the smell of hair tonic. As they taxied out, Mitch still explaining things, Carrie noticed a red light flashing. "That light..er... on the dashboard...is it OK?"

Mitch glanced down. "On the console? Oh, yes absolutely, just the alternator. It's a loose connection, don't worry it happens all the time actually. I'll recycle it." She cheerfully flipped a red switch off and on. The light went out.

"Oh!" *Flying is just a computer game.*

Mitch called for departure, lined up on the runway, throttled-up. Almost immediately the little plane took off. Carrie stared out of the window, watching the airfield shrinking beneath them. To her surprise she felt a rush of adrenaline. As they levelled out amongst clouds suspended as though in a solution her spirits soared. She felt slightly breathless. Wow! This, she thought, was OK. OK indeed. Better than lolling around in bars. Better than champagne and sex. This was original flying. Libidinous, joyous flying: just as the pioneers might have experienced it.

"I love computer games." She murmured, watching the dirty, polluted environment below her transforming into something magical and desirable merely by the angular distance. "Wow and wow."

They flew for an hour. Mitch repeated her instructions tirelessly and Carrie blundered around, sometimes pushing the controls in the right direction, often not. Unlike a computer the Cessna had no pause button.

In spite of this Carrie became more and more enamoured by the smooth joy of flight. She wheeled, she soared, she pitched and jarred. And, even while Mitch murmured, "gently, gently,' she knew this was going to work. That she would be able to fly, would be able to bring her husband's plane home. Would make her money there. The smile on her face grew rounder and rounder. Her spirits lifted higher and higher as the little Cessna pushed through spiffs of white cloud. Carrie could imagine dying this way. Dying from the tumultuous unadulterated joy of living.

"That was very good," said Mitch, as they walked back to the school, across a car park that looked more like a bombing range. "Not bad at all."

As part of a reconstruction program a number of buildings on the airfield had been pulled down, preparatory to creating a new terminal; then either the money or the enthusiasm had run out. Piles of rubble were interspersed with craters rough enough to puncture tyres, brick ridges appeared at the edges of unexpected crevasses and everywhere indestructible dust covered cars. The new terminal remained a paper exercise but the pilots, teachers and students of the old schools cramped into shared spaces and only the cars benefited: their area being larger, even if considerably less smooth, than before.

In the corner, next to the foundations of a destroyed edifice, Carrie saw a rusty purple Peugeot. Untaxed and with one window slightly collapsed, she was nonetheless sure it was the same car that had chased her. She stopped in surprise and told Mitch her road rage story, stating with certainty: "That's the same car."

"Might be," replied Mitch unenthusiastically, fiddling with her watch, "but there are loads of purple Peugeots. Absolutely loads. Everywhere."

"Oh," said Carrie discouraged, "but I'm...sure," her voice tailed off impotently as Mitch strode ahead of her into the office.

In the office Janie wrote out the bill on paper decorated with planes, and suddenly flying didn't seem so cheap. On top of the original hour was a landing fee, V.A.T. and an indispensable thing call 'Club Membership.'

"I'd better find that missing money," thought Carrie.

By the time Carrie left the school the light was fading and the red sky had darkened to a deep azure, littered with grey clouds just slightly tinged with pink; reminding Carrie of a salmon shirt she had accidentally washed with Ignatius' socks. Out of these slithered an amazingly Gouda-cheese coloured moon, which illuminated the sky around with a cold orange radiance. Carrie was forced once again to marvel at the beauties of the country she left behind. Perhaps, she thought, she really had under-estimated the loveliness of the British countryside. Perhaps the depressing newspaperman had overstated the country's destruction. Maybe all nature is as indestructible as early adventurers found the jungle. She felt surprisingly, vividly content.

Across the rubble strewn car park the purple Peugeot gleamed at her invitingly and she turned towards it, drawn by the power of the moon and blatant curiosity; she was sure this was the same one.

She'd hardly gone 10 yards when a girl brushed past her. Half turning to apologise, Carrie saw the girl was almost naked, covered only with a banner which read 'Leopard Club'. Bare feet zipped over the car park craters, as the girl sped noiselessly past the Peugeot and crouched down behind a bush. Carrie stopped in surprise, wondering if she should offer her some help, a lift, some clothes...anything. However, before she could move, a completely naked man with whiskers reminiscent of a West Highland terrier also charged past her, waving two luminous marshalling batons.

Carrie giggled nervously, and the man stopped. "Fancy some directing?" he asked, his lips quivering like a dog sniffing scent.

Carrie shrank back towards the Peugeot mute, but at that moment the half dressed girl leapt out from behind the bush and, aiming an air-kick at the man, disappeared off into the darkness at a provocative canter.

"Must go," yelled the terrier, "power up that left engine." And, his batons waving like furious fireflies, he too pounded off into the darkness.

Carrie abandoned the Peugeot, scurrying off to the safety of her hire car. Was it the moon or was this why pilots nicknamed the place Bigamy?

When Carrie returned to her cousin's house there was a letter waiting for her from the insurance company, forwarded via the lawyer's office.

> *Dear Mrs Nordsuitlaan,*
> *We refer to all your letters from the 13th November to date, in which you asked for a payout of your husband's policy 12845Z.*
> *As your husband's body has not yet been found, we would normally need more time to ascertain that he died in the helicopter crash. However, this is not the case in these circumstances.*
> *Unfortunately, in this case we have discovered from our records that your husband was not insured for death, only for injury.*
> *Therefore, unless he is alive and injured we are unable to assist you any further.*
> *If you have any queries please phone this office in normal office hours.*
> *Yours sincerely......*

"What!? Rubbish!" Carrie shouted violently, banging her fist on the table although there was no one there to watch her. Tears started into her eyes. "Nonsense! Rubbish! I signed the cheque myself."

Grabbing the phone, she rang the lawyer's office in Cape Town, her fingers shaking so violently that she misdialled and had to start again. Mr Barbar was working late, expecting her call, and came to the phone smiling soothingly. "Yes, yes, Mrs Nordsuitlaan, I have spoken to the insurance company. The policy conforms with accepted standards. You were insured for injury and death, your husband only for injury. Clients often have the same problems with their car insurance. Why only the other day........"

"But I paid the premium...Ignatius told me it was for both of us, for death and injury..He TOLD me ..couldn't you explain to the company?"

"I'm sorry. The position is beyond even my powers of impeachment."

Carrie felt very cold. "You mean..?"

"Yes, it does. Nothing. No compensation. Nada," averred the lawyer, laughing lightly. "You have my sincere commiseration. Your position is indeed most clearly unenviable."

"Yes it is. But I don't understand. Why would I need full insurance, while he only had injury cover? The most risky thing I ever really did was travel in an African bus."

Mr Barbar laughed politely, adding, "insurance forms can be obscure."

"Shit!" Snorted Carrie suddenly shivering, "yes, yes that must be it. He was terrible with paperwork. Of course. Yes. Yes. Thank you," she replied automatically, putting down the receiver.

But the question remained: yes Ignatius was a risk taker, yes he was bad with paperwork but he was also a businessman and knew the importance of insurance. Why would her life have been insured and not his?

Flying even when his Canvas is Rent

The large, moustachioed pilot followed the taxiway down to Nairobi's longest runway, noting, as he and his passenger passed the wind sock, that it drooped like a eunuch's prick. The outside air temperature beat fiercely down on them as they joined the queue of aircraft waiting for departure on the runway. He set the altimeter. They were more than four thousand feet high, and still the sun burned through the canopy of the little Cessna 152 like desert spray. The pilot reached for the water bottle in his door-pocket.

"Oh, may I have some too?" Asked the man at his side, his face wet with perspiration, his big body sagging in the heat.

"Sure, it'll help keep our weight down," remarked the pilot chattily.

"I'm sorry?"

"Nothing, only it's after being a warm day and the little Cessna doesn't go jumping like a stag in fresh snow in this kind of weather. Hot weather's about as useful as tits on a boar hog to the smaller members of the Cessna family."

"Oh," replied the bemused passenger. He stared out of the window as the pilot talked into a hand-mike and taxied out onto the runway.

"You ready? I'm steady. Let's go!"

"Fine."

"Spectacles, testicles, wallet and watch!" While the passenger's eyes dilated in surprise, the pilot crossed himself and then let down a stage of flap for greater lift.

He pushed forward the throttle, and the little aircraft trundled down the long runway. On and on it rumbled, the speed hardly increasing at all. On and on, on and on. The far end of the long runway drew nearer. The Cessna seemed less and less inclined to lift off. At last the pilot could bear it no longer, he jerked back the control stick as hard as he could. The obedient little Cessna made a gallant attempt to jump into the air. It struggled upwards for a brief moment. Then failed. As the end of the runway approached the little plane and its human cargo sank disconsolately back onto the earth again and rolled into the dust of the overshoot area. The Cessna ground to a halt bring up a small spurt of stones. The pilot swore.

"What happened?" asked the passenger, wiping his face with a large handkerchief.

"Well," concluded the pilot, picking his hat from where it had fallen on the floor, "either we were too heavy, or the air was not dense enough, or someone put this airfield too high up in the mountains."

"Oh," replied the passenger, "shouldn't you have known about that before we attempted to take off?"

"Yup. Fair case of thumb-up-bum and mind in neutral. Fancy a drink?"

Weather does more Business in Winter

The next day it rained, heavy tropical rain with big droplets and cold damp air which seeped into your bones. Carrie yearned for Africa. The beautiful autumnal leaves had fallen off the trees and made a slippery mush on the streets. The stalks on the side of the road looked like an opposing army of knives. However, she was still keen to get on and learn to fly so Carrie drove down to the airfield through pouring rain, certain there must be something she could do. Mitch was drinking coffee, reading the papers, and was surprised to see her arrive.

"Hello Carrie, bit optimistic actually. Didn't Janie ring you?" She glanced at Janie, who rolled her eyes in reply and started plaiting her hair. "There's not much we can do today, unless you fancy some ground school. I'll have to charge you I'm afraid."

"How much?"

The girl winced apologetically. "Forty pounds an hour; school charges."

"£40!" Generous bank manager or not, this was a very additional, additional extra. "How much is coffee?"

As Carrie drove away, Mitch watched her from the window. "You know," she told Janie, "she's been asking about a purple Peugeot."

Janie was fiddling with the radio, trying to find a suitably raucous channel for her current turbulent emotions: the boss had been in the office again ordering her around and wanting things. "Oh, yeah?"

Mitch's gaze strayed across the stony craters to the small car at the edge of the car park. "Absolutely. Apparently Ben tried to drive her off the road."

"Oh, yeah? Fuck, this radio stinks. Why?"

"God knows. If I had money for every one of Ben's subversive brain cells either I'd be a millionaire or he'd still be a pilot."

Janie stopped fiddling and looked at the instructor. "Yeah. Anxiety freak! Okay I'll find out if you like. You know he'll do anything for me; the love washed my car last week." She smiled teasingly.

Mitch frowned, irritated that, as Janie said, the boys 'would do anything for her'. Mitch believed in the equality principle: no man did anything better than she did it herself. However, the question of Ben bothered her; why would he have behaved so indiscreetly?

It rained steadily for almost all the rest of the week and on the one day when it wasn't raining, the winds were too strong. Eventually, ten days later, the weather was good enough to fly. Carrie drove her car enthusiastically down to Biggin Hill. She was met by the fat man.

"Hello," she said, scratching her brain for his name. "Mitch around?"

"All right? Would you like a cup of tea?" replied Dave.

"Coffee? Yes, thanks." This was a bit better, it looked like she had chosen the right school afterall. "Black, one sugar."

"Oh, hot and sweet like your men."

"Umm. Is Mitch flying?"

Dave rubbed his hands together, making a bowing movement which would have seemed impossible with such a large stomach. "Well, you see it's like this ..er..sorry what was your name...?"

"Carrie Nordsuitlaan."

"Well you see Car-ie, it's like this...oh, there's the kettle..just a minute..not trying to put you off but .."

He busied around. Eventually Janie came downstairs.

"All right," she said, "has Dave told you?"

"Told me what?"

"Oh, sorry. I'm afraid Mitch's not here today, these frigging airline pilots, you know. So you're flying with Dave today. She apologises but, you know, she was on standby. Did she tell you this is only her part time job?"

"No, she didn't."

"Aw. Welcome to Bigamy Hill! It's always like this. Hey Dave, cheers, ain't you making me one too..fat git. I hate men, don't you?"

Dave gave Carrie her coffee. He began a story about faulty engineering, but soon slipped over to topical jokes. "Do you need a pee, Carrie? Or would you prefer Euro-nating? Heard the one about Uri Geller and the plastic fork?"

About three quarters of an hour after Carrie had arrived Dave looked at his watch. "So, now Carol, how far have you got in the syllabus?"

"I've had a trial lesson."

"Oh, right, tell you what; I've kicked the tyres so let's go light the fires."

"What?"

"I've checked out the plane already, so we'll just go shove off shall we? Get on with it, like. Anything special you'd like to do?"

"You're the boss," she said, giving him her cup. "whatever you say."

They squeezed into the Cessna, Dave's bulk emphasising how little space there was inside. There was no preflight checking with Dave. Without waiting for Carrie to strap in he started up the plane, motioned her towards her headset, talked on the radio and taxied out at a fast running pace.

"Gotta get ahead of the queue," he murmured, winking at her.

He called the tower. "Bigamy Tower, Echo Yankee request departure off 29."

"Roger Golf Echo Yankee, reading you fives, wind 210, 15 knots, state your intention."

"Echo Yankee, happy with 29, ready for departure."

"Roger Golf Echo Yankee cleared for take off on 29. Break. Golf Alpha November hold position on 21. Confirm holding."

To Carrie Dave said, "they won't let just anyone take the out-of-wind runway, but Ken and I are like that." (He twisted his fingers, letting the control column go so that the nose dropped, as did Carrie's stomach). He winked.

They flew over to Brands Hatch because, Dave said: "everybody wants to fly there. In a helicopter we could land, but we can still scare the pants off the bast...er them. Let's do it. Yaahooo!!"

Down he went, swooping past the racing circuit so low that Carrie thought he was going to shake hands with one of the drivers. Just as it seemed impossible to avoid hitting the car, Dave pulled up hard and they catapulted back into the air. "Woohoo!"

Without another word Dave pushed the nose of the plane steeply down again. Hurtling towards the ground, the airspeed building up and the rev metre off the scale, Carrie's stomach collided with her brain. Then, just as the propeller started chopping trees, Dave yanked the stick sharply back; the little Cessna leapt for the sky: Carrie's brain and stomach descended into her shoes. Upside-down Carrie's shoulders stretched her seat-belt, while her eyes watched the roof. After a final burst of G-force, Carrie's nose now grazing her knees, the loop was looped. Carrie gripped the sides of the plane and thanked her helicopter flying for a strong stomach.

"Hey, Karen, you're OK," shouted Dave, thumping Carrie on the shoulder, "I don't usually do that with my female students, they scream too much! But you liked it, hey. You know, I've never had an aerobatic lesson. Not one! Literally taught myself. Pretty good, hey!"

"Oh," Carrie replied. Then "thanks," as he finally let her have a go at the controls. She flew around, while he called a friend on his mobile, shouting to be heard and occasionally correcting Carrie's over-ambitious movements. When it was time to go back he took control.

"Great flight," he said landing, "you're doing well."

Walking through the derelict car park Carrie noticed the purple Peugeot again. She asked Dave who owned it. "Well, you see Carol," he said, rubbing his hands together and bowing over his stomach, "put it like this...it can't be a pilot; he's literally colour-blind!" He laughed, his belly wobbling contentedly.

Carrie went upstairs to pay. Janie greeted her warmly, while twisting her hair into a plait behind her head. "All right lover? How was that? Guess it was good, isn't it." She fumbled for a hair clip with one hand.

"Yes," said Carrie, "by the way, in the car park.. that purple Peu...?"

"Janie," said a voice from another room, "get me a coffee, and ask Mrs Nordsebrand to come in here will you."

Janie dropped her hair and stuck her tongue out at the office wall. She made a face at Carrie. "Fagin 'ud like a word," she said, tilting her head at the opposing wall and mouthing 'fat git,' "he's in there. Wanna coffee? Hot and bitter like men?"

In the small office, behind a large desk, sat an aging skinhead. He did not get up but waved her to an opposing seat, like a man batting a fly. In spite of the half-inch cut topping his gaunt frame, he soon revealed himself to be a born company man.

"Good morning, Mrs Nortsowman, take a pew. Mitch tells me you're interested in some kind of deal...we can help..this company believes in its students. A company without students is, if you'll forgive the phrase, like a fish without a bicycle; a sentiment I know you'll understand."

As he began to enumerate the massive perks that came in return for paying £5,500 in advance, Carrie glanced out of the window. There in the building site, bumping erratically across the cavities, was the purple Peugeot.

"Oh," she said shocked, jumping to her feet, "wait! I'll be back."

John half rose in amazement as she leapt out of the room and down the stairs towards the car park, only to find that she was too late; the Peugeot had already entered the main road and was driving away.

"Rats!" she said. But even as she cursed herself she wondered what she was hoping to effect by catching the Peugeot driver.

Pilots gain Reputation from Tempests

Carrie returned to Peckham thinking about money, John's slim deal on advance payment, and purple Peugeots. Before she'd even parked the car Roberta was opening the passenger door.

"Where have you been?"

"Flying. Why..."

"And, more's the point, what have you been doing? The police were here looking for you! You know I don't mind having you to stay.."

Carrie picked up her bag, locked the car, and made her way towards the house; Roberta following, her nose almost in Carrie's shoulder like a small, angry dog. "...but I don't expect a barrage of policemen to turn up every time I open my door. I've got a position in the neighbourhood to think about. If I start getting house-calls from.."

"What did they want?" Carrie asked, closing the thickly painted, wooden front door.

"They didn't tell me. Wouldn't tell me! They said it was routine, part of an investigation; but we know from films that they always say that. They left a number for you to call. They wanted to wait, but I wasn't having that pair of heffalumps humping around, colliding with my furniture. Besides they were a right pair of God's drop-outs..."

Carrie stared at Roberta's definite handwriting, cutting out her voice. DI Kundera and DI Jones and a number. What did they want? Was this something to do with Ignatius's death? She put the note in her bag; she'd think about it later. Later; it would wait.

The next day God was on Carrie's side; the weather was sunny and calm and Mitch was at the airfield. She gave Carrie a check list. Made her check out the plane thoroughly, and do the start up and taxiing checks herself.

"OK, it seems hard now," Mitch said talkatively, "but you'll thank me later for this good basic training, believe me. I thank God I was taught properly from the start, not like some of these jokes who teach now. Start smart, last long." But when Carrie asked who owned the purple Peugeot Mitch shrugged, fiddled with her left ear, said there were always strange cars in the car park, and became taciturn.

They flew for five hours that day; an hour at a time with ten minute breaks. By the last hour Carrie was exhausted, her mind was spinning and she could barely remember her own name; let alone understand the complicated concepts Mitch kept bringing up. As they flew back to airfield Mitch announced, "I've got a sore bottom."

"Why? Have we been flying too long?"

"No! It's you. You're flying out of balance. Look at the ball." Mitch pointed to a sideways spirit level on the console. "See! Even my beads are drifting!"

Carrie laughed. "That's all. You're weird."

"Don't you believe it," said Mitch. "You'll remember that far more than if I just told you to fly in balance. But now I have a treat for you."

"What?" Carrie asked uneasily. The only treat she really wanted was whisky and her bed. Still she had asked to learn quickly, and Mitch was a thorough teacher, no gainsaying that. She shook herself awake.

"Stalling," said Mitch excitedly. This was obviously something she enjoyed.

"Which is?"

"When your plane stops flying because the wing has too high an angle of attack. It's something you're likely to get into when you are showing off to friends, either because you are flying round their houses or because you are chatting away and not concentrating. Getting into a stall won't hurt you, if you have enough height to recover, but not getting out of it will."

"Not just a headache then?"

"Absolutely not," Mitch said, closing the throttle and easing the stick back, raising the nose. When they were just about standing on the tail, the Cessna began ducking and shaking. Carrie felt the floor was sliding from under her and didn't like it. She grabbed the throttle and stuffed it forward. The little plane gave an upward lurch of surprise, paused for a moment, it's propeller beating the air with ineffectual fury, then the nose fell left, and with a brusque flick the plane plunged down toward the ground, corkscrewing madly round and round. Mitch's pearls clattered against her headset. Carrie seeing the world blurring by as though she was inside a washing machine felt extremely queasy.

"Oh my God!" She screamed, "we're going to die!"

"Don't worry," said Mitch calmly, as the world fizzed by, "you've just put us into a spin. Good thing we were high."

She closed the throttle and pushed the stick forward, putting in full opposite rudder; the plane juddered, shuddered, stopped and straightened. Her pearls flopped back into her shirt.

"It's OK, we were coming to that in a later lesson, you just anticipated me by a few hundred hours! Spinning used to kill them in the First World War," she said brightly, as she recovered to straight and level, "but now we practice it as a matter of course. Look at that! We lost 1500 feet!"

"Oh, is that good?" asked Carrie shaken, really wanting that whisky.

Mitch seemed rather amused. Flying is a computer game with wings.

"You are doing well," she said, predictably, as they taxied in, "we'll go on to circuits next. You'll need a medical from a CAA approved doctor before you can go solo."

"Thanks," said Carrie sarcastically. Another cost.

"This might be the moment," said Mitch, "to talk about insurance.

Nothing concentrates the mind like an unintentional spin."

Carrie shivered. Insurance again. The ever present ghost of the flight.

"Although," said Mitch, "you can actually never be sure with insurance. It's all in the detail. One man I know is a very good example of that."

"Oh?" asked Carrie, both wanting and not wanting to know.

"Yes, he and his business partner dealt in helicopters. They could both fly, but Jed was a CPL, sorry professional pilot, and an engineer, so he did all the buying. The other guy, James, was the money. But actually Jed was swindling James. He would tell him that he had bought a helicopter for more than he actually paid and that he had sold it for less than he got. Kept the difference. Clever. But the company was failing. Eventually James wanted to be rid of this loss-maker. He talked to Jed, but Jed was no rocket scientist, actually, and James soon realised that he was being cheated. An argument ensued and Jed killed him."

"Killed him!" asked Carrie shocked, "the bad pilot killed the good pilot?"

"Absolutely!" Mitch replied, puzzled that Carrie seemed surprised. "Actually it usually happens that way. Anyway, Jed got to thinking he could dispose of his partner's body, and make money at the same time. So he put James at the controls of the helicopter, flew it out into the channel and dumped 'em! Jed's wife picked him up.."

"In a boat?"

"I assume so, unless they had a Duck! Anyway, he went back home and, a few days later, declared his partner and the helicopter missing. He even went to the lengths of forging James's writing in the tech (sorry technical) log so the flight was legal. When he told the police the company was losing money, they were easily convinced it was a case of suicide. But the insurance company...well, you know how they hate to pay out.."

"Yes," said Carrie, unconsciously palpating her hands, "I do."

"Absolutely. They did loads of investigation. They were round here constantly. Asking this and that. Checking every lead. Then nothing. Finally I heard around the clubs they were preparing to pay out, but just before they did one tiny thing gave him away...do you know what it was?"

"I imagine he had a row with his wife and she turned him in."

"No, she was loyal actually. This was something so tiny that, even though he thought he'd covered everything, he'd forgotten it."

"What?"

"Well, apparently, last time they'd renewed the insurance they noticed pilots with a hundred hours paid lower premiums. Jed had thousands, James had ninety. So, they decided James would do another ten with Jed covering. They'd actually done ten flights, but one of those was only fifty minutes, so James was actually ten minutes short of being covered by the insurance. Someone in the firm suddenly noticed it. Just before the final pay out, actually."

Mitch laughed. Carrie was absorbed in her story and the delighted raconteur had no idea how much angst she was causing.

"Good old insurance, 'eh. Better than the police any day. Never miss a trick on these frauds. They must have seen hundreds, actually. Probably the guy got promoted. They refused to pay and Jed went nuts. He rushed around to their office yelling and screaming (an inappropriate emotional response!) The secy got alarmed and called the police. He's doing life now. All over ten minutes."

Carrie's palms began to sweat and she felt queasy. She was thumpingly aware she still hadn't called the police, her mind felt paralysed by insurance. She focused on Mitch again when she heard her say. "...until tomorrow then."

"Oh. You're not away?"

"No, actually I'm only a co-jo at the moment and my schedule's light...but I'll be a captain soon. Still reading Flight International from the back..." Mitch grinned, quite unaware her audience was not listening, but instead was sitting at her elegant rosewood desk in Cape Town, signing an insurance document where her husband had marked a pencil X.

"It's a bit boom and bust in the flying world," Mitch chattered on happily, "late 80s jobs galore, 90s nothing. What do you say to a newly qualified commercial pilot? 'Hamburger and fries, please'."

Carrie stared at her blankly. Then, returning from Cape Town, she slowly realised that Mitch was telling a joke. "I haven't heard that before."

Mitch didn't seem to have noticed her absence as she babbled on as cheerfully as before. "You will. Pilots are notorious for repeating jokes"

"I noticed! Dave..."

Mitch laughed. "Actually he's better than most. Loves flying and 'ud be an airline pilot but can't pass the exams. After a while people are embarrassed to ask 'what next': aware you've passed your train-by date. Instructors get paid peanuts and you know how much responsibility monkeys take!"

Carrie smiled, brought out of her conflicting pains. "Oh? And does this monkey find it worth it?"

"Ha ha," said Mitch, "actually it is; I love it. But profit...Zip! And now we're becoming European! You know the game: bureaucracy rules OK."

Mitch began to talk politics, apparently enjoying the subject as much as flying. Carrie remembered why she preferred men. Men make jokes, women make conversation. Women were so serious, so political and involved. Carrie wasn't sure clever women really knew how to have fun; although Mitch clearly liked to talk.

The Lightning Pilot

"What did Ben say?" Mitch asked Janie after Carrie had left, sliding half a buttock onto the girl's desk and balancing her coffee on her knee.

Janie played with her calorie chart, annoyed at being disturbed in the middle of counting her points. She'd lost her place and would have to start all over again; but it was no use saying anything to Mitch, who was thinner than a skeleton with anorexia.

"Anxiety freak! He really pisses me off you know! He asked me to lend him some money. Christ I can hardly make it through to.."

Mitch felt like slapping her. "Absolutely. But about the road rage and Carrie? What did he say? Why'd he do it?"

"Oh, that. Shit! You know Ben, he mumbles and that until you don't even listen properly. Something about a photograph and no wonder he got $100. Should've been more, he said. And you know him, he always thinks he's hard done-by. Always thinks everyone's looking down on him. Even if they only pass him on the street he sees their scorn! So, he opened this package..and now he knows a thing or too and he's going to show them he isn't a nobody to be fucked around. Only $100! That's larf! And he's asking me for a loan! Fucking cheeky...with Fagin..."

Mitch ground her teeth. "Why did Ben try and run Carrie off the road?"

"Oh, he wasn't really. Only, you know, he saw her and he thought he'd warn her, or scare her, it was hard to tell which. Or he'd been shooting-up... Something about..oh, I don't know, it gave him a shock to see her alive! He kept going on about about how he wasn't anybody's fool and they had really under-estimated him."

"Who?"

"Oh, fuck me Mitch I don't know. Why don't you ask him yourself? I've had a fuck load of him and his moaning. Sorry, I need to concentrate. I've got to count my points before Fagin gets back and asks me to do something stupid."

Mitch sighed and, slipping off the desk, walked to stare out of the window. Below her, it's abandoned-drunk look more poignant than ever, was the purple Peugeot. She knew she'd have to go and see Ben herself, but dreaded it. Last time had been so frightful, so difficult; they'd nearly come to blows. Initially she'd felt tender towards him, even maternal, but later he had become tiresome and obnoxious. Mitch couldn't understand his slide into adolescent debauchery. He'd had a great career ahead of him. Then one small problem and he lost it, went rapidly off the rails. Living in an air-raid shelter and surviving by petty criminality, when he had been on the path to flying a big jet out of Gatwick or Heathrow. It made no sense to her. None. She left her contemplation and went to prepare the next student's lesson.

Coffee Spells Disaster

The next few days Carrie flew uninterruptedly with Mitch. Mitch's serious thoroughness and striving for perfection got Carrie solo in 12 hours. Mitch bought her a bottle of champagne. "Good," she said. "Very good."

Every day before Carrie left the house, Roberta would ask if she'd rung the police yet. Carrie became adept at finding another excuse. "Oh, they were engaged." "Both the DIs were out, you know how busy policemen are these days." "They're on holiday." Until Roberta gave her an ultimatum. "Either you ring tonight," she said, "or I'll do it. I'm not having them hanging around here again, as though I'm the criminal."

With that pulsing in her mind, Carrie drove down to Biggin Hill three days after her solo, only to discovered that Janie was alone.

"Hi ya lover, like a coffee?"

"Why do I think that spells disaster?" Carrie put down her books.

"Excuse me?"

"Nothing. Where is Mitch?"

Janie twisted a finger in her hair. "Ah. Sor-ry, I'm afraid she's left."

"Left? Left what? You mean...LEFT! As in no longer here? But she can't..I mean only two days ago she was here."

"Yeah. Sor-ry, lover, there's a bit of a story to it...have you got time?"

Carrie snorted. Time. That was the only thing she did have plenty of, but Janie was explaining that her life was 'go, go, go twenty-four seven.'

"Why's Mitch left?"

"Oh, yeah. Well, it's Dave, you see. She thought it was out of order."

"Dave's sick?"

"No, he got the sack. You know, Mitch went 'that's unfair' and Fagin went 'no it ain't' so she left. She's freelancing at White Waltham. She said to tell you in case you wanted to go there but I don't know, depends where you live, don't it. So, the gossip!"

Carrie didn't want to know, these business internecines bored her. The only thing she clearly understood was that both the instructors had left, which meant more problems for her. She bent down to pick up her books, but Janie was ahead of her and hot to spill scandal. "Yeah, it's all coz of the purple Peugeot in the car park."

"Which purple Peugeot?" Spluttered Carrie, straightening up, books forgotten, suddenly alert.

"Oh, its gone now, you know, police took it after the murder." Janie had a drag of coffee, certain now she had Carrie's interest.

"What..which murder? Whose is the Peugeot?"

"Well, it's a bit complicated, you see. Now Ben, you know, he's one of those guys who hang around at airfields; you see them all the time, always helpful and attentive but you can never really see what they're there for. Nice, quite sexy even, he'd been an instructor here but he took too much dope...you know sometimes he didn't come in at all. Fagin couldn't stand it. Not that he does much himself, lazy bastard, but he expects the rest of us to work like fucking dogs..."

Carrie shuffled her feet, hoping to get Janie back on track. Janie took another noisy gulp of coffee.

"Well, he fell out with Fagin and had nowhere to go, so he started sleeping in the old air-raid shelter in the woods, left his car here. People borrowed it. No keys, wires job. You know. Dave borrowed it lots. Even Mitch. Even little Mitch!" Absently she got out a brush and started inspecting her split-ends.

Carrie nodded. "Go on."

"Oh, yeah. It was funny really, Fagin used to let him fly. Then suddenly something happened. Fagin went paranoid. No more flying. Fagin changed the locks, everything! Wouldn't even let the sodding engineer in, coz' he was a mate of Ben's. He was fixing Fagin's planes and John made him pee in the bushes. Weird all right! And Fagin took Dave off salary, paid him to fly only. Dave was right pissed off, so he started doing some work for Tony, in his Cessna. Fagin didn't like it so he went over and nicked the guy's wheels."

"Wow. Isn't that illegal?" Carrie hadn't completely followed Janie's tortuous story but she was drawn in; when men stole wheels in Africa it was serious business, not this kind of temporary child's play.

"Yeah probably, and you know what Dave did?"

"Kicked the tyres? Lit the fires?"

"Eh? Oh! What are you like! No he stole the wheels off one of John's planes and flew away. John went ballistic! Wanna coffee, lover?"

"And?...the Peugeot? And the murder? Who was murdered?"

"Oh, Ben. Murdered in the woods. Dead in his little hovel surrounded by golden autumn trees. Shame really, he used to clean my car and everything. Anyway, that really did Fagin in. He was as paranoid as a parrot after that, sacked Dave completely. The rozzers took the car."

Carrie felt sick. That evening she rang the police.

Flying Boots and Spurs

DI Kundera was a soft spoken, polite man who happily agreed to interview Carrie at Biggin Hill rather than in Peckham. "Actually," he joked, "that suits us rather well, though we're not from the Flying Squad. Don't worry this is only routine. Just a few questions."

After Carrie's thirteenth hour, with her third instructor (a 'flying boot', who thought there was only one way to fly; the army way) she met DI Kundera and DI Jones in a small briefing room at the school.

Roberta had exaggerated. Far from being heffalumps, DI Kundera was an exceptionally thin, swarthy young man and his colleague, DI Jones, was a ballesque, bubbly woman with red hair, a south London accent and a discreet chin stud. Both were wearing regulation short-sleeved shirts in spite of the climate: presumably so they could at any given moment take off in a 15 mile chase without over-heating. They had a good rapport, Kundera finishing Jones's sentences and Jones unconsciously acting out his phrases: like TV news presenters.

"Just a few questions, Mam," said DI Kundera. "We're investigating the death of a man killed at the back of the airfield and there seems to be a slight connection with yourself."

"Oh?" asked Carrie, slipping into an orange plastic chair, relieved that this had nothing to do with Ignatius, "the owner of the purple Peugeot?"

The officers exchanged glances. "Yes, you've heard of it?"

"Sure. Janie, the receptionist, told me about it."

"I see," said Jones, while Kundera continued. "Did you know the man?"

"Nope. Only I think he may have tried to kill me..road rage..."

"Oh. Road rage." DI Kundera looked only slightly interested, while Jones brought out a picture. A slight, young man with short red hair in a pilot's uniform. "This is him," Kundera said helpfully. "Do you recognise him at all?"

Carrie wasn't expecting to recognise him, so she glanced briefly at the photo and away. Then something pulled her eyes back to him. "Um..."

"Yes?" Kundera was alert. Jones was tense.

"Have you another picture of him...only something...I'm not sure?"

DI Jones brought out a host of pictures, which she showed to Carrie, including one of Ben with his red, tangled dreadlocks, in an engineer's overalls. "More photos," explained Kundera. One was of the boy with Mitch. Both standing arms crossed defensively.

"My instructor," Carrie said.

Jones crossed her arms and Kundera murmured, "they were friends."

"Look," Carrie said eventually, "it could be. I met him once, twice maybe. My car was broken into and a guy, who had those odd red plait-things, who also sold perfumes in the schools, stopped to ask if I was OK. But it might have been someone else, you know..." She shrugged her lips but knew it was Ben.

The detectives got excited; they knew too. "When exactly was that Mam," asked DI Kundera, "how long ago? Was your car locked?"

"Did you lose anything from the car?" asked DI Jones, "anything at all?" "Actually, he did do counterfeit," Kundera added.

"I don't think so. I thought it was kids looking for cash."

They took down a few details, then DI Jones brought out another photograph. "Do you recognise any of the people here, Mam," Kundera asked.

Carrie looked down at the photo. Blinked and found herself blushing. She looked up at the detectives; one, then the other. She wondered if this was some kind of trick. "Of course I do. That's me and Ignatius. Our ..our wedding photo."

The detectives exchanged glances again. "We found it in the Peugeot," said Jones, "we traced you through the photographer," continued Kundera, "and finally through Mr Barber, your lawyer."

Carrie stared at the wedding photo. She felt like crying. There was Ignatius at his best; she too, pretty, slender, her blond hair caught up in a bun, her face shining with happiness. And shitty Sissy, who had somehow slunk into the picture too: ugly cow. She sighed. So much had changed in the intervening years. So much hope destroyed. Enthusiasm debunked.

DI Jones put her hand softly on Carrie's shoulder. Carrie looked up, realising that she'd gone into a coma of thought. "Are you all right?"

"Sorry." She forced herself back to the present. "So, you think he took it from my car and put it in his own? It might have been in my bag." She shrugged. "When I left Africa I took everything portable. But why? Why steal it? It's not worth anything."

"Actually," said DI Kundera, "at this point in time we don't know." "We are working on it," Jones nodded.

After a few more questions the detectives left and Carrie had another lesson with the Flying Boot. His catch phrase, apparently caused by despair at her imitation of flying, was: "Hey ho. Back to basics!"

Then she drove home to Roberta's questions.

The Flying Boot lasted a week, during which the thought of Carrie going solo again turned him pale with fear. Then he too was gone. John explained he wasn't quite used to civilian life yet. "He's gone to the airlines." John said sweetly. "They are really snapping up guys like him."

"He said the engineering bloody stank," Janie elucidated cheerfully, "and he called Fagin fucking cheap! Which he is.."

Carrie's fourth instructor was called Steve. Steve was a cool dude. So cool he was quite happy for her to go solo without flying with him first.

"If you are good enough for Mitch, you're good enough for me," he said helping himself to a piece of toast, "want some? There's some great jam?"

"But that was ages ago, and I only flew solo once."

"Say again? Coffee? Hot and sweet like your men?"

"I've only been solo once."

"Ah yeah but the Boot said you were fine, bit undisciplined but fine."

"Eh Stevie-lover," Janie broke in, "if you're going flying could you be a pet and pop this video down to Mark at Rudehill, there's a fiver in it for you."

"I'm only doing it coz I love you," he said hopefully, blowing her a kiss.

Redhill, known locally as Rudehill owing to the volatile air traffic control unit, was a beautiful grass airstrip sandwiched between Gatwick and a large hill. Applications to become a satellite airport for Gatwick had floundered on local opposition and had left behind heavy discontent and eccentric closing hours. As they flew down there Steve looked out of the window and commented: "It's a case of thumb up bum, mind in neutral."

"Say again?" Carrie said, pleased she was becoming a pilot in speech at least.

"Go with the flow, don't try too hard! Relax. Let your body do the flying. This is a skill: not like reading a book. Flying is just another way of chilling out."

Steve called the airfield and was told to 'stand by' by the controller.

"Stand by?"

"Wait! He probably needs a Juliet Romeo. We'd better start circling." Steve's finger drew a circle. "Couldn't organise a fart in a bath this lot!"

Over the radio they heard a distraught ATC yelling. "All aircraft landing or taking off stand by. Listen out and do not transmit at once! One more problem from you lot and I'm shutting the radio indefinitely!"

"Humm," said Steve, "all stations normal with Phineas Fag at Rudehill's Air Tragic. Circle on. We'll get even more angst if we try and slip in unnoticed."

On the radio the controller had changed, the new man sounding no less fraught. He was soon berating an unfortunate pilot who couldn't see the airfield. "Lost. What do you mean lost? You shouldn't be coming here if you don't know your way. Don't you know we are Prior Permission only?"

Eventually they did get clearance to land. Under Steve's directions Carrie taxied round to the cafe. "I'll tell'em you'll pay the landing fee when you finish, so off you go and enjoy yourself. When you've finished go to the tower, pay the bill and come back over here and pick me up. OK?"

Before Carrie could reply, Steve was waving at someone inside the cafe and walking. She called tentatively on the radio, trying to reassure herself that the people on the other end were only human and probably very kind.

"Redhill Tower, Golf Echo Echo Hotel Juliet request taxi for solo circuits," she said, speaking slowly and clearly into the microphone.

"Golf Hotel Juliet, reading you fives, taxi for Alpha one, hold for the two six runway, QFE 989, QNH 995. Caution work in progress on southern taxiway and a fire-truck chasing a loose deer on the perimeter, so taxi via Echo one for a one nine hold, to continue," came back in fast-flowing radio crackle.

Carrie gawked. She stared silently ahead, noticing a helicopter on the far side of the field, which appeared to be imitating a trout caught on a line: nose-up, kick, tail-up, yaw. As the helicopter instructor recaptured straight and level, the ATC said dryly in Carrie's head-phone; "I've got two balls but neither of them are crystal! Golf Hotel Juliet did you receive my message?"

Carrie did her best but now her mind was full of men sitting on large illuminated balls. '..er..Runway 26, .er...C5 hold...er... Hotel Juliet."

"Roger GOLF Hotel Juliet, how many on board?"

"One ..er...Hotel Juliet..er.. Golf Hotel Juliet."

She started to taxi but hadn't gone far before the tower was back.

"Golf Hotel Juliet, do you know which direction is North?"

Carrie said nothing, searching around for the compass.

"Golf Echo Echo Hotel Juliet Redhill Tower, I repeat do you know which direction is north, because while I am working like a one-armed paper hanger up here, you appear to be heading south?"

"Hotel Juliet." She replied obligingly, hoping that would halt the babble. Instead it increased.

"Golf Hotel Juliet did you hear my warning that the southern taxiway was closed? That is CL-OS-ED? You do understand English?"

"Er... ." She knew there had been something about deer.

"Golf Hotel Juliet do you read?"

"Hotel Juliet."

"Well then GOLF Hotel Juliet, why are you taxiing south? Turn around and taxi in the opposite direction."

"Er, sorry..er..wilco."

This she tried to do. But, rather shaken by the tower's invective and the fact that she was about to fly solo for only the second time, as she turned she ran off the taxiway. Her nosewheel stuck in the grass.

This really got the air-traffic controller going. You could almost hear his behind-the-scenes cry of PILOTS! CRETINS!

"Golf Hotel Juliet did you read the NOTAMS before coming here?"

NOTAMS? NOTAMS? Carrie thought back to her flights with Mitch. They had consulted the NOTAMS then. 'Notice to Airmen.' They were sort of road warnings for airfields; this was closed, that was changed etc. But since leaving her care Carrie hadn't seen one.

"Negative.... Hotel Juliet."

"Well, Golf Hotel Juliet," came back the tower now all slick sympathy, "I suggest you taxi back to Redhill Aviation and ask your instructor to show you the NOTAMS before you go sticking your nosewheel in my grass, which was NOTAMed off as soft and wet and, therefore, unsuitable for traffic."

"er..Hotel Juliet, I'm stuck."

"Stuck! Stuck! Golf Hotel Juliet is stuck! You come here from another airfield, without knowing which way is north, without reading the NOTAMS and then you get your nosewheel stuck in my wet bits and close my airfield. Hotel Juliet shut down and go and get your instructor. Redhill General Broadcast: all the runways are closed, all traffic to hold....."

Carrie walked back to the cafe.

"Ah don't worry," said Steve, cool as ever, "they're just a nasty old bunch of queens here at Redhill. It doesn't make any difference. Next time we come here the old faggots will be treating you like a long lost friend."

"I don't want to come here again. Ever! They had a general broadcast about me!"

"Negative, you do. General Broadcast is closer to General Love than Major Cock-up. Don't fret. Now let me have a quick word with young Jonnie boy in the tower and we'll have you off solo again."

As they flew back, Steve told her that in the ten years he'd been flying it had always been the same. "Rudehill has a reputation around the world; ignore it. They'll all die of heart-attacks long before we do. Attitude is all. Now balls in the middle my sweet." Tapping on the balance indicator, Steve sang her a relaxing song.

Through the weeks Steve was joined by Tim, and then Clive, who was replaced by Mike, and then another Dave, a man who started every flight with the phrase: "Let's go play!"

John said a high turnover was usual in flying schools. Janie explained Fagin was cheap and fell out with all his pilots.

Carrie missed Mitch. When she asked Janie how she could find her, Janie mentioned she and Mitch had both been interviewed by the police.

"But nothing," she said. "I thought it would be more, you know, exciting. But they just asked a few questions and that was it. They talked to Mitch longer, but then they would."

"Why?"

"Oh," Janie undid her hair from it's bun and began platting it, her face tinged with scandal fever. "Oh, didn't she tell you she had a thing with Ben?"

"A thing?" Carrie thought she understood but her stomach heaved (why does emotion always attack the stomach not the heart, she wondered) and she wanted this spelt out. She couldn't quite believe it. "What thing?"

Janie looked wicked. "They had an affair. And Mitch was married at the time. So you can imagine the police liked that one."

"Is Mitch divorced then?"

"No, her husband was killed. Driving to the airport! Ironic in't it."

"Long ago?"

"Two years. She'd stopped having the affair by then. And then Ben got into trouble and left. Anyway someone like Mitch is hardly going to hang around in an air-raid shelter are they?"

Carrie shrugged, feeling incomprehensibly sad, her stomach's lurching turning into an anguished ache.

"And," said Janie, her voice dancing like snowflakes against a light, "you know she visited him the night he died!"

Carrie wandered away. She wanted to think about this. Of course there was no reason why Mitch, who was clearly a private person, should have told her student anything, but Carrie felt let down. As though Mitch had pretended to be a better friend than she really was. For a wiser moment Carrie wondered if someone of Mitch's integrity could really have had an adulterous affair, let alone be implicated in a murder. She could have put the idea down to Janie's obvious lust for scandal, but woman-like she preferred to believe that the paragon had done something wicked, thereby reducing herself to the level of ordinary mortals. It was then an easy step down to deeper suspicions. Very easy if you can't resist flirting with the romance of failure.

Steve had left by the time Carrie was ready for navigation; John said suavely he'd become a little too relaxed; Janie explained that the police had been around asking about a stolen laptop. Instead Carrie had Tim, an ex-driving instructor, who wore white socks and navigated by road.

"I fly IFR," joked Tim, "I follow roads."

Carrie looked blank. "Very funny; not."

"Not heard of Instrument Flying Regulations? IFR?"

"Oh, OK I get it now."

Tim sighed. He wasn't sure if Carrie was just a blond bimbo or if she was really very clever and pretending. Hearing that she spoke four languages he had asked her to teach him Spanish, adding wittily, 'of course the best way to learn a language is in bed'. Without even a smile, she had replied that that was true and that she had taken loads of books to bed before she got fully fluent. Still, even if she was dumb, she had nice legs and wore shirts cut low under the arm without a bra, so if he leant back when her arms were on the control column, he could see everything almost up to the nipple.

Tim taught her the art of satellite navigation, which for him was the antidote to getting lost. Everywhere Carrie flew (following the roads or not) Tim tuned in the GPS and soon she was an expert.

"You can't use it for your test," said Tim, "that will be dead reckoning only, but don't get too exposed. Sarah, your examiner, will be bound to use the GPS, steaming after those satellites to make sure she doesn't get lost herself. Tell her you know nothing about it, and you'll be just A.OK."

Knowing this, Carrie wasn't even nervous on the day. She sailed through the navigation test, finding even the most obscure points exactly where they should be. When Sarah came back she congratulated Tim.

"Well done, Mr Instructor," she said, "that girl was great. A1 pass. I think she might be the best person I've ever examined. And the pundits say women can't navigate. Well! I could tell them a thing or two."

Even Carrie's General Flying Test turned out to be similarly breezy. The examiner had just come back from a meeting about European Union changes to the flying licence and was far more interested in discussing this on his mobile with various other examiners, than in testing Carrie. After a quick flight in the local area they returned to the airfield.

"Look," the examiner said, "I'm going to stand down here on the airfield and watch while you do a couple of circuits. OK?"

Carrie looked out of the window as she landed, (rather brilliantly she thought) but the examiner's back was firmly turned, mobile to his right ear, blocking out the aircraft noise with his other hand. When she taxied over, he too congratulated her on a fine test. "Excellent," he said, "women always make good pilots. Now, you make the cheque out to me..."

So, Carrie thought, this is it. I've got the licence. I know how to fly. I know how to navigate. All I need is a few maps. Off I go to Florida and find my fortune. Hurrah! The sound dropped like a helicopter in autorotation.

Every day Carrie almost booked her flight to Florida. Every day she walked to the phone. Every night she went to bed without a confirmed ticket. She tried ringing Mitch for advice, but found that she was in America. She asked John, but he recommended a box. And she still hadn't heard anything from the police. She tried ringing, but was told that both detectives were away on holiday.

Roberta didn't believe it. "Yeah," she said, "sure! They'll be back and you'll be gone and I'll be done for murder. So much for doing good deeds for relations."

If the Pilot Slumbers at the Helm

The airfield base was small and squalid compared to the luxurious Nairobi office. It didn't even have good access to the airstrip, the builders having chosen the longevity of shade over utility. But, as the Chief Architect had explained to the Chief Flying Officer, this place would only be used by pilots and therefore did not need anything more than the basics. Consequently the Chief Flying Officer spent most of his time in Nairobi, only coming here when it was necessary to discipline his staff.

Now he sat on the worm-eaten chair, staring angrily at the pilot sprawled over the plastic sofa. He'd been fooled here, that's for sure. The guy'd come with great references but he was an idiot. And that ridiculous over-the-top moustache! Not only did he know nothing of planes and performance but he couldn't navigate either. He was like a joke-pilot, a send-up, a..a..he sought for the word..con..car..something; damn! Then reminded himself he was a man of action and must be expected to forget mere words.

When the boy had had the simple job of taking some freight to a near-by strip, he got lost, landed on a military airfield instead; just as the President was touching down. Then he was caught doing things to the President's daughter that even her husband might have balked at: and she hadn't complained. If the Chief Flying Officer hadn't had some pretty influential friends, the bloody idiot would be in jail, or more likely dead. He had to go.

"OK, mate," the Chief said, standing up quickly so the old chair rocked like a ticking dynamo, "well it looks like things haven't worked out. But we'll pay for your flight back to the UK. Can't say fairer than that."

"Yes, its a shame; better to be a shameless dame than a dameless shame," said the pilot carelessly, stubbing out his cigarette on the arm of the sofa, so the plastic shrivelled and gave off a nidorous smell. "I feel jolly old Blighty calling me home. A ferry company is begging for my services and I just can't let them down. Write me a reference, will you. I always crumple up like an actress on her first date at the sight of that lovely shiny paper. "

The Chief Flying Officer shrugged and drew out his pen. Then he glanced up at the pilot, his expression changing, becoming what internet-educated Carrie would have seen as Machiavellian but to the Chief himself was simply wise. He scratched his neck, where a nasty rash of prickly heat was attacking.

"Agh. A ferry company, you say. Well. All right, buster, it goes against my honest nature but I'm a kindly man. More. I'm going to give you a present. A little job, something specially suited to you and something you can fit in with someone else's expense account. Capice!"

"Too good," murmured the pilot. "Too good."

Stretching the Sainsbury's Bag

Carrie didn't usually worry about the future; shifting Sainsbury's bag avoidance providing her with the best results. But she had recently received some rough phone calls from the bank. The assistant bank manager's assistant even questioning the existence of the plane "on which they were placing so much of their hopes". She had to fetch the plane now. She couldn't afford more experience. She'd have to hire a companion. A cheap companion pilot. Pity Ben had been killed; this would have been just the job for him.

She asked a few of the instructors. Most refused, but a couple said laughing: "Cool job! We'll crack it or die in the attempt! I've flown to France and the Atlantic is only a bigger channel! Only I'll need to be back in a week."

Hearing variations on the same phrase, Carrie realised that searching for a ferry pilot amongst the instructors was like looking for candour in the council.

She rang the CAA, nicknamed the 'Campaign Against Aviation', and began a round of mechanical voices: "Please enjoy the music while you hold," "you are 12th in the line, the average length of call is 5 minutes," "we are working regardless of the weather to help you." Wafted into what Carrie saw were indeed the tears of bureaucracy, she was finally told that if there was a man there who could help her, he was away on holiday. "Please call again soon".

As an addict of computer games she knew it must be possible to solve the dilemma: planes were no doubt ferried day after day across the great shark infested sea, without being eaten by club wielding giants, but it certainly didn't feel like it.

She went into the flying school bar and ordered a whisky. As she played with her whisky and tried to clear her head, a lean, elderly man sat down next to her on a bar-stool, noting her whisky and her sour expression.

"Bad day, darling?" He asked sympathetically, leaning over and rubbing her shoulder.

"More like bad future!" She said, not objecting to the darling or the shoulder because he was so old.

"Oh? Not a problem with getting to the solo stage is it...we've all been there, my darling." He had a long face like a horse, with kind, lived-in eyes, his eyebrows drooping in silent sympathy.

Carrie snorted. Having spent the last few months in this flying environment, she had perceived that most pilots judge all life in relation to flying. If you are cross it must be pre-solo; if you are happy it must be immediately post-solo; if you are smoothly content you probably just got your licence.

"No, ages ago," she said, adding blasphemously, "it's really rather more important than that."

Colin's eyebrows shot up. He knew the way women confused important issues and trivia. He'd seen his wife beside herself with tears because her parrot had died, while when she drove the car into the side of one of his planes, she'd merely remarked that it was metal and could be mended. Strange creatures women. Perspectives quite off.

"Can I help, darling? I'm Colin Larfman. I am a pilot myself."

Carrie restrained a second snort of laughter. Oh, well, that's the answer then: 'pilot power, the solution to every situation'. He looked a little old for a trip across the Atlantic, but she did need someone, even if the best she could find was an aged bar-prop.

"You might," she replied a trifle wistfully, "but I'm really looking for an experienced Atlantic flyer."

"Atlantic Flyer, wasn't that the Wright brother's plane?"

Even for a pilot that seemed a rather obscure answer. "No, I mean I want someone to fly with me from the USA in my Warrior. I've been asking around amongst the instructors here but...."

"Oh, them," Colin said dismissively, squeezing her shoulder, "they couldn't find their arse with both hands. But... A ferry pilot for a flight across the pond, there I can help you. Didn't anyone tell you there are agencies?"

Carrie stared. Here was her computer wizard.

"No. They probably didn't know. I asked the manager too, John at .."

"What Fagin? Tighter than a gnat's chuff! Christ he'd bite your leg off if he thought you had a pound coin in your socks but he wouldn't tell you the time unless you paid him."

"Oh."

"Tell me what you need? I have a host of pilots, all about as useful as daffodils but serviceable nonetheless."

Carrie, glad to have a sympathetic ear, explained how she came to own a small Warrior in Florida, and what she wanted to do. Colin listened intently, making comments.

"Funny of your man to buy a plane without flying it first," he remarked. "Especially a pilot. Pilots, my darling, understandably don't trust engineers. Put it in a box; God knows what it will be like."

Carrie was adamant. She wanted the adventure and felt in her heart that the trip would do her good one way or another; maybe a fourth husband, certainly money. He promised her some details and they arranged to meet a week later. Carrie hoped he wasn't just another pilot who talked.

Roberta sneered when she heard the details. "You met a man in the bar! And then he solved your problems. Great. How soon before you meet again in some sleazy hotel? He's sorry but his wife is ill. And anyway she doesn't understand him. Yeah! Forget it kid, I've been there."

"No! It wasn't like that at all. You don't understand."

"It never is, honey. And you haven't rung the police recently. For all you know this Colin may have murdered Ben and created a meeting with you. You trust him and then....wommoom! Sack over head!"

When Carrie met Colin a week later the flying school bar was again empty and desolate. Colin kissed her on the lips like an old friend, and Carrie wondered for a brief moment if her cynical cousin was right.

"Why is it always empty in here?" she asked Colin, looking around the bare tables and silent chairs. "How do they survive? Don't they need drinkers?"

"Survive I don't know, but it's the era, my darling. The modern flimsiness of man. The no-drink, no-do culture. When I was young flying school bars used to be full, so full you could hardly squeeze in. Beer flowed, men drank all night and then got up and did a full day's flying; I feel sorry for you young girls now. Those were the days when men were men, pansies were flowers and sheep were afraid. I remember when I flew at Bigamy.."

"Perhaps it's just they've got better beer at the local pub," broke in a young man, walking in from the school.

"Excuses," said Colin dismissively, turning his back. "Now, my darling, we have work to do."

He gave Carrie six CVs. The first one was a girl called Hazel Brown.

"This is a girl," she remarked, then, remembering Mitch, felt guilty.

"Ya-um, I've given you two girls. I thought it would be cheaper and easier; you could at least share a room. They tend to be more reliable too. Which is that one...?" He leant over, moving the paper with one hand while manoeuvring his glasses across his nose with the other. "....Oh that is Hazel, she is the most experienced of the whole bunch, probably."

"Hum," sniffed Carrie; since he didn't know about her hidden agenda he was naturally flying with only half a tank. Pilots, like all physical men, tended to be rather naive in her experience.

She read Hazel's details quickly. She was 45. Divorced. American. Schooled in England but had worked everywhere. She knew the ferrying side of Africa well, which might have been a factor had Carrie not decided to sell the plane in the UK. Hazel's hobby was microlight aerobatics.

"Does she have a death-wish, this one?"

"Eh?"

"Microlight aerobatics!" Carrie screwed her face into a facsimile of fear.

"Oh! See what you mean. She's good. Tests the things to their limits but no crashes. A thinker and totally dedicated to flying. The story is her husband said 'it's either me or the planes' and she replied, 'no contest.'"

"Yeah," Carrie said skeptically, reflecting that that underlined what she always thought about women not recognising comfort when it hit them. She put Hazel to the bottom of the pile.

The next one was an older man whose age was quaintly written as 50+.

"Very experienced, my darling" said Colin, "very experienced."

"Umm, is there something about these pilots..they seem a bit rare, not quite what you'd expect in a pilot. Not quite like my instructors."

"Well. No. But you know you can't expect ferry pilots to be airline pilots, present or future and, besides, the situation is a little difficult."

"Howso?"

"Well, you see, ferry pilots are free birds. They travel alone and they don't like taking passengers, even, well especially really, the owner." Especially a woman, Colin thought, but he didn't say that to Carrie. "So these are a select group..the ones that said 'yes'."

"Great!" Carrie said, understanding immediately, even though he shilly shallied around the subject and repeated himself a few times: these boys didn't want her, only her money. Funny, she thought, how she'd been on these shores of life before; and last time it had cost a lot.

The old boy was called Jim. He was a specialist in seaplanes having ferried more than a hundred. The CV said that he had had only 2 incidents."

"Two incidents?"

"Like crashes but not so bad."

"I know what an incident is, I wanted the details."

"Oh, well they are quite funny really."

"Really?" Clearly this man was not an owner. Carrie had not forgotten Fagin's £4,000 insurance excess.

"Yes, the first one was when he was flying a Lake Buccaneer from Goose Bay to Reykjavik. It was one of those sleet ridden days and he shouldn't really have started the trip at all, but he did (perhaps he was in a hurry to get home) and now the weather was deteriorating. Getting worse and worse, terrible blinding rain, awful conditions. He was flying on instruments. Then the first VOR failed. He still had the artificial horizon but when he glanced at the ADF he realised that that was down too, and the second VOR. It was getting dark and suddenly his compass began to swirl. He thought everything that could have done, had gone wrong, until he glanced at his fuel gauge..." He paused for dramatic effect but Carrie was ahead of him.

"Low?"

"Empty! He decided to put down on the sea and try and radio for help on his only remaining instrument, his VHF radio. He was shaking as he landed and then he saw..."

He paused again.

"God?"

"A wall! The harbour wall, he'd flown right into the harbour without realising it. "

"Lucky he didn't hit a boat. So the plane was saved?"

"Not sure my darling, but he was anyway."

"Oh!" Definitely not an owner.

"The second one was equally exciting. Again he was between Goose and Reykjavik, well past Greenland. The weather was as clear as a bell, crisp and clean, none of that pollution that we get in these over-populated parts. He could see Iceland, well the outline anyway. He was singing. Everything was perfect, except the winds were much stronger than forecast. As he battled on he was watching his fuel gauge. Finally he knew it was no good, he would never make it to land. He only had one chance. So he called up search and rescue on the radio. He was lucky, there was a ship nearby, and it could divert the short distance to where he was."

"Wow. He landed on the ship?"

"No, he landed next to it, they sent out a lifeboat and he climbed on board the ship from there. He never even got his feet wet."

"And the plane?"

"Oh, well that joined the flotsam and jetsam in the sea. It was insured."

"Great planning," Carrie murmured, putting him even further down the pile than Hazel Brown.

The other girl was quite different from Hazel. She was younger, only twenty-eight. Unmarried, but had a child. Was trained in the military; then they asked her to go to Bosnia, six months after the birth of her son. She was looking for other flying jobs more compatible with being a young hands-on mother.

"What will she do with the boy while we travel?"

"Her mother looks after him. I think she lives with her own Ma."

"I'd have thought there were more suitable jobs for a single mother," Carrie said. She suddenly imagined what it would be like to travel with Sissy sister-in-law, inconsolably missing her little darlings.

"Maybe." Colin, while, like most pilots, extremely nosy and fond of gossip, was not judgmental on other people's morals and behaviour.

The third man was young and single. He'd been at Oxford Training School, then straight into an airline. Unfortunately after 10 years, just as he got his captaincy, the company went bust. Even now he was only 32."

"Sounds OK."

"Yes. I haven't met him, he's probably charming. At the moment he works in the bar over at the terminal, but he will get back into the airlines when they start recruiting again. Until then he is looking for a bit of different flying. His only drawback from your point-of-view is his lack of ferrying experience. And he was a bit hesitant about single engines; he asked

ATLANTIC WARRIORS

Carrie put him above Hazel and looked at the other two. One was an Irish airshow pilot, fortyish, married, no children.

"Seems to go together; ferrying and aerobatics."

"Yes, airline pilots aren't really suited for this type of individual work. They are more team men; warm cockpits, several engines and no risk. Men for repetition. These ferry pilots are the hard men of flying, the seat-of-your-pants flyers, the adventurers, the pioneers. The romantics."

The last man, Rhum, was 40, divorced, three children. Chess player. And then the CV said enigmatically 'at least one East European wife.'

"What does that mean?"

"Oh, well, he's rather a character. The type to beat the computer at chess but wear odd socks, if you know what I mean."

"Not really."

He's very intelligent; loves flying but somewhat eccentric. He ran away from home at some young age, taught himself Russian and chess somewhere on his travels and then ended up marrying an Eastern European woman for money. They got out of the USSR and he learnt to fly. Somehow he also got paid for playing chess. Now I think he's been rumbled. He began marrying women to get them out but since the wall came down he's rather lost his market."

"Sounds innovative. Nice character?"

"Unusual. If he was a woman you'd say he was an air head."

"Good thing for a pilot."

"Say again?"

"An airhead..flying..it was a joke."

"Oh, yes, very funny, my darling."

Carrie put him next to the airline pilot and looked at the airshow pilot.

"What about him?"

"Kieran O'Toole. He's a character and a half. Big man. You'll have to see him. You'll like him, he's spent a lot of time in Africa. If I told you the stories about him and by him you wouldn't believe me. I don't believe half myself. One story is that he was flying a Stearman when, desperate for a pee, he set down in a field on a slight slope. In spite of the lack of brakes on the Stearman, he thought it would be OK: until he turned around midstream and saw the Stearman launching itself down the slope towards a ditch."

"Ha. Sounds like Kieran and the 'Russian' are brothers."

"No, Rhum is more up-to-the-moment, Kieran more a 'showman.' But there are things in common. Which lads do you want to see?"

"I'll see them all except crasher, sorry incident-man, I think his luck is running thin."

[76]

In a Calm Sea Every Man is a Pilot

Another week ate into Carrie's, and the bank's, meagre supply of money and then the first of her pilots arrived. As soon as Carrie opened the door, she knew he was the airline pilot.

Tall, slim and mousey-haired, he walked with a straight, military bearing but kept his eyes on the ground. When he said 'Hello' his hand shot out from his side like a cannon ball. He grasped her hand with his tanned one, as though she was giving him a life-line, and held on far too long, apparently unsure how to let go having made the contact. She took her hand away.

"Hello, Clive Somerset." He said raising his eyes to the level of Carrie's chin. "Sorry, late. Wheels in garage, had to come by horse taxi." He laughed heartily and crossed his arms defensively.

The moment he saw Carrie, Clive wished he hadn't come. When Colin told him a widow woman wanted to fly a plane back across the Atlantic he'd imagined some nice, middle-aged woman with fat arms, who would sit beside him admiring his style. Not this tall, blond sex-bomb with her young skin and athletic body. Still, it would be something different, and interesting flying. If only she'd been a bit uglier. At least she couldn't fly so he would be the boss; unless she liked him...ouf...his feet turned to the weakest rain-sogged clay.

For a moment they both stood smiling, Clive at Carrie's chin, Carrie at Clive's eyelids. He shifted his weight from foot to foot, discreetly glancing from her chin to the seats. He knew it would be rude to sit down unasked, but he didn't want her to stand so close.

"Sit down, please," Carrie said. "Would you like a coffee?"

"No, ...thank you," Clive bobbed politely at her chin, sitting down nervously, neither on the edge of the sofa nor fully into its depth. He rocked slightly as he sat, making Carrie feel that he was ready at any moment to spring back onto his feet. As his eyes zipped up to her chin and back to the ground, Carrie began to feel agitated. Picking up his CV, she tried to be light-hearted.

"You've been flying yonks."

"Say again." He dropped his gaze to the floor.

"You've been flying a long time."

"Yes," his eyes flew up to her chin. "Er, 15 years, three months and a week yesterday. First solo on 17th birthday."

"That's good. You've got lots of hours. 8,000?"

"7,969. Shouldn't be long there." Gaze still up.

"No doubt. I've got 50 something hours myself. I've just finished my licence. Originally I thought I could bring the plane back alone."

"Oh." Gaze definitely down. Drat! A pilot! Why was she so pretty?

A strangely tense atmosphere filled the room. Clive kept his thin arms tightly crossed, his legs poised to spring. Carrie couldn't understand it; usually men flirted easily with her and she responded well. She made another attempt to put him at ease, giving him a smile that would have caused any of her ex-husbands to jump across the water. Clive buried his head in his arms.

"What makes you, an airline pilot, want to ferry a small aircraft?"

Clive took a deep breath. Here goes. "Oh, adventure. Experience. Been lucky. Thought might try slumming it a bit."

Tactful, Carrie thought, before hearing his abrupt laugh again and realising he was making a joke. 'Won her over there,' thought Clive. Women like humour.

"Would you be happy flying a single? I see you flew four engine planes."

His head bobbed up and down and finished up looking at the floor. "Yes '74s. But do aerobatics regularly. Yak 90, that's single. Water is the problem but guess we'll have all the kit."

"Umm. Do you have anything yourself?"

"Got an immersion suit and a hand-held ELT."

"ELT?"

"Emergency Locater Transmitter; so one up on you there."

He laughed again. Then stopped mid-laugh and began coughing. It wasn't a good idea to laugh at beautiful women or employers. They didn't like it. He stared intensely at her chin. "Guess there'll be one in the plane anyhow? USA and all that?"

"I guess so. How's your navigation? Small planes are different from Jumbos," said Carrie, pleased with herself at what she considered to be a pretty well-informed question.

"Oh, yes. Old school me. Dead reckoning was how we did it. Map and compass. Nothing else. Not like this lot now; mobile phones, you know, can't navigate for toffee. All used to getting directions by phone." He laughed again, desperately signalling another joke.

Carrie had had enough. All this nervy jolting around was making her queasy. She told him she had a few others to see and she'd let him know.

"Right. Right," he said, jumping to his feet like the shot spring she'd expected. "Be off then. See you soon. Er...Good luck...er..whatever."

He gave her another of the nervous hand-grips, shot one terrified look at her face and, after she'd removed her hand, banged into the door in his haste to be away.

"Oh, sorry," he gasped, flinging himself down the steps in embarrassment. If only she could have been darker, older, fatter and a little bit less attractive. And not a pilot.

Carrie wanted a drink. She remembered this feeling; it was just like being married to her second husband. She poured herself a whisky and then telephoned Colin, desperately looking for reassurance.

"He's a good pilot," said Colin, "it's just human freight he has problems with, not planes."

"What about human freight employers?" she asked.

Colin was so diplomatic she could hear him smiling over the phone.

The next one scheduled to arrive was Geraldine, the single mother, and as Carrie put the phone down to Colin, she heard the door bell ring. Outside the door, standing on the step, was a tall woman in her fifties, made taller by her use of long stiletto heels. She wore a pencil skirt, with a tightly fitting jacket over a pink silk shirt and several rows of multi-coloured beads. In her hand she clutched a Maggie-Thatcher handbag.

"Hello?" asked Carrie surprised. Clearly not the 28 year old Geraldine.

"Hello," said the woman, and her voice was soft and mellifluous. "I'm sorry to surprise you like this, but Geraldine has found another job and she asked me to come in her place. May I come in?"

"Oh! Of course, so sorry," Carrie stammered, wondering if this overtly feminine, middle-aged woman could really be a pilot. "Come in, please. Have a coffee? Would you like a biscuit?"

"No, thank you," the woman smiled, undulating into the room like a model on the catwalk. "Watching my waist-line so other's don't have to."

She sat down on the sofa, her legs neatly to one side, and stroked her skirt. "I am sorry to spring wildly upon you. Only this morning the Air Ambulance called Geraldine. She knew she'd be a fool to turn that down, although she was looking forward to your trip and I think you girls would have clicked." She smiled again, conspiratorially. "She asked me if I was interested. I've more than 14 thousand hours and I'm currently unemployed." Shutting her eyes, she clasped her hands in front of her chest. Her handbag slid down her arm, twisting at the elbow. Regretfully she disentangled herself and, after brushing the area with a handkerchief, placed the gently on the floor, next to her matching shoes.

"Airlines! They discriminate terribly against women. It's terrible! Awful! I don't know any women with my experience on 747s and yet can I find a job? Can I?"

She smoothed her skirt down again, her face suddenly drawn into painful emotional lines. As Carrie watched, she got out a powder pack and looking in the mirror, puffed delicately around her nose. Upset, she redid her lipstick.

'There was never yet fair woman but she made mouths in a glass,' thought Carrie, remembering long internet evenings in Cape Town.

"Sorry," the woman said in a trembling voice, fluffing her fringe and re-combing her hair, "it's so...so unkind...I get so emotional. Perhaps I will have that coffee. Thank you, dear. I suppose it's too early for a little accompanying sherry?"

Carrie poured her both and gave her a biscuit, which she nibbled at delicately, leaving red lip stains where she touched.

"So, tell me about the trip. When do we start? I've flown most places, Africa, America, the world, well you can see that from my hours. There's really not much I don't know about flying..I began in Zim.."

"Sorry Mrs..Miss..I'm afraid I don't know your name."

"So sorry, my dear. Cary Carlise, but all my friends call me CC, I hope you'll do the same. We will be friends. I feel it already." CC gave Carrie a profoundly superficial smile.

After talking for an hour, eating all of the nibbles in the house and drinking four cups of accompanying coffee, all in the most dainty manner, Cary Carlise left. Carrie rang Colin again, extremely glad she'd scheduled the remaining three pilots for the following day.

"Colin?" she asked. "Do you know anything about a Cary Carlise? Only she came in place of Geraldine. There was something...something almost..odd about her, like an actress playing a part. Tell me I'm imagining it. She's certainly highly experienced."

Colin chuckled lecherously. "So, Gary's turned up again has he, darling? The old dog! The old dog! I wondered when he would."

"He? Are you saying Cary was a man in drag? I don't believe it, she was so.. well so feminine." A thought struck her. "Are you suggesting a man can act a really feminine woman better than a woman could. Quaint. I love it."

Colin loved it less. "No. He's all woman now. He wasn't once though. He used to be a Rhodesian air force pilot, had some kids too, then he emigrated. Worked over here as a pilot for a large airline, before suddenly deciding to have a sex change. But, while he was changing, the guys in the cockpit knew what was happening; they refused to work with him. He was made redundant. Anyway, after he became a woman, he (sorry she) started working again with a small airline. And well, my darling, you know what us guys are like," Colin gave another, rather pleased little chuckle, "well, not to put too fine a point on it, he/she slept around. The boys thought she was one hell of a goer and soon she had slept with most of them.."

"They thought she was a woman?"

"Of course," spluttered Colin outraged, "there's nothing kinky about pilots. Anyway, it just happened that the small airline sent some pilots, including Cary, to work temporarily with the large airline and, not to put too fine a point on it, the guys from the large airline recognised Cary as the man he no longer was..and told all his sex partners about it..Well! They realised they'd been sleeping with a man and well, not to put too fine a point on it, they weren't too happy. He got the sack again! From one sack to another! I think you get my meaning." Colin chuckled again.

The first of the three remaining pilots to be interviewed was Hazel Brown. Carrie had talked to her on the phone. She had a mature, responsible sounding voice and Carrie pictured a stolid, serious-looking woman with thick legs and pronounced features. Consequently, when she answered the knock on the door and saw a tall, slim, short-haired blond girl, she didn't immediately connect her with the voice.

"Hello?"

"Hello," said the telephone-voice. "I am Hazel Brown."

"Good Heavens."

Hazel looked surprised. "You are Carrie Nordsuitlaan?"

Carrie nodded, amazed that Hazel had pronounced her name correctly. "You weren't expecting me? Colin Larfman definitely said 10.00am sharp on the 10th."

"On, no no, I was. It's just..I mean I was expecting..no nothing."

Hazel walked in and Carrie felt relieved. There was something in the way she strode into the room, looking around, taking command of the situation, which exuded competence and strong efficiency. Carrie wouldn't have been at all surprised to hear that Hazel had been head girl at Benenden. "Coffee?"

"Please." The professional woman accepted a cup of coffee (strong and black, and no doubt like her men although she didn't say so) and sat down at the table, opening her briefcase and bringing out some papers.

"I expect you'd like some references. I brought a couple, but you can have more if you like. I also did a rough plan of what route I thought we would take, and a few scenarios - you know, length of time en route, diversions if the weather gets bad and so forth. I brought you some useful phone numbers; you might like them even if you choose one of the other pilots."

She handed Carrie a sheaf of papers. She was surprised that Carrie was so young but other than that she made no judgment. As Hazel knew from her own experience, it was not what you looked like but how you acted that was important, although actions themselves could sometimes be detrimental. She allowed herself only a second to dwell on something as irrelevant as a past incident in her life before returning to the business in hand.

"If you do decide to employ me, it will be a first for me too. I've always previously flown alone." She smiled at Carrie. "I'm glad you are a woman, I think it might be difficult flying eight hours a day with a man."

Before Carrie knew what was happening, the efficient woman had her poring over charts, discussing the best possible routes and likely climatic conditions at this time of year.

"Normally," said Hazel, "my pay includes expenses, so I just go, go, go. I fly 14 or more hours at a time, sleep in the plane or camp down somewhere on the airfield, and I'm through with the whole trip in a matter of days. My record is Van Nuys in Los Angeles to Cape Town in six days; it was a twin of course, much faster than yours. I don't suppose you'll want to go like that, though, since you're partly being a passenger. I imagine you'll want to sleep in hotels. Yes? And, before I forget, since you are a pilot I assume you'll want to fly some of the legs. Yes? That's fine with me, as long as we agree that I'm always pilot in command. If anything goes wrong, I make the decisions. I'm sorry to come on strong about that, but I think it's just as well if we know where we stand from the beginning. That way there are no misunderstandings later. Now when are you thinking of leaving? How long will it be before you can let me know whether you have chosen me?"

Carrie murmured about 'others to interview', but already she saw that the efficient woman was too strong for her. This would be Hazel's trip, with Carrie as a passenger. Carrie wanted to remain in some semblance of control. Anyway weren't men better at practical things?

As Hazel was leaving, Carrie asked her curiously. "What made you learn to fly?"

"I like machines," Hazel said, standing so still she seemed like a British train. "I like the purity of them, the instant response of their actions. I like the control of man over mechanics and his environment. And I the sensation of flying, the excitement and the challenge."

She smiled suddenly, and there was an intensity in her face, a shining light in her eyes that Carrie hadn't expected. "You can see I've thought about it; asked myself the same question."

When Hazel left, Carrie had a cup of strong, black coffee, and felt depressed. Hazel was too much for her. She even caused Carrie to question herself. Was her life a little trivial? Her constant search for a rich husband a little insubstantial? Nothing would fluster the efficient Hazel. That would make her an excellent ferry pilot but would they have fun too? Wouldn't evenings be spent merely flight planning? Carrie recognised Hazel; the Boadicea of flying, chariots exchanged for Cessnas.

Impossible to go down that route and survive, Carrie instead began to wonder about Hazel's ex-husband. What sort of man could he have been? A push-over or Hazel's equal? Was their home life a constant battle for domination, or did she walk all over him? That they might have had a successful, happy marriage Carrie could not imagine. Her own first husband had been her idol; strong, sensitive and kind, he was an older man who had treated her like a favourite daughter, but he had died.

Her second marriage had also died, although the husband hadn't, after their disastrous visit to Holland. His parents were neither the mad ravenging cheese hounds her father had imagined, nor wallowing in luxurious splendour, as she had hoped, but millionaires who loved money far too much to part with it. In spite of owning several factories across the country they had no car, only bicycles, and would always travel by bus when possible. "Taxi" was a swear-word in their house.

Their house was a monument to 1950s durability; beds were narrow and spartan, and meals basic. But for Carrie the coup de grace was delivered with the bathrooms: unheated, unventilated cupboards with water leaks, which trickled down the walls and burnt or froze, but scarcely washed, the people inside. When Carrie left their house, knowing that nothing would come Kees's way until her 'fit and fifty' in-laws died, something in her marriage died too.

The Russian arrived next. A strange bubbly little man, shorter than Carrie and quite plump, he twitched energetically as he spoke. A flap of skin joined the top of his breast-bone to the point of his chin giving him the appearance of a pelican. His long, brown, curly hair started at the back of his high forehead and gave the impression it was about to slip off backwards. He wore odd socks, one green, one red, above his pumped-up, race car sneakers. But he had a strange, undefinable charm that made Carrie warm to him immediately.

"Hi," he said, examining her and the room with lightening glances. "I'm Roman but call me Rhum." He kept his hands in his pockets, but he smiled. "You want to start ferrying planes back from the US for money 'eh?"

"Well, just one so far."

"Yeah, that's what I thought when I did my first ferry trip, but it's like LSD, you know. You do one and then you want to do another. You're hooked. You can't help it, it gets into the blood. I've thought of doing it for investment myself but then..I'm not the money-type really. I like the adventure but, well, cut the crap, I'm not one for long term planning. For me it's here now, gone tomorrow. Nice house you've got here. Victorian I guess around 1870?"

"It's my cousin's."

"Oh, yeah of course you are from sunny SA aren't you? You sound rather English to me, none of those oy sounds. Did you emigrate?"

"I married a South African but he was killed in a helicopter crash." It wasn't the whole story but it did for now.

"Shame. I'm a siwk myself..."

"SWINK?"

"SIWK. Single income with kids, though they live with my ex-wives. I like the egg-beaters myself. A lot of pilots don't, but I think if it flies it's good. I like birds too. I used to be an expert on Russian birds. Speak any Afrikaans?"

"Some, I had Dutch before and it helped, it's a bit like baby-Dutch, which suited me. You're Russian?"

"No I'm a Cunian, that's from Manchester, but I speak it. That name Nordsuitlaan, I've heard it before. I think I met a pilot of that name in America. Your husband fly ferry too?"

"No, he'd never been out of Africa."

"Oh, my mistake then. I'm terrible with names, only some hit my memory. I must have got it mixed."

"Coffee?"

"White and sweet like my women. Yes I speak Russian, French and English fluently. Spanish, German and Polish well and smatterings of other things including Dutch. Zal wij in Nederlands spreken?"

Carrie started to correct him, "zullen.." but he was still talking and she didn't bother. Her desire for grammatical accuracy had been a problem with all her husbands.

"I prefer the grandeur of the German and Russian intonations to the Dutch guttering," Rhum continued, "but I expect you agree. Most Brits find the 'Kaas Kop' rs and gs a pain. Give me a fluid, flamboyant tongue any day. So when did you want to bring the plane back?"

"As soon as possible."

"Magic. I'm free at once. We'll need a few clearances and presumably you don't have a ferry tank yet? Are we going all the way to SA, or just UK?"

"Just to the UK. I've arranged hanger space at Biggin Hill."

"B.H. Not a bad place, I used to teach there myself once. Is that how you know the Col, sorry Colin?"

"Sort-of. I met him in the bar."

The Russian's eyebrows flew up towards his slipping hair, reminding Carrie of the moustache on a palindromic head. "Is that so. I never thought the Col was the type to go picking up girls in bars. Looks far too solid. Still people have thought me religious, so. Cheers." He gulped his coffee.

The last interview of the evening was Kieran O'Toole, but Carrie nearly put him off, as she thought the clever, light-hearted, single Russian would be a fine companion for the trip. She assumed he must be able to navigate, though he hadn't come across as nearly so awe-inspiringly prepared as Hazel Brown.

Carrie was comparing these two pilots when the door opened and

Kieran O'Toole swept into the room. He was indeed a big man. Cowboy boots, tall legs in jeans, and a long black, leather coat. Even his twirly aviation moustache was ridiculously large and blond. Everything about him screamed aviation pioneer except his peroxide streaked hair, which whispered aging playboy.

"Hello," he said, sweeping off his dark glasses with his left hand. His right hand outstretched, his confident smile beaming into her eyes, "I hope you don't mind my coming in like this, but your fine speaking cousin was on her way out and she let me in. She told me to tell you she'd be back late and not to wait for her for dinner."

"You must have had quite a conversation."

"I'm a good listener. Always have been. It was one of the traits that attracted my wife to me, my silent thoughtful way of listening to everything she said. I think she was in hurry (your cousin that is, not my wife who is a thoughtful woman herself and seldom in a hurry). I was standing on the doorstep finishing my cigarette and she wanted to tell me not to smoke in the house. She has an interesting line in speech, your delightful relative; she told me if she discovered I'd been smoking in her house she would reduce my head to the size of an undernourished tomato and stomp on it, so naturally we started talking, if you follow my wild crazy verbiage. Pure pioneer's language."

He smiled at Carrie and swept his hand up through his hair. She couldn't be certain but she had the feeling he just peeked a look at himself in the mirror behind her head.

"You fly yourself, Colin tells me. Let me see your hands...ah yes aviator's hands. You will become a Pilot of the Purple Twilight. I can tell, just from the way a person walks, if he's going to be a good pilot. I've done most jobs and I used to be an excellent instructor, but time moves on and I felt the need for something more challenging. This will certainly be more demanding. All my previous Atlantic trips were in twin engine planes or bigger, but I'll enjoy this. We'll go VFR all the time I presume?"

"VFR?" Carrie groped for this term in her mind.

"Visual, no instrument flying. IFR I follow roads and there sure ain't going to be any roads out in the Atlantic. Anyway, I'm sure you'd prefer to see the view, and frankly I never trust those small plane instruments. Dog's dinners committing liberticide against the pilot. Colin tells me you are from Africa. Splendid. I love Africa. I did some of my finest flying there in the days when men were men and pansies were flowers! The stories I could tell you; indeed will tell you. When do we start? Soon? I was supposed to be going up to Scotland to look after the birds on Eigg and Muck, but I cancelled the trip. I'd so much rather fly your little Warrior back from the jolly old US. Do you want to talk tactics or shall we have a drink? If you've no better idea I have a yearning for a hotel bar. Odd I know but sometimes I'll be wandering down the street and I'm overcome by an intense desire for a nice sleazy little hotel bar. Ooh ha hotel bar, a cry from the jungle."

Later Colin asked Carrie which pilot she favoured.

"Hazel seemed the most organised but I'm not sure we'd have fun, the nervous one was so nervous he'd wear me out. The Russian was probably the best but he is a bit dreamy, I'm not sure if he really knows anything about flying. You were right about Kieran; big man."

"He's got good references."

"Yeah." References meant nothing to Carrie. "Talks a lot. Energetic."

"That type of pilot usually is quite energetic, not like instructors," said Colin sourly. "Those, my darling dear, won't do anything at all if they're on salary, unless they are hour building towards the airlines, then they'll fly in the worst pea soup and leave you as soon as they get enough experience to be useful. Otherwise they move slower than a French farmer's blockade."

"Maybe I'll take Cary Carlise."

"Over my dead body," spluttered Colin huffily, "my agency is straight. Besides you don't know where he's been or where she'll be looking!"

"No advice then?"

"I don't know girl. Sleep on it, that usually helps."

Colin knew better than to give advice to a woman; they were creatures of multiple moods. In one mood they'd be thankful and happy; five seconds later they'd be screaming at you. Never give advice to women, that was his motto, and he'd been married 33 years: all his wives had stayed friendly.

Carrie spent the night awake, tossing, turning and debating; could the Russian really navigate? Would Hazel be fun? Would Kieran talk too much? Was she sane enough for the nervous airliner? Around 4 o'clock in the morning Carrie finally decided on the Russian.

"I think," she told her cousin, who wasn't listening and didn't care, at breakfast the next morning, "I think he will be the most interesting and something tells me it won't just be remunerative but also terrific fun. We may even have a romance."

Carrie danced around the kitchen, glad to have made the choice. She accidentally spun into the table. "Oops."

"Sit down, for Gawdsake. I hate liveliness in the morning. If you want to dance, get me another coffee."

"Sorry, it's just..."

"Yeah, sure it is, great. Just shut up and sit down."

At nine o'clock Carrie decided it was late enough to ring Colin. "Hey

Colin, I've decided. It's going to be the Russian. You were right to tell me to sleep on it, although I did more thinking than sleeping."

"Hello my darling. I am glad you've made your choice. Only it's the wrong one," chortled Colin. "Rhum rang me only a few minutes ago to tell me he's withdrawing from work. Apparently he's found himself a girl-friend, and more importantly a girlfriend so rich that he can buy planes for himself."

"Oh," Carrie was deflated, "but why?"

"You know women," Colin explained obscurely, "her husband says he can't afford to divorce her, so they've come to an arrangement. She has promised to treat your Russian to an advanced aerobatics course."

Carrie acknowledged defeat. Wondered for a moment about Hazel Brown, then dismissed her. The nervous one was too nervous, Cary too genderically uncertain. Which only left Kieran.

So Kieran O'Toole it was. She would have to hope that he would grow quieter when he knew her better, Carrie thought, fondly imagining that Kieran was the sort of person affected by the desires of others.

A Kiss through a Veil

Carrie pounded anxiously around Gatwick, ticket in hand. Like Ben a year before she was invisible to the passing punters, hurrying to their futures. Unlike Ben she was driven by fury. Where the Hell was her pilot? She didn't want to check in without him. He could keep her amused with flying anecdotes and they would discuss the trip. Get down to tactics, which had been somewhat lacking so far. She pulverized her heel on the Gatwick linoleum in frustration. Was he late or was he not coming at all?

Just as Carrie was starting to imagine the scene where she took him to court for compensation, the inevitably inconvenient thought popped into her mind: she remembered where she had last seen the wedding photo. Ignatius and Carrie were about to leave Cape Town to go bush and she wanted to take the photo with them. She noticed it wasn't in its silver frame. Ignatius, when asked, had replied that he was having it copied so that his family, who loved her so much (yeah, right: especially Sissy no doubt) could have a copy each. And, in spite of that atrocious lie, she'd forgotten about it; never thought about it again.

Carrie was on the edge of despair, torn by thoughts of photos which might be important (should she contact the police?) and longing to get even with that damn pilot, when Kieran swanned up. He strolled over calmly, oblivious to her adrenaline rousing emotions. On his head a Stetson topped reflective Ray Bans, a mobile enhanced his black leather waistband, and a pair of lizard skin boots complimented his dark green calf-skin jacket. Dangling from his shoulders was a bag so huge that Carrie could never believe it would fit in the small plane, let alone feel it was justified when she had scrimped up a light back-pack; only the minimum amount of clothing to prevent herself going stark naked, and hardly a stick of make-up.

"There you are," he said, beaming at Carrie as though she'd been lost, "I've brought all my navigating tricks and all of those little things a pilot and traveller should never be without: spectacles, testicles, wallet and watch." He crossed himself as he spoke. "Well, well, we'd better be thinking about getting our flight if we don't want to miss it. No use hanging around now hoping the captain will be after offering a place at his table, for those days have gone out with the flying boats. But there we are, the beauty and romance of travel has left these shores never to return...."

"Where the Hell have you been?" Carrie spat angrily, all thoughts of photos leaving her head, "it's less than an hour before the flight goes. I'd given you up for dead. If we miss the flight it will be your fault and I'll expect my money back."

"Oh, you poor thing," he said, "it'll be the early morning start that's upset you. The sooner we get you on board with a glass of champagne to warm the toes, the better."

Smiling happily he led her up to the check-in desk. Carrie was exasperated, but she'd chosen him so she thought she'd better make the best of it. "You'll have to live with your sins for a long, long time," her father had said the very last time he spoke to her.

On the plane Kieran was charming and courteous, helping her settle into her seat, making light conversation and, when she went to the loo, disappearing.

Carrie came back to the seats to find them both empty. At first she thought he too had gone to the bathroom, perhaps to have a surreptitious smoke. But when, after four hours into the flight, she still hadn't seen him and his untasted food lay beside her in its plastic dome she began to imagine he was indeed an Irish leprechaun, who could come and go at will.

Just as the stewardesses were getting the plane ready for landing, seat-belt signs on, girls walking down the aisles checking buckles and backs, Kieran reappeared.

"Ladies and gentlemen please take your seats. We will shortly be landing at Miami International."

"Where the Hell have you been this time?" Carrie snapped. No longer considering him some celestial being. "What have you been doing?"

"Oh, I just popped up the front to chat to the boys. You should've joined us, you'd have loved the company and the stories. The Captain was a first rate man and his First Officer was a lady, a lovely young girl. You'd have enjoyed chatting to her, she's only a young'un but apparently she's wanted to fly since she was three years old. Imagine that, three years old and already knowing how her life would pan out. I'll bet you weren't like that and for sure I was a heady young beast at three years old. I was after being a soldier like my great-grandfather. Now there was a man. A hero. Killed for his part in the Post Office riots. Do you know your Irish history?"

"No."

"Well, never mind, we're landing now, but I'll keep your education in mind for one of those rainy days where we're stuck in Florida, or further north. Ferrying a plane in March, I ask you! It makes you wonder about the imagination of a southerner."

He smiled again and began to buckle his seat belt as they heard the familiar klunk of the undercarriage kicking down from the wings. The plane landed and they taxied in towards the terminal. Kieran signalled his approval of the pilot's landing.

"Not bad, not bad. Myself I'd have come in a little shorter and stopped at an earlier exit but you know what these airline pilots are like. Far too much imagination."

"Ladies and gentlemen we will shortly be deplaning..."

"De-plane-ing. Deplaning! Why can't they say disembarking?" snapped

Carrie, tired and irritable. Flying might be a computer game to Mitch, but Carrie felt far from heroic: rather a substitute on the bench of life.

"Ah, my dear Carrie," said the well-seasoned traveller, "bitter and twisted with a spark of lime, this is not nearly so simple. Do you disembark from a bark of frailty? Do you de-plane from Planet- E? What happens if your barker is a dog or your planet is G? Why don't you simply get off?"

Once they were through customs, a surprisingly easy formality with Kieran, whose charming breeziness seemed to bemuse customs men as much as Carrie, they proceeded towards the Car Rental Hall.

"Which company do you favour?" he asked. "Personally I always like Avis. The trick with them is to ask for the smallest car. They never have it of course, so they are forced to give you a bigger car at the lower price."

"I haven't brought my driving licence." Carrie said, "I thought we'd save money and go by bus."

"By bus? Well, it almost intrigues me enough to try it, but this, my love, is America, home of the free, where you only travel by bus if you can't get credit and even then not in Florida."

"I haven't brought my driving licence," Carrie reiterated stubbornly. "I didn't think we'd need..."

"Lucky I've got mine then, Petal. Now, here we are with the nice girl from Avis."

Indeed, the whole time they were talking he had been leading her through the mass of wandering people, unerringly towards the Avis desk.

"So, my darling, what will it be? A Fiesta from Leicester, a Rover from Dover, a purple Peugeot from Fontainebleau..."

Carrie jumped, but he was smiling flirtatiously at the girl from Avis and she decided it must have been a co-incidence.

Kieran did get his larger car for a smaller price; with larger car insurance which went on Carrie's already over-used credit card. She had plenty of time to regret leaving her driving licence behind, deciding to have her cousin and Fed Ex repair the omission before the next spate of car hiring: Kieran was a terrible driver.

Climbing into the car, the first thing he did was start to play with the alarm system and stereo. "Gadgets! Americans love 'em. Look at this, darde-dar, boom, boom and up it goes. 400 channels and here we can turn the speakers around so you can hear it outside. We can have a picnic and still hear the music, doesn't that appeal to your romantic heart? I'm surprised we don't have a bar; all bar none as the actress said to the bishop. You don't get this when you hire a car in jolly old Blighty, now do you? While here it's as standard as the car itself."

He smiled at Carrie, still looking at her as he put the car into gear and shot out of the lot, nearly hitting another car coming down the central aisle. The other car braked sharply, the driver honked furiously and Kieran, supremely unaware, swept on, remarking "Americans are so noisy, I find a couple of weeks in their company and I'm longing to go back to the tranquillity of the old homeland. Not that they aren't the best and most hospitable people but it's all yak, yak, yak; how they can chat, those dear old Americans."

Kieran dashed through red lights, changed lanes without indicating and swerved around corners, while remarking how much he liked the wide American carriageways. "Marvellously spacious place, the US, one thing I particularly like is that right hand turn on red without traffic light indications. Ha ha tidily bar, only heavy indications. No subtlety there; you'd understand that well. Now which Heavenly hotel did you say we were making for?"

Fumbling with the map, which seemed to have half the streets missing, Carrie told him they were going to one of the Best Westerns. "I booked it for tonight only, hopefully we'll be on our way tomorrow."

"Best Western, wonderful! I've always loved the irony of staying in the Best Western on the Eastern Seaboard. Such comedians the Americans. Different sense of humour than ours, to be sure, but no worse for that. I find I rather warm to their childish nature. You have that in yourself too and I think it's an excellent point, we all need a touch of the child. I'd like a child's touch myself! My goodness! Look there is our hotel already. How much swifter is the enjoyable life."

They dropped their bags at the hotel, inspected their rooms, and Carrie began to think about dinner.

"Dinner," said Kieran, "didn't you eat on the plane? How about a bit of exploring? We've got things to see downtown, or even up and mid-town for that matter. Miami here we come. Let's go and view."

Taking Carrie's arm, while singing a couple of bars of 'Downtown', he led her through the huge, warm parking lot to the car.

"Marvellous, isn't it," said Kieran his eyes searching the parking lot for the car, "they take away your car, those valets, but do they bring'em back? Of course not. This is America, home of exercise bikes and walking to the Chrysler . Does your car cry slurs? Do your bikes sing blues?"

"Are you ever silent?" Asked Carrie exasperated.

"I am constantly. Shame I can't say the same about you; however I like your light chatter. Many may not, but I'll tell them to take their evil thoughts elsewhere. It will surprise you in one as silent as me, but I'm a great supporter of idleness in chatter or in life."

Kieran drove out of the car park, down a ramp, straight across the highway without looking, and turned screechingly left. To her relief, Carrie saw they were facing the same way as the rest of the cars. He set off at a fast pace, towards some distant settlement of twinkling lights. She imagined they might be looking for a bar but she was wrong; for Kieran, exploring meant an investigation of the sex shops.

"Americans are pretty tame," Kieran pontificated, "not like the French. Now the old Europeans know how to present their sex and really make it raunchy, but the Americans, and the Brits for that matter, far too prissy; it's all suggestion. They never really get down to it in any proper manner? What do you think? I'll bet you tried a few African numbers in your time?"

He stopped talking, apparently waiting for a reply. Carrie stared at him, her brain flipping over his words, like fly-paper turning endlessly on a wheel. This was not how she had foreseen the growth of their relationship. Eventually she said, "Kieran, you are too much."

"Oh, mum tub, my little dove, no opinion on the big black Dick? Well wait and see, you'll soon find I'm right."

With that he pulled the wheel severely right, skidding to a halt outside a blank looking wall with a green door, hitting the curb as he did so.

"Bloody hire cars," he said in a rather amused voice, "they're always hitting things!"

Carrie examined the blank wall, wondering how Kieran could possibly know there was a sex shop behind the facade. In the London she remembered sex shop windows were full of red hearts and frilly knickers. In Amsterdam scantily clad girls looked bored in shop windows. If there were any in Africa they certainly weren't out in the bush, where she had spent most of her married life. Here there were no windows.

Kieran grabbed his cowboy hat from the back of the car and strode towards the open green door and through hanging plastic tendrils, which hissed and rustled as though complaining about their callous treatment. Carrie followed him with mounting curiosity. She'd never been into a proper sex shop before, although she had once bought a blow up doll for a party. Only one of her husbands, The White Thai, had taken her to a brothel in Chiang Mai where she had danced, in an innocent, mocking circle, with some of the girls; thong shod Essex girls without the handbags. Her first husband had enjoyed it immensely; but died before he could further her education.

Once inside she was disappointed. The place reminded her of a discount record shop. A man sat on a raised box. He took the money but also prevented any less desirable customers from leaving without paying. His large, tattooed arms suggested it wasn't worth challenging and the arresting height of his box gave an extra dimension to his authority. Carrie hoped Kieran wouldn't find it irresistible to find out if he was really as large as he looked.

Kieran, magnificent in his cowboy boots and hat, and anyway tall enough to ignore the challenge of raised men, swept past him to the rows of sex objects. They were laid out in high sided cardboard boxes reminiscent of Christmas shopping. Carrie expected to see rubber spiders, or jelly bean filled umbrellas. Instead there were plastic pouches of naughty underwear, and a diverse selection of dildos from large black to small green, some of which came complete with electric wiring. One actually stated, "battery not included." Carrie started to snigger. Kieran looked at her haughtily.

"Very important for some people, you know, to have these on tap. These aren't so much an entertainment as a medication. You ask my friend here, isn't that so?"

The tattooed cashier looked up from his magazine. Eyed Kieran silently. Disdain in his eyes. His look would have been menacing to anyone less than Kieran but nothing seemed to fluster the Irishman. He shrugged, and moved on past the boxes to the magazines and videos.

"Now, look at this. See what I mean about Americans being prissy. All these pictures and not a bondage magazine amongst them. Bondage Monthly; bound to please."

He turned to the cashier again. "So, good fellow, anywhere my friend and I can watch videos?"

The man's nose and lips sneered, while his eyes remained bored. "Not together."

Kieran sighed gustily. "Boring! So American! Come on my darling, let's see if we can find anywhere a little more liberal."

He minced out of the shop, so provocatively that Carrie found herself smiling at the man and muttering polite, "thank yous" as though she was in a greengrocer's. She rushed out after Kieran, followed by the blank, challenging, stare of the cashier.

Outside, Carrie felt the sudden shock of the darkening highway. In the UK now, pubs would be opening, in Cape Town there would be music, dancing and vibrant life, here there was just the whoosh of machines passing down the hot, black tarmac. She got into the car and Kieran lit a cigarette. As he over-revved the engine and bumped away from the curb, alternating between zoom and brake, she consoled herself by blasting the neighbouring cars with 400 channels in succession.

Driving down the dusky road, the regular pulse of the overhead lights strafing the car, Carrie felt an acid depression signalling desperately.

"Can we stop and have a beer. I feel the need."

Kieran swerved right immediately. Narrowly missing a gatepost, he plunged into the dark behind the shadowy outline of a box-shaped, wooden house bearing a single sign: BAR. The car's wheels crunched noisily on the loose gravel like a child eating cereal.

The bar door opened off the highway and was closed because of the heat, air-conditioning turning the room into Arctic cold. When Kieran opened the door, the people cloistered inside looked up angrily, like a room full of babies interrupted from cryogenic sleep. Hostile faces watched Kieran and Carrie walk across the room, past the pool table to the bar. Two men held up cues aggressively like weapons. The air was tense with the dislike of foreigners.

"I don't like it here," whispered Carrie, "can we go somewhere else?"

Kieran, however, shrugged her off, refusing to be intimidated. He walked up to the bar and ordered a Bud light for Carrie and a glass of milk for himself. The atmosphere became positively quartz.

"We don't serve milk here!" The barman spat. "And I'll need her ID."

"In that case," said Kieran lightly, "I shall take my business elsewhere. Good-day to you gentlemen." And swinging on his heels he left the bar with the same slow provocative walk he had used to enter. Carrie scuttled after him.

"So much for your bar," said Kieran, as they skidded over the gravel back to the car. "Luckily I remember another one on this road, The Pelican Inn. I think you'll find it rather more alluring."

"Why did he need my ID?" Carrie asked, "does he think I'm a drunk?"

"No, young. He thinks you are under 21. You can't squeeze a quart into a pint pot but every year above twenty comes in halves for a woman."

"Wow," Carrie grinned, ignoring Kieran, "nice man!"

The Pelican Inn was a remnant of former days. With Southern Belle architecture and spreading balconies, it looked as though it had once been a private house for the Miami elite. Now, though, it had a worn but appealing tackiness. The car park was lit by old-fashioned, runway-style, flame lights. In front of the house were deep steps and banisters decorated with plastic Christmas lights, which led up to a wide wooden verandah. The planks, curled with age and the damp heat, reminded Carrie of rows of question marks.

Pushing through the double doors, they entered the bar. Kieran's boots tapped like a dancer across the polished wooden floors as he avoided the threadbare rugs, flung down with haphazard accuracy.

The bar filled the former ballroom and spilled on out onto a terrace overlooking a river, which emptied into a distant bay. There was no air-conditioning and the swinging doors fluttered in the heat like aging southern belles. Carrie walked out onto the terrace, feeling the warmth increase as she left the twirling fans of the ballroom. In the distance she could see a little bridge lit up and shining out of the darkness. Every now and then a small boat would come down the river, its wailing horn resonating across the water. Then the middle of the bridge, with its line of red lights, would gently stagger up into the air, hold its angular line until the boat had passed underneath momentarily blocking off the lights, and slowly jolt down again in stages to its original position.

A barge with a JCB on top drifted out lethargically into the flickering reflections on the black river. It appeared empty but, as Carrie wondered if should she shout: "Barge overboard," the digger arm moved. Slowly it went across the barge and down into the water on one side, pulled back like an oar, then lifted up again and over to the other side again, heading towards the bridge.

"Have you seen that?" Carrie gasped as Kieran joined her, Bud in hand. "The JCB is rowing the barge."

"There was a man who washed planes, On Canada's deepest plains. Said he to this pilot, 'be wise,' For only a judge can devise, When the water is pulled, Or the puller is watered, Then will he have beer for his pains."

He gave her a Bud, winking as he limericked. They clinked their bottles and the JCB rowed on down the river.

"This is nice," said Carrie relaxing, hoping they could find something in common for the length of the trip.

"Umm. My romantic soul scoured it out last time I was here. Another ferry trip, but that time home (or indeed home-away-from-home) alone."

Something large flew past them in the dark and she felt the movement of warm air as it beat its wings. "What was that?"

"A pelican. Look at the shape. Feel it in your face. A pelican at full stretch is larger than our little Pontiac Grand Am. And it carries 13 litres in its beak. Think of that, my little ferry flower, just think of how many gold shekels you could spirit away in there. However, you might ask why it wasn't asleep at this time of night..."

Carrie only half listened to his words, feeling the blanket of Florida night air and hearing the clack, clack of some nearby night insect. She was momentarily aware she was on the start of a great adventure. Thank you, husband, she thought. This is great. This adventure will lead, who knows where, but certainly to financial resuscitation. She raised her beer bottle.

"Here's to the us and the trip Kieran."

Kieran clinked his bottle against hers a second time. "To satisfaction!"

When they got back to the hotel, Kieran discovered there was a Singles Party in the Amelia Earhart Bar. "Better check it out," he said, "I'm always interested in seeing people at their most basic."

"Personally I'm for bed. Tell me about their baseness in the morning."

Fortunate in Fort Lauderdale

Early in the morning Kieran drove Carrie, in his slipshod way, over to the airfield to see the Warrior. As they entered Ford Lauderdale Airfield Carrie was amazed to see that her plane was not one of just a few; it was one of thousands. The car drove past rows and rows of parked planes before they arrived at the salesman's office and stopped outside.

Mr Footsie's office was a slatted pine bungalow, a design replicated many times across the apron. Each office had a wooden entry portico but emphasised its uniqueness with a different paint scheme. His welcoming banner declared 'Footsie's Sales - Be Fortunate in Fort Lauderdale'. Carrie felt depressed; she was only one tiny mite in a world of plane sales and she had imagined herself something rare and unusual.

From the porch they went through a wooden door with a mosquito screen, which swished crisply as it opened. Carrie was again struck by the chill of air-conditioning as they entered the office.

"It's cold," she said, at the same time as the receptionist greeted them.

"Yes. Intense." The girl smiled, seeing this as a compliment. "Mrs Nordsnootiland?"

"Yes. This is Mr O'Toole, my pilot."

The receptionist gave him the once over and apparently found him average. "Y'all OK? Mr Footsie's waiting for you. Love the accent."

"She knows what it's for," remarked Kieran irritated, "and it's not just for pissing through."

The salesman, a thin, balding man with an eager air, was ready to greet them in his office. He jumped out of his chair, hand out, smiling delightedly as he purred at his guests.

"How ya doing? So nice to meet you Mrs Naughtysodlan. Please sit down. So sorry to hear about your husband. What a nightmare for you, my most sincere condolences. He was such a charming young gentleman, I must admit I found him one of nature's truly delightful souls..."

"You met him?" asked Carrie, astounded. Halted, half sitting. "When?"

"When he made the purchase, naturally." Mr Footsie was going to say more, something about her husband's companion, but stopped, realising he was giving news breaking information to his listener, and remembering that a wise man says few words.

"Charming.." he repeated, floundering. His smiling flashing on and off his face like a passing shadow. "Unfortunate.."

"When exactly was that?" asked Carrie.

Embarrassed, Mr Footsie moved stiffly towards his desk. He flicked through a blue folder, similar to the one Carrie had been given by the lawyer.

"Ah, here. The 2nd of March last year, just over a year ago."

"Oh," said Carrie, her stomach churning uncomfortably. She recognised the date. Her father's funeral and the only week in their marriage that she and Ignatius had been apart. She had assumed that Ignatius had spent the week in the bush; now it was suggested he had been in Florida, buying planes with her money. Why would the salesman lie? The wedding photograph with Sissy swam up again, but her mind refused to make any logical connection. "Oh!" She repeated vapidly.

Glad to have finished that conversation, Mr Footsie returned to his polite inanities. "Now. Can I offer you something to drink? Coffee? Something cold? No? Please sit down."

Carrie collapsed the rest of the way into her chair, her mind burning like an Australian forest fire. Mr Footsie himself sat down carefully but with some relief. "Now, you'll want to see your plane soonest. Let me call one of the boys to bring it up."

"No need," replied Kieran, who had not sat down, smartly pirouetting on his heels, clicking his knuckles behind his back. "We'd like to see it where it lies. Ten fathoms deep, my father lies; the plane of God upon his eyes. Point it out and we'll go down there."

Mr Footsie stood up, shocked by such brusqueness, his smile switching off and on once again. He started to remonstrate, then suddenly shrugged and pointed lethargically to a distant part of the huge airfield, reminding Carrie obliquely of her father's West Highland terrier who would run for balls with bigger dogs, but when the longer legged animals got to the ball first would walk off, pointedly turning his back as though he had better things to do than play so childishly.

"There! You can just see the row in the distance. It's on aisle Green, stand number 568," he said, "you can drive down there, if you really want to. Come back afterwards Mrs Nordsnootile and we'll discuss the paperwork."

They walked out of the office, Carrie knowing that 'discussing the paperwork' meant money. Kieran was silent, reversing the car quite thoughtfully out of its parking space.

"Keep an eye on the numbers will you. This is the Green aisle. I hope it isn't the green of innocence. Any idea what instruments the machine had in it when your husband bought it?"

"How could I?" She almost spat the phrase, stunned that Ignatius could have spent a week in Florida without telling her, without even mentioning it. It was seven months before he died; there was plenty of time to have told her. Her mind drummed out thoughts, back on the repeating wheel and she could not concentrate on what Kieran was saying.

"Pity!" muttered Kieran. "Dealers are notorious for selling a machine with good instruments and then swapping them for dogs when the deal is done. Just like the pimp with the blind bishop."

As they drove down the aisle Carrie started to feel sick. They went down Row 200, Row 300, Row 400. Here there were lines and lines of small planes, grass growing up around them. Some were in a fair state of repair; others had wings that trailed the ground; one or two had fallen onto their noses. Most did not look fit to fly. Finally she saw 500 and then 560.

"This is 560, it must be along here."

"Yup."

The planes here were just like the 200s, 300s and 400s. Bracing herself, she thought that at least now she knew Ignatius had seen the plane she could assume he had bought a winner. Ignatius was a man who knew about engines and airframes; latterly he had talked of little else. Probably he been meaning to tell her about his trip and purchase, but the time just hadn't been right. Maybe it was a present for her; he had died before her birthday. Yes, that must be it. A birthday present. He loved her. He did. She resolutely put any doubts out of her mind.

Finally they found 568. It was a blue and white Warrior, paint sparkling in the sunshine and apparently in fair shape. The grass had recently been beaten down and lay flat and tangled like Ben's unkempt dreadlocks. Carrie waited silently for Kieran's opinion.

He stopped the car and walked over to the stand. Walked around the plane. Opened the cowling. Put the key in the door; discovering as he did so the lock was broken. Looked inside. Started moving the seats and crawling around the machine. Reappeared and dropped down underneath. All the time without speaking. Eventually she could bear no more. She jumped out of the car and went to join him. He was sitting in the pilot's seat, moving the controls about, watching the ailerons flapping on the wings through the window, as though mimicking turns in flight while remaining securely anchored to the ground.

"So? So? What do you think?"

"Well, it's a dog, but I'll fly it. At least until I've seen anything to stop me. Why have a dog and bark yourself? The first run will be the tester."

"What do you mean? What's it worth? How much can I get?"

Kieran took off his hat and looked at her through his shades. Carrie saw her reflected image and didn't like it.

"Well my little business woman, you can get what the market will give, but what I mean is that we should be safe to fly the old dog across the pond, or aren't you as worried about your life as you are about the money?"

"Yes, of course I am," she snapped, "but..." She stopped. She wasn't quite sure where her buts were going. She'd been wrong-footed. "Damn. I'll take the car back." She said and climbed out of the plane.

They packed their belongings into the plane, sorted out all the details with the salesman: insurance, parking fees for over a year and the Export Certificate of Airworthiness, all of which seemed to be almost as expensive as buying a new plane, and which cut into Carrie's small profit. By the time they'd finished with the salesman and worked out a flight route it was nearly 11 o'clock. Carrie wanted to be away, but Kieran was ready for a sandwich.

"It'd be 4 o'clock in the UK," he pointed out, "and I'd be having my tea and cakes. So just a sandwich and a cup of coffee and then we'll be off. Got to keep up the blood sugar levels. No point in making a pain out of pleasure, as the actress said to the bishop."

"Umm," Carrie said dryly, drinking a glass of tap water.

At last they were ready. Kieran got into the pilot's seat. "I'll do the first leg," he said, "I expect you'll want to fly from time to time but I want to see how the little donkey bucks before we get too far from young Arthur Daly here."

"Arthur Daly?"

"Someone on British TV, a salesman you can't trust but never mind. I'll just listen to the ATIS (canned airfield information to you) and then we'll call for start-up. Listen to that lovely southern drawl; real tall-Paul drawl. Fort Lauderdale Ground this is November 2122 ready for start-up, I have Bravo."

His speech came out in a wave so Carrie wasn't sure if he was talking to her, listening to the recorded airfield information, or talking to the tower. Somehow everyone understood their bit, and they finally taxied out, following a yellow painted line towards the long, tarmac runway. Got their take-off clearance and were ready for departure on runway eight (the US version of compass heading zero eight zero).

"Well," he said, turning to her and adjusting his Ray Bans, "this is it! The start of your great adventure. Off into the Apple Pie. Lakeland here we come. You ready?"

"Yes."

"Well, quick check. Spectacles, testicles, wallet and watch!" He crossed himself. "Then chocks off! Bombs away. Let's go and get Daddy!"

Leaving Fort Lauderdale they turned left and headed north towards Lakeland. For a while they flew along the deserted beach where the Warrior's shadow dipped in and out of the dunes like a great grey predator flying in formation. Smaller birds skipped away from the pursuing shadow and Carrie wondered if they saw the Warrior as a vengeful eagle. Kieran told her tales of sea fog coming in faster than rats before lava. Reaching the Hillsboro' Canal they turned inland and headed for Lake Okeechobee, a huge stretch of water which dominated the horizon in front of them.

"Impossible to get lost here, you'd think," said Kieran, "a huge lake ahead, and then the mass of railway lines (some deceased) but people have done it. Here in the Everglades people have disappeared, never to be seen again. Whole flights indeed. The saddest one was a little Trauma-hawk with its control stick broken off: the student was pushing forward, while the instructor was pulling back. The instructor's mouth was full of water; he'd been screaming as they went down."

"Oh!" said Carrie, looking out at the innocent Everglades shimmering in the afternoon sun, wondering if this was what she wanted to hear right now. Was he trying to make her nervous?

When they reached the lake Carrie was swamped by its vastness. 35 miles wide at its largest, it is a quarter of the width of Florida and it seemed that they were surrounded by every inch of that 35 miles. Everywhere there was nothing but water. If they had an engine failure here it would take some swimming to reach the shore.

"Water, water everywhere but not a drop to drink," said Kieran, "or as the actress said to the bishop if it's holy water how come it doesn't pour out the holes."

Carrie was about to suggest to Kieran that they climb higher, to give themselves more chance of gliding back to land rather than ending up like that instructor and pupil in the Everglades, when he said. "Well, we'd bet-ter try out your water nerve. We'll go low in the middle of the lake... For you it will feel just like being over the Atlantic. You won't be able to see any land, you'll think you are alone in a huge, unforgiving ocean. You'll get the feeling that yourself is the only person in the whole world, and that if you did spear in, no one would know or care; Ocean Depression, as we ferry pilots call it."

He smiled in her general direction. "You know they could see this lake from space? Alan Shepherd, who of course you know was the first man to go up into the big black abyss of eternal night..."

"I thought it was Yuri Gagarin or even a dog..." Carrie cut in, but Kieran waved away the Russians as unimportant.

"Ol' Al...he looked out of his little portal and what did he see..Lake Okeechobee...never mind the Wall of China..he saw jolly old Okeechobee and he knew he was in space. What did he say? He said OK I see OK cho I be! Ho ho A nudge is as good as a wink to a blind actress.. "

They swooped low over the lake and Kieran started swearing.

"Look at that damn altimeter! This dog is carrying some garbage I can tell you. That flipping artificial horizon and the turn and slip. Goddamit! The whole plane is full of rubbish. Shall I drop it here in the lake and let you collect the insurance?"

"Thanks but no thanks. Is it really that bad?"

"See for yourself. Look at that...now, are the wings of the plane level or are they level? Then you look at the artificial horizon and what do you see...we are in a descending turn to the left. Rubbish! Look at the turn indicator ...straight as a die; seems fine, but then I turn and what happens...still straight as a die. A pup! This dog's got puppies. I'll tell you what..you ring that damn 'amster when we get to Lakeland and get those instruments replaced or this pilot is going home. Get the picture?"

Carrie saw the picture and she didn't like it. Whatever had her third husband been thinking about when he bought this plane? And yet he'd seen it; tested it perhaps. It made no sense. For a moment she thought nostalgically about a container to ship it home and no Kieran.

Behind Lake Okeechobee they passed an Indian Reservation. Carrie looked out for signs that this preserved a different way of life but to her disappointment there were no tepees, no totem poles, only houses and cars. They climbed up to 1500 feet and flew on past Lake Placid, Lake Istokpoga and followed the railway line to Lakeland. As they approached the area, Carrie could see more lakes; everywhere there were lakes, Lake Wales, Dundee Lake, Lake Handcock, Lake Alfred, Lake Pierce. Flat, wet circles that swelled out like play-dough. It was although they had already reached the Atlantic and were looking at tiny islands between swathes of water; rather than the other way round. Carrie tried to think out a joke; in Dutch a lake is a 'meer' and 'meer' also means more: meer meer, more lake. She told Kieran but he only grunted, concentrating on landing.

Ahead the airport spread out like a flat black cross amongst the many pools. It seemed apt to Carrie that the first airport they landed on should look like a symbol of death and rebirth. Just like another computer game: talk about synchronicity.

On runway thirteen Kieran bumped the Warrior down "just to test," he said, "the state of the undercarriage."

"Not," said Kieran, "that that's enough of a test. This dog's a dodo! The Dead Dodo Cult! Cult indeed? Lucky I don't have a lisp! As for Mr Footsie's suggestion about an engineering base, you might as well ask Dennis Nielsen for a good butcher. A recommendation worth a farthing in the 22nd century....."

Carrie cut out Kieran's voice, concentrating on the approaching LinkLong Engineering base. This looked like a huge, open sided car-port. Angled into the prevailing wind, it allowed the breeze to keep the planes cool even in the intense Florida summer. On one side there were square wooden legs some eighty or hundred feet high and from these rolled down long, reinforced blinds, acting like doors or wind-brakes. Above, a tin roof (whose light weight metal emphasized the case for rebuilding after a hurricane) was attached to a concrete hangar. Below this a wooden platform jutted out into the void, surrounded by an iron balustrade. Underneath and to the side of the platform were huge hydraulic pistons, which raised and lowered the plane-carrying working area. Thus engineers could work on two levels, still protected from the heat and wind. The platform was currently empty and had been pulled up for the Warrior to taxi underneath. However, it hosted the tendrils of a square, wooden engineering frame, which dangled into space and pulsated in the breeze like a sliver of balsa wood on a spider's web.

Taxying in, aided by an engineer with reflective batons, Carrie longed to shout "more reverse thrust" like the Biggin nudist, but felt no such eccentricities could exist here in this haven of work.

Unwillingly leaving Kieran in charge of the plane, Carrie went to phone the evasive Mr Footsie. He was loathe to replace the instruments, insisting that her husband had seen them and tested them. Carrie refused to believe him. He prevaricated. She became persistent. Finally, after she had invented a hungry journalist friend and threatened to sue, he agreed to replace the artificial horizon and the turn and slip, but not the altimeter. That, he said, her husband had bought separately and put in himself.

Coming out of the office Carrie heard Kieran's dulcet tones surrounded by happy laughter "..and the Dutch girl cried to her British boyfriend: 'oh how I love you, lake and lake everyday'!" Basking in their merriment, Kieran said. "See what I mean! A joke absolutely made for Lakeland.. more mares than you can count."

Carrie booked them into another Best Western, where they could wait for the arrival of Federal Express. At least that was Carrie's plan. Kieran, however, was not a waiting man.

"We'll have to hire a car," he said. "I'll ask the engineers. This being the good old US, there's bound to be some company prepared to bring a car out here and take it home again when we fly away. We'll go and experience the flying scene at Winterhaven, land of the sea..."

"No way!"

"What? You don't want to see Winterhaven? You an apprentice pilot! You budding little pilots haven't lived, more importantly haven't really flown, until you've experienced the thrill of the bump of floats on water, until you've piled along on the step, then ware, ware away...great juddering oracles..lucky I haven't got a lisp... of magic. You'll love it."

"I don't care! I can't afford love. Everything costs money and I don't have any. I'm sure there's something we can do here. A museum, a play, a theatre, computer games, anything," said Carrie defiantly.

"A museum is it? You'd put money first before living itself? Well then my lovely, I'll be off to see what I can find, who and where; time to spare go by air, time is short, fuck any sort. You put your little tootsies up in the hotel and I'll be back as soon as I've found a path to Winterhaven. Who knows, we might even take that bus you're so keen to experience."

Carrie went up to her room feeling down but relieved to be alone. How could this trip, which had held so much hope, be turning out so bad, so painful: so expensive? For a moment Carrie verged on the edge of depression, but she'd been there before and she wasn't going to let her emotions lead her to Hell again. Damn them all! Hoping Kieran had got lost, she picked up the remote. At least TV didn't cost anything, although there was an option to pay for porn channels.

Less than an hour later, just as she was being invited to buy a self-cleaning cat litter, with a paw cleaning ramp and cat privacy tent, Kieran called from his mobile.

"Hello sweet-cakes, have I got something for you? I'm in the piss house, one hand on the phone. Guess where the other one is? Come and check it out. All your fantasies will be rewarded...As the actress said to the bishop 'cross my palm with silver and you'll shiver in my palms."

"Kieran! Don't be silly, I can't go into the gents!"

"Oh, you little sex fiend!" Kieran laughed. "I was hoping you'd join me in the bar!"

Carrie reluctantly left her room, dubious of what Kieran might have on offer. She got out of the lift and dallied for a moment in the movement-sensitive lights, sniffing the scent of newly washed nylon carpet. But entering the bar, Carrie saw Kieran wasn't alone. Sitting by his side, in a high-edged booth on the pseudo-leather seats, also drinking milk, was a very young blond girl who for a second struck a cord of remembrance in Carrie. For some reason she thought about Sissy-in-law. Then Kieran shouted, destroying her rumination.

"This is Charlee," he said, waving his hat in the girl's direction, so close he disturbed her hair with the wind, "Charlee's an angel...."

The girl laughed and Carrie winced.

"...and the angelic angel Charlee has offered to drive us to Winterhaven, isn't she just the cutest little ol' lady you ever did see? "

Carrie winced again at his imitation southern accent, but the girl giggled. "Hi," she said cheerfully, "I'm Charleen."

This giggling cheerfulness persisted through the drive to Winterhaven, in Charleen's open-topped red sports car. She dropped them at the sea-plane base and, with a thumbs up, a grin and a swish of lovely blond hair, drove off.

"Well done, Kieran! I've no idea how you did it but well done."

"Oh," he said, "either it's just my natural charm attracts the lassies like flies to sand-paper, or perhaps I just opened my wallet and there she was. While others are going around committing liberticide against the proletariat, Kieran is sowing the grains of human love and admiration. The attractions of snakes to their tamer.."

"Yeah, sure. Lice to a head. Locusts to wheat. I know. Perhaps you should call her your financial squeeze," said Carrie wittily, simultaneously wondering if that didn't more accurately reflect her own present state. "You didn't offer her a ride then..or have you done that already?"

He looked offended. "I never shit on my own doorstep," he said obscurely and hurried up the steps into the seaplane base.

Charlie Brown's Sea World was, like Mr Footsie's House of Fortune, a plank-built structure with wooden steps up to an entrance portico. As Carrie stepped onto the colonnade, surrounded by advertising posters, Kieran pointed at a picture of a SeaBee and suggested they share an hour's flying.

"That'll keep the price down for you," he said sweetly, charging off to book the hour before she could reply.

While Kieran flew, Carrie walked down the jetty and leant on a lichen soaked rail, aimlessly watching fishy shadows darting through the muddy green water. Her mind was full of unconnected thoughts. A wedding photograph that turns up in a dead man's Peugeot. A unaccounted week in Florida. A plane bought. A house sold. A dead husband with no corpse? No insurance cover, or, at best, insurance on the wrong person. And why didn't Ignatius tell her? He was a risk taker but this was apparently complete madness. Perhaps he had gone mad, hence the low-level torque turns that killed him.

Her journey no longer seemed like a great romantic adventure with treasure at the end of the rainbow, but instead a flight on a broken wing with painful personal and financial ramifications.

She heard the rattling roar of the Super-Cub engine (it seemed the Sea Bee was away having some engineering done). Kieran was returning. Looking at her watch, she saw they'd hardly had 15 minutes. Perhaps he felt guilty. It didn't seem like Kieran but she might have misjudged him.

The Cub water-taxied in toward the jetty, swung around for mooring, Kieran jumped out and took Carrie's hand, propelling her uncontestably towards the plane.

"How ya doing?" yelled the pilot greetingly over the engine noise.

"Oh, fine, thank you," replied Carrie distractedly, trying to look at him and step into the pitching Cub all at once.

"Now my little licheese, step carefully and in. That's it, like a water born baby. You have a good time. I agreed with Charlie here to give you a longer flight than me. After all I've done it before and although it's wonderful for me, for you it will be the opening of your eyes, the first taste of paradise, the cream which smooths down the strawberries of fate. Have fun my little girl. Enjoy. Enjoy.'

He was still talking as they taxied out, lips moving but the sound lost under the noise of engine and wind. There were no headsets.

"He's a character, that Keer-raan, real class act," yelled Charlie, pulling up a cord which led to the water brakes. "We need this for taxying," he explained as they edged away from the jetty.

"Yep, he's a quaint guy," he continued, urging the plane forward on to the step. Carrie felt a strange sensation in her back as the plane tipped forward and high on its water skids, skipping lumpishly along the water before finally achieving enough lift to grudgingly ease into the air.

"Ok, you got control. Expect it to be heavy on the rudder, you got pontoons instead of wheels and it feels like daddy's got his boots on!"

She took control gingerly, uncertain. The plane immediately yawed right. "Left pedal!" yelled her instructor, "bootfuls of it! Oh you 'spam can' pilots! Use ya fucking feet!"

She stuffed her left foot almost down to the floor and suddenly they were flying straight. "Fab!" he screamed back, over the noise. "You got it."

They flew around, did some turns and then some rather bouncy lake landings. After a while Charlie took control, to do some manoeuvres he felt Carrie ought to experience, and she looked out of the window at the scenery.

"Hey! Look down there!" Charlie banked the little Cub to the left so Carrie could get a good view of something on her left, although she had no idea what. "There's a couple getting it away. Think we'll go cool that little game!"

Saying that, he swooped low along the lake, popping up just over the edge and practically touching the side of an open, red sports car, zipping immediately overhead the couple. Clothes blew up everywhere in a flurry like snow flakes including a pair of lizard green cowboy boots.

"Yahhooo!" Charlie yelled, "did you cop that chick's yam yams?!"

"No."

Looking back, Carrie could see an arm reaching out to replace the roof.

When they got back to Charlie Brown's Kieran was sitting demurely in the school, chatting to Charleen. He welcomed Carrie with a wave. "Meet Charlee here.... of course you've already met her, silly me aren't I the girl! But there's things you don't know. Charlee's an aerobatic pilot, oh aeros I love the feel of the wind rushing past while the engine holds its breath..."

"Oh," said Carrie, "Kieran didn't say you were a pilot. Have you got a licence?"

"Yeah, I do. He doesn't. He's kinda cool about me..."

Kieran cut through them both. "...she'd love to take us flying tomorrow, so I've arranged for her to come to the hotel and pick us up. Shall I ring you, or thinking about it Charlee, why don't we go back there now, have a drink and then you'll see where it is for the morning."

"Do you got my number? All right. I've gotta visit mum but it's like almost on the way. Do you wanna stop there first?"

"Absolutely," said Kieran, "to the hotel!"

Charleen shrugged and Carrie was surprised to see she looked rather put out. "Okay," she said, "it's your shout!"

"It is very kind of you to do all this ferrying around for us," said Carrie sincerely, getting out of the car at the hotel. "Thank you very much."

"No problem. Like, you know, I wanted to meet you," replied Charleen smiling enigmatically. She left with a kiss on the lips for Kieran and a wave.

"Hum," Carrie said, sardonically. "She seems to know you quite well Kieran. What did she mean about she wanted to meet me?"

"Oh. Probably I sang your praises from Heaven and back. So naturally she wanted to meet this woman of the stars, of the realms where midnight hardly stutters across the universe. This Donna, this lightening in the celestial stars. Show me such a woman, young Charlee cried, and I will drive you to the corners of the untrodden earth."

"Ho."

"Now," Kieran recalled, "I don't believe I've told you the story about last time I was ferrying here in sweet Florida. A work of genius or I'm not the prince of pilots. So, I must just email the female; call home ET but then we can settle into Denny's with a delicious Surf and Turf for the tum and delight for your ears."

In Denny's, Carrie ordered a steak and Kieran, as he promised, ordered surf and turf; a huge lobster and pounds of steak, with many plastic packs of mayonnaise, sitting on mounds of lettuce, carrots and bread mixed with more mayonnaise. Sliced white bread on the side.

As they sat in their mauve faux-velvet booth, their faces wrinkled by colours from the patchwork table-lamp, Kieran began. "Well, last time I was here in little wee Land of the Lakes I did not have the benefit of this marvellous superfluence. Hence I had to visit one of Florida's finest supermarkets for something cold and cheap to munch in my grotto, while accompanied by the gentle face of the land of a thousand channels; none anything to compare with the good old Blighty Beeb. There I was, getting out of my old, humble hired car, when I see, on the opposite side of my car, a man. Not a large man but nonetheless a man. And there was something else special about this man. Not his looks. No indeed, for now I can scarcely remember those. Nor the shape of his head, although I do remember his eyes. Those eyes were bad. Not bold. Not brave but bad.

Scared. Crazed."

Kieran took a bite of turf and continued thickly; his mouth full of brown and white gunge. "Nope. The special thing about this man was that he was carrying a gun."

Kieran stopped, tensed, an inspired look on his face. Carrie was about to say, 'why not? Guns are legal?' when Kieran let out a huge fart.

"Ah the great Botty Burp! Weapon of the proletariat against the bourgeoisie. Bliss in India is a dry fart! Better out than in, as we say in China. Now where was I? Ah yes. The man had a sawn-off shot gun! And sawn off shot gun says to me, it says, a man with no good intentions. Indeed his tension was definitely not IN for me. Now, you are making me digress off the point. The point is this man was clearly considering pointing his gun at me. So what did I do? Did I jump back in amazement? Did I hollar in surprise? Did I flick a chop in his direction? No I did none of these things. I simply turned and walked away, and you know what happened?"

"No."

"He went and pointed his gun at an old couple in front of my car. He clearly decided that they were a better target than me."

"Wow!" gasped Carrie, "so what did you do?"

"I got back into my car and drove away. Clearly this was not the supermarket for me, with all these coke heads hanging around."

"Oh," said Carrie.

Charlee's Aeros

In the morning Charlee returned to pick them up, sticking her face around the door of their breakfast joint some ten minutes after her intended time of arrival.

"Hi guys," she said, "like you ready? I'm mega."

"You're early," said Kieran, "pre-ETA. Come and enjoy the delights of a wonderful mug of good weak Florida coffee."

"Yeuch. No way Hosé. Grosses me out to the max! Let's go, Kieran. Like, you know, I gotta plane at ten."

Kieran smiled, without moving. "Come and have a quick one, no point in making a pain out of a pleasure, as the actress said to the Bishop. Here I've ordered you an orange juice instead. Orange juice for a juicy piece of poppet."

Charleen sat down, unable to fight Kieran. "OK! OK! Just one buster but, like, no longer. I get shat on if I don't, like, take the plane out when I say. I'm not, like, a lastminute-dot-com person, you know."

She brought out a pack of cigarettes, extracted two, put them in her mouth, lit them both and gave one to Kieran, pressing the other to her lips, while managing to hide them from the hotel staff. Carrie felt challenge in the air but couldn't quite fathom the reason for it.

"Do you work at the school? Are you an instructor?"

"Yeah Carrie I do. It's wicked." Charleen put her thumb up.

Carrie could hardly believe it. This girl looked like a 12 year old bimbette, but was obviously better at flying than Carrie. "Really. How interesting. What made you want to fly?"

"Oh," said Charleen, "Oh, dunno Carrie. Like I didn't, but like, you know fuckit, my dad disappeared and, you know, when I was seventeen he walked right back. Took me up Carrie. Like, it was wicked. Intense! And well, like you know, Carrie, coz he was an aerobatic pilot I did it too. Now it's cool."

She drew on her cigarette, blew a smoky bubble and smiled so angelically in Kieran's direction that Carrie felt a thump of emotion. An indication of a hidden agenda? Another mystery?

North Piri Piri airfield was huge, tarmac and full of runways. As they approached the airfield Carrie noticed the scent of diesel. Little planes and helicopters filled the air around them. They left the road and drove for a mile, before passing under another road and then through a tunnel under a runway. Finally they came out on the far side of the airfield. Charlee drove up behind the school and parked between a rubbish skip and a Cessna, squeezing in under the high wing.

"Duck or grouse you guys," she warned giggling as they scrambled out of the car under the wings. "Like I saw that in a real intense English pub in L.A."

They walked through a crowd of Cessnas and Pipers on the way to the reception, some attached to large round stones with cords, others already untied and awaiting a pilot. The other side of the airfield Carrie saw a collection of helicopters, parked on individual wheeled pads which were being pushed out of the hangar by a man on a small tractor.

"Wow, how many planes does the school have?" Carrie asked, "it seems awfully big."

Kieran gave himself a quick once over. "How did you know? Oh, you jest. Forgive my young friend," said Kieran, "she's used to baby British schools, all grass and failing engines. There you're lucky if the local council allows the airfield 200 movements a month, whereas here you have thousands each day, isn't that so Charlee, Oracle of the Americas?"

"Yeah, awesome Carrie..." Charleen began while Kieran continued. "...at least 100 planes here but that makes it only a small place. I remember when I was out in good old LA, home of freedom and the ornamental orange, the airfield had 300 planes and 100 helicopters and that was only the local..."

"Are there really...."   "Well, Carrie, I mean it's like.."

Kieran forged on oblivious to girlish interruptions. "Ah, young Carrie you forget the price difference. What did you pay in good old Blighty, £80, £90 of your foolish, man-made pounds? Probably more. There is, as the wise oracle tells us, one born every minute. You should have asked me for my advice, but enough of that running after water under the bridge. Here in America, good old land of the free enterprise, you pay $30 in jolly old LA and something only slightly more than that laughable sum over in this East Coast Heaven. I would have thought that you with your little bourgeois love of your shekels would have come burrowing over here to do your flying...."

By this time they had reached the reception and Kieran strode up to the desk. "Well, my lovely girl," he said to the receptionist, "I believe we are having one of your delightful planes with sexy Charlee here for a spin of high class aerobatics."

"Hi guys. Lurve ya accent. Y'all Australian?"

"I, my darling, am from that little green land struggling against British colonial power, just as your ancestors once did here to give you the monumental and blissful existences you now enjoy."

"Oh, y'all British?"

Kieran sighed and remarked that he was a vessel cut in half, from the cruel rages of casting his pearls before mere porcine recipients. The receptionist stared at him and got to the matter in hand.

"Y'all late. Y'all lucky the next guy's punched out. Ignorant horse!"

She gave Kieran the keys, his belief that such rules as timing and paying didn't apply to him was reinforced. Saying he needed to check her flying, Kieran went off in the Aerobat with Charlee.

"Many are called but few are chosen," he remarked handing Carrie his hat, "take my tit fer they also serve who can't be bothered to wait."

"Thanks," said internet-obsessed Carrie, about to tell him she recognised the misquotation as Milton when the receptionist said, "I luv the way y'all Brits quote Shakespeare, y'all so educated."

While Carrie walked down to the river, Charleen taxied away from the school. On the runway Kieran took control. "So what will it be babe? Sex in the straps? On your back, Jack? Bit of what you fancy, Clancey? Spectacles, testicles, wallet and watch. Here we go babe."

He took off, lifting the plane quickly and holding it low to the ground to build up speed before pulling back sharply as the end of the runway passed beneath them, climbing straight up in an apparently vertical climb, levelling off and then rolling sharply. Much to the consternation of the ATC, who remonstrated over the radio; ignored by Kieran.

Charleen was used to this. "Like, Kieran, I wanna work like my hammerhead. It's not like, you know, I'm freaked out, but my lines are definitely not cool. No way Hosé. Incidentally, babe, why didn't you, you know, like, tell her who I am?"

"Who are any of us? Who are you? Who am I? Who are we? Do we any of us have that insight...Now; the sensuous stall turn, the heliographic hammerhead....oh American, oh English, the cool tongue of a thousand nations all inexplicably varied in their expiation of the lingua franca.."

"Kieran! Like you know what I mean. He's like dead now. Do we gotta keep it secret? I mean, you know...I'd like to talk with her. Like, you know it would be cool swapping stories."

"Dead? What is dead? Is a dull man alive? Does a hero die? OK doll. Inverted spin. Flick. Smooth and sensuous as your favourite dick."

As he spoke Kieran put the plane into a roll, stopping it roughly as they reached the inverted. The little plane juddered slightly.

"So here we are, upside down; nothing on the clock but the maker's name. Ahhggg! Aggh we are going to die! Help! Help! Feel that stuttering stall coming in, ooh-er feel that vibration, better than a dildo, the shudder and the judder and then full left rudder and wh-oof. We're in and down and round and round. A right hand spin inverted. Yawing left. Rolling right. Oh the pleonasm! Oh the dream. OK it's yours. Recover."

Charleen had been expecting that; an inverted spin is deceptive, requiring the opposite input from a normal spin. She knew Kieran would be hoping either she'd been lulled into torpor by his voice or that she'd think they were in a right hand spin. If so she would have put in left rudder, which, since they were inverted, would simply put them into a flatter spin; as they only appeared to be spinning right and were in fact spinning left. In fact she put in full right rudder and brought the stick firmly backwards, keeping the ailerons neutral. The little aerobat, juddering and stuttering, stopped spinning. She rolled back to level flight.

"Wicked! OK buster. If you don't tell her, like you know, I shall. I got'er for a flight, don't I. And it's my secret too, ain't it."

Carrie walked back from gazing at the steam, thoughts flitting uselessly in her mind like a fly trapped behind glass. Ignatius's plane purchasing clearly hadn't anticipated these engineering hold ups. It was unlike him to have bought a plane with defects; perhaps he hadn't had much time. Maybe he was thinking of moving them to America. She wished he was still alive. She missed him. Her mind focused on the beautiful flowers on the edge of the tarmac; what a blue colour. He did love her. This must all be some mistake, a mistake easily resolved, plus the return of her money. Probably the lawyer had mucked up and would suddenly find another account. He and his creepy, collapsing office didn't look too efficient. Those flowers were amazing, incredible, what did they live on, sitting there amidst the fuel fumes? Oh Hell, why was she who enjoyed the easy life being forced to think so much?

In the school building Carrie had a coke from the drinks machine and sat down with a copy of GQ Magazine to see what men thought about, if they thought at all, or if they just made noises in sports stadiums.

When the aerobaters returned shortly after noon, she heard the lilting humm of the Lycoming engine and walked to the window in time to see the little Cessna land and taxi off the runway. The aerobat moved fast, the rudder waggling back and forth like an excited dog's tail as they zigzagged down the taxiway. She went out onto the tarmac, expecting it would now be her turn to fly with Charleen.

Kieran halted in front of her in a screech of ill-treated brakes, killed the engine and jumped out of the plane, running straight back to the rudder. He shook it disparagingly.

"Just look at this," he shouted to Carrie, although she was almost at his elbow, "look at this fucking piece of American Apple turnip. Useless, quite useless. I thought we were going to die. I thought of you depending on me for your livelihood. For your trip. For your fortune. I thought all that was going to end. And Charlee! Charlee. What was she doing during this piece of fandango? Was the girl praying to God? Was she fixing the machine? No! She was calm, she was sitting, she was waiting for me to get us out of trouble. Lucky I was there to save us or who knows what would have happened. Death of a hero, disgust of the fans."

"What happened?"

"Happened! Happened. You ask so lightly what happened. Just look at this, look at this rudder...don't you see...? That you need to ask, you a pilot, is a sorry state of affairs..."

"Whats'all happened, guys?" asked the receptionist joining them.

"Fucking thing!" said Kieran in a voice of high disapprobation. "Piece of American rubbish. The rudder jammed, but luckily I managed to free it with my foot. I wouldn't let you fly this apple pie, Carrie. Not if it was the last plane on the airfield. Sorry! You and Charlee darling will have to paint the sky some other time. It's a shame but better to be shamed now than ashamed later, as the grave digger said to the gold digger."

"Gross!" said Charleen, her little face pink, willing Kieran to Hell but unable to cross him, knowing he was preventing her from being alone with Carrie, "to the max! Kieran, you got your foot stuck under the rudder pedal. Like heels aren't the cool gear for aeros."

"This plane," said Kieran, "is a dangerous liability. Come my children. This is no place for the freedom fighter."

"Y'all have a nice day now," said the receptionist.

Heart of Fool's Gold

When they got back to LinkLong, Carrie imagined that everything would have been done and they would be ready for lift off. They went over to the mechanic's office with a certain air of expectancy, ready if necessary to fly away immediately. In fact only the instruments had been FedExed over. Carrie's cousin had rung to say she couldn't find Carrie's driving licence but suggesting that if she showed her pilot's licence perhaps that would do, and 'not to ask her again because she had better things to do than keep running around after her nearest and dearest'.

"Quite a character, your cousin," remarked the engineer, swinging the tendrils of the engineering platform around his arm so the wooden scaffolding above shuddered and swayed as though a hurricane was coming in. "Quite fucking, scuse-my-French, frank ain't she. We had a bit of a talk..."

"Heart of fool's gold," said Kieran, "left by miners....taken by adults.."

"She left you a fucking-scusem-French message. Said the heifer's lumps were back, wanting contact. Makes no fucking-scuse-French sense to me."

He tapped his head suggestively.

"So," said Carrie, refusing to be deflected by cousins and police-persons in the UK. "The plane's ready?"

"Yeah," said the engineer, "and no. We got your fucking-scuse-French, instruments but we need a credit card number before we start work."

"A credit card number? But you've got the plane."

"Yeah, and what am I going to do with that little barker 'eh? You didn't think I'd fly it did you? Fuck-scuse-mFrench, am I a suicide merchant? Couple of questions though: one about your ferry tank..."

Kieran looked interested. "What about it?"

"No can do. The FAA man's got chicken pox and we both know that you can't go, fucking-scuse-mFrench, flying all the way over to Greenland with tanks and no FAA check."

"Call another FAA man then," Carrie said, surprised he hadn't thought of that himself.

"Ain't one. There's only two in, fucking-scus-French, Florida, one's on vacation and t'other's sick. You gotta ring up Portland Maine, they've got another fella up there, get the fucking-scu-French, work done in Bangor. I'll do the instruments here though, you'll need them on your way up north. In the, fucking-scus-French, snow!" He shuddered.

"Do we need a ferry tank?" Carrie asked.

The engineer snorted. "Depends if you want to reach, fuckings-French, England! Takes time to swim." He laughed humourlessly. "What range do you think your fuckings-French barker has, 'eh mam?"

Carrie said nothing, trying to remember if range was number of flight hours or distance; she knew it was related to fuel and consumption.

He continued, "731, fuckings-French, miles, that's what! And the fuckingFrench pond is approximately, fuckings-French, 5000 miles. So, Mam, you, fucking-French, ain't going to make the trip, even via Greenland, without some 50 gallons or so in your, fucking-French, ferry tank, not unless you buy some oars and start paddling." He laughed.

"And number two?" cut in Kieran, bored by this display of knowledge .

"All those holes in the inside..it's like..they've been cut, you know, they're not torn, far too, fucking-French, regular. Think the old bin could have been used for fucking-French drugs?"

Kieran laughed this time. "That old dog, do me a favour! If that's after being the best they can find in the aviation highway, they'd never be able to afford the street merchandise."

"OK, keep your cool. I'm not into no, fucking-French, illegals you know."

Carrie thought about ringing her cousin, to see what the detectives wanted but, discovering the time difference was bad, left it. It would wait.

When the bill came, a couple of days later, Kieran laughed again.

"Wow!" He said, "well, they saw you coming. Nice cost for such a little amount of work. No wonder he asked about drugs. Bump, bump goes the till. Up, up, up the hill. Far, far, far too late to call the Old Bill!"

Carrie went to scream at the engineer and eventually did get a small reduction. That it wasn't enough was clear by the happy way he waved them goodbye.

"Y'all come back and see us, when you buy your next little Frenchfucker." He and Kieran smirked at each other.

They taxied out, and lined up on runway twenty seven. Carrie looked down the long black tarmac and thought of South African roads; long, empty and perfect. Kieran, sitting on the right hand side, chatted to the air traffic controller.

"I'll do this take off," said Kieran to Carrie, "practice my right hand seat flying then the rest of the trip will be yours, if you can handle it."

He held the Warrior on the brakes and put on full power. Letting the brakes off sharply, they trundled down the runway.

"Pah, not exactly a fart in a bath, is it, your little life giver; your future; your baby."

He lifted off and immediately started swearing. "Pants, Pants what a dog. This thing's full of poopies. Look at the ASI...Lakeland tower Warrior 22November request a pattern and landing..."

Carrie looked at the air speed indicator and saw they were registering nothing, even though they were clearly travelling at more than 60 knots. She felt sick. Another problem. This didn't look good. Another cost.

"Warrior22 is this an emergency?" returned the tower.

To Carrie's surprise Kieran replied with, "negative. Just a brief pit stop." To her he said, "spare me from rank amateurs."

"What?" asked Carrie, baffled. "What do you mean? The airspeed...?"

Kieran didn't reply.

"Roger Warrior 22, runway twenty seven in use, land at your discretion. Call ready for re-departure."

Kieran did a pattern without speaking, concentrating on the speed outside. Brought the plane round gently onto finals and landed fast, putting on the brakes quickly and bringing the Warrior to a slow crawl by the first exit. Jumped out, leaving the machine running. He went around to the left wing, pulled off the pitot cover and got back into the plane; waving it angrily at her.

"So much for your preflight check," he spat. "You left the pitot cover on. That cover's supposed to stop flies crawling into the airspeed indicator. No wonder the poor little dog wasn't barking, its mouth was all sealed up!"

"But you were doing it!" Carrie broke in, "you told me you wanted to.."

"No excuses! No justifications! Just get these things right in future. A mark of a good pilot is admitting he's fucked up. All right I have control. No more thumb up bum and mind in neutral. I'll taxi us around, we don't want to lose any more time. You can do the take off. Bloody dogs and amateurs. Give me a professional any day." He shot off at an Olympic sprinter's walk.

This time take-off was uneventful and they headed north towards Wilmington, North Carolina. The Warrior again passed over lakes; Harris, Griffen, and Yale passed under them, while they headed for Lake George, Crescent Lake and the coast. Once again water was dominant, as though the land was mocking her, teasing her imagination about the trickey ocean voyage to come. Kieran mentioned this was going to be a much longer trip than he'd planned for.

"You don't seem very well prepared, my little Cherokee," he murmured, putting the plane into a steep dive: to test the wing strength. "If we get any more delays I'll have to start charging more."

"I don't seem very well prepared. Cheek! Who is the expert here?"

"Ah, expertise. Many have made that mistake. The myth of the bourgeoisie committing liberticide against the poor proletariat. Still, since you've learnt to fly, you'd better show me your expertise. This may take some adjusting to after the Cessna. Ever flown a low wing? There are those who never fly high wing and others who scream the low wing is the abomination of the weight carrying pilot. You have to experience both and then have an opinion. Oh! Not so rough; smooth and sensuous, treat the plane like your favourite dick. Percy. Mr Cock. Ah, ah."

Kieran started to sing; something about she never loved me quite so much when I treated her well. Carrie flew, while he took the map, tuned in the instruments and every now and then struck his hand into an arrow-like pose to show which direction he thought she should be flying in.

"Doodbeedoobe do..she loved me when I made her blue.." Left arrow, "and when I took her mother down, her love was worth another crown." Left arrow, "and oh so great was her adoration, when I had slept with half the nation. LEFT LEFT for goodness sake don't you know which side is left? Another case of thumb up bum and mind in neutral. OK you've had an engine failure...land somewhere..."

As he spoke he closed the throttle, and pulled out the carburettor heat. Reacting rather well, she thought, considering she hadn't had much experience, Carrie aimed for a field, without trees and animals, looked for wind direction and prepared her approach.

"Good Lord. No! No! No! that won't do....try that one on the left."

"Why not?" Carrie was exasperated.

"Don't argue with me. Argue only on the ground. That should be your life's motto. Many pilots have died arguing in the cockpit. Respect! That's what we need here. A bit of respect."

She looked at the field he had chosen. "Your field's full of sheep."

"Irrelevant." He murmured and began singing again. "Respect your pilot lest you die at his hands."

"Bollocks," Carrie snarled, hating this particular pilot, wishing she'd been able to have the Russian.

Kieran sang. "Bill and Ben, flower-pot-men, one got laid the other was slayed. Do you ken the flower-pot-men."

Finally they got to the coast at the Matanzas inlet. Kieran took control and dropped so low they were level with an elderly renovated Fort. Carrie saw the Stars and Stripes flapping away in the sea breeze.

"That's Fort Matanzas," Kieran, ever ready with knowledge (right or wrong). "Built in 1740 on the site where the Spanish cruelly massacred French soldiers in 1570. And why did they do that, my little reborn? Was it to consolidate their power, was it in revenge for a previous killing of Spanish? Of Indians loyal to the Emperor-would-be King Philippe? No, it was an opening move to establish a colony in Florida. Death for power, power for money, money for gain and chicks for free. Simply Spanish Imperialists committing liberticide against the French proletariat."

Carrie looked at the small fort with its stone walls and imagined a scene full of bloody, dead French soldiers. Was that where 'scuse my French' came from, perhaps? Her fucking engineer had definitely made a killing.

"Bill and Ben," sang Kieran, "Bill got laid, was that fair..."

The Warrior's shadow flitted along the sands of Anastasia Island.

Carrie saw seals in the water, but the Warrior slipped by too quickly. A few people on St Augustine waved, or cursed; fists in passing shadows.

After Jacksonville they headed out to sea, avoiding the coastal curves. Kieran told her about Florida sea fog, which came in so fast he had only been saved by following the sound of a fog horn up a side channel, thought to be haunted. Here the fog had mysteriously disappeared, the air was clear and the weather balmy. "We all have a guardian angel. Mine works well, yours probably harder than most. What a job for a dead man."

They radioed Savanna, Jacksonville, Charleston and Myrtle Beach, but no one seemed interested in the little Warrior heading north. At Cape Fear they turned across Smith Island, and ran into a patch of light mist.

"Virga!" crowed Kieran. "Like the virgin on viraga, never touches the ground. Oh joy, an eternity of virginity far better than a vision of virility."

After three and a half hours flying, the DME told them with digital accuracy that Wilmington was 10 miles away. Carrie searched for it across the greying, sun-drying sands and pools left by the receding river. Turning up the inlet, Kieran gave the airfield a call.

"Very different from the old UK," he said cheerfully, "far more frequencies and much more relaxed, hardly any need for standard language at all. Eyes down; you've got your undercart, eyes up; your cart's retracted. Wild women's words 'eh. As the blind man said when he saw Heaven. Hello, Wilmington. N2122 we have Delta, inbound to you for landing. Look forward to trying out your great facilities."

"Roger N22," said a girl's voice. "Reading you fives. Runway twenty three in use. No traffic. Call finals."

"Fives?"

"Strength five...as clear as a bell and as loud as the nun's excitement," replied Kieran.

In the distance through the shining air they saw the harsh outline of the airfield's long dark runways. At the far end were a concoction of grey hangars surrounded by small red and blue houses, like a herd of elephants standing amongst a flock of brightly coloured birds. It was, like so many American airfields, virtually deserted. Only a couple of small planes taxying towards the departure end of the runway.

"Oh wild!" said Kieran. Carrie wondered if he was talking to her, the airfield or himself. "I love these empty airfields, so long and hard; as the actress said to the bishop. Notice they don't give us QFE here in the old US; all landings done on the jolly old QNH. QFE about as useful as tits on a boar hog in the good old USA. And that would have confused the jolly old Bishop."

As they taxied in, Kieran asked the traffic control girl, "so Wilmington traffic my love, which TBO can you recommend?"

The air traffic girl came back promptly. "I'm afraid I cannot recommend any of the TBOs," she said.

For once Kieran and Carrie were united in laughter. "Well," replied Kieran, "just tell me which one I can meet you in this evening."

"I'm afraid I cannot recommend any particular company," she replied smartly, rectifying her previous mistake.

"Yeah, typical," said Kieran to Carrie, "no sense of humour those Americans. Anyway she's probably 40 years old and 40 foot wide. Besides why would I want another companion, when I have your light jolly chatter to keep me amused. We'll try this one, it looks fine."

"What's a TBO?"

"Hello! The lights are on but no one's at home! Didn't they teach you anything at school in The Great Colonial Power? A TBO is an FBO, Fixed Base Operator, but at the terminal, where they give you a car to drive, look after your plane and treat you like a king at all times."

"For a price no doubt."

"Ah, that little bourgeois spirit rearing its head again. Go lightly through the wicked skies and ask not when your Daddy lies, believe him when he tells you that ..." Kieran began to sing again.

They chose a TBO in a recently painted blue building with large viewing windows above short, brick walls. Inside, the reception-girls clustered into a pine corral with broad counters in the middle of the room. Carrie thought they looked like beautiful animals herded in to protect them from the brutish customers. One girl, with model's arms, leant on the desk-top and asked in a southern drawl if they were from Canada.

They seemed extremely impressed when Kieran replied he was flying this tiny plane to England. Several asked if he needed any luggage, which led to many jokes from Kieran about baggage, luggage and garbage, boots and hoods. They gave him presents, which they said other pilots had left behind. Another girl, a long-legged, long-haired blond with deep-set eyes, suggested he borrow her car.

"I don't need it tonight," she breathed, smiling extremely sweetly, "I've got my boy-friend's."

Hum, Carrie thought, they could have had Kieran, if she hadn't needed him herself. Still it was useful to have the car, and this time Kieran decided not to look for sex shops. Indeed, when they met in the long, modern, pinewood bar for a pre-prandial drink, he suddenly became extremely charming and, telling Carrie he used to belong to the Magic Circle, began to perform tricks.

"See this..." he said, taking a dime from behind her ear. "Now, what a beautiful acoustic organ. I said acoustic...watch my lips. Have you got a Franklin?"

"A Franklin?"

"Funny, I'd have thought you of all people, my little money worshipper, would have known what a Franklin was. A Franklin is a 'C'. One hundred lovely little purchasing dollars, my soft, white dove, is a Franklin."

"Oh! Yes I have..."

"Show me!"

Carrie opened her purse and let him see the note adding, ".... but I'm not having you tear it up and then replacing it or something like that."

He sighed. Leant forward and took a second dime from behind her ear, which he presented to her.

"Funny place to keep your money! Where is that spirit of adventure? I can see it is true the plane came as a gift, you'd never have allowed that much money out of your sight. Very well, my pigeon, I will use my own Franky, but the trick loses something that way."

"Not for me," Carrie said, while Kieran, obviously changing his mind, took a 'Franklin' from the barman and tore it to pieces, only to restore it and give it back to its owner intact.

"Shall I tell you the story of my life? How I was found under a cherry tree, how a good woman took me in and made me hers. And I made her life, which once was dull and unenviable, full, fun and the envy of all her compatriots."

Carrie laughed. "You! A story teller!" She moued sarcastically, "I don't believe you! I thought every word was Gospel truth."

"Many have made that mistake. But seriously, all the most interesting people tell stories; and that may or may not be akin to telling lies. But you, my little world-seeker, you of all people shouldn't be afraid of fabrication when it suits your purpose. It might even make you a fortune."

Carrie frowned, finding this too superficial. "Wouldn't that be just an admission that my real life was dull, that I had to lie to invent a better one?"

"Not at all! All lives are dull or interesting in parts, but what makes the difference is the way the owner portrays it to others, the lilt he gives it...are you following me. The lights are on, but is anyone at home?"

"Yes. Yes I am." Carrie, interested but wary. This could be closer to the way she had imagined the trip; a learning experience and more lively than surfing the web.

"Now," Kieran said, "the story of La Grand Therese?"

"Who?"

"The greatest deception of the nineteenth century. Completely true. How a young girl, who came from lower than nothing, arrived at riches purely by using her tongue and making up stories. Convincing the elite of the French Third Republic that she was an heiress."

"And... go on." Carrie liked this idea. She hoped he might go further, give her some tips on painless money-making. He could perhaps increase her internet-stimulated knowledge of history, psychology, economics and other subjects.

"Oh, well she got caught in the end." He yawned. "Now, to cement what I say, I shall buy you dinner this evening. Which little candle-lit bistro shall we grace with our presence? Which haven of eleganthia? I know just the place: the hotel dining room. So cozy. So chic, and above all so close. And besides, I seem to have acquired a Franklin."

He waved one in front of Carrie's face and she laughed, intrigued; where had it come from, was it the barman's or was he just fooling? It was only when she went to bed that night and counted her remaining dollars that she realised she was a hundred short: that it was her 'Franky' that had paid for their dinner. While wondering which Magic Circle he had belonged to, she also realised she couldn't prove it or get her it back. Just you wait, Mr Kieran, Carrie thought irritated; charm tonight, tomorrow revenge.

The next day the cloud base hung low in the sky. Carrie surveyed the gathering gloom and wondered if Kieran would be prepared to fly. Apparently he was, since, after his breakfast of steak and eggs, and her coffee, he drove her over to the airfield, pointing out that he was saving her bourgeois heart by letting her have a free car.

"I suppose by rights," he said, "I should be charging you rent for letting you ride beside me in this borrowed car, the present of my sweetheart and admirer in the TBO."

"Hum, don't push your luck!"

"Push me luck! That's an interesting thing to say to a superstitious pilot about to fly off into cloud. If you weren't going to be there at my side I'd say you were wishing me harm. But then you're not the little sweetie to do such a thing, are you my little dear? Even if you know nothing about TBOs or post office riots."

"Are you superstitious?" Carrie asked. "I heard that about Irishmen but I'd have thought pilots were more men of science."

"Irishmen! Superstitious! Men of Science is it? How many hours did you say you had now? 45 or 50 in flying and how little in life? I think you've still got a bit more learning to do."

They arrived at the airfield and Kieran went to check out the plane, while Carrie paid the bill to the girls in the pen. After a few minutes he was back in the office again asking the girls if they had any "gaffer tape".

"Gaffer tape?"

"Thick strong tape."

"You mean duct tape?"

"Duck tape it is honey."

Curious, Carrie followed him out to the plane. He was lying under the Warrior's wing attaching a pencil to the back-underside of the right aileron, another already graced the wing's leading edge.

"What's that for?"

"I told you it was a dog. The bow wow seems to be pulling left, I'm evening up the wings by biting into the airflow. Bet you'd never have thought of that my little innocent."

"You're right. It couldn't have anything to do with...." She stopped, suddenly uncertain. She couldn't help remembering what the engineer had said about the holes in the aircraft and drugs. Combine that with the missing money. Could Ignatius have bought drugs with her missing money? Could there be some packets of heroine taped onto one side of the fuselage, making it pull right? Was she innocently carrying contraband? It wouldn't be the first time someone stopped for smuggling said they knew nothing of the merchandise. Or that no one believed them. Kieran hadn't a clue her thoughts had turned in such a direction.

"What? Would you be suggesting I might be too heavy compared to your little levitating body, and the plane is lilting left?"

"No, of course not!"

"I thought not. Good thing I'm here."

She left him to it, wondering why she didn't mention the drugs idea to Kieran. Or if bits of pencil attached with tape would really make any difference to the stability of the Warrior. Still, as Kieran would have said, 'is there any point in having a dog and barking yourself?' The common sense part of her that made her able to fly (and fall for rich men) warned her he was pulling a stunt. The imaginative side saw Kieran as a drug smuggling aid to an Ignatius who had somehow avoided death.

They left Wilmington around midday, with assurances from the weather men that the low cloud was only regional and as soon as they got further north along the coast they'd be into blue skies and light sunshine. They crossed the Cape Fear railway line and river and headed over the Moores Creek National Park never getting above 500 feet. All around them seemed to be the tops of trees. A huge unending sea of dark green pine, whose branches looked challenging, rather than inviting, and certainly not suitable for a precautionary landing.

Contrary to the weathermen's predictions, the cloud grew denser and lower as they went further north. Far from flying out of trouble, the Warrior was driven closer to the ground, trying to stay below the tendrils of grey cotton wool that clung to the tallest trees, obscuring their vision. Every now and then they would get into a clearer patch and Carrie would grow hopeful, then a swathe of mist like an old man's beard would creep in below and with a curse, Kieran would turn away to remain in sight of the teasing trees.

Soon they were creeping along just above the foliage, so low that Carrie noticed a parasitic buddleia growing in a lightening blasted relic. Everywhere around was forest, not even a track suitable for a forced landing. Kieran for the first time seemed seriously disturbed. There was no singing and no stories. He adjusted and readjusted the instruments, as if to convince himself they were really flying much higher and more safely than he knew to be true. Eventually he could not bear it any more.

"I'm sorry," he said. "This is crap."

"That's OK, I like the view down here," Carrie said.

"Mary mother of God save me from amateurs. We're turning back to the airfield," he swore and dialled up the VOR radial for Wilmington.

"Wilmington November 2122 returning to you due to appalling, Warrior-defeating weather. Request joining and landing instructions."

The ATC had heard everything before, and merely informed them that landing was on runway five.

Once on the ground, Kieran regained all his light charm and danced back into the TBO, keen to tell the girls he had missed them so much he couldn't tear himself away. But all Kieran's flirting couldn't get the girl's car for a second night and Carrie had to pay for the use of the TBO one. Spitting, she saw her profits whittled down a little more.

As they were about to leave the airfield for the hotel there was a commotion outside. The receptionists poured out of their pen and jostled the pilots already by the window, peering out and making remarks. Even Kieran, intrigued, walked over to see what was happening. Carrie joined him, staring out at the parking bay. A large silver warplane from yesteryear, with a high peaked nose tilting back to a stiletto tail, taxied in and stopped outside the TBO, its tail shuddering like a wet dog.

"What's going on?"

"It's an invasion by an Invader," said Kieran. "One of those classic aeroplanes we would all love to own but mostly can't afford, so it's left to the rich amateurs. I think we'll wait and meet the pilot. You may find he'd be happy to let you sit on his knee in the cockpit or even fly. Who knows what your gorgeous charm may do to these wild, crazy American pilots?"

"Thanks."

Carrie watched as the doors of the plane swung open, and a woman climbed backwards out of the cockpit. A small, rather broad-based body with elegantly coiffured blue-black hair and a pink eye-patch matching her flying suit. As she turned Carrie noticed that in spite of being around sixty she had a very pert, almost lifted bust.

"That's the owner," said a TBO girl next to Carrie, "like, she's Mexican or Polish or something...her husband is loaded. He likes young dolls, so he says to her, like, you know, I'm 65 and I'm having babes but, like you know, no divorce, no way Hosé. Weird 'eh! No one fucks my head up like that, even my boyfriend...not like he's rich or old. Wayne's OK, he's class...."

Carrie lost interest. A man was climbing out of the plane and she realised she knew him. He was the Russian-marrying ferry pilot; her choice. So this is what happened to him.

"Hey," she said, "that's Rhum."

"Oh, do you know him?" asked Kieran, cheesed off. "Rum name Rhum. I once had a dog called Brandy but I had to give him a way he was much too bloody randy..."

"Sort of..he's the you if you weren't you, if you see what I mean."

"I can see clearly now the rain has gone? No I don't see. Clarify, my little darling. Tell us here of your passionate embraces, of unrequited love, of torn breasts and rent passions..."

"Oh! I interviewed him to come out here, but he was too busy. I guess this is with what..."

"Ah, whom, surely, not what," breathed Kieran, "but now it is clear. Young Rhum is a ferry pilot, not a sherry but a ferry pilot although his girl may be a cherie, and certainly wears a cherise eye-patch. We must wait and chat, learn and tell. I foresee tonight will be fun."

Rhum unfortunately didn't recognise Carrie until he was reminded; which, Carrie felt, reduced her already low street cred with the TBO girls, but gave Kieran rich delight. The owner of the plane was The Baroness de Vocov, an imperious woman who treated everyone, including Rhum and Kieran, as though she was a Hollywood star and they were on-set lackeys. Carrie wondered if this was the result of arrogance or merely because she had years of giving orders behind her. Clearly she had not learnt that money could not buy everything.

"Fetch my bags," she said to one of the TBO girls, handing her the keys. "And put them in the car. Rhum will show you."

She then swept off, picking up a box of matches, and didn't reappear for an hour. Carrie and the Russian had a cold drink from the machine, while he awaited his mistress's pleasure.

"I'm sorry I couldn't acknowledge you," said Rhum, "the BV doesn't like me to have lady friends."

"I interviewed you for a job," Carrie pointed out, sitting down on a mock Scottish tartan sofa and picking up a glossy magazine, "that hardly qualifies me for a position as your lady friend."

He sat down opposite her, across a small table, and produced an oblong box from his bomber jacket pocket. "No, no of course not, but you are a beaut. Would you like a game of chess?"

"I'm not very good," Carrie said, but she put down the magazine.

"No. Of course not. Unless you were grand master level you wouldn't be able to beat me anyway. Is that your little Warrior? Nice. Nice colour. Are you going on to NY next?"

"Yes. Thanks. And yes again."

"I always carry a chess machine with me. Usually I beat the machine, but this way you and the machine can pool your assets against me. Sometimes I do lose this way. I've remembered where I met your hubby."

"Oh. I'd forgotten you had met," said Carrie startled, her mind absorbed with Rhum's keenness to destroy her fragile chess abilities. Behind them Kieran flirted with the TBO girls.

"Give me your hand," Kieran said to one of the girls. He massaged it in his grip; back and forth, back and forth. "I'm a Martian: I'm just like you, I eat like you, I sleep like you, there is only one difference between us...my sex organs are in my hand!"

The girl, screaming with giggles, pulled back her hand and the others all looked at it laughing.

"Yeah, it was in Africa," Rhum told Carrie, setting up the board. "I'd finished a long flight and was winding down, when he came over with an American girl I know."

He picked up a white and a black pawn, shuffled them behind his back, and held out his two fists. Carrie studied his wrinkle-free hands, taut like a well-filled sausage skin; the fingers bloated to about twice normal size. She wondered whether a scratch would ooze out white gunge in the place of blood.

"American girl?" She asked, choosing the hand that turned out to hold the black pawn. "Was she a pilot?"

She played her knight in response to Rhum's first move, wondering why this normal sounding encounter with Ignatius made her feel queasy.

"Yes. How long do you stay in Wim?" Rhum asked, taking her knight.

"We leave tomorrow." She risked her queen, wishing she wasn't. "Check."

"Good move. BV and I are off early am. Oh, check mate. Bad luck. Best of three?"

"OK. What was her name? The pilotess I mean."

Rhum set up the board again. "Oh..God I'm bad with names..I'll think of it in a moment...funny name...like a fruit or a flower. I can see her. Blond. Quite small but long legs. Young. Cute. Check mate again! And MacGuffies!" Rhum made an illustrative gesture.

By the time the Baroness was ready to leave, Rhum had beaten Carrie five times. "Do you beat the Baroness?" she asked, frustrated.

"Umm," breathed Kieran tiring of the TBO girls, "beats him hard, beats him long. Hard and full makes full and hard."

The Russian ignored him. "Oh, I wouldn't play with BV, I'd have to let her win. I have tact."

The four of them had dinner in the shade-filled courtyard of an international restaurant in a forest outside Wilmington, which Rhum had discovered. It occurred to Carrie that these spreading branches were probably from the same trees that had prevented her leaving Wilmington this morning. Wiping her chair with a handkerchief before sitting, the Baroness told Carrie Rhum's forté was finding restaurants.

"Dear one," she barked in the manner of deaf people, oblivious to Rhum's contiguity, "he's a bit of a wet jacket but totally reliable, and that's rare enough. I realise that nowadays the affection of servitude is dead and buried, but I don't need to be reminded I pay for loyalty."

"Yes," Carrie said slightly embarrassed, uncertain how to respond. She came from a different generation, with less money, more introspection. "I'm sure you're right but personally, I think.."

"Holy Cat!" The Baroness Vocov spat away whatever Carrie was going to say as irrelevant. "There's no need for this openness. In my day, you never spoke of it: now everybody is an expert. Get it! Get the picture? Dear one?"

Ting! Ting! Ting! Baroness Vocov, growing impatient as older people will, had put her knife to her glass. Carrie fidgeted uncomfortably on her chair, blushing at this method of getting attention. But the waiter, unflustered, floated over with the menus, smiling benignly.

The Baroness took a quick glance at the text and sighed. "Rubbish. Disgusting! Why Americans never learnt how to cook beats me. Plenty of 'em. Plenty of non-Americans here too; but cooking. Bleah! Young man I'll have a Dover sole, lemon...don't ruin it with your usual American sauces. OK."

"Yes, Mam," the waiter said, and Carrie wondered if there was an edge to his politeness when he added, "you may."

The Baroness heard only the subservience. "Give the others what they want! They probably like your muck, it takes time to develop good taste. And money."

Carrie, not hungry any more, ordered a salad but Kieran delightedly enjoyed asking for Surf and Turf, with extra ketchup and sauces. Rhum ordered chilli con carne, with just a small glance at the Baroness to see if this fitted her criteria. Apparently it did since all she said was, "Surf and Turf. Americans. So hard to find a good pilot these days."

"So, Baroness," asked Kieran, leaning forward ingratiatingly, "how do you find the Invader, pearl of the American Orient?"

"Pearl of the American Orient?" She spat again, bits of Dover soul making a last escape across the room. "This idiot a friend of yours Rhum? War Plane, that's what!"

"Of course..." began Kieran but the Baroness was ahead of him. "In 1945 my Invader carried 4,000 lbs of bombs inside and 16 rockets outside. Pearl of the Orient! Hah. Practically blew Korea out the water! That's what."

"Yes, but in Pearl Harbour.." began Kieran.

"Pearl Harbour was the 7th December 1941," interrupted Rhum, "the prototype of the Invader didn't fly until the 10th July 1942."

"Attaboy!" said the Baroness. "Others can say what they like about your brains Rhum, but I've never found you a fool."

Kieran ordered a Guinness and gave up. For the rest of the evening Rhum and the Baroness lectured Carrie on why the Invader was a far better investment than the Warrior.

"Rubbish, these modern planes," snarled the Baroness. "Tin rubbish. When the Invader was built men knew how to make aircraft..."

"Built when men were men, and pansies were afraid," began Kieran, returning from his Guinness, "when engineers were inspirational and planes were solo creations instead of concoctions by committee...."

"Rubbish! I hate cliches, especially the flying phrases. Worst of all. Damn pilots. So hard to find a good one these days."

"Lekker dag," called Carrie to Rhum, as the party broke up.

"BBFN," replied Rhum.

Watching the Vocov tribe turn towards their hotel, Kieran sneered. "Of course Rhum is a fucking poofter! No MAN would allow an old bag like that..."

"You're joking! You don't really think Rhum is gay?"

"Undoubtably."

"Impossible! He's multi-married. Got kids."

"In itself proof," countered Kieran.

"So, much married means not the marrying kind!" Carrie asked sarcastically, opening the door into the hotel. "I had three husbands and I'm not in the least bit gay."

"Neither gay nor humorous," said Kieran dismissively, "but definitely woman. Women need marriage. They don't necessarily enjoy it once they get it but they crave it like a drug. Frankly I'm not sure it's even good for them, but that's not the issue here. Take it from me, your case and his are different. For Rhum, in the macho world of flying in which he wishes to preside, he is more fortunate being a polymath-husband by inclination."

"But he doesn't strike me as..."

"Why do women constantly have to probe the depths? Why not let men have their secrets in peace 'eh? Politics, you know, had no foibles until women and their insistence on 'The Truth' became involved."

"Rubbish!" said Carrie, irritated and finding her voice pitching higher. "You are putting the honesty of women into a demeaning format, which makes it seem like a sin. Politics should be up-front."

"You think so, my little beetle? Even to the extent of stripping down the private lives of individuals. Would you like to be told that Dennis Thatcher tied up his wife and beat her every night and that such treatment allowed her to go freely into the world and terrorise nations? Is that the politics of honesty you women so espouse? Don't you think if people had known about that it might have reduced her effectiveness in the brutal world, which only needs a few secrets to protect it and maintain the status quo?"

"But now you are being ridiculous, extreme..." Carrie walked along the corridor, prickling with indignation.

"What are extremes but logical conclusions, my little heart beat? Find me an extreme that stands alone and I will find you to be the best aerobatic pilot in the Eastern Seaboard. But enough of this tittle tattle and faradidle, we must be thinking seriously of the job in hand and the future, not juggling in this light way with levitations of Thatcher's sexuality."

"No..I.." Carrie wanted to prolong the conversation but Kieran was a master in the art of talking (or not) about any subject under discussion.

"Goodnight, my little heart-beat," said Kieran and, slamming his door shut, left her staring at the blandly painted wood.

The following day the weather was beautiful. Thanks to Kieran's renewed flirting, however, it was almost noon before they left North Carolina and the sun was high in the sky. Taking off on runway thirty four, they turned north and followed the coast through Onslow Bay up to Moorhead City. Here they flew along the false coast inside the islands over the Pamlico Sound, a natural harbour of water protected from the Atlantic Ocean by a long spit of thin islands.

"Good place for seaplanes," remarked Kieran, "protected from the weather like the nun in the monastery; nothing visible to the jealous God of the seas. Easy seas and easy sighs, give God and man many lies." He began to sing again, while Carrie thought about Colin's constantly ditching ferry pilot.

The Warrior dropped height and skimmed along the sands between between Norfolk and the Chesapeake Bay Bridge, 'the longest miracle of engineering,' said the ever informative Kieran. Under his instructing hand (left arrow, left arrow) they passed over the Delamarva Peninsula, kissing the water in Delaware Bay. Carrie watched their shadow, as the little plane flew low-level over the sandy undulation and smiled to be flying here in the sunshine above the wreckage of life. She was a darting carefree silver bird in the spring light.

Up the coast, past the high rise gambling dens of Atlantic City. Kieran told stories of free buses to the city, free gambling money to start the passion. "They'll do anything to entice the human flotsam and jetsam to get sucked into the gambling virus. Gambling with bodies not with money, lambs to the slaughter not to the pasture. Over to the west is Philadelphia, home of Shakers, those who abuse the humble zip. Button wearers and the Amish."

Carrie steered the small Warrior past Neptune, Ashbury Park, Long Branch, Red Bank and Sandy Hook, watching the ant-like traffic crawl: even at 500 foot you could feel the frustration. Kieran (left arrow, left arrow) sang about the Headmaster of Roedean who: "had a wee one, useful only for keyholes and small girls' weeholes." Left Arrow. Left arrow.

After four hours flying they entered Lower Hudson Bay and made their way low-level along the Hudson River, under the vying skies of Kennedy traffic, up towards America's most beloved city, New York.

Carrie felt a surge of happiness as she realised their arrival coincided with the setting sun. Looking ahead she could see the town, swathed in a redgold glow; not the pinkness of pollution often seen in London, but a warm light which shimmered like spangles on the buildings. Intense, she thought laughing, surreal: I'm becoming American.

Leaving the sea behind them, they flew up a wide channel, which narrowed as they left the bay and entered the river. Getting closer, Carrie could see the that Hudson itself was aglow with the same reddish orange light. Dancing on the waves, the river full of tiny fires. Above them the orange light merged into a deep blue, darkening with height. Nearer still the buildings began to reveal individuality, climbing out of the fires to stand above them like eerily reflective spirits. This, Carrie thought, I should have been seeing with a prospective husband. Such a romantic scene could hardly fail to bring on a string of proposals. Still, more optimistically, travelling with Kieran had been an eye-opener, proving her husbands hadn't really been that bad after all; even the divorcee.

"You've got JFK on your right, Newark on your left and if you took the right fork up the East River, you could wend your way to La Guardia," Kieran informed her. "But we take the left fork into the Hudson proper and ..look there's the World Trade Centre...it's almost crushed really isn't it..from this angle..it hardly even looks tall...but wait until we see the Lady of the Harbour....my babe..."

Carrie blocked out his voice and watched Manhattan reveal itself as a combination of shorter and taller buildings, indigenous to their own districts. Here the shorter, older ones clustered on one side of the peak, while over there, further down the peninsula, the tall younger ones stood forming a solid guard against some external enemy. There was greenery too, almost black in the setting sun. Carrie was shocked to realise she had previously considered New York to be merely a bank of identical silver high rises.

Kieran gave a position report at Staten Island and the American emblem of liberty passed a short way below them, her arm and crown gleaming in the sun; a green-gold woman in the fiery chocolate river. They swept over what seemed to be glistening torrents towards the George Washington bridge. The cluster of squat buildings on the peak of the island now became a host of different shapes and forms in the sunset, unknown and unidentifiable by her but inescapably unique. The taller twin towers, over to the west of the island, stood out red in the quiescent sun, but catching a dying ray's reflection they held a long silver streak down each building; like a spear through blood.

In comparison the lower eastern environment look stubby and short. Where were the areas she had heard so much about? 'Greenwich Village,' 'Downtown' and Brooklyn? She laughed at the way the West Side buildings spilled over to the edge of the river. She wished she could identify those tubby buildings reflecting the ruby light back at her. What was that small, older looking building, maybe a church, tucked amongst the silver stretchers. As they took the left fork up the Hudson, she wondered which bridge was that on the East River, joining a promontory on Manhattan to another island. Her body resonated with the excitement of the warm, orange glow. They flew on to Palisades Park and turned left, leaving the Hudson and crossing the New Jersey Turnpike and a smaller tributary of the Hudson towards Teterboro.

It was nearly dark as they flew over the airfield, the wings were now just shadowy blocks against the twinkling lights of New Jersey, the static lines giving them a hairy appearance. The Warrior flew over the main runway, where something large was just touching down, and lined up for finals on the shorter one, used for less space-hungry craft. Carrie landed with a bounce and a bump.

"Hoho," said Kieran, "and how many landing fees will we be charged for that one I wonder? One, two, and baby makes three as the Father Confessor said to the nuns."

Carrie taxied the Warrior across the tarmac, beautifully relaxed and content despite Kieran's comments. It was fully dark now and she followed the flickering blue taxi lights to the over-night area.

"Park next to the Lear," commanded the air traffic controller.

"Wilco," said Carrie, to him. "Lear?" She asked Kieran. "King Lear was that? These air-trafficers think you know every type of aircraft."

"Lear Jet," explained Kieran, "not exactly an obscure plane, I would have thought; but to you, sweet poppet, the long white aircraft sitting next to the long blue one, just over on your right."

She grimaced. Probably, she thought, he couldn't tell a roan horse from a strawberry chestnut. She didn't risk asking though, remembering that Irishmen often have a sort of magical way when it comes to horses: although that might not extend to Irishmen born in Clapham.

Parking her tiny plane next to its larger companion, Carrie mused whimsically on what lies and stories her little piston engine would tell its svelte neighbour that evening. And what sort of evening this would be for her: sex clubs and fraught anxiety? Or Kieran telling stories and being a charming, delightful companion; while removing money from her ears and her wallet. With Kieran it was never possible to guess in advance.

They collected their cases. Carrie stood for a moment on the wing of the Warrior, breathing the scent of a living city night; the smooth softness of the darkness, accentuated by an occasional cold breeze which prickled her skin; the smell of diesel; the continual flashing of lights and the invigorating hum of distant traffic. 'The bees that tease in the high Pyrenees'. Here there was no warm buzz of cicadas, but instead the stimulating strength of the achieving world. It was strange, she mused, that your body appreciated all these different sensations, identified them, stored them, and recognised them again. And yet she could hardly put words to this percipience.

She heard the tisk of a match and smelt the tang of sulphur as Kieran lit a cigarette. Her dream broken, she was turning to shut the little Warrior's door when a voice behind her said: "Carrie! Carrie Nordsuiterlaan. My God it is you. I can hardly believe it. What are you doing here?"

Carrie looked up and there, climbing out of the Lear, was Mitch, wearing a short sleeved shirt in spite of the evening cool, arms sticking out like a cockroach's legs, Ray-Bans hanging from her pearls.

Carrie 'de-winged' with an energetic bounce. "Mitch! Good Heavens. What the Hell...?"

Like lightening Kieran was there, flashing smiles at her side, one arm lightly placed around her shoulders, cigarette between his fingers, the other stretched out in greeting. Full charm in place and oozing.

"Well hello, I'm Kieran O'Toole, young Carrie's pilot, splendid to meet you. Is this your Lear Jet? Do you mind if I have a look..you know I used to fly one of these for the Baron de Montapusy, therein lie a few stories, which I can bore you with later but you'll be interested...."

Before Carrie could focus on what was happening, Kieran had swept Mitch off into the Lear, leaving her with a few words from her instructor.

"Carrie," she said, almost physically resisting Kieran to give her instructions, "could you be a dear and wait for my man? He's on his way over here from the terminal. Just let him know I'm still up here and bring him up to join us, will you? Thanks. Sorry about this, actually.."

They disappeared into the Lear (King or jet,) while Carrie stayed on the tarmac staring in a bemused way at the little black opening which had swallowed them from her sight. She could hardly believe Mitch had been there and was almost able to convince herself it was nothing but a dream. Certainly there was no appearance of Mitch's man.

Since she spoke both English and Dutch, Carrie wondered if she was waiting for Mitch's 'man' as in husband. But her husband was dead; unless she'd remarried. Carrie knew all about that. Maybe Mitch, like Carrie herself, found it hard to live without a man. None of her own husbands had been perfect, but they had been male, and at the time that had seemed enough. Now, though, it no longer seemed so. She needed more; but what?

Across the tarmac a young man ambled her way. A tall, dirty-blond, he stooped right, like a man carrying the world's pain on one shoulder. Around his neck he wore an Ascot cravat. Carrie felt a lilt in her stomach. Her eyes followed his arrival; could this be Mitch's husband? This familiar shape. This man, a little older, more bowed and less lively, was Kees van der Pick, Carrie's second, and still living, husband.

"Carrie? Christ!" His guttural accent reminded her of heavy butter.

"Just Carrie will do," Carrie quipped wittily, pilot-like. "Hello Kees, long time. Mitch says to tell you she's inside the Lear."

"Oh!" (It sounded like Ho.)

He looked at the girl in front of him silently, seeing her beautiful face again. Of course he hated her for what she did to him, but you couldn't deny the power of that face and the strong, springy body. He sighed. Outside so good; inside all bitch. All bitch. He knew rabid dogs with kinder bites.

Carrie remembered that silence as one of her former husband's annoying habits. He seldom asked questions, just waited to be enlightened. She wasn't going to say anything. She refused to make life easier for him: she hadn't forgotten how much he cost in alimony.

"Yours?" he asked eventually, indicating the Warrior.

Carrie nodded.

"Expensive? Cost a lot?"

"No."

"Oh?" (Ho.)

"A present from my husband." Carrie spoke defensively.

"Oh! So you are OK already."

"Yup. I'm fine. You?"

"Sure. I'm good so to say.'

They were silent.

"So," Carrie said, "you remarried?"

"Married? No way. Once was enough already."

"But..Mitch?"

"Mitch? Mitch the pilot? My wife? No way. She's a one husband woman. She's my co-pilot. I guess you don't know it: I am a pilot, so to say."

Carrie gaped at him. Of all her husbands the second was the least practical, the most airy-fairy. Throughout their marriage he'd never done a day's work and even the idea of him winding the clock was enough to make her laugh. Now he was flying planes.

"You're joking? A pilot?"

"Yeah. Already a while ago I make my private licence. Many cost but much discounts I wangled."

"Oh."

"In the absence of money you've got to light the fire in your own belly, hé. OK, my airline transport licence I haven't completely made but I fly. My commercial licence have I made. Then I meet Mitch. She asked me, was I wanting to accompany her on this trip up the coast. Hours building and for free."

"Is this Lear hers?" Flabbergasted Carrie had visions of Mitch owning planes across the continent. Skinny, pearls and now jets? It was enough to make you hate her.

"Oh, no. No, already...before she was making her airline job, she employed pilot of the owner was, so to say. Now sometime, when not working at her other job, she makes flying jobs on her old boss. He said she was number one pilot he had; at number two price."

Carrie felt strangely sad. Why half price? Because she was a woman? Kees, however, had started talking and seemed to be enjoying himself. "Here in America is such much flying..and all sorts of schemes they have...all very complicated, so to read. Will we go take a see inside the Lear? You shall be wanting to see the controls."

He scrambled ahead of her up the little ladder and disappeared into the plane. Carrie followed more sedately. Her mind pulsing, not only with thoughts of her husband and flying, but of Mitch. Kees had said she was a one man woman, quite the opposite from what Janie had indicated. So perhaps... Oh, who cares, thought Carrie suddenly cross: bored of her thoughts. Who gives a damn, I wish everybody would leave me alone. All I want is money and, right now, a very strong drink.

In the cockpit Kieran was draped leisurely across the Captain's seat, telling stories about his Lear Jet days. As she approached, Carrie heard: "...and the plane crashed into the side of the carrier. We all thought Mountapusy was dead...but then I walked into the bar and there he was, drink in hand. He'd gone straight through one of the port holes and ended up on a stool just by the bar...and you know what, the barman treated him to a free beer..."

She heard Mitch and Kees laughing and wondered if they believed him. Mitch certainly seemed quite taken with him and he was putting on the charm at the moment.

"There you are," said Mitch to Carrie her voice full of excitement, which might have been caused by Kieran or the Lear Jet. Her face was a little pink. "Bit different from the Warrior. Or the Cessna we started in, actually. Have you seen this...."

She enthused over the controls, the instruments, her flight out, and various modern additions until she noticed Carrie's poor response and realised she must be tired. "Shall we go and have a drink?" She asked.

"Excellent idea." Carrie murmured, already turning towards the door.

Descending down the Lear jet's narrow steps, they walked towards the white and blue terminal strobe lights. Kieran was surprised that they were allowed to amble openly across the airfield without an escort, but Mitch explained she came here so often she was almost part of the staff. She changed the subject and was asking Carrie about her flight, when Kieran suddenly realised he'd left his hat back in the cockpit.

"Silly old me...first the hat then the head. If I didn't 'spectacles and testicles', I'd forget my watch. Don't wait for me girls, I'll be the tickling of a ferret's fanny."

Mitch gave him the key, remarking she didn't usually lock it because there was always security on airfields but here, so close to New York, she thought it might be safer.

"Oh, no!" Carrie said, "what shall I do? My door won't lock, it's broken. The engineers at Lakeland allegedly mended it but it's gone again already. Should I go back and check it?"

"I'll check it on the way past" said Kieran, surprisingly helpful.

"You do seem to be having trouble with your plane," said Mitch, "Absolutely awful. Kieran was telling me such stories. Perhaps you'd be glad if it was stolen! But actually Carrie, if you'd like me to look at it in the morning, just to give it the once over, I'd be happy too. "

"Yes please," gasped Carrie, surprising herself by the relief she felt at Mitch's suggestion, "especially...."

"Especially the lock? I'll have a look, but actually you'll probably need a new one."

"Oh," Carrie had been going to say 'especially inside the wings', but

Mitch forestalled her and suddenly Kieran was back, his hat now firmly on his head, changing the subject and making flirtatious jokes to Mitch. Still, she could show her the following morning.

As there was no alcohol at the airport, the pilots took a taxi across the George Washington Bridge to New York City. There was a choice of that or the Lincoln Tunnel, but Kees insisted the bridge was cheaper.

"Better not go under the water," said Kieran laughing loudly, "or Kees van der Cloggie will be looking for a dyke to stick his finger into."

None of the others laughed.

The taxi was tiny. Even with Kieran in front, the other three could barely squeeze into the cramped space behind the divide that protected the driver from any passengers enraged by his inability to navigate or speak English. "All boot," said Kieran, "no spurs."

"Trunk," corrected Carrie's ex-husband.

Shutting the doors activated a recorded message from John Doe: "asking you to go on the rampage for safety; buckle up in the back."

"Belt up in the back," yelled Kieran, "as the vicar said to the monk."

Kieran's directions got the taxi driver lost, infuriating Mitch who took over map reading from the back. Eventually John Doe deposited them in Time Square; not a square at all but a tall street, full of offices, Disney shops and flashing digital news.

"Thank you for travelling with John Doe. The good news is you'll remember to take your things with you when you leave."

Time Square, once notorious for porn shops, had been either bought or cleaned up, the hotel prices rising in reflection. However, people on the sidewalk still drank from bottles encased in brown paper bags.

"I'm not staying here at this price." Carrie cried as they questioned a hotel receptionist. "Forget it Kieran. Pay yourself or we look elsewhere."

Kieran muttered about suffering the bourgeois spirit in a cheap place, or living on the doorstep of life, but Kees interrupted him. "Such much cost, I think Carrie is right. New York has horrid expense."

Carrie looked around at the flashing neon and the underfloor-heating-steam escaping from manholes; little foggy rounds in the wet street. Smoky depression and a flashy pilot. Things had been improving but now with rising costs and Kieran's pugnacious humour they were ebbing away. She longed to be alone with a whisky. A sidewalk sign said: "Raise Plow."

"Raise plough, fall heart," thought Carrie, absentmindedly walking out into the road, looking in the wrong direction.

There was a barrage of shouting and klaxons. "Out the fucking way!" yelled some nervous New Yorker, the heel of his hand hard on his horn.

Hardly aware of the noise or Kees' voice yelling in warning, Carrie felt Mitch grabbing her arm, pulling her back onto the pavement. It was lucky, she thought, Mitch had the reflexes of a helicopter pilot. Like Ignatius? A memory flashed in the depth of her mind, to be immediately forgotten.

"You OK?" asked Mitch's voice from a distance, while Kieran could be heard saying: "reflexes of lightening and wit like thunder..thus God and man conspire to wonder...."

"Yeah, guess so," said Carrie, staring blankly at the moving traffic and wondering if she had made an oblique attempt at suicide.

"Look," said Mitch, jovially unaware, "actually we've got a couple of beds for the night. You can join us, but you'll have to camp. What you think?"

Carrie, now back in the real world, didn't hesitate. "Great. Thanks."

"But first," said Kieran, "some exploring."

Carrie's reperked heart sank back: was he really going to inflict porn and sex shops on Mitch?

"Time Square," said Kieran, "is not the haven it once was for the poor sinners of Satan. Some think the Reformation was not a triumph. Amongst these I could number Bloody Mary. I think we should search out a hotel bar in some sleazy neighbourhood and watch young Mary at work."

"You know someone everywhere," said Carrie ironically.

"I'm sure you do," Mitch remarked with friction, no longer enamoured by Kieran. "But actually we are for beer and dinner. If no one has any better ideas I'm for something cheap and cheerful. What do you say Carrie?"

"Fine by me," she said. Kees adding, "is good."

"So," said Mitch excessively polite, "will you be joining us Kieran?"

Instead of answering, Kieran took her hand and kissed it lightly, smiling into her eyes.

They had dinner in a stretch hamburger joint where you could eat as much as you wish for $10. Sitting in a plastic-leather booth with their own reduced sized juke box Kieran (now recovered from Mitch's behaviour) enlivened their meal by telling stories of his exploits during ferry trips. Mitch contradicted him, muttering 'exaggerations'.

"With such bad luck, Kieran," Mitch acidised, "it sounds like you shouldn't be a pilot at all actually. These kind of things never happen to me."

"Luck the fool's fuck," joked Kieran. "Many have made that mistake. Few are intelligent enough to see, though many wear glasses."

"Is that an Irish expression?" asked Kees, coming back from the steamer for a second time, his plate piled with salads. He tried to get past Kieran's chair which was blocking his path. "Sorry Kieran, can your stool move in?"

"Excuse me! Can I push your stool in," simpered Kieran, flipping his wrist effetely. "As the choirboy said, Master Bates is so lucky."

Kees looked puzzled. Then, reverted to Kieran's previous conversation. "We have a similar saying in Dutch," he said, "'het geluk, het lekker stuk'. Luck the tasty piece. Not so schatje?"

Kees smiled conspiratorially at Carrie, 'Lekker stuk' was not as innocent as it sounded in translation. She felt the tension between them but wondered why Kees bothered; Kieran was not someone who blushed at swear words.

After dinner Mitch took them to her sixty year old godmother's Upper East side apartment. It was empty because she was living with her fifth husband in Connecticut. She had kept the flat in case the marriage didn't work out. Carrie liked the idea of a fifth husband.

This time the recorded message in the taxi gave them a welcome from "Donna Farely, hit the high-spot for safety: buckle up." She also told them they might open or close the windows at their convenience and "here I am back again with the welcome news that you should not forget your belongings."

The doorman greeted Mitch like an old family retainer. "Why, Miss Mitch. So nice to have you here again. Will your friends be staying?"

"Absolutely, Paulton. But I promise they'll behave than the last lot."

"Miss Mitch, all your friends are a complete delight."

"Humm," said Mitch, as they went up in the elevator, "he only says that because last time, when they sprayed the lift with fire extinguisher foam and the lobby (and a couple of stuffy gents) with champagne, my godmother gave him such a great tip it was actually worth a month of stuffy yuppies."

As they left the elevator, opening into a private vestibule, Carrie pulled Kees aside. "Is Mitch a bit grand? This is quite a place! Almost a palace."

"Depends how you look at it," said the ever-defensive ex, as they slipped into the apartment behind the others. "So to say, I ponder not all her money made from flying was."

Mitch looked around the echoing apartment. "Actually, it looks like we're a bit short of beds, my honeys. I'm only allowed to stay here on condition that no one but me uses her room. But there're two other beds; the drawing-room futon and the spare room double. Fight it out between you."

"I have never," announced Kieran, "shared a bed with a man, and I'm not starting now. And while, me darling, I'd be very happy to have you in my room, I'd prefer one where I could attach electrodes to your nipples, so I think I'll take the futon."

"Oh," said Carrie shocked, "but that leaves...surely you boys...I mean I don't think..really..."

She looked at her ex-husband in despair and noticed he looked unfazed. Angrily she realised that for Kees the pain of an uncomfortable night's lodging was far outweighed by the joy of a nickel saved.

"Oh, all right," she muttered, "let the old devil ogle me if he wants to."

Kees said nothing and smiled.

Carrie stayed in the kitchen as long as she could, having another coffee, a brandy and a glass of water, hoping Kees would fall asleep before she retired. Sooner or later she knew she would have to go to bed. Eventually she could think of nothing else to put off the moment. Why was it that men were always available when you didn't want them; never when you did?

She opened the door of their shared room. Kees was already in bed and was waiting for her, light on, his arms behind his head, smiling at her discomfort. He wasn't even pretending to sleep. She sat on the far side of the bed, her back turned. What was she doing here? Flying a plane full of drugs with a maniac pilot, and now sleeping with an ex-husband. Shit, her life had gone dreadfully downhill. The only place lower was jail and it already looked as though that might be the next stop.

Depression was threatening to overcome her when Kees said: "Tell me what does a dog judge?"

She looked up irritated. "What? What dog?"

"I suppose a dog might a bone judge? Don't you say?"

"What? What dog? What judge?"

Carrie realised she was talking Pigeon English, led astray by his speech; next she'd be shouting. In spite of herself and the awkward situation she felt a hiccup of laughter, which she suppressed viciously.

"The magnificent Kieran told me his wife a dog judge was. He is something unique to see. He hasn't exactly fallen on his mouth."

"Oh Heavens!" Carrie snorted. "She judges at dog shows. The dogs don't do any judging." This was ridiculous. His English was odd but surely better than that. "Anyway that would mean Kieran had married a dog."

"You think a dog would have more sense?"

She turned and looked at him suspiciously. He winked at her. The tense swelling that had held the room exploded; so did Carrie.

"If Kieran on his mouth fell," said Kees, improvising because she was amused, in spite of the still smouldering anger in him, "he'd bounce back from the hot air forsure. Float up to the moon on his own fabrications."

Kees loved proverbs, something which had originally attracted and later infuriated Carrie. She remembered one of Kees's benefits was his playfulness: even though his idea of humour was usually more childish than subtle. She felt drawn towards him.

"How did you meet Mitch, Kees," she asked. It seemed so unlikely; that strong, straight-forward woman and her gentle, joking ex-husband.

"Ah," replied Kees, "very complicated is. You remember Oma Linda?"

"Of course."

Oma Linda Koolkop was a batty old woman who lived in The Hague, in a house full of cats. No one visited her because of the appaling smell, but she had treated the miserable and neurotic Carrie far better than any of Kees's saner relatives. Carrie remembered her affectionately.

"Well, she married," said Kees, already starting to laugh. "She married and moved to America, bringing all the cats with her...and you know what he for a living does?" Kees was laughing so much he could hardly reply. "He fucks dogs!"

"What? Oh you mean breeds," said Carrie; the Dutch for breed is fokken. She doubted Kees had forgotten; another little joke, understandable in a country where the Royal Family own the Palace of Loos.

"How on earth do the cats manage?" Carrie wasn't laughing; worried about the cats and kind, but mad, Oma Linda.

"It's a farm, they all fuck, sorry breed, already. Oma Linda has baby twins too."

"Clearly catching! But how old was she? I thought sixty at least?"

"No, but middle fifties or late already. A triumph is for Dutch farming methods, hoor. For sure, schatje. For sure. But really schatje human beings and animals need love to thrive. Oma Linda and her cats were loved, now they make babies."

"Um," said Carrie, amazed this naive man had once been her husband. "Sounds more like IV. And how did this lead to you meeting Mitch?"

"Ah, well I staying with the family was, Mitch's friend wanted to buy a dog, so we all meet at the airfield. Dog too."

"Did she buy?"

"He. No, he want dog to protect his air raid shelter. But then quarantine problems and I don't know. Very complicated. I only listen with half an ear."

Carrie was startled. Could Ben have accompanied Mitch on a trip to the US before he died? Or did she know lots of people living in air raid shelters? Their affair must have gone on longer than Janie had told her. And yet Kees thought she was a one man woman. Puzzling.

"When was this exactly? Can you remember his name, Kees?" she asked, smiling suddenly, thinking it was lovely to gossip in the dark; something unknown to a girl without friends. Then she heard a stuttering snore, and remembered how tiresome men were.

In Chapter Eleven

Kieran and Carrie left New York the following morning, heading up the coast towards Bangor, Maine. She looked down at the sparse tundra beneath her, and could hardly believe she had left Africa for this, its frozen counterpart. Here the land was still undulating and, until they were past Manchester and Boston, had large towns and villages. But as they flew further and further north the land changed, becoming flatter to their right towards the ocean, more mountainous to their left. Here there were few habitations, instead many low lying lakes.

She let Kieran fly and chat along as normal, but hardly listened to a word he said. Her mind was full of the awesome co-incidence of meeting her living husband, let alone sharing a room with him and finding he was in the process of becoming an airline pilot. It gave her a spooky feeling and she was half glad to slip away in the morning. Surprisingly for Kieran, who was usually extremely bad at getting up in the morning, locking his door and taking his phone off the hook when they had planned an early departure, he had been knocking at her door at seven o'clock this morning, all impatience to be away. Mitch was still in bed and she hadn't been able to check the plane before they left. Men! There was no understanding them. She should know. Still, perhaps the futon had simply been uncomfortable.

As they flew along the wind increased, and increased. As a gust lifted her up and dropped her down she swore. "God!" she snapped, "this is rough. Did we leave New York for this?"

"Yes child, and lucky for you I'm such an early riser and like to read the metars or we'd be taking off in this. The wind isn't only here you know. Long though the distances are, this little bit of wind has been running with us all the way, only here the countryside is so much flatter and more barren and so it gets bored having nothing to do and decides to knock us around. In New York it was distracted by all the other goings on."

She laughed. Kieran did have good points. He might be an arrogant, self-centred kink but he had some absurd ways of expressing himself, even funny. She felt strangely cheerful this morning but decided not to try and analyse why.

As they went further away from New York the countryside became sparser and gradually whiter. They passed Manchester, Berlin and by the time they reached Waterville the countryside was completely covered in snow, albeit snow that had trouble lying on the scrubland and gave a strangely mottled appearance to the ground.

"Over there," said Kieran, "waving his hand past the left window, are the Appalachians, great white monstrosities of the East. From them we have wind effect which, with the clouds, is humping us up and down like a veritable whore's drawers on a Saturday night."

He called Bangor Air Traffic Control. To Carrie's surprise they replied calling him Lear Jet 22N.

"Well, well so much for the intrepid Americans!" said Kieran, as once again they were thrown around by a gust of air from the mountains. "They think all little planes should be tucked up in bed. You'd like flying a Lear Jet, and, since this is as close as your ever going to get, revel in the moment."

"How do you know? I might..."

"I'm Irish, me darling, don't forget we Paddies see things that you jolly old Jonnies miss completely. Now where did they put that darlin' little runway ...? Ah there it is, another two miler for the ten or so planes a week that fly here."

There it was, frozen in front of them. A long dark streak in the mottled white surroundings. Carrie wondered if they had gritting lorries to clear the runway, or under-tarmac heating. Or did they have a thousand maids with mops? Kieran lined up with the black rod ahead.

Bangor was completely empty when they landed. Neither a plane nor a person in sight. The engineering base was closed. Kieran left her, saying mysteriously he had some business to do in air traffic.

"If you can see any fuellers, fuel up. Otherwise I'll be back shortly."

Carrie wondered if he was off to find another Charleen, another 12 year old look-alike blondie. Charleen, having slipped into her mind, stayed there for a moment. She'd seemed so familiar. Like a celebrity you know only from their image, not from their character. Or the haunting memory of knowing a relative, a face from the same gene pool which stirs your instincts but still has not penetrated your conscious thought. But whom? Kees had the same blond colouring; the White Thai had swarthy, olive skin so he was out; Ignatius had the same shaped eyes but he too was dark. Anyway she was American.

Carrie waited. No one materialized and she wondered if they ever would. The airfield had the appearance of a long-disused railway station. Some distance away from the Warrior, across a snow covered lawn imprinted with animal and bird footsteps, was a stolid, brick tower which looked as though it might once have housed carriages. A low undulating wall, with valleys that suggested gaps in the thawed months, divided this from the apron. Here the 'keenly cuffing wind' (Gurkha Colonel's Afghan diaries) had howled around, chasing feathers of snow into huge fat cushions and piling up banks of bizarre forms, so the wall seemed to be wearing a thick, protective duvet. The only sound was the wind in the gaps, like a giant sucking air through missing teeth.

All the buildings were closed, the windows black and uninviting. 'The lights were not on and there was no one at home.' There was no hidden hearth inside those buildings, only the spectres of the past; grey bearded ghosts punching tickets for passengers who never travelled but joined in the general squall. It was bleak and very cold, and she was glad she was wearing her immersion suit. She'd put it on at Teterboro much to Kieran's derisive amusement; he immediately pointed out that the Hudson was the largest water space they would cross that day.

Knowing Kieran's habit of mysterious disappearances, Carrie fully expected not to see him return until daylight had gone, so she climbed back into the cockpit and closed her eyes. A moment later he was there. Mocking her.

"Hello, the lights are on but the pilot's sleeping on the job. I wasn't long was I? Short and sweet like your men? Many have made that mistake. It's OK. They haven't really gone bankrupt; they're just in Chapter Eleven. And they'll take us but they're not open until tomorrow. So we can stay here after all. I've booked the hotel."

"Who? What? Chapter eleven? Sounds like a book."

He put his hat on her head and drew down the edges until she looked like an eighteenth century maiden. "Very sweet!" he said. "Sweet and virginal, but not for long." For a moment Carrie thought he was going to kiss her. Instead he let go of the edges of the hat, which flipped back and fell into the plane. He fumbled in his pockets for a cigarette.

"Well you are a little pet, aren't you. Remind me to tell you my story about the morons, oops my lisp, watch my mouth murmuring Mormons. Nod's as good as a wink to a blind ferret. The engineers are not out of business, as I had feared with this deathly silence so rare on this one of America's finest, but merely having a holiday thanks to their precarious financial state. So we'd better leave our little Warrior here. Aren't you aching to see the lovely beautiful hotel. The way they work in this country, we'll be here at least another week. Which reminds me, we need to talk about money."

Carrie waited, holding her breath. If he asked for more money, she'd decided, that was it: he was out and she was finding another pilot. She might even call on Kees back in New York. Even if she had to fly the plane out of this ghost station herself she was not giving him a penny more. But before he could say more they were interrupted by a man in an incongruous dark uniform, with gold braid on the sleeves and what looked like a station-master's hat.

"You can't leave that aircraft there," said the security guard. "You know the fuel office isn't open, so I don't know why you're sitting there so smart."

"I'm sorry," Carrie said, "I didn't know."

"Humm," he grunted disbelievingly, "move it to the apron, that's where it ought to be. As you well know."

Carrie taxied the plane over a crisply frosted layer of snow to the apron, while Kieran finished his cigarette. By the time she'd got all the bags out, he'd ordered a car on his mobile and they were ready to leave for the hotel.

The hotel was only just outside the airfield but it might have been transported from an Alpine ski resort. The building had the low swooping roof, wooden beams and small windows of a ski chalet. The entrance was marked by logs, neatly piled to mark out a path of Tyrollean gravel. This had been swept, although the snow had ventured back in a couple of icy spots. In front of the door the stones merged with red tiles, also predominantly free of snow. Kieran dropped Carrie and her little bag at the end of the walkway to a porch, decorated with cow bells and alpine dolls, and went to park the car.

The dusty-glass hotel doors were surrounded by wood, and decorated with carved flowers, more girls in alpine dresses, and indistinguishable animals. A cow bell, balanced on the top, clanged as Carrie pushed the mid-door wooden plank and hurried into the lobby. Inside burned a large open fire.

"Phew, thank Heavens," she said, rushing towards the warmth.

"Not used to our cold then?" Asked a middle-aged man behind the wooden reception desk. His triangular face and concave glasses, which perched on the rim of his nose, gave him the appearance of a newt. "You will be if you stay long enough."

"Just one night."

"Ah. You're with the man in the hat."

"Yes."

"What's happened to him then?"

For a moment Carrie didn't understand, then enlightenment came from the raised wrinkles on his forehead, which were obviously questioning. "Oh, you mean where is he. He's just parking the hire car."

"Higher car? Higher than what?"

"Hired. You know not ours, lent, paid for with money."

"Oh, shit! The rental car! Yeah, you Brits sometimes confuse the Hell out of me. What was it Oscar Wilde said, 'one nation two languages?'"

"I thought it was one nation divided by two languages, by Bernard Shaw," said Carrie apologetically but remembering her internet days, "but I'm probably wrong."

"Yeah," agreed the receptionist, "you are. Definitely Wobbly Wilde."

Kieran and his bags walked in, only now as well as his huge duffel bag he had an extra two cases dangling from his fingers.

"Tidily pom, tidily pom," he sang cheerfully, "one for me and one for you, baby's sweet but my she's blue."

"Have your suitcases been breeding?"

"Very funny, my pet. Travelling with you is one continual hoot of laughter. No! I always keep a few lock-ups around the country for storage. It helps to keep cold and warm clothes apart you know. Peck em up, put 'em down, why my baby, wears a frown." Kieran sang. "I'm just doing a little shuffling. No point in being a ferry pilot if you haven't learnt to shuffle. The two-step was invented by a merry ferry pilot."

Committing Liberticide

The next day it was minus twenty degrees centigrade and the plane refused to start. Carrie, wearing a borrowed balaclava, Kieran's spare woolly hat, an extra sweater from the hotel shop, and swathed in coats, sat in the Warrior and pushed the starter button in vain.

"It's cold poor thing," said Carrie, her light tone hiding her fear that it might never start again. "I know what it feels like!"

"Fucking old dog," said Kieran, opening the cowling and hitting the starter motor with the folded end of his Swiss army knife. "I'd have thought an animal like this could swim the Atlantic doggy paddle. It doesn't need a pilot like me, used to verve and fire in his machines. People ask me to fly their classics and I ...."

"What shall we do?"

Interrupted from his developing monologue, he lit a cigarette. "We, me little angel, are going to have to push this wee doggie across the whole airfield to that hangar over there.." He indicated a far off place with his large gesture. "...so we'll be nice and warm by the time we get there."

'We' meaning just Kieran and Carrie, plus the grumbling security guard, pushed the Warrior across the snow-slowed tarmac. Puffing slightly, her feet slipping, she asked Kieran. "Won't the engineers help?"

He laughed, gasped and they stopped for a break. "No, I asked them but apparently their insurance cover doesn't start until we reach the concrete outside their hangar, so they'll help us from there."

"Great! That's about 2 feet."

"That's right! It's a case of engineers committing liberticide against pilots. Call for the liberticide-nappers!"

Eventually, panting, sweating inside their clothes in spite of the minus twenty degrees and exhausted they reached the 2 foot limit. However, not only did no engineers appear, neither did the doors open.

"What's going on? Why don't they open the doors?" Carrie panted.

"Dunno," said Kieran lighting another cigarette and taking a desperate gulp of reinforcing fumes, "why don't you go in and ask them?"

He wandered off quickly, as the security guard started to remonstrate about his smoking. Carrie went through an old metal door into the hangar.

"Hello," she said to a group of men, who, tools in hand, surrounded an exposed engine, apparently working, "the plane is here. Can you open the doors and get her inside? We need to start working soon, I want to get away tomorrow."

Someone hidden behind another plane laughed.

"Tomorrow! Tomorrow is it!" Said an accent Carrie recognised rather well, having spent so much time with Kieran. Bloody Irish, she thought, they get everywhere.

"Yes, tomorrow!" said Carrie into the void, trying to keep calm. "Time is money."

He came out from the back of the hangar, a small dark man with an infectious twinkle in his eyes. Carrie, however, was as immune as the inoculated.

"You must be Mrs Nordsnootiland. I'm Seamus, Chief Engineer, but you can call me Mister O'Brien. But you'll not be after going anywhere tomorrow, so you won't. We've got to put the tanks in, check over the engine and airframe, and t'en you'll be flying back to Portland to get an FAA check. It don't happen overnight you know, even with help from The Irish. Besides 'tis far too cold to open the doors today. We'll just have to leave your little aircraft outside until tomorrow, so we will."

"What? You are joking," said Carrie rising into a frenzy.

"Joking is it? You wouldn't be wanting my men to get the cold, t'en t'ey'd never be able to work at all. We have to be careful with t'e sickness, so we do."

Looking back on it, Carrie thought he might have been joking, but she was in no mood for humour. She had not only spent a recent night in the same bed as one of her ex-husbands but she had just pushed a far from light, light-plane from one side of the ice-blasted airfield to the other, while the engineers stayed in the warm coziness of the hangar. Carrie didn't even bother to think about logical arguments. She just screamed. She said a lot of things and most of them were not complimentary to the Irish, to the Americans or indeed to anyone involved in flying. By the time she'd finished the hangar door was open and the plane was being pushed into the warm. Kieran followed, stubbing out his latest fag against his boot.

"Well, done, little 'un," he said, cheerful as ever, "I knew your cool, tactful charm would win over these receptive Americans."

Carrie breathed deeply, but it wasn't over yet.

"I guess," said Seamus, his eyes still twinkling with malicious glee, "t'at you've got the forms, haven't jer."

"Forms? What forms?"

"Well, you'll be needing t'e forms before we can start work. Didn't anyone tell you about t'at?"

Carrie went ragged. "You've known for over a week I was coming. Ever since we rang you from Lakeland! This isn't a surprise visit. Goddammit! Why didn't you get these forms yourself?"

"Well, me darling, many people talk but action is rare. How could I be sure you were coming until you arrived?"

Carrie considered screaming again, but Kieran put his hand on her shoulder quite gently but restrainingly.

"So, what if the forms are sent? They should arrive tomorrow?"

"Oh, well maybe, but you know what the post is, so you do...and tings here is particularly bad...especially since the snow's set in." Quite a few of the engineers were listening now, tools hanging from their hands, smiles of anticipation on their faces.

"Where do we get the forms from?" From the resoluteness of Kieran's voice Carrie knew he too was seriously annoyed, but to strangers it appeared that he was just mildly interested. "Do we need to drive to Portland or is there a nearer place?"

Seamus shrugged. "Portland's the only place I know and I've been living here for more than 10 years. And you'd better be off yourselves if you want something today. T'ey shut at 3, don't they now. And t'ey'll not be after waiting for t'e likes of you." And having had his say he walked away.

Kieran looked at his watch. It was eleven, they had four hours to get to Portland, which was 100 miles as the Warrior flies, but more like 150 by car, and then there were the lower American speed limits.

"Anyone got a Mercedes I can borrow?" he asked into the silence. Then to Carrie. "OK, come on kid, you're going to see me really drive."

They went out to the hired Pontiac Grand Am. He stroked the roof.

"Well babe," he said, "you are about to have the drive of your life."

He exaggerated. He drove just as badly as ever but faster, down roads which were almost entirely two or three lane highways but nonetheless surprisingly full of traffic. They scraped into the FAA compound at 2.30pm only to be told that the FAA man was having lunch and they'd have to wait until he returned.

For half an hour they sat drinking cans in the public area of the FAA building. Every few minutes either Carrie or Kieran asked the receptionist if the FAA man had returned yet. Her reply became more and more exasperated with every question. "No! I'll let you guys know. Really! I will. I will! OK!"

At three o'clock the FAA man came back. Moaned a bit at having to give the forms out now when the office closed at 3.30. Suggested they came back tomorrow. But, faced by Carrie's anger and Kieran's coolness, relented and gave them the forms, warning them with dire prediction that they only lasted for a month and then would have to be revalidated.

Carrie drove back to Bangor in silence, surrounded by snow. Even licenceless it seemed a lot safer than Kieran's driving. Kieran wanted lunch but Carrie refused angrily, not allowing any liberticides herself.

"Wow!" said Kieran. "Watch out for that guy. He was close. Those American drivers! Didn't you see it? You must be tired. Drive like I fly; smooth and sensuous. Feel the stick like your favourite cock; aah, ahh lovely. Perhaps we should stop for a bite to eat. '..Maybe a bite or stay for the night..' Your blood sugar must be low. Perhaps I should drive for a bit;

there's nothing to beat sensuous driving."

Carrie watched the relentless road silently. The passing trees dragging her back with snow-cold arms until she petrified under the heavy grey sky. The good mood she had felt yesterday had definitely passed and yet, to her surprise, she discovered she still had the strength to find it almost funny; to be amused rather than irritated. Something was changing in her: if she'd been like this before perhaps she wouldn't have been so quick to divorce Kees.

They arrived at Bangor just before the engineers stopped work for the evening.

"Well," said Seamus, locking the hangar door, "looks like work will have to begin tomorrow, so it does." Whistling, he crunched over the crisp snow to his car, the forms dangling from his hands like an empty bag.

The next day Seamus did start work on the Warrior. Although Carrie was tempted to sit in the hangar watching him work, certain he would slacken off without her harsh eyes willing him on, she agreed to accompany Kieran on his explorations.

"I've got to meet somebody," Kieran explained as he reversed the car out of its parking spot, "but there's no reason why you shouldn't come too."

"Another blond?"

"Funny! I'm a ferry pilot. Sometimes I do a little business during a trip. So, if you could for once in your life be tactful and not talk about money, it would be appreciated."

"Business?" asked Carrie, wondering if he was freelancing on her time. "What sort of business?"

"Certainly none of yours, sweet cakes. However, before your nose does a cartwheel across your face! Each time I come through I sell a few friends some of those things you can't get here in North America. And this time in particular I'm fulfilling a commission for a friend."

"Is that what your case is full of? 'Things you can't get here in North America'? I should be charging you petrol, oil, wear and tear for transport and my time."

"It's because you pay me so little I have to do work on the side. Talking of pay....." Carrie turned on the radio very loudly.

Once in Bangor Kieran cruised, until, stopping suddenly, slewing round and sliding along the impacted ice, he forced the drifting car into a parking spot. The wheels scraped aggressively along the curb. Beyond the snow filled path was a tall, shiplapped building with no windows. Another sex shop perhaps?

Kieran opened the trunk. Inside were the two suitcases from the lock-up and a large, sellotaped cardboard box.

"Take this will you," he said, handing her a box so tall she could hardly see over it. He took the cases and motioned her to follow him.

Stomping across the slithery sidewalk they entered the building by a little door, whose curved lintel made it appear almost Georgian. On Kieran's instruction she dropped the box inside the door and they climbed up a splintering stairway, lit by cracks in the roof. Emerging into a well illuminated bowl, Carrie saw they were at the top of a stadium. Long, backless bench seats ran in tiers all the way down to a stage, separated from the audience by a wall of reinforced glass. Below them, on the stage, students, whose t-shirts proclaimed 'Bangor Braves', were playing ice hockey, opposing a team of 'Ontario Owls'. Most of the seats were empty. Carrie sat down.

"Go Maine! Go!" yelled a very fat young woman, several rows in front of Carrie. She bounced up and down in her seat, frequently leaping to her feet. She seemed to know all the players by name and interspersed her 'Go, Maine, Go,' calls with 'Hit it Jonnie." "Slam them Randy!" "Wallop 'em Hunter".

"Bet she's a hit on Saturday night when the players are tired," said Kieran, sitting down beside Carrie, "come on boys give it to me hard and full."

Below the reinforced glass was a strongly made wooden barrier, into which the hockey players catapulted at full tilt; very often. Outside the glass, substitute players sat on two rows of shiny brown benches, awaiting their turn.

"Go, Maine, Go," the girl yelled. "Stretch 'em Sammie!"

Where, Carrie wondered, was the person whom Kieran had come to meet? Was it the loudly yelling girl? She wasn't blond. Or slim.

"..of course I played ice hockey myself at Crystal Palace, when men were men, and pansies were blooming terrified," said Kieran, taking off his hat. He whirled it around on one finger and replaced it on his head. "In those days we didn't have all that padding you see these web-wasted weaklings wearing..."

"Go, Maine, Go. Wallop 'em Hunter! Whatsat? You must be kidding!"

"I didn't fall they way they do now. Excellent sense of balance, not like this lot. A whore has more chance of keeping her panties on a Saturday than these weasels of beating their Canuke cousins..."

Thump! The Team Captain cannoned into the glass. Krump! Another two players toppled over him.

"God," said Carrie shocked, "this looks dangerous."

"How about a hot dog? I think my blood-sugar level is falling."

The fallen players stood up and the referee was doing something with their sticks, but Kieran was more interested in buying a hot dog from the mobile vendor. "Here, want one?" He passed Carrie a hunk of bread, dripping with ketch-up, mustard and relish. He didn't ask her for money, but chatted away to the vendor while the game restarted. Carrie got the strangest feeling he was placing a bet.

"Go, Maine Go! Hump'em hunter! Slash'em Sammie!"

"I played with The Eurotrash of course," Kieran said, sitting down heavily beside her, "great team. We always won, being internationals, well Italians mainly, with me as the Irish contingent. No Irish, no luck, as we used to say in the home bogs. Keep the home bogs steaming! With my Olympic foresight and their financial acumen your Jonnies from Blighty never got close to even licking our boots..."

"Go, Maine, go!"

"What was that all about?" Carrie asked as they cruised back to Portland in the fading evening twilight.

"Gambling and gifts, my liberling. Favours for friends. Aid from Africa. Nothing but a bit of a flutter, as legal in Ireland as the President of Potcheen but here as frowned on as an elderly heroine in her last play; there is nothing to understand in America and nothing to confuse. 'Coming Vicar?' asked the nun as she stirred the teapot with her other hand."

The Importance of a Fan

The next two days were an agony of waiting, but on Friday morning the aircraft was ready. Seamus, like the previous engineers, asked why the inside was full of holes. "T'ose holes were made for som'ting," he said, "and they're not after being air-conditioning."

"I know. Anything else?" Carrie snapped abruptly.

"No. It's done. But I'd put a little more t'ought into its previous use if I were you, Mrs Gnawd-tooter-land."

They had to fly to Portland to get the tanks checked. Kieran, having one of those Irishmen's premonitions he talked about, insisted on ringing the FAA in Portland before they left.

"Oh, hello," the FAA man said, "yes, I remember you. You were lucky to catch me, I was just leaving for the vacation. I'll be glad to look at your plane on Tuesday afternoon."

This time it was Kieran who lost his cool. "Tuesday! Tuesday! If there is any chance that I am not in Greenland by Tuesday I will come and personally take you and your office out of Portland and throw it on to the green slopes of Ireland!" He said, "and I won't be alone."

The FAA man agreed to wait until noon. "But then," he said, trying to regain some pride, "I'm off."

They bowled out of Bangor like the Bullet train. Seamus, twinkling as ever, hoped they'd have a nice trip (something which, looking back on it, had the status of a threat). His men watched them taxi out at speed. "Shame," said one, "to always be in such a hurry. You miss so much."

The Warrior took off and they turned immediately south.

"Tiresome to go south to return north," murmured Kieran. For a moment Carrie thought he was about to revert to his plea for money, but instead he began playing with the ADF, muttering a cat had better direction finders. They quickly left the more civilised area around the airport and plunged into mile after mile of densely wooded landscape. Looked at from above it was very beautiful, although spartan. Some of the tree canopy looked like broccoli, sprinkled with snow like iced vegetation. Every now and then there would be a break in the broccoli, and a river would cross their path running down a deep valley. Here there were occasional settlements and, joining them, the odd partially visible track.

"Not a very social place to live," Carrie remarked.

Kieran looked up from the map. "Here take this. Trappers probably." He passed her the map without stopping his speech. "Or people who don't want to be with people, there are plenty of those. When I was in my teens I used to go every year to Norway, not just to see the great lights, the gods committing liberticide with the stars, but to be alone from the constant rush of people who never leave you alone. Did I tell you I was a teacher at that time? Ah a thankless job. Preaching my jewels before swine, I gave of my best and did they listen, did they learn..?"

"Perhaps they couldn't find the jewels amongst all the bullshit."

Whatever Kieran might have said next was prevented, because at that moment the engine stopped. Dead.

It gave a couple of splutters. Seemed to be slowing, revived and then, with a short thud, thud, thud and bonk, stopped. The noise evaporated. Carrie almost felt the quietness. She hadn't noticed the engine was loud; until it wasn't. She could see the yellow tip of the propeller. In front of the cowling an elegantly shaped, ellipsoid paddle cut through the horizon. Silent. Still.

A cold chill went through Carrie's stomach. For a moment she couldn't believe it. But for that stationary propeller. It occurred to her they were about to find out what did get trapped by those trappers below.

Damn my husband! she thought. Why didn't he buy a twin?

Kieran was suspiciously silent.Out of the corner of her eye Carrie could see he was doing something down by his boots. She ferverently hoped he wasn't praying. Or lighting a candle.

The Warrior glided on quietly towards the trees. Carrie stared at the approaching branches. Then miraculously, as suddenly as it had died, the engine sprang back to life.

"Always," said Kieran, apparently unfazed but with what, by that stage, Carrie had come to recognise as the counterfeit calm of relief, "reverse the previous action."

He explained he had changed fuel tanks and the engine had stopped. When he returned to the first tank it had automatically started again. "Thank God for Lycoming engines," he murmured, "they start better than they stop."

Carrie thought that would be it, but the Irish-genie in Kieran wouldn't leave him; throughout the rest of the journey he switched the tanks back and forth, to see what happened. She watched these investigations squirming, keeping her eyes glued to the fuel pressure gauge. Occasionally he left the engine switched over too long, and pressure would drop, followed by the engine quitting, restarting as soon as Kieran pushed the lever to the other tank.

"Obviously the engineers did something wrong," Carrie said crossly, "why don't you leave it until we're on the ground?"

"Ah, young 'un! Never assume, always experiment. Without trials how dry our life would be."

"Fine. It's the dryness of our tanks I'm worried about."

At Portland the FAA man and his large bunch of associates (how many engineers does it take to pass a ferry tank or, in this case, fix one) discovered that only the left tank lead was running fuel to the engine, the flow from the right tank flow being interrupted by an air bubble that had lodged in the pipe when the ferry tank was connected; neither the right tank nor the ferry tank were feeding the engine.

"Lucky we weren't over the pond," said Kieran, "that would be the downing of the Warrior and the drowning of its pilots: all to be mere merry ferry-men fish-food."

Carrie, listening to him describing the problem to the FAA inspector in elegantly graphic detail, wondered if her husband was responsible for this problem too. Could this really be just another 'normal' mistake?

Dropping Down with Costly Bales

As they flew back from Portland the dusk closed in softly, deceivingly, with little flurries of dry rain which teased their eyesight and mocked their visual navigation. The temperature dropped steeply towards the dew-point and Carrie, watching the encroaching weather, suggested they wait in Bangor until daylight. But now Kieran was suddenly keen to hurry, insisting that sleet makes buffoons of brave pilots. They dashed to the hotel, picked up their things, paid the engineering bill, which shocked Carrie terribly but which she hadn't time to argue about, and took off in haste to Moncton, New Brunswick.

It was not a long flight, just under two hundred miles, but here the land was seriously barren, with scrubby bushes and oblique angles where the snow dissolved into grey-green silhouettes and white-blue lakes. Carrie was again glad she was wearing her immersion suit. It wasn't very practical to wear this torpid rubber over her clothes, but it did prevent the cold, wet air from outside seeping into her bones and turning her mood into a brown quagmire.

As the dusk deepened, the darkness emphasized the barrage of ice crystals hitting the window, now divided into two lines, zooming past the Warrior's windscreen like relentless white missiles. Carrie saw how easy it would be, hypnotised by the indomitable weather, to fly on into a mountain, never noticing the change in terrain. She forced her impetuous eyes to study the figures on the GPS screen.

After passing the Saint John River there were no more large towns; only an occasional twinkling light below in the black carpet, probably more little trapper hermitages. The snow was heavier now and thicker bands pressed on the Warrior's windscreen, gripping the glass like a stream of flat, white bubbles. Watching the diminishing view ahead, Carrie wondered why she had agreed to leave Bangor. Was it simply that 'why have a dog and bark yourself' belief again?

Kieran tapped the moving map by his knee and watched the little plane edge across the grey expanse. "Marvellous the GPS, how did we fly without it? Seat of the pants! Damn that, sister. Give me the old movements and the mapping cinema."

On and on went the streams of frozen water, mesmerising the pilots into a snowy trance. Only the background noise of the radio stopped Carrie feeling she was alone in the world, alone with a repetitive dream. From that crackling interference of static, interspersed by spectral voices, she came to believe she was approaching the airfield, and really did have a chance to make it home. Others did. Why not her too? Kieran talked endlessly but she heard little of what he said, concentrating instead on the snow, the radio and her thoughts.

Passing Sussex, Kieran made the first call to Moncton.

"November2122 pass your message."

After he had given their details, Moncton replied with the unexpected: "Warrior22November we have no record of your approach."

Carrie forced her gaze away from the stupor-inducing repetition ahead and looked inquiringly at Kieran. "What does he mean, why should he have a record of our approach? Is he PPR?"

Carrie knew from Redhill that some airfields in the UK required prior permission. That hadn't seemed to be an issue in America, but this could be a first.

Kieran said, "all Americans are idiots."

"Oh, do you think that's it then?"

"As sure as Belfast is in Ireland."

The tower gave them landing information and then asked them to confirm they were landing at Moncton. Baffled, Kieran replied in the affirmative. However, as they called finals the tower informed them that they were in Canada; they should have filed a flight plan and that if they landed they would have to suffer the consequences.

"Warrior 22November confirm your intentions."

"What a load of balls," said Kieran, "what do you want to do, my little carrot? I don't suppose it will be any more than a smack across the wrist."

"I don't want to go back," said Carrie, her gaze glued to the airfield as though it might suddenly disappear into the mist. "They're not going to put us in jail are they?"

"Come off it! This is America...sorry Canada, land of the free."

They laughed, and continued the approach to runway six. The Warrior came down low over the Petitcodiac River, its frozen, glinting monster's jaws dripping with snowy saliva. Carrie wondered if the choice lay between being gnashed to death by the river or being eaten alive by the Moncton ATC.

Landing they skidded slightly on the wet snow but, before Carrie's heart could skid too, the Warrior steadied itself and they taxied off the runway at the first junction. Here, though, as well as the normal "Follow Me" van they were joined by a short, red, 1950s fire truck, which escorted them all the way to the customs apron.

"Do they think this is an emergency?" Carrie asked, watching the unnecessarily large group of firemen gathered in the truck and suspecting this might be one of the most exciting things that had happened in Moncton for a long time.

"No, my ferry flower, they think we are illegal aliens, refugees from the cruel spoke of American law. Wicked miscreants absconding with US dollars and Mexican mushrooms. Pilots of the purple twilight."

Carrie was wondering if this had happened to him before when she remembered the drugs in the wings. 'Oh, my God Ignatius. What have you done to me?'

On the customs apron they and their escort were met by a supremely irate lady who had (she indicated) been pulled out of her bed for this landing. Since it was just past seven o'clock in the evening Carrie doubted it. Nonetheless there was a 100 dollar fine to pay for the International Crime of no-flight plan. She spoke a few words with the driver of the fire truck and he drove away giving them a cheery wave.

"Welcome to Canada," he shouted ironically, "did you think it was still one of the colonies?"

"Oh, he's a smart arse," said Kieran, "everybody likes a tight arse but no one likes a smart arse..."

"Another $100" Carrie moaned. "My life is one of ever increasing costs."

The irate lady (pulled from her bed) turned with lightening accuracy and said. "If you don't meet the customs regulations you must expect to be fined. I am not a normal customs agent, I am a special lady!" $10 per minute special, thought Carrie.

The two pilots stood on the tarmac while the Special Lady diligently searched the plane. Carrie's stomach heaved like a plane in turbulence when she found the holes. Saying nothing but looking closely at both Carrie and Kieran, the Special Lady tightened her lips and went to her car to fetch a torch.

Climbing inside the Warrior, she pushed the right hand seat forward, so it pressed on the wheel and forced the elevator into a thumbs down position, squeezing her stately torso between the ferry tank and the holes. She peered into the darkness of the wing, torch light flitting back and forth along the spars like a Nazi search beam.

Well, thought Carrie, this is it. Will we have drugs before us? That is the question. She looked at Kieran hoping he might have something to suggest, but with no one paying him any attention he was already bored. Bringing out his cigarettes, he had lit one before the Special Lady realised what he was doing.

"This is an airport!" she declared angrily, sending him off to the terminal with a guard.

"You stay here with me!" she instructed Carrie, climbing back into the plane to resume her investigations. Eventually though she emerged, red and rather breathless, but certain that nothing nefarious had been attached inside the wings.

"Very well," she said, "I think you have merely been foolish. As a goodwill gesture I will reduce the fine to $60 Canadian. But remember International boundaries are there for your protection."

Carrie found herself thanking her as though it was her fault. It struck Carrie that Kieran should have known this was Canada. However, her pilot was way ahead of her and was already laughing at her famous geographic ability.

"Well, Mrs North South Land, rather well named are you not! It is like this: if you put America at the bottom and Canada at the top and draw a line between them what do you get..?"

Moncton was where all 'Atlantic Crossers' have their equipment checked for its search and rescue avoiding potential. In previous years many light aircraft had left North America without sufficient survival equipment or expertise to get home. The subsequent distress signals and rescues had cost the Canadian tax payer a lot of money. Hence the obligatory pre-crossing examination.

Having survived the Special Lady's spar search Carrie wondered what revelations might come next but in fact they sailed through this further inquisition with laughter. The inspectors commenting that they had three times the amount of survival equipment necessary and twice the number of radios.

"How do you fit it in, with that 100 gallon tank and the rest? I bet you're sitting on his knee," Carrie heard again and again. In the end the checkers decided that the Warrior was 20 lbs over weight and its crew would have to dump some things here. Kieran immediately asked Carrie what she could leave.

"Nothing."

"What nothing? Of course there is something. We all carry the flotsam and jetsam of non-necessity with us on a daily basis, now for you I would suggest..."

"Speak for yourself, Kieran. I brought the minimum. Look at my bag compared to yours." Indeed his luggage sitting next to hers, made Carrie's little duffel bag look like an unfed waif beside its richer cousin.

"Tell you what," said one of the weight checkers, "I'll give you $20 for those cowboy boots; although I'm cheating myself really but I like to help a fellow aviator."

"$20? $20! I bought those for $100..."

After negotiation Kieran did leave just one of his three pairs of boots and one of his leather jackets, although he promptly declared he would expect Carrie to reimburse him at the other end. "At the very least," he said, "you could give me your body, skin for skin, leather for leather! Oh, I love the rasping feel of leather against the skinny parts...the slash of the lash..rummmph."

The hotel in Moncton was one storey modern: long corridors all with identical plastic-smelling, washable carpets and anonymous beds; doors which lead to rooms without character but with strong, hot showers and TV. This hotel was one of a breed, a race of residences which always have a gym, a jacuzzi and an ice machine no matter where they are or what the temperature. The clientele were also from an ilk; travelling salesmen, tax collectors, and young couples who found the cemetery too cold.

Next door was one of those breakfast-any-time-of-day joints, reached by a long wooden verandah running along the side of the hotel. Carrie bought a copy of USA Today from a vending machine attached to the wall. Inside there was a choice of booths or a long wooden bar for diners eating alone. False floral decorations were placed in significant areas of the room and hung from timber ceiling beams.

Sitting on a stool by the breakfast-bar Kieran began to give the assembled eaters his expert opinion on the weather in Canada, hunting in Canada, being Canadian and Canadian life in general. Carrie wished Mitch had been there to make snide remarks.

'So nice for the locals to get this inside gen..."

She smiled thinking of the girl and her lessons and realised she missed her; her honest straight-forward attitude, her genuine skill. She suddenly wondered why she hadn't asked Mitch to fly with her instead of Kieran. Too late, of course. It simply hadn't occurred to her before. Why do the best ideas so often arrive after the deed is done?

The waitress came along the bar, coffee jug in hand. "Hi guys? Two? Cawfee?"

"Yes, thanks." Carrie accepted a mugful of brown water, knowing the taste would be closer to muddy streams than beans. Kieran examined her short skirt and brown tights with the eyes of a connoisseur.

"You guys ready?"

"Do you have any bread, sweet-cakes, for the humble hungry?"

"Sure. Do you want white, whole wheat, rye, light pump, dark pump, poppy seed, sesame roll, nut loaf, sour dough or regular?"

Carrie said she'd have regular, whatever that was, and an omelette. Kieran on the other hand wanted eggs, sunny side up, fried bread - white, fried sausages, bacon, beans, mushrooms. "Although I must not have too many or it won't leave mush-room for anything else." And tomatoes.

"Ok, one regular breakfast and an omelette."

"I'm on a sea-food diet," said Kieran, "I eat all the food I see."

The waitress smiled automatically, without listening, and went to process their order.

"Fried food," said Kieran, "is so good for you. Recent studies show that men who eat plenty of fried food live far longer; take the Canadians, for example, they love fry-ups, barbecues and loads of good healthy fat, lard even, and they live well into their hundreds. Last time I was here I talked to an old boy and how old do you think he was?"

He suddenly stopped. Kieran had recently begun doing that, convincing Carrie it was done to ensure you were listening, although why that was necessary to him she couldn't imagine.

"Well...what do you think? What...what..."

Carrie shrugged. "I don't know. Seventy?"

"Seventy?!Seventy?! She says seventy." He looked about at the surrounding munchers, none of whom were paying much attention. "That is what she calls old! Now you sir, how old are you?"

The old man next to him looked up. "Fifty." Kieran had clearly been hoping to hear something older but he didn't pause in his monologue.

"Fifty! A boy!" said Kieran, "a child. This fellow was not fifty not seventy, not one hundred. This man was three hundred years old. Three hundred years old! And a scientist. He'd studied everything there was to study in his three hundred well used years. He'd seen all the medics come and go and you know what he said to me? Do you? He said, 'as I was saying to my father last week, we've lived fair lives coz of the fat we eat.' That's what he said. And this man lived on fat. You know that. All types of fat. Goat. Cow. Whale. You name it he'd eaten its fat."

Kieran paused for a sip of coffee and one of the benched eaters said, "my wife's fat! I wonder if he'd eat her!"

There was a thundering waveburst of laughter from the men around him, one man smashing his huge fist on the counter, while another jagged the speaker in the ribs. Kieran as ever was unawed.

"You say that my good Canucks, but I have eaten human flesh and I tell you there is less lard on a fat woman than on a whale. Fat is good for you, especially smoked and with red wine...I was in Africa at the time...."

Carrie finished her breakfast and wondered if she could persuade Kieran, now drinking another coffee and delighted with his audience, however mocking, to leave. She looked out of the window and watched a blue, high wheeled jeep draw in. As she vaguely wondered if driving a high wheeled vehicle felt like hovering a helicopter she saw Mitch at the wheel, looking like an Astrakhan dog in her high collared fur. Kees climbed down from the suicide seat dressed like a Cossack.

"God, they get everywhere!" Carrie said aloud, albeit with mixed feelings. Kieran followed her glance. He glanced at his watch.

"Good Heavens good Canucks, how the time flies when you're enjoying yourself. Sorry to leave you gentlemen. I enjoyed our little chat and I hope we are able to renew it soon. After all I have to be careful; you may be able to count on three hundred years but I have to use wisely my portion of mere one hundred and fifty." And doing his usual spectacles, testicles, wallet and watch, he swept out with Carrie in his wake.

Outside, Mitch was getting a copy of USA Today from the vending machine. She saw her former pupil and waved. "Hi ya Carrie, Kieran."

"Hey! What you doing here?"

"We've brought some parts up for a stuck Herc," Mitch said tucking her shades into her pearl-string.

"Stuck up Merc? Mercedes?

"Herc. Hercules. And stuck, not stuck up. It was taking freight to the north and broke down."

"You might say," said Kieran wittily, "you were heroes for a Hercules when it took fright in the north."

Mitch sneered, tucking the paper under her arm. "We're going to be following you around. After a couple more trips here, we're going over to Iceland and then to the Faeroe Islands to do some deliveries."

"Rather grand to be doing deliveries in a Lear Jet!" Carrie said, thinking Mitch made the Lear Jet sound like a delivery van. "Expensive!"

"Yeah, maybe, but it's just another flying vehicle to the man that pays!"

"Well, my little blue-bottles," said Kieran, "I shall look forward to tinkling the ivories with you somewhere en route and listening to all your jolly little pilot exploits, but for now adieu. Farewell. Farewell, adieu. Come Carrie!"

He strode purposefully towards the rental car, getting into the driver's seat as usual. Carrie was a bit slow following him, thinking she ought to say 'Hello' to Kees in case he felt hurt, when she noticed he was already at her side. He took her arm in a harsh caress, saying to her in Dutch. "Wees voorzichtig schatje. Ik vertrouw hem voor geen cent." (Take care, darling. I wouldn't give a penny for his trustworthiness.)

Carrie looked at him, surprised. There was a lot wrong with Kieran as a travelling companion, but nothing that she would consider harmful to her safety. But Kees was nodding his head emphatically to emphasize his warning.

"So to say as I know he is not a good man, already," he said.

"What do you mean?"

"Just believe me. I promise not to say more. Take care."

"But...wait..."

"Come on Carrie, I'm leaving," yelled Kieran. "Get your arse in here!"

"Don't shout at me," Carrie yelled back. She climbed into the car completely fascinated: what could Kieran have done to shock Kees? Not that that was hard to do; most of their married life had been spent stressing Kees's shock absorbers.

Kieran over-revved the engine and bumped away down the polymath carriageway towards the airfield. Carrie laughed happily.

In Bangor, Seamus had told them that the Northern Canadian route would be the clearest at this time of year and, in spite of his significantly useless engineering abilities, they trusted in his weatherman skills. So from Moncton they flew off towards Wabush, intending to fly on to Frobisher on Baffin Island the next day; the northerly route into Greenland, with a shorter sea crossing but higher mountains making it a far bleaker passage.

West from Moncton they crossed the Northumberland Straits and over Prince Edward Island, the smallest province in Canada. North east to the island's tip they flew over Cap Gaspe, past the Anticosti Island to Sept Isles in Quebec.

"See the French influence," said Kieran, "I stayed once at Sept Isles, but the ghosts spoke a sort of strange patois and I didn't like it, so I moved to Gasper where you can smoke like a man."

Carrie laughed. Once again she found him amusing. She looked at him intently hoping to discern evidence of some crime. Presumably only midway crime, since Kees wouldn't have let her travel on with the man who murdered Ben. One does have some obligations to an ex-wife-who-paid-alimony: though less than to one who still owes.

Here the countryside was low and rugged with slashes of water, as though it had once been a host of high mountain ranges which time and the feet of giants had worn down, until it became harsh hills with wet wrinkles like an old man's neck after shaving. Below them the fjords were frozen and looked beautifully undesirable. How much easier to watch from above, like a hawk examining its prey, than to be part of the crystallized life below.

Wabush, Labrador (where the dogs come from) was a sixties town. Built for the tin mines, it had no roads and was accessible only by plane. The day before they arrived there one of the snowed in and interbred inhabitants had, they were told, killed a girl in a sexual skirmish. She was found tied to a chair, hanging up-side-down from the ceiling. Carrie suggested Kieran could have had the same problems if he'd been born here.

"My little darling, you have a wild sense of humour. Whatever I might like to do with women, which, I would like to stress, you have neglected to find out, it does not include unwilling ladies. Indeed what I do with my girls in the depth of the night releases them from the strictures of the day. I free their minds from the subjugation of convention, by showing them the bondage of freedom and the freedom of bondage."

"I think," Carrie said, "you dominate them with your will power."

"You mean my willy power!" said Kieran, "as the actress said to the bishop there's more skill in a willy than will in a skillet."

Landing at Wabush couldn't have been more different from their landing at Bangor. Half the town had turned out to watch them arrive. Keen aviators criticised with fanatical interest as Carrie bumped the Warrior and all its kit down on the hard tarmac. Kieran jumped out of the plane as soon as they reached the apron, his hat firmly on his head, his boots swinging in dancing strides, delighted by the attention, however unexpected. He strode past a waiting policeman, ready to entertain the crowd with the details of his flight. A man called out of the crowd.

"Are you going to play for us tonight?"

Not in the least disconcerted Kieran shouted back. "Certainly, name your game. I prefer dominoes."

The crowd roared with laughter, while the man screamed back. "Name your instrument, I prefer the sax."

"I only play it with my wife," said the canny Irishman, "give me a Guinness instead."

"Where's the rest of the band," yelled another Wabushite.

"What band would that be?" returned Kieran, "the only band I never left was the band of gold my wife gave me."

It seemed somehow that due to a mix-up of faxes, emails and telegrams, the inhabitants of Wabush were awaiting the arrival of Pink Floyd; instead they got Kieran, and perhaps they were pleased by the substitution. Kieran became a four day celebrity. For four days he strode around, tall and debonair in his hat and boots. On day two he bought a whip, cracking it wherever he went turned his fame to infamy.

There were two hotels in Wabush, standing opposite each other across a small road. Carrie chose the cheaper hotel, irritating Kieran. Stronger now, Carrie told him to bin it, waiting to see if this led to a return of Kieran-price wars. But, absorbed with being a superstar, Kieran allowed the problem to pass with unusual tolerance.

The houses in Wabush sat in a rigid grid pattern, streets marching north and south or east and west. Made of wood and raised on breeze-block-like local material, the houses faced each other across snow beaten paths. At the edges of the path the snow was still new and fluffy, while the middle was bare and down to the ice, like an old carpet worn by many passing feet. Perhaps there were pavement edges hidden under the snow, since here, like New York, there were signs which read; "Raise Plough," here with the English spelling. Most houses had little ladders going up to their doors, left open, in spite of the cold, so the insiders could watch the progress of the almost-Pink-Floyd Kieran through his fandom. Kieran doffed his hat and waved happily.

However, after a couple of turns of his stage, even the publicity conscious Kieran decided the minus twenty degree temperature was too much for his fans, and wishing them all a night of sweet dreams, or better still a night of sweet adventures, he returned to the warmth of the hotel.

All night it snowed and snowed and in the morning it was still snowing.

"We," said Kieran searching hopefully out of the window, "are going nowhere. Even the Twin-Otter 'bus' service isn't flying in today and if a Canadian Twin Otter don't fly then you can be sure the weather is bad. The gods of snow having committed liberticide against the earth-bound proletariat: we are going nowhere."

Nowhere except round and round the airfield. Having cleaned the snow off the plane with a brush (Carrie brushed, while Kieran helpfully smoked) they taxied the Warrior to the compass rose to check the magnetic tilt this far north. To combat the cold, Carrie pulled on the heater. As they taxied around she began to doze off, slowly dropping under the ether. Kieran lent over and shook her shoulder.

"Wake up! Wake up!"

"Umm, what, just a few moments.."

"No. Wake up. Are you OK?"

Groggily Carrie realised she was not in bed, that she couldn't sleep here. "Guess so. I just couldn't keep my eyes open."

"Carbon-monoxide poisoning."

"Eh?"

"CO_1...far worse than CO_2...didn't you know that carbon-monoxide has an affinity for haemoglobin...?"

He was defeating her. Mitch might have told her these things long ago but by the time she'd got through the Steves, Daves, Tims and Rays all this information had left her mind. "No."

"Never mind, get out and walk back, that should clear your head. Leave the door open. I'll taxi this little death trap back myself. From now on we don't use the cabin heater. OK!"

Carrie walked back to the terminal while Kieran, clearly unaffected by carbon-monoxide thanks to years of puffing on cigarettes, returned the aircraft. Later she checked the carbon monoxide monitor, a cardboard Kieran-necessity with a sensitive centre supposed to warn you of impending danger. Far from being the black she expected, it remained a healthy orange. However, it had passed its renewal date six months ago. She wondered if she should regard this as suspicious in light of Kees's warning, but couldn't take it seriously; after all Kieran had saved her from possible poisoning.

With nothing to do in the small hamlet of Wabush and no longer worried about the possible possession of drugs, Carrie's mind became exercised by her main problem; would she make it safely back to Biggin Hill? Could there be a connection between Kees's warning and her husband's strange purchase? She explored every crevice of her brain, desperate to find some devious link but could see nothing in common between Kieran and her third husband except they were both tall pilots, who smoked and loved flying in Africa.

Each morning for the next couple of days they explored the avenue of shops, a full sized version of the Dodge City game her step-sisters had owned. All in a line, they were built from local wood, with slatted shutters on the windows. Each shop had a raised platform with banisters for tying horses. An older version of parking meters, Carrie wondered, idly imagining Dodges tied for a fee, a bucket by the radiator.

Apart from playing pool there was very little to do. Wabush, population 1005 (1004 since the death of the girl) became the centre of the universe for the Warrior pilots. Kieran's already huge fame gained royalty status when he sauntered into a gun shop wearing a black leather hat, a leather jacket and black flying suit and demanded to buy a gun, explaining it might be necessary to kill animals if they had an engine failure and were forced down. In contrast to America's reputation for letting anyone buy a gun, nobody here would sell one to Kieran.

As the snow continued they checked the weather for Frobisher and beyond on the hotel computer. The northern route was going to be impossible, deeply embedded in recently fallen snow. Instead they decided to abandon the north, take the only break in the snow storms, and make a dash for Goose Bay in Newfoundland.

This was a flight of less than 200 miles over the same wrinkled and lake filled country they had seen before. Here, though, the lakes had French and Innuit names rather than the English and Red-Indian of the south. Lac Joseph and Atikenack Lac and others twinkled with icy silver lights at the passing Warrior.

This too was barren countryside with little respite. Carrie thought about the bush pilots who flew here. She remembered reading about a pilot whose plane had crashed whilst on an emergency mission. When they were finally found, many months later, the pilot was still alive but the nurse and patient had disappeared. The pilot said he had given them a decent burial. Although the pilot never admitted it, most people believed he had eaten his dead companions in a determined effort to stay alive. Looking at the miles and miles of frozen tundra in every direction, Carrie understood.

On the way to Goose Bay Kieran flew up and up towards the stars, testing the Warrior for its ceiling height. It made 10,000 feet only with engine groaning difficulty.

"Bloody Dog! We might as well ditch the damn dooley right here! You do realise the mountains in Central Greenland are 11,000 to 13,000 feet high don't you?"

Carrie said nothing. She felt mulishly annoyed; it was a bit late to be saying this now, practically on the edge of the Atlantic.

"So? What are we going to do about it...your bloody plane."

"You're the pilot, that's what you're here for...to bark.."

"Yeah and for sure little money..."

Just as he was about to go off on the money hike he stopped. Carrie looked at him and saw that his normally ruddy complexion had gone green. He lent his head against the window. "Are you OK?" She asked.

"I'm just feeling a little dizzy. It will pass."

"Oh! I feel fine. It must be smoking, makes you susceptible to the altit.."

Kieran ignored her. "We'd better go down to a lower altitude. You fly," he said, before lapsing into a somnolent silence.

Carrie stared at this corpse-like creature next to her. "Kieran?" No reply. "Kieran." Nothing. He was still breathing but shallowly. She grabbed the map. Hurriedly ascertained her position she turned towards Goose Bay. He didn't look as though he was ready to die. Mitch had told her about altitude sickness and it did seem like a temporary condition but... She began to descend, slowly because she couldn't remember if it was better or worse for him to lose height quickly.

As the Warrior glided gently down towards the rocks Carrie pulled out the carb heat control. It made the cabin warmer but nothing happened to the rpm. Indeed to her tortured mind the engine started sounding pretty rough. She pushed it in and out again. Nothing.

Typical, she though, a half dead pilot and the engine plays up. Experimenting she pulled on the cabin heat. Immediately the rpm dropped slightly and there was a hiccough from the engine, as though it was ingesting gulps of ice. She waited a moment and then, when she pushed back the knob, the engine ran more smoothly. After a couple of tests Carrie was certain that the pipes were mixed up. Another present from the 'Chapter Eleven' engineering company that would have to be fixed. Fix, Carrie mused, had the same root as finance, plus the X from expensive!

She wanted to point out these confused pipes to Kieran but he was leaning forward, his head dropping on his hands uninterested in the niceties of any engineering other than his own body. Still at least he was not dead! She dialled up the frequency for Goose Bay. "Goose Bay this is November 2122."

Goose replied, "welcome November22, what a lovely accent!"

Carrie flew down the middle of a valley, watching the sheer rocks beside her, hoping this was Happy Valley and not some teasing delusion. (Happy Valley! Sounds like a drug attack). She laughed. Scared she was also excited: it was all up to her now. What if she was lost? Were the sides of the valley too close for a turn? Her pilot slept in his seat. She saw the water ahead; could she have missed the airfield. What then? Out to sea and turn back, but where? Then to her relief she saw in the distance long black lines dissecting the snow and felt a shaking rush of adrenaline. She'd found it! Without any help from Kieran. She was learning, growing, becoming a real pilot. She landed on runway twenty six and, as instructed, taxied in towards a parked Archer ready to kiss the ground.

Behind her she heard another plane landing. Quicker than the Warrior it soon caught up and taxied in almost on her tail. Turning, she saw that it looked more like a boat than a plane, with a pusher engine on the roof and great floats below the wings. It parked next to the Warrior and the pilot, a short, bald headed ancient baby, jumped out, running enthusiastically towards her, his hand already extended. Carrie watched him proving himself unarmed as she unlatched the door. Otherwise, of course, she might have got out her gun (had Kieran been allowed to buy one) and shot him. Instead she opened the door.

"Hello," Carrie said, feeling slightly silly, "you must be that pilot of the sea-plane-thingie. Sorry I don't know...." Her lips quivered and she realised she was shaking, tension evaporating from her body like sweat.

"Lake. Lake Renegade. Jim. Jim Thomas."

She giggled spasmodically, unable to stop her vibrating sensory glands. Relief was mixing with amusement as she realised this was the first ferry assistant she had turned down. The incorrigible Ditcher, whose incidents still filled her head with sinking thoughts when she was doing her flight planning.

"Great to meet you," Ditcher said with a younger, taller man's energy, "I thought at first you were Randy. But he's an Archer and I see now you're a Warrior. What a difference in 20 horses 'eh."

"Yes, indeed," she said grinning. "Yes, yes. I am definitely a Warrior."

Kieran had recovered enough to light up a cigarette. He jumped out of the plane delicately but full of bonhomie. "Hello, Kieran O'Toole, how's the little Lake been in these winds? I remember when I last flew one...in 79, I took one out to the Middle East for a sultan's son who wanted to learn. I ask you, a seaplane in the desert. Almost as ridiculous as Isabel Eberhardt, who died of drowning in the desert...."

Carrie left the two pilots to their memories and went to make sure Goose Bay wasn't also in a different country. In the terminal she met the Archer.

"Hello," he said, stretching out a broad, gloved hand as she walked in, "you must be the Warrior. You flying with Kieran?"

"I own the plane," Carrie said rather stiffly, put out. "Kieran's my pilot."

"Yes, I heard someone was doing a two-up. Must be difficult. Especially man and woman. I'd rather travel man and man. But rather still alone."

"Lucky I didn't ask you then," she replied tartly and the Archer, whom she later discovered was a very nice man, began apologising madly. "I didn't mean....er."

"No," she smiled primly, "of course not."

She brushed past him to the planning room, knowing she was behaving rudely; but suddenly she didn't want to talk to anybody. She wanted to be alone with her thoughts. With her stress. This was it! Here they were at the edge of the Atlantic. And Kieran had failed her. Her pilot had passed out. There was no one left for her to rely on except herself and the Warrior. "Life is a journey, travel it well," which after-dinner speaker had quoted that? Not that it mattered now.

Nothing else must now go wrong or it would be fatal. Vital and fatal. Her Warrior, her only asset in the world, on the edge of the ocean. Ready to start an over-water trip which would either bring her safely home with loads of profit; or send her to join Ignatius at the bottom of the ocean.

The weather got worse and worse. Day after day filled with snow, which only seemed to stop for the night before starting again at dawn. Even when the snow abated the cloud hung low over the sea, preventing any movements from the airfield.

Carrie tried to find things to do, to keep her nervous mind off the future. First it was a trip with an Innuit taxi-driver around the town. But although Goose Bay was a little more exciting than Wabush, it was hardly stuffed full of theatres. Then it was shopping in the long, warehouse-like superstores. Kieran took pictures of white painted, stone houses decorated with colourful plastic butterflies and birds. Finally it was a day spent washing the Warrior.

"Well," said Kieran, smoking while Carrie scrubbed her plane, "if your little dog won't start, we can steal the Vulcan Bomber on the apron. You could fly it around the airshow circuit. On second thoughts I could do it for you, and you could pay me. Hey let's do it! Let's do it in the road; oh I just love those hard iron manholes; as the monk said to the bishop, as they sang in the chapel, there really is no substitute for the full blown organ."

"Pass me the soap will you," ordered an irritated Carrie.

"As the nun said to her sister, wears the soap, doesn't it?"

"So, my little petal," said Kieran on the fourth day of bad weather. "Shall we harness up our little Innuit driver again and go visit the outlying posts of old America. Find those legendary whore-houses tucked away in the goosedown of the downside of Goose...hire the man for the day..hire the whore for the hour...no question who costs more. Oh for the love of a laidye..."

"No!"

"No? How no? What is that little word, so strong and silent like the finest pilot, what is that for NO?"

"I can't afford it and besides I'm sick to death of looking at that ugly house with the plastic bees on it."

"Birds, butterflies...I don't remember any bees but clearly you had a confusing sex education. What then pray shall we do to fill our idle hours? We have examined the area for sex shops and found it lacking, we have searched...."

"I'm going to the Flight Planning room to check the weather. Then I'm going to join Ditcher and Archer for a coffee and then I might read my book. I don't care what you do, as long as it doesn't cost me money!"

"Well, there's an excitable little dog owner, a poodle in a puddle, a madam in a muddle...what will you do in the Flight Planning Office without your mother, guide and pilot? Come let us away to the met and planning man for he will tell us how the days shall span."

Reading the weather in the very well equipped Goose Bay Flight Planning Office, Carrie began to understand why most ferrying is done in the summer. The weather charts showed days and days of low pressure. Fronts pushed across the Atlantic in quick succession, giving them weeks of low cloud, high winds and poor visibility. Typical March weather.

"Not very good," said Carrie, recognising all these things from her meteorology books. "Look at those tight isobars; severe winds." In spite of her underlying anxiety she was rather pleased with how much she remembered, but even that wasn't enough.

"Wild variation here on top of the world, 'eh? The pull of the poles," said Kieran, "this amount of variation is only normally found in a woman's heart!"

Archer saw Carrie was looking puzzled and he showed her his map. "Look on my chart," he said. "See the practical difference (the variation) between true and magnetic north. In the UK the variation is only 4° or 5° so it's hardly relevant. But here, much closer to the North pole, there's a huge difference. Take my planned route, for example; here at Goose our variation is 29.5° west, while over at the Greenland tip it's 32°, by the time we reach Reykjavik in Iceland we have 24°. So, when I draw a line from origin to destination, my original track is about 040°. Now add the variation and my magnetic track is 070°, almost East. Quite a difference! Extra problem now, what do I do with the changes in variation between the points? Its a difference of 8°s between Greenland and Iceland."

"You could take an average," Carrie suggested, hoping that sounded well-informed and intelligent.

"Good! Or you could give yourself two tracks, one to the tip of Greenland and another for the flight to Iceland," explained Archer. "Either way that magnetic pull can easily confuse the unwary."

"I see," said Carrie, wondering why she hadn't been aware of this before. "Thanks. If we ever manage to leave this place I'll be a whole lot wiser. What about the weather, any luck?"

"Just here," said Archer, pointing at the advanced synoptic chart, "we might find a chance. There's a break in the constant stream of fronts and I think we might get a ridge of high pressure we could grasp. Might be tomorrow, but looking at the speed of these two warm fronts..."

"Slow," affirmed Ditcher.

"Slow! I don't think they'll be past until the evening and then we might get a break...I'm prepared to plan for the day after tomorrow."

"I'm always ready," said Ditcher cheerfully, "if the weather clears I go."

Yes, thought Carrie, and we know what's happened to you in the past. Never mind the fuel quantity, look at the quality of the breeze!

"Why," Carrie asked, "is the quality of forecasting so much better up here?"

"Ah," twinkled Ditcher, "don't forget here it is a job, while in the temperate lands it's more of a hobby!"

"Well boys," chimed Kieran cheerfully, "if we're not flying today how about retiring to the bar for a few get to know yous?"

"Sure thing," said Archer kindly, "I don't drink but I'd enjoy the conversation. I always bring a book on these trips but talking to other pilots is like a thousand stories."

The four of them made their way over to the airfield bar. Archer was staying in the same hotel as Carrie and Kieran but Ditcher had brought a tent, which he pitched in the hangar under the wing of a freight-carrying aeroplane. He stopped in there briefly to fetch his glasses.

"The engineers are good guys. Always helpful with a spare razor and things I've forgotten," said Ditcher cheerily, smoothing his hand over his bald pate. "You may not realise it," he told Carrie, "but us bald guys still have to shave the face. Ironic 'eh. Where I want it, it's gone, but where I don't need it it grows."

"Ah," interrupted Kieran, "just like the activity of the elderly actress and her admirers."

"Isn't it cold in the hangar?" asked Carrie, thinking of the freezing temperature outside and unable to contemplate staying in a tent in such weather.

"Oh, no, it's heated. The engineers couldn't work in there otherwise. It's a nice temperature. Bit noisy but I sleep like a baby anyway."

"What would you like to drink?" Carrie asked Archer and Ditcher, as they settled themselves into some orange plastic chairs in a fluorescently lit bar with all the decoration of a Stark house.

"Nono," said Archer, "let me. I insist. I think I owe you one for my rudeness when we met. It was quite unintentional."

"Oh..no I," Carrie began, blushing, but Kieran broke in. "Never believe a man with an un. I'm all for intentions; good ones are dull, bad ones are bliss but all can lead to great satisfaction that you don't get from an un. Glass of milk for me. No, I'll go wild in your honour and have one of those pale, gleaming replicas of cat's piss you Americans call beer."

While Archer went to get the drinks, Kieran, leaning back, balancing an orange chair on its back legs, began his worst moment story, obligingly lengthening it so the missing part of his audience had time to return from shopping.

"I was flying over the Pacific," said Kieran, "I'd left San Fran for a stopover in Tahiti and on to Auckland, stuffed (and when I say stuffed I mean stuffed! Stuffed like a Christmas goose whose family hadn't eaten for a week) with fuel. I had tanks pressing on my hat, coming out my ears, fighting with my elbows. There I was, out of sight of land and suddenly I felt something wet on my right hand. I looked down and what was happening? What was? Fuel was gushing out of the right tank, into the cockpit and over my arm. Luckily I'd thrown my fag out the window (you should have heard him scream)." Kieran undulated foppishly, exaggerating a flamboyant wrist. "Oh, I am a girl! The fuel was pouring around me like foam in a Jacuzzi (and I mean a JACUZZI) and I knew I had do do something now or go up in the biggest (and I mean the BIGGEST) ball of fire you ever did see. Fireball committing piloticide against O'Toole. The autopilot was broken, so I took off my seat belt and tied it around the steering column to keep it in place, while I climbed into the back. Carefully! (How did you climb, people ask..carefully I say). I climbed over the seat to the tank. The cap had broken neatly into two under the pressure and was about as useful as tits on a boar hog. So I took off my boots, luckily they were made of good, strong leather, and I twisted them into a long, strong plug and shoved it right into the depth of the tank, with the feet of the boots just resting outside. And that held it for the whole journey. But I tell you there was no chance of me dropping off to sleep by mistake that night. So young Carrie you know the moral of that story."

"Always wear strong boots?"

"Never give up until you're dead. I always meant to die with my boots off and on that occasion I nearly did!" Kieran stopped for applause.

The Archer told his story leaning forward, his hands on his knees. "My worst moment was when I was ferrying a Warrior like yours," he smiled at Carrie, "to the Seychelles. It was misty and just getting dark. I was following the ADF track and it showed dead ahead. Dead ahead. I knew the island should be showing up in front of me and there was nothing. No lights, which was what particularly worried me. I looked at my fuel. I still had enough for another hour, but I knew that if I didn't see the island soon I wasn't going to make it. I couldn't turn back and there was nowhere to go. I said a little prayer. As soon as I did, as soon as I let myself be guided by God, I was possessed by an overpowering sensation that I was too far to the right. I knew I must track left. It went against all my training to do so when I saw the ADF pointing in the way it did."

"Always believe your instruments," cut in Kieran explanatorily.

"Exactly! But in spite of that I turned. I went left, and after a quarter of an hour or twenty minutes the island suddenly appeared out of the mist. I said a thank you to God, but if I hadn't changed my course in spite of the instrument, I wouldn't be telling you this tale now."

"Creepie," Carrie said shuddering, while Kieran asked what was wrong with the navigation instrument and when it was last checked.

"The engineers couldn't find anything. Night effect maybe or coastal effect or simply evil spirits."

"What about you?" Carrie asked Ditcher, "what was your worst moment?"

"Mine was more human," he said, twinkling at her, his hand feeling his bald pate as though fearful of finding a hair growing there. "In the 70s I was flying an Ag Cat down to Saudi via Syria and Iraq. Three of us in convoy and all the necessary clearances tip top. Going through Turkey I had engine trouble. I voted for the return hop to Ankara, leaving the others en route. In fact it was only a small electrical problem; false indication. So, I told the air traffickers and they agreed to do all the clearance re-sending. Off I popped. Just past Aleppo on the Syrian border, when blow my tiger, if there wasn't a Mig Fighter on my port side. Waggling his wings. Other side; sure as Mum there's another. Two choices. Follow them or be shot down.

No need to guess which I did! I followed them back to their military base outside Aleppo; landed. The guns were on me, and all these blighters with tea-towels on their heads. Most alarming! All tall guys too. No one spoke a word of English, of course. I held my hands up and followed the big guys."

"What do you say to a man with a tea-towel and a machine gun?" Asked Kieran, answering himself: "Sir! No place for Inshallah here!"

Archer looked slightly shocked and Ditcher carried on. "We got to the terminal, a hut really. Inside was some Big Wig in another tea towel.

'Where are your clearances?' he screamed at me in English. I explained. He didn't believe me. I had visions of spending the rest of my life in a

Syrian jail. Thanks my friend."

Ditcher took another beer from Kieran and drank deeply.

"He was screaming at me. He got somebody on the phone; soon he was screaming at them too. It could have gone on for ever, but I saw the chess board over in the corner. I wandered over while he was lambasting the lackey. Unfinished game. There was an obvious move he'd omitted to make, would have got white out of trouble plus given him check mate against black. Dummy! I made the move.

'Hey, you English!' He yelled at me, although really I'm from Scotland, 'what you doing?'

'Oh,' I replied, 'if you move white queen ahead of the rook...'

'Allah! Do you play chess?'

'Of course, all ferry pilots do.'

I nearly said I could see from the board he didn't but wisely held my tongue. No use insulting the enemy when they have the upper hand, especially when they dress in wash-cloths. He yelled. 'Ayeah. If you beat me you can have your clearances. If you don't...Inshallah.'

Luckily I won, so we'll never know what might have happened."

Atlantic Dogs of War

In the morning, when Carrie tried to start the Warrior's engine, it coughed, made a few game attempts at turning over, and collapsed exhausted. Kieran moved her out of the way and tried instead. It still wouldn't work. Carrie felt like crying. Now of all times, when they were just about to cross the shark-infested ocean with great white giants ahead, the Warrior decided to quit.

"Humm," said Kieran, "piece of rubbish. The dog's starter motor's gone to Heaven to join the rest of it and the man that bought it."

"Oh! Is that it, again. Thank Heavens."

Carrie was relieved but not surprised. After the freezing in Bangor, followed by dubious engineering, you could feel for the troublesome little plane; used to the warmth of Florida, it hadn't asked to come trundling off to the frozen wastes of Canada.

"OK," said Kieran, "you'll have to hand swing it."

"Hand swing? The plane?"

"Not the plane, you donkey, the propeller! You'll have to pull the propeller through by hand, it's like an old car handle. It kicks the motor into action. OK, just pop out and swing the prop."

"Who me? Carrie the Colossus? Look at the size of my muscles?"

"It isn't muscles, it's technique. Oh, for goodness sake! Watch this. Leave everything off for the moment. No mags...just check the magnetos are off, aren't they? Good."

Kieran went to the front of the Warrior and started to demonstrate how to hand-swing a plane by pulling round the propeller. He put one leg delicately forward to balance his body, then putting all his weight on the back foot he put his left hand up to the propeller and pulled it sharply down, bringing his weight further back as he did so in order to keep away from the cutting edge of the propeller.

"Right, see how easy it is! OK, now your turn. Keep your other hand clear."

Carrie tried. She lent in towards the Warrior, put her left hand on the propeller, while holding her right behind her. She balanced her weight on the back foot. Pulled. The propeller tripped a couple of inches and flipped back to its original position.

"No, no, no, not like that. Sensuously! Follow my body, as the actress said to the Bishop. Use your body. You're activating an engine, not dusting a picture. OK. watch again."

Kieran flicked the propeller, it buzzed round. "See! Perfectly easy! Try it again."

Kieran took Carrie's place in the cockpit and shut the door. Carrie tried heaving again; the propeller managed half a turn before falling back. Tried again. Same effect. Behind the glass, his sound channels cut off,

Kieran's hand became verbose. After a while he couldn't stand the silence any more. "Come on," he shouted, leaning out of the door, "pull! Use your f...ing weight!"

To Carrie it soon became obvious that, technique or not, try as she might or not, her muscles (and probably her self-preservation instinct) would not let her pull that metal propeller through even half a sequence, let alone past the firing point. Despairing, Kieran sent her off to ask the kindly Archer for his assistance.

"After all," he pointed out unflatteringly, "I would prefer an experienced pilot in the plane if I were going to pull the propeller. I mean what would you do if the plane started and began rolling towards me..."

"Pull the throttle back and put the brakes on."

"... so I'd better sit in it while he pulls. Besides, think what it would cost you if I lost a hand or an arm...."

The Archer came over and agreed, unwillingly but with good Christian spirit, to pull the prop. This time the propeller turned freely and once the mags were switched on the engine fired happily and spun round unaided.

"Wonderful!" Kieran enjoyed the performance so much that he shut the plane down and asked Archer to do it again. "We need to make sure it will start every time. Never take a first request as the true answer, as the dancer said to the censor."

Archer smiled without judgment, even laughing when Kieran, who could never resist a challenge, discovered he was a Mormon and began asking him questions designed to annoy him. "Are Mormon's allowed to tie up their wives? I've heard they get regularly beaten and buggered."

"We are allowed to do anything within the loving family bond," Archer said, "but that doesn't mean we do."

"But it's very restrictive being a Mormon isn't it. Of course we all think lucky old you with your twelve wives..."

"I only have one, that being in line with the American law."

"Yeah sure, but your wife has eleven sisters, right?"

"Wrong..."

They wandered away to the bar and Carrie fussed around the plane. She put her handbag on the front seat and was moving things around in the back, trying to ease the life-jackets out from where they had slid down between the folded, stored seats and the extra fuel tank, when she heard the airport golf-cart purring up towards her.

"Hello, Mam," said a young man in a fluorescent yellow jacket with fat silver stripes, "are you bleeping?"

Carrie stared at him. She was used to pilots approaching her and saying odd things, but if this was a pick-up line it was a rare one.

"What?"

"Your ELT. Has it, like, gone off? The noise is on the radio. All the Search and Rescue boys in Newfoundland are on alert. We've pinned it down to you."

"I can't hear anything," said Carrie, wondering if she'd gone deaf.

"No, like Mam, you can only hear it on the radio."

She leant into the plane and switched on the radio, tuning to 121.5, the emergency frequency. Something was pounding away at a high enough frequency to give a dog a panic attack. The marshaller poked inside the plane but the built-in emergency transmitter was switched off. The Warrior looked innocent.

"Perhaps the handheld?" She opened her bag and pulled out the rectangular, orange portable. The restricter pin, which should normally stand proud on the top of the transmitter, lay on its side. As the portable came clear of the bag, the pin slipped off the orange body and dropped onto the dark tarmac with a slight plonk, bouncing into a water drain. The boy and Carrie stared hopelessly after its disappearing shape.

"Oh, my God," he said, "like what now? The noise is driving all the Labrador units crazy. They'll kill me."

Carrie thought it was more likely that they'd kill her, envisaging a pack of Labradors licking her to death. She grabbed the ELT and hit it a few times against the tarmac, hoping the jolts would silence it.

"Man, that won't work," remarked a helpful spectator who'd joined them, "these things are meant to sustain a plane crash, you know, a bit of tipping won't stop it."

A second spectator, also stopping by to help, suggested a bucket of water. While he and the first spectator argued, the young boy went off to get some water.

"Won't work, man," said the first spectator contentedly. "Boy! I mean these things are designed to survive boat crashes, they all happen in the water, don't they?"

"But this is different, this is placing it in a restricted bucket of water."

"Look man, you know, you drown if you fall in the sea or I hold your head in a bucket, don't you. Like where's the difference?"

By this time Kieran had realised that something was happening out on the tarmac and was back at Carrie's side; the ever-ready hero. He grabbed the ELT and poked at it. Nothing happened. He pulled the aerial off. Transmissions continued. He dropped it in the bucket of water, which by this time the boy had brought over. Transmissions continued. Eventually he took an axe to it, spilling acid all around the airport. Transmissions finally stopped.

"Well, my little angel," Kieran said, "travelling with you is one jolly jape after another isn't it! I don't like to point this out," he added mendaciously, "but I never have any problems when I travel alone."

Carrie went for a walk.

After five days of hanging around the met office, Archer's forecast break in the weather finally arrived. Although the clouds were not exactly puffy little white ones in an aquamarine Heaven, they were at least no longer on the deck. With a cloud base of around 1500 feet and a visibility of 10 kilometres, the pilots decided the weather was good enough to give it a go.

"Are you sure?" Carrie asked nervously, "don't take any risks with my future."

"Well, liberling," replied Kieran in true confusing form, "although I know you don't place much value on life, I rather think those other boys do. So we'll see if your plane is worth as much or as little as their lives, shall we? Let's go for the blow. Let's dive for the sun..."

They flew out of Goose Bay, through the lower extension of Happy Valley into Lake Melville, and out of Canada by Groswater Bay. While Archer and Ditcher, directly on their way to Iceland, challenged the icing levels and flew in cloud at 2500 feet, the Warrior stayed low under the cloud base.

"We all know about this dog's instruments," said Kieran. "Besides, it gives me a nose bleed to fly too high, and while they can put ice down their backs to stem the bleeding I've an aversion to cold cloudy stuff." He began to sing.

Carrie felt alternately elated and terrified. Here we come plane and all; romance, adventure, money and still 5,000 miles of water to cross.

"Suppose we have an accident," Carrie asked, "would you save me first?"

Kieran smiled his charming smile and told her she had already answered the question by asking it: which he certainly had done then.

Ten minutes out of Goose the GPS failed. Carrie saw the screen fade and go blank. She tapped it hopefully. "What's happened to the GPS?" She asked, hoping Kieran had some sure fire explanation.

He looked over and nodded. "Um, useful as tits on a boar hog those GPS nightmares. As the actress said to the Bishop there's nothing like a grey face when you're looking for the colour of your dreams. Luckily we have our two ADFs, but we may still find ourselves in the wrong channel at Simutac. Deadly! We'll have to wait until we get to Greenland to see."

"Great! Shall we go back? Perhaps there's..."

"Too late! Too late...Goose draws away, the weather goes grey; as does the GPS. When it's got to this stage it's deader than a Mummy's grandmother. No screen no use; no mama no cry. We'll use the other instruments but clearly it's all part of the cur-dog's sickness. I wouldn't have bought this plane if I was paid to! And," he added, unconsciously echoing Colin, "your husband was a pilot. Odd 'eh?"

After half an hour they were out of sight of land. For the next two and a half hours they flew without seeing anything but sea and cloud, and cloud and more sea. Above them, hidden within the dense grey atmosphere, and slightly ahead owing to their greater speed, were the other pilots. Both men kept contact with them over the radio, encouraging them with news of the better weather which lay ahead.

Carrie looked at the too close sea and hoped the little engine would stay the course this time. What had made her pilot husband, a man who often said aviation was an expensive time-waster, invest in a Warrior? At least, she thought dramatically, if I die out here I'll be able to ask him in Heaven: if he's been allowed in.

Two and a half hours after leaving Goose Bay, the cloud above them finally began lifting and dispersing. At first it just seemed lighter. Carrie felt her mood rising with the increasing illumination. Then she saw bits of blue appearing in the between the clouds. Gradually those patches joined up until there was an unbroken blue desert above, which merged into the sea all around.

"Enough to make you blue," sang Kieran, animated by their emergence into good weather. "I'm so black in the sack and it's pink in the sink when you pee..."

Carrie pulled the cabin heat on and watched the rpm drop on the gauge. She put it back in and saw the revs go up, pointing it out to Kieran as she did so.

"Have you seen this?"

"Oh, yes, I've been keeping an eye on it. I meant to ask an engineer at Goose to look at it but it clean slipped my mind! Clearly those half-brains at Bangor got the pipes mixed up. It's easy enough to do if you're a proletarian intent on committing liberticide against the rich. Or just simply inefficient and half witted. After all, both pipes are the same colour, same shape and end in similar places; although not, as they obviously think, the same. We'll get it changed at Narssarssuaq."

"They couldn't have done it on purpose could they? I mean first they try and kill us with a dead engine and then this..."

"Well, I know I'm very important but why, my little floosie, would anyone want to kill you? Especially now your husband is no longer alive to benefit from the insurance. Just incompetence, if you ask me. "

Carrie gasped. "What do you mean?" But Kieran was singing again and ignored her. She told herself it was just co-incidence and Kieran speak; he couldn't have known about the insurance mix-up.

After three hours of nothing but sea they passed the 'Point of No

Return'. Now the distance back was too far for the amount of fuel still in the tanks. Here they were in the middle of nowhere, with only the option of going forward. Saying goodbye to the Archers and Ditchers, Kieran changed frequency to Narssarssuaq.

"Nothing on the radio," said Carrie suspiciously, "all very quiet."

"Umm, my little sweet cake, Narssarssuaq is not exactly Virgin Radio you know."

He called the airfield, now they were within radio range. Narssarssuaq knew, of course, that they were coming, since they had filed a flight plan half an hour before leaving Goose Bay. However, to Carrie's surprise and Kieran's derision they came back with a brusque reply.

"N22 Narssarssuaq Airport is closed, state your intentions."

"Oh, my God," said Carrie, "not again. What now?"

"To put down in the sea on your doorstep!" was Kieran's immediate response. "A guest dying from ingratitude at such a host!"

Carrie expected the same kind of abuse you would get at Rudehill, but Narssarssuaq was unfazed. The air traffic controller kindly informed the approaching Warrior.

"We can make a special exception and open the airfield for you, for a price, but it is Good Friday and a national holiday. State your intentions."

"We'll come and pay," said Kieran, and turning to her he said, "another place saw you coming. Didn't you know it was Easter this week-end?"

"Who is the Catholic here?" Carrie spat at him, very unhappy about this further in-road into what no longer seemed like profit at all.

"Catholic, protestant; you sound like Northern Ireland...did I tell you my grandfather fought in the Post Office Riots..."

"Yes. Many times."

She stared out of the window, watching the still line of the sea. Nothing but sea in every direction and now they were forcing themselves upon an unwilling airfield. If they could find it. If the airfield really existed. Was this her great adventure? This constant battle with incompetence and those who wanted her money. (What money?)

Gradually Greenland's crags and fjords shimmered into view; at first just a hazy outline and then, as they got nearer, sharply clear against the horizon. While before there had been miles and miles of sea, now it appeared that the future held miles and miles of unbroken, inhospitable rock, leering over sheets of cracked white ice. Somewhere here was the Cape of Desolation, named by sailors. Carrie searched the relentless highlands ahead for Bluey West One, the fjord Earnest Gann had written about as the entrance to Narssarssuaq. She knew that, now they had lost the GPS, they were dead if they got the wrong passage. Kieran was also looking, fiddling with the ADF.

"Of course," he said, "if we don't find Simutaq and get the wrong fjord we're doomed. If, instead of going up Skovfjord and Tunugdllarfik, we accidentally stray into Bredefjord or Julianehåbsfjord that's it, we're stuck. No turn, narrow channels! We haven't the lift to climb out or the fuel to get back. We'd just have to land on the pack-ice down there, get out the dingy, if there's any sea, and do what we can. I've heard with immersion suits and a dingy you can probably live almost an hour without too much pain."

"Get the right one then!" Carrie snapped, no longer in the mood for Kieran's romanticism. "I thought that's why I paid for so many instruments to accompany us on this trip, so we didn't get the wrong one."

"When they work!" Remarked Kieran, shaking his head, "when they work. Let's just hope Simutaq and Julianehaab haven't got their signals mixed up, NDBs you know...very unreliable, as indeed you might expect from non-directional beacons..very unreliable. That's why we all changed to satellites...although even those can be turned off at the maggot-President's whim..."

"Great!" Carrie looked at the emerging layer of icebergs angrily. "Great!"

However, as they neared land Carrie was captivated, and lifted out of her misery. The ice layer was impregnated by incredible colour, a sapphire blue Carrie had never seen before, somewhere between aquamarine and turquoise; a colour she later discovered didn't reproduce properly in photographs. It was (according to Kieran) the result of ice melting and being refrozen over and over again. Perhaps it was really the purity of the sea or the contrast with the silent grey crags ahead and the dark, jewelled blue sea shining up from beneath. Larger icebergs butted on smaller icebergs and some nudged over them, submerging their smaller fellows into the ocean; others had partly merged, as though a mother was bearing ice-blue babies.

Carrie looked through the gulfs, down to the darker blue depths below. Was this what her husband had bought the plane for? Perhaps he had imagined they could one day fetch the plane together, take it back to Africa and en route experience such purity of colour together. Or did he imagine her sinking into the frozen, unfrozen black blue water, never to surface again: while he took the insurance payout. She could almost feel the strong colours closing over her little light blue Warrior. For a moment she fought against the compelling temptation to push the stick forward and simply plunge into the unknown world below. A memorial flight in ice! A romantic gesture to love.

The air was so clear, it seemed somehow stiller than even the highest pressure day in winter in the UK. Carrie wanted to experience it on her skin. She opened the little storm window but it was impossible to feel any-thing but a tunnel of coldness.

"I wish we were in a Tiger Moth now."

"Bloody cold! Not to mention the ferry tanks you'd have to carry in that one," said Kieran. "I once took a wing walker up to 10,000 feet in the Alps and I can tell you the predominate feeling was cold. What was the pre-dominant feeling? It was cold."

Kieran sang.

They went up the channel Kieran assured her was Bluey West One.

"Where is Earnest Gann's shipwrecked boat?" Carrie asked nervously.

"Probably fell apart years ago," Kieran remarked.

"Or been stolen I suppose," she retorted cynically.

"Stolen? Who by? It's not exactly crowded with vandals and thieves up here you know, my little poppet. Even Narssarssuaq only has a population of a hundred."

He sang a few bars of gypsies, tramps and thieves.

Carrie said nothing, watching the steep sides of the channel, hoping they were in the right place. She could not imagine what it would be like to crash here, knowing there was nowhere to go and that you would be lucky if you lived an hour. Accompanied in your last hours by Kieran. That would be something else!

Carrie looked ahead and saw a totally straight line where frozen fjord met Atlantic sea-water. "Wow, look at that ice line, it's so straight."

Kieran mused whether the ice was strong enough to hold the Warrior. "Shall I try a touch and go? Looks pretty thick to me," he said, "what do you think, shall we risk it? The worst that can happen is we have a long walk to Narssarssuaq and catch the next (if any) plane home."

Carrie said nothing. They flew on over the ice towards the airfield. In summer this would be water. Gradually, after what seemed to Carrie like miles of ice flats gleaming in the sun, the airfield came into view. The first obvious thing was the long tarmac runway which stood out from the snow like Lake Okeechobee from outer space. Carrie's relief was enormous.

"We're in the right place," she gasped.

"Sure," said Kieran, once again suspiciously semi-silent.

At Narssarssuaq there was only one way to land the aircraft, 08 from the fjord, and only one way to take off, 26 towards the water. The reason was a huge mountain at the other end of the strip; landings too fast or too long met solid rock.

"All landings here are good ones," said Kieran lyrically, theorising as to whether a glider could dive over the top of the mountain and still manage to land on the runway. "Probably," he joked, "you'd have to be pissed to plunge onto the piste. Imagine a little American flying school here on a busy summer weekend; would there be queues? More than in the Manchu dynasty. Oh queu-er!"

Although Narssarssuaq had an NDB it was restricted and there were no fully approved radio aids at this airfield. The approach plate declared: 'Day time and good weather only' for landing, with an additional warning: '..take offs and landings must not take place when cloud base is below 1500 feet or visibility less than 5 statute miles.' Seeing the way the mountain captured the clouds and held itself invisible, Carrie understood: unfortunately others were not so convincible.

Kieran reduced power and speed and the little Warrior descended elegantly through the cold, dense air. The ice got nearer and so did the rock at the far end of the runway. They made a low level approach across the ice field to the runway.

"Here's my chance," said Kieran, "to practice my short-field landings for real; only... if I drop too short we have a cracking icy skid, not a mere skedaddle, to the runway...better to skid on ice than slice the kid...as the actress said to the axe murderer."

Kieran applied full flap and they bumped down onto the runway just after the numbers. He applied the brakes gingerly and they slid gently to a halt, furlongs from the rocky promontory at the far end of the airfield. "Easy as farting in the bath," remarked Kieran, "and you were worried and sweating in the cold my lover-ly."

He taxied in and parked the plane next to a closed hangar. There were no other aircraft anywhere on the apron and the air traffic controller gave them no advice.

As they jumped off Warrior's wing Carrie noticed it was warmer here than in Canada. True the sun was shining, but it had shone in Moncton too; there the air temperature froze exposed flesh, here it only took your breath.

"The North Atlantic drift," said Kieran, when asked, "identified by Benjamin Franklin, who as we all know gave his best signature to be used on the $100 bill and his name to the Frankies restaurant for their hot dogs. Same Gulf Stream as we have in good old Blighty, only here we are a bit more to the North..."

There was just one customs man at the airfield, who was also air traffic controller, security man and tourist guide. He laughed delightedly; a man whose dull Good Friday had been enlivened by the arrival of a couple of tourists and an extra $100. Kieran, feeling as close to a twinge of guilt as someone of his personality could, asked the Cheerful Customs Chappie if there was anywhere to stay.

"There's the hotel, but that is expensive and they're always running out of food...it's all tins and no forward planning there. ..pppp you know.

Prior planning prevents piss-ups! We respect that in aviation, why don't they observe it in hotels?"

Looking out at the surrounding snow and ice, flying forever into the distance, Carrie could see why they had no food. The Cheery Chappie chatted on. "....You might feel like going on to Iceland today after you've fuelled. I've got the weather and it don't look good for the next few days. I rather think we won't have another clear spell until Monday." He paused but Kieran said nothing. "Or you could stay with my friends on the edge of the barracks. You," he said to Kieran, "could stay in the barracks, but I think you're lady friend here might not like it."

"Lady friend!" screeched Carrie, while the Cheerful Chappie chuckled, now from embarrassment.

Kieran put a huge arm around her shoulders. Carrie noticed the smell of leather, mixed with male sweat from his jacket, and aftershave. He gave her a reassuring hug.

"So! Tell me about your friends," said Kieran to the Cheerful Chappie, "they sound like our sort of people. I'm just too tired to fly on today, and you know what they say about a tired pilot! Know your limits that's what. Never let commercial considerations push you on..."

His smile challenged Carrie to insist, but she knew Kieran was even more determined when challenged. She shrugged, not yet ready for out-and-out war, and actually agreeing with his analysis: she didn't want a tired pilot either.

"OK, then," said Cheerful Chappie, "what about your plane? I can ask the boys to put it in the hangar, they won't charge much."

"Great. I'll go and have a word. Is there an engineer around? We're having trouble starting; I don't suppose a new starter motor will cost much will it? And there is a little problem with the pipes. Oh, and I noticed the primer line has come loose on the right forward cylinder. If this was a dog it would have been in tins for his cannibalistic relatives by now..."

Cheerful Chappie laughed again. "There is Rob, but ask him yourself. If you ask me and it goes through the company, we'll have to charge company rates..."

Carrie went purple. More costs and mainly the result of having to redo a previous engineer's work. What was her husband thinking about getting her in this situation? Kieran, too tired for a tantrum, went to ask the engineer to swap the pipes and look at the cost of the other repairs.

Narssarssuaq was a row of ex-American-army barracks. The customs man led them up the man-made steps through the snow to the line of wooden huts. Carrie thought he was joking when he said: "This is Narssarssuaq!" But that was all there was. A couple of lines of communal quarters in deep snow, with trodden snow paths between and a large aerial on the mountain behind. The village was bleakly beautiful, like a Christmas card with its thick cover of snow and the huge towering backdrop mountains. But beautiful in the way of the desert; the result of its isolation, its still, craggy harshness, and its extremes.

It seemed to Carrie that this area of the world was either sea or ice; rocks or snow in every direction and as far as the horizon and beyond. Here it was possible to imagine that the world had ended and mankind must start again. Carrie remembered what she'd been told about Danes liking beer. She could see that this virginal beauty could easily send you to the edge of madness; could cause a longing for the clutter of rubbish. She imagined drunk Danes throwing beer cans in the snow, just for the pleasure of polluting their own paradise: perhaps she just didn't have the right temperament for environmental elegance.

Cheerie Chap's friends were a British Danish couple, who were there for some reason Carrie couldn't quite fathom. Anna worked in the hotel, but Carrie found it hard to believe she'd left the UK and come to Narssarssuaq just for the pleasure of working in the tiny, scarcely used hotel. Knut apparently spent his time shooting small birds with an automatic rifle. When Carrie said she thought it was extremely cruel, he pointed out that he could have used the sub-machine gun he kept in his end-of-barracks house.

End of barracks it was; stuck on the end of the long wooden army quarters it had doors and windows on one side only, and four rooms. The Cheerie Chap led them into the main room, through a small porch where one could stamp the snow off ones shoes or change out of boots. Carrie took off her boots and walked into the room in her socks but Kieran, after a cursory tapping of his leather boots, strode onto the rush-matting allowing a few offerings of crystallised snow to drop as he walked. They lay in piles until they dissolved into small, wet pools in the warmth of the gas heater.

The main room had a sofa and a couple of chairs, a desk where Knut's papers lounged in random piles, a small bookcase, a large Calor gas heater, a tall wooden cupboard and three doors. Each door had a blanket draped from a curtain rail to keep the warmth inside the room. One door led to the kitchen, where Anna had already started to prepare something with a strong fishy scent. She put her head around the blanket to kiss the Cheerie Chappie.

"Hey, Jo. How's things?"

"Terrific. Yours."

"This 'n that. I'll come and chat tomorrow."

He winked in an approving manner and Knut got up from his desk to shake hands. After a quick introduction, the Cheerie Chap said he must be back to his post, "in case we have any other surprise parties!" He kissed Anna again and left the interlopers with a wave of his hand: they and their $100 were already past history.

Anna returned to the kitchen, the bulky brown blanket dropping heavily back into place like a theatre curtain. Knut gave them each a beer, sitting on the sofa that would later be Carrie's bed.

Knut was a large bear. Six foot six with square shoulders under a thick Jersey, he made Kieran seem fragile. Carrie imagined that being heavily bearded was essential living in Narssarssuaq, where supplies could only come in by air from November to March and, even in the warmer months of the year, only after a long sea voyage from Denmark. Certainly saved on shaving cream. Restless young woman as she was, Carrie could hardly imagine why anyone should want to come out to this desolate place to live; no wonder he wanted to persecute the birds.

"Straight from Denmark," he said lifting his bottle in welcome, "each beer costs more than $10 US. Gold is less useful here. Sometimes we eat local food, but we wouldn't drink their piss. Only Danish or Czech beer, unless the freeze gets really deep. Ice after April means drink from the pail."

Carrie laughed, but he frowned, puzzled by her amusement.

"Do you like fiskefar?"

"Fiske fuck in far waters..." said Kieran.

"It's cod," continued Knut, ignoring the interruption, "from the huge shoal bank off the west of Greenland, but a Danish recipe. Greenland isn't known for its great culinary variety. Here we do it boiled and with a mustard sauce. You are lucky coming in March. We only eat fiskefars in months with an 'R' in them."

"Oh," said Kieran, "no refrigeration? It used to be like that in Ireland with oysters, but now stomachs are harder and refrigeration is better."

Knut, who had taken an immediate dislike to the volatile Irishman, again ignored him. "Afterwards we have Bondepige med Slor."

"Bondage pig meets slag!" said Kieran. "I love it...the slash of the whip on the whoring pig, slags disciplining the mind and body...tote that pork, bound that bale..."

Knut gave that special patronising laugh that nationals reserve for foreigners who have made a grave linguistic error; delightedly he began to correct Kieran. Carrie was overpowered by a strong sense of deja vue. Could it be that we in fact keep living and reliving our identical lives over and over again, separated only by a blank curtain which sometimes breaks, giving us the view of last time? Could her life or lives be forever intertwined with Kieran's? "Oh, God," she thought, "I hope not!"

"Bondepige med Slor," Knut was continuing proudly, "translates to your language as 'Peasant Girl with Veil!' In Denmark we make it with fresh apples, rye bread and whipped cream, but here we make it with dried apples from our store room, black bread, butter, chocolate and we use a milk substitute."

"Bread and butter pudding," said Kieran, "I know it well. I prefer spotted dick. Is it a disease? Is Muffin the Mule an offence?"

"Doesn't the milk substitute...er..change the flavour?" asked Carrie quickly, "you ..er..seem very proud of your foodie heritage."

"Ah. Here the air is so clear, we live outside, all our food tastes well. More delicious than anywhere in the world, even with inferior ingredients. Greenland is the best place for food lovers."

"Oh! That's unusual," she murmured.

Anna came out of the kitchen. Physically she was the opposite of Knut, a short and wiry woman, while in character she was a down to earth, basic animal who enjoyed living off the land.

"So," she said, "you two lovers or not? If you don't want to share the futon there is the sofa bed, otherwise that's it. What do you want?"

"I'll take the sofa bed," Carrie said.

"Fine!" she said and showed Carrie where the linen was kept.

As they pushed the curtain aside, entering Anna and Knut's spartan bedroom, Carrie felt a spasm of culture shock. Here there was only a bed, one chair each side and a table; no ornaments, no books and nothing to give it a personal edge. Carrie took joy in things, even when she couldn't afford to own them. These people had money enough to buy guns but clearly wished to own nothing that was not utilitarian. It seemed the desolation outside was matched by the imagination inside.

Carrie went back into the main room, leaving the bed-linen on the floor. Anna made up Kieran's bed on the futon, in a room with no furniture except a television, a huge pile of videos dumped on the floor and a large black wooden music centre which Anna said Knut had made himself from local materials.

"With any luck," said Kieran watching Anna do his bed, "the bears won't attack in the night, but if they do Carrie, my little Cassius Clay junior, you can come and share my futon. We can Botty Burp together. No bear would dare attack me after a session of Botty Burping!"

"Thanks, I'll keep that in mind," said Carrie as icy as the island.

"To be sure," said Kieran, "you'll bear that in mind, just as I will bare you in my mind dancing with the bears. Oh the broad-breasted delight of the barely covered buttock."

After a few Danish beers Knut became lively, and began telling hunting stories, each more gory than the last. Nothing daunted, Kieran also began to invent a few more post office rioters in the family. There was eventually a lull as each monologuer grew bored with the other's monopoly, then Kieran said, "so, Carrie babe why don't you tell us the story of your first husband."

She jumped. "What? Why?"

"Well, there must be a story there. What did you tell me he called himself? Ah yes. 'The White Tie.' Very colonial! A nineteen year old girl goes out to Thailand to marry a forty nine year old bachelor, and a couple of months later he is dead (black Thais at the funeral no doubt). Pretty suspicious. Especially with number three now also on the trolley. If I were Kees I'd be thanking my lucky stars I could still look up and see them!"

Carrie gasped outraged, keen to defend herself, but Knut was also intrigued now. "Ah, true love then. You met, married and he died. How sad. I am a romantic."

"Sounds financial to me: you young blond, me rich oldie, " said Kieran. "Why didn't he marry a local girl? If he was living in Thigh-land he must have had plenty of takers. I remember when I was in sweltering Bangkok, a girl invited me in..of course I never pay for what so demonstrably is for free....but she asked was it shell or sea...."

"Yes, yes," said Knut bored. "But this was different. Love? Was it not Carrie?" His bear's face lit up with a sudden illuminating glow.

"Yes." Carrie said, her throat constricting, although she no longer knew if she'd really loved any of them: such is time's healing capacity. Perhaps in the beginning. Perhaps she'd loved them all once; but each time a lover leaves you lose a little of yourself, until the last is only a ripple in what now amounts to your happiness. She was left a vacated Sainsbury's bag in the wind.

"Ah!" said Knut, with only one wife and no knowledge of failed marriages or departed lovers. "And where was the meeting?"

"In Thailand."

"In Thailand? Go on, why were you there?"

"Oh. I was backpacking. I was travelling alone and almost out of money. Getting to Bangkok had been more expensive than I'd realised. I thought I needed to get on to Australia if I was going to get a job. Then someone told me the embassy was interested in employing girls with good languages, so I went for an interview."

Carrie took a sip of beer, part of her wondering why she was telling these strangers her story. And Kieran; strange but not a stranger. She could have avoided the issue, made a light joke but instead she chose to go with the flow, to reveal a little of herself and her life. She continued. "The woman liked me, but didn't have anything for me. They wanted local girls. She thought I could get a job up in Chiang Mai; there was a language school up there supported by the embassy. I liked the idea of that. Chiang

Mai was cheaper than Australia, but more colourful. I took the train. But as I slept my bags were stolen. I only had the money in my purse, and it wasn't much. Then I was a bit of a fool. I say that looking back; at the time, of course, I just acted."

"Ah," said Kieran, "we all have 20 20 vision in hind..."

"Yes, yes, Kieran, we know..." muttered the exasperated Knut, "go on Carrie."

"When I got in to Chiang Mai, I said to the assembled multitudes of samlor drivers (a sort of cart with a foot-running or bicycle-riding puller. They also had tuk tuks with an engine, but they were too expensive). Anyway, I said to these samlor drivers. 'Who will take me to this address, but not cheat me (you see I'd heard they used to go around the houses to get extra money) I've only got 45 Baht.' So, there was a competition and one guy won. He, I guess, understood he was getting 45 Baht for taking me to the address. Stupid of me! Cultural mistake!"

"Bekacs?" Kieran suddenly spouted, bored of being ignored. "That's the name for them in Indonesia, comes from the sound. I remember I was doing a ferry from Oz and.."

"Ssh, Kieran," said Knut sensitively, "I like this story. Go on Carrie."

"The address was hard to find, we went everywhere. You see in those days Chiang Mai wasn't as it is now. It's grown a lot since. In those days it was a quiet backwater town, mainly reeds and tracks beside the river. Old Oriental houses. Romantic old trees with trunks which twisted around each other and leaves that swept the ground. It was lovely. An environmental fairy-tale. Anyway this driver, or rather puller, wore himself out with running up and down and around, through the reeds and under the leaves. Finally he told me the place did not exist. I think he thought I'd just get out of his cart, pay him and disappear, but no way. 'It must exist,' I said, 'the British government told me about it. It must exist. Try again'."

"Determined my little pigeon,.." began Kieran.

"Desperate more like. What was I going to do with no money and nowhere to go in Chiang Mai? I wasn't exactly littered with friends in the country, or out."

"Stick to the business," commanded Knut, "be quiet Kieran! No more interruptions. I want to hear the story."

"So brutal these Danes." Kieran stroked his hair, affecting pain.

"We were arguing, the puller and I. He was saying..." Carrie made a spirited effort to imitate a Thai samlor driver's accent, "... 'get out my 'umlor, pay me money, or I call police.' I was saying he was a liar and a cheat, 'take me to the address! I'm staying in this cart until you do!'

Then out of nowhere a man appeared. He came up to us and I was immediately nervous. Police, I thought, and I was in trouble. No money. Even my passport had gone. And no Thai-speak. But the man was friendly and he spoke English. In fact he was English, but he was so tanned, so localised, I didn't know.

First he asked me if I was English. When I said I was, he nodded and asked the driver in Thai if there was a problem. The puller-driver started all faladiddle of a story, which, although I could only guessingly interpret his gestures, I knew was all balderdash. I kept trying to break in. The new man couldn't help smiling then, but he silenced me with his hand. Gently. Kindly. Eventually he said to the driver, in English this time. 'Never mind that address, take us to this one.' And he climbed in beside me. Three minutes and we were there; a lofty mansion with peaks and scrolls. Something that would have fitted into an archaic parchment without any extra decoration.

At his house, which was something he hardly knew he'd got himself," - Knut flicked his hand at the irrelevance - "sorry..at his house he paid the driver 100 Baht, which immensely pleased Mr Samlor, who went bobbing off, pleased as a driver who's just been paid 100 Baht for a 10 Baht job.

Then the Englishman turned to me. 'Do you know what that address was?' He asked, raising his eyebrows so he looked quite saturnine. 'Where you were so intent on going?'

'A language school,' I replied coolly, wondering who he was and what his business was with me. 'I am still going there for a job, not least because I must pay you back the 100 baht!'

He started laughing abruptly. There we were standing outside his palatial wooden Thai house with its curving balconies and templesque side houses, and this stranger was creasing up, tears pouring down his face. I felt like an idiot. I turned around to go, but he took my hand gently and stopped laughing. He looked at me deeply with his brown eyes. Thoughtfully.

'Who told you it was a language school?' he asked, his handsome face still suffused with glee, but twinkling now rather than laughing.

'The British Embassy in Bangkok.'

'Wow!' He reflected for a moment and then he chuckled again, but with a different, amazed almost wondering tone.

'Well, my sweet,' he said, putting his hands on my shoulders and looking straight into my face, 'it is in fact a brothel. But if the British Embassy in Bangkok (he imitated my way of speaking,) thinks it is a language school then maybe they are giving it some subsidies. How quaint 'eh, the ways of bureaucrats! Still never mind them. Come into my humble abode.'

I wasn't sure about this, especially after the shattering information that

I'd nearly turned up to ask for a job in a brothel, so I said. 'Look, hang on a minute, I'm not a groupie, I'm not a whore and I...'

He started laughing good and proper then, doubling up with the joy of amusement. 'I almost wish I'd let you go and get the job! They certainly wouldn't have known what to make of you at Madam Mangoes. It's OK, though, welcome to the one country in the world where it's so easy to get sex, no one needs to force the unwilling. I want something different from you.'

He stroked my cheek with the back of his closed fist."

"Typical man," lisped Kieran, "I knew there'd be a catch."

"Shut up Kieran!" said Anna, whose blanket had been pushed aside so she could listen from the kitchen. "Go on Carrie, what did he want?"

"Marriage."

"Ah," said Knut, "so it was love at first sight."

"Not exactly. His mother had just died and she'd been worried about him living alone out there in Thigh-land (his term,) so she put a proviso in her will. If he wanted to get a penny of her money he had to marry an English girl. He didn't like the only ones he knew already, so he decided to take a risk with me. We were married. He got the money, then six months later he was dead. Luckily for me he hadn't had time to get through all the money she left and he didn't make a will leaving it all to the flousettes."

Carrie finished abruptly. Remembering The White Thai made her suddenly feel like crying; something she hadn't done for years. Death is harsh, but memory is kind, allowing you to forget the pain unless reminded by certain actions, questions. He had been so mature somehow..so...gorgeous, so kind, so different from these people with their harshly spartan ideas of how to live. The White Thai knew how to live well.

"Ah," said Knut, "I still think he loved you at first sight, just like I did with Anna. What did he die of?"

"An ulcer. He was only 49." Carrie thrust away the thought that her life would have been so different if he had lived.

"Oh," Knut stroked Anna's hair sadly.

"You're a pet," said Anna, and went back behind her curtain to finish making dinner.

"So," asked Kieran, "if your first husband left lots of lovely lolly, how come you are down to only a small plane? Someone over-spent somewhere!"

"Good question," replied Carrie, "I wish I knew."

Next morning the cloud was so low Carrie couldn't even see the beautiful mountain that dominated the end of the runway.

"Well," said Kieran, "that weatherman-cum-customs-cum-security guard (oh what bliss to come so often in so little time) knew his weather. Looks like we'll be stuck here for a couple of days. Shall we walk down to the airfield and see what goes. What's the buzz? What's a happening? Who are you? What have you sacrificed?" Kieran sang.

On the airfield a Sikorsky S76 helicopter was running up its engine, causing a thick cloud of snow to cascade across the airfield. Soon the Sikorsky was completely obscured. Only the red beacon on the tail boom, flashing compulsively through the white wall of crystals, remained visible.

"Are they planning to go somewhere?" Carrie asked Kieran as they watched the flake tunnels dancing in the helicopter vortices.

"I doubt it. If they were even thinking of lifting, they'd have done so without causing that blizzard. Did you know the IRA used to put talcum powder on the helipads in Derry, to prevent the army helicopters from seeing enough to take off or land. That's why they just come straight in and land. Chalkout or whiteout, if you can't see when landing you crash. Let's go and ask in the tower."

Thinking it must have taken a lot of talcum powder and wondering if Kieran made up half these stories, Carrie said nothing. She followed him up the outside steps, to an Air Traffic Control hut so cramped it was hard to believe they weren't in some small provincial airport, rather than the international airport of Greenland (pop 55,400, biggest island in the world; if it is an island). Carrie had expected to see the Cheerful Chappie, but apparently he was having the morning off and another guy manned the tower. As she jumped off the steps and saw him, surrounded by a sanded pine console, he half rose in polite welcome. "Goote´ Morning." His sing-song accent could have come from any of the Scandinavian countries.

"Hi ya," Carrie replied in unison with Kieran's "Morning. I don't suppose you'll have much work today. All the little Warriors and Archers are keeping themselves in the hangar..."

While Kieran chatted aviation to the ATC guy, Carrie looked out of the window, wondering if the weather would ever clear. Would they make it back to Biggin Hill, or be forced to stay here forever, sandwiched between Kieran, Knut and the frozen sea? She was so deep in her thoughts that it wasn't until she heard Kieran saying: "Bloody Joker!" that she realised something interesting was being discussed.

"What's that?"

"Just some half-brain from Iceland on his way to the US, thinks he's going to stop by here in his King Air! Dumb mutt! Look at the weather!"

Carrie looked out at the compressing grey clouds, strabismal against the cruelly gleaming snow, and the helicopter now stationery on the apron. As her vision cleared she saw the mountain at the end of the run-way two thirds shrouded, and wondered. She knew the only airfield aid was not supposed to be used in anger, but perhaps the guy was in trouble and thought this was the best of bad options. Kieran clearly believed he was just a fool taking a chance.

"Is he coming?"

"See-més so," said the ATC looking out at the mist as though expecting to see the King Air there. "He filéd a plan-n. But still no call. Of course we wait, will he comé?"

"Of course."

They didn't have long to wait before they heard the static on the radio followed by the broken voice of the King Air pilot. He crackled, 'inbound with 20 DME to run.'

"What's 20 dme?" Carrie asked Kieran.

"Naautical mil-lés," answered the ATC, "that-sa pilot's way of say-ing it; dist-ance measur-ring equip-ment."

"Oh, of course."

"Humm," said Kieran, "would you like me to speak to him?"

The ATC shook his head; more than his job's worth presumably to get Mad Kieran on the blower giving his all to the listening birds. To the King Air he said: "King AirN6543 we are VFR only and the runaway is below limits. Plea-sé state your inten-sions."

It struck Carrie that ATCs did very little else apart from asking pilots their intentions. They must be a wow at home: "Darling, do you love me? Please state your intentions."

The King Air pilot replied that he was coming in to land.

Inside the traffic hut the tension was growing. The young controller had never had anything like this to deal with and he had no idea what to do. Meanwhile outside in the foggy, snowy sky there was one lost pilot, who didn't seem to realise the potential trouble ahead. The pilot called long finals, but a glance at the QDM direction indicator on the console showed he was in fact 45 degrees off. Then the pilot called short finals, a few moments later he popped out of the cloud going at 90° to the runway and towards the mountain. As they watched he flew close above the roof before disappearing once again into the cloud. Carrie gasped with shock and ducked.

"Wow," breathed Carrie straightening up, "that was too close!"

"This man," remarked Kieran sagely, calm as the legendary Chuck Yeager, "is going to crash!"

"The ADF," explained the ATC defensively, feeling the pilot's problem was his responsibility, "it doesn't work well in this weather."

The pilot, who must have seen the hut flash by, called again. He was going around and setting himself up once again on the approach. His voice seemed to shake a little and reverberated around the tiny hut.

"..going around, ..around,.. round..nd.."

There was silence, both in the hut and on the radio. Then after tense seconds which seemed like minutes he called re-established; the direction indicator showed he was only 20 degrees off heading.

All three inside the hut were silent, watching the direction indicator needle as it fluctuated left and right, apparently hunting for sound.

The pilot called once more; 10 degrees off. Then silence. Nothing. Nothing. Nothing. The three watchers sat inside the hut waiting. Carrie noticed that the ATC was pulling bits of skin off his fingers. However, when he spoke he seemed calm, and apparently thought the King Air must be able to land safely; he said nothing more into the radio. Kieran, on the other hand, remarked the pilot was probably dead.

"The dead aren't very chatty, you'll have noticed. Mummy, mummy can I play with grand-dad? No darling, you've already dug him up three times today."

Then they heard an eerie, whining sound over the radio.

"Fucking pants!" said Kieran immediately on his feet, ready for action, "his ELT's gone off. Listen!"

Carrie recognised the sound from her incident in Goose Bay. The ATC picked up the radio and called the King Air. "King AirN6543 are you on ra-dió. Sta-té your positio´n and intentio´ns."

There was no reply.

"King AirN6543 aré you on radió. Staté your positio´n."

Still no reply.

Kieran said, "for God's sake man he's crashed. Sound the alarm."

Unwillingly the ATC pressed a red button on his console, activating the siren which spiralled up in a great wail of sound that alerted even the rocks, and no doubt put the Dane with his automatic rifle off his shot at some last remaining song bird.

Out in the snow the whole population of Narssarssuaq, who seldom had this much entertainment in a year, started emerging from their barracks, keen to see what was happening. In only a short while someone was back with the news.

"They've crashed down there on the pack ice. The pilot's OK but his passenger is dead; hit his head on the instrument panel. The plane's a mess. I wouldn't like to be that guy when he next meets his employer!"

"Come on Carrie," said Kieran, "let's go." And he jumped down the steps of the hut in his haste to be out at the scene.

As Carrie followed Kieran down to the crash site she saw Anna and

Knut, who were also going down to see what had happened. The four joined up, Anna immediately falling back in line with Carrie and talking, apparently continuing a discussion she had just been having with her husband about the crashed plane.

"It's dreadful," she said, "absolutely awful. Painful. Frightening."

"Yes, I know..."

"To think such a thing could happen here, of all places."

"Yes, I know..."

"Such injustice. Such unkindness. I've never been so shocked in my life. The whole thing is a complete fandango."

"Yes, yes," Carrie said soothingly, thinking what a soft soul she must be to be so upset about someone else's accident. Most people secretly rather enjoy the excitement even while they empathise with the pain.

"The suffering and just over such a small mistake."

"But it was foolish to come here without warning and in such weath..." Carrie began gently, hoping she would see the pilot was not without blame.

Anna gave a gasp! Clearly stung by such injustice.

"But they did have warning! They knew, they had been informed by letter and by telephone and still they behaved in this terrible manner. And it's not as though they have someone to replace me.."

"To replace you?" Carrie asked confused. "I don't understand. I thought you were talking about the King Air."

"Oh," said Anna, "oh, no, terrible of course that he should have crashed and all that, but I was talking about the gits in the hotel. They have given me a warning. Me! Their best worker, their cleverest and ...they were lucky to get someone from England and not just one of their parochial locals..."

"Oh, I see," Carrie said.

The plane was not as badly smashed as Kieran had predicted. The propellers were all curled over like flower petals in a child's toy, the wings had folded upwards and looked like cardboard but the body of the plane remained intact and solid. The two men, one alive one dead, had been taken on one of the airport golf buggies up to the hotel but there was still blood on the seats. Kieran nudged Carrie and pointed to a scarf dangling over the back of the arm-rest.

"Strange," he said, "how everyday symbols bring out the piquancy of a situation. Yesterday that was just a scarf someone wore around his neck, now it is a scratch on the surface of one man's mortality, an indication that an object continues its existence long after its owner has passed his fragile sell-by date."

Carrie nodded. Death seemed to follow her around, she thought.

At the back of the plane the rudder had twisted, pulling the fuselage into a curve which made it look flabby, like a toy made of malleable foam.

Knut said the plane looked like he felt and cursed his guests for making him drink most of his remaining beers last night. Anna said nothing, still thinking about her manager at the hotel. Kieran started to explain, from the position in which the plane was lying, exactly how it had crashed.

"It looks as though he came up here, .." he rushed off behind the plane, shouting so the group could still hear him, "looks like white-out. You notice he was in line with the runway, which is good, but just too low...it'll probably be his defence, he'll suggest that the navigational instruments were undermined by sea effect, which indeed they may have been, but then that is why this is day and VFR only...."

"Will he be prosecuted?" Carrie, the only one listening to Kieran, asked him. "For coming uninvited as it were."

"Hard to say. International Aviation Law goes up and down like a whore's drawers on a Saturday night. I'd guess it might be a matter for the US FAA since it's an American registered plane. Of course the passenger's estate may sue..."

That evening Kieran lent on the wall next to the kitchen entrance, holding the curtain up by his head, and asked Anna how she came to be living in Greenland.

"Excuse me for committing such a bourgeois liberticide in my curious quest for knowledge, but it's not every day you see a young British girl living in a barrack town of a hundred men in the northern arsehole of the world. As the bishop said to the actress, what is it that made you fasten your seatbelt my dear?"

Anna came into the main room from the kitchen, taking the brown curtain from Kieran and hitching it up on a nail so she could keep an eye on her Svinemorbrad med Gronlangkaal. She took a draught of her beer.

"I used to be a nurse," she said, "I do sometimes help out here if and when necessary."

"Darling," Knut broke in, "you don't have to..curiosity only..you know.."

She smiled at him. "I know, but I think they'll understand. Don't you?"

"Umm, yeah." Knut looked as though he'd rather go and shoot small birds.

Anna went on, either like Carrie earlier thinking conversation with strangers was almost agreeably irrelevant, or really wanting to unburden herself. "I was a night nurse..."

"I thought you got that from a bottle," Kieran laughed. "Were you the genie in the bottle?"

"No," Anna said seriously. "I mean I worked as a nurse at night, in the geriatric ward of a large teaching hospital. This particular night we'd had a busy time, lots of old women screaming for new bandages and singing to get attention. None of the patients had slept all night. Usually we got some time to rest, but that night it was go, go, go all night. All night. I was pooped, and fed up. Before we went off duty we had to give all the old dears their breakfast and then, while they were eating, the shifts changed and the new nurses came on. I'd taken the trays around to my noisier patients and then I got to Mrs Emery. As I approached her bed I noticed she was ignoring me, which was unusual. Normally she perked up at the sight of food. Poor old biddy, eating was almost the only thing she could do unaided. Anyway, I got to her bed and what did I see? She was dead. Excuse me."

Anna went into the kitchen to check her stew. The audience was silent, even Kieran. Anna had spoken so matter-of-factly they were all slightly shocked.

"It's fine, it'll be a while yet before we eat. OK so, as you know, when someone dies in hospital it's all form filling and worse. You have to stuff their holes literally and metaphorically. Well, you know, it had been a long night and I was tired. I didn't want to have to go through all that bureaucracy and bodily nastiness. So, I thought I'd leave it for the next lot. After all they had a whole shift to fill. I drew the curtains, propped her up in bed with her tray, as though she was alive, put her hand on the plate, as though she was about to pick up the bread, and went down to the nurses room to take part in the handover. I knew when the next nurse took over she'd find her dead and think the poor old biddy had just snuffed it, all excited at getting her nosh. The new lot came in, no one noticed she wasn't still alive and I went off home."

Anna drank some more beer. "I wasn't the first to do this, you know, night nurses often..." her voice tailed off. No one spoke and she went on.

"...but unfortunately and unusually, the consultant came to do his rounds early. Consequently the old biddy's daytime nurse hadn't been to look at her before he started on the ward. Even so, it should have been all right really. Anyway, he went into her curtains with his tribe of students and just as he was leaning over saying patronisingly: "Now Mable how are we this morning?" when, bong! She had a rigor mortis spasm and wham! She hit her tray away from the bed and all her milk and cornflakes went over the consultant! Yep!

Was there Hell to pay, when they found out that she had died earlier? It wasn't any good me explaining. The relatives found out too and the hospital wanted a scapegoat....anyway, I saw a job in the paper for a hotel in Narssarssuaq and even though I didn't know where it was, I applied."

She took another draught of beer. "And now the bastards are warning me. Shit. I'm too good for this place. Too good and too clever. Perhaps I'll leave; take my life out in your plane."

"She do not mean it," said Knut, when she went back into the kitchen. "But they've hurt her at the hotel. Mentally I mean. Tonight we eat Kraasesuppe med Melboller (giblet soup with dumplings) and Svinemorbrad med Gronlangkaal, (spare ribs of pork with stewed cabbage). This is one of our favourites."

The next day the weather again hid the mountain under a damp cloud. Kieran suggested a walk above the airfield. Carrie remembered Kees's warning and wondered if she should be suspicious. After all Kieran, with his manicured nails and streaked hair, hardly looked like someone who liked mountain walking. At the same time, she reckoned even the most desperate criminal was hardly going to do away with her here, where the tiny population knew of everyone else's smallest move. To kill her, then leave without her in her plane, was just a little too close to the edge of hope.

Apart from Kees's warning she had no reason to suppose Kieran was after anything other than money: more money. Perhaps, she thought, Kees imagined Kieran might hold her down in the snow until she produced her credit card. Much good that would do him! Kieran was more likely to get his cigarettes out.

The snow was ice-rink hard on the path behind the airfield. As they climbed further, however, it appeared that only the superficial crust remained crisp and their weight took them through the top layer, sinking into a pit of deeper snow, whose wetness enveloped their boots whilst the sides froze instantly. Each footstep became a six inch valley. This combined with the steep ascent, made walking progressively harder. Lifting her feet high, Carrie swung her legs like a trotting horse, her heart beating and her lungs restricted by the cold, so that her breath came out in jolts. For Kieran it was worse. A smoker, a large man and an unfit one, Kieran found a gentle stroll in those lung-catching mountains exercise enough, and their pace was definitely mature. Ice crystals hung on his peroxide moustache like twinkling fairy lights. Once at the top Kieran brought out his cigarettes and took a desperate puff.

"Woof," he said, "but these fags do you good. There's no doubt you wet non-smokers won't live a quarter of my life."

He threw the butt into the pristine snow. Carrie watched it fizzle and disappear into its melting silhouette, before the snow closed over and left it to pollute the future.

As they climbed out through a wet layer of haze they found themselves in clear air. Cloud below obscured the airfield but above that and into the glassy distance were the cornucopian colour shades of the Greenland highlands. Where the snow had fallen off the steep angles, the area looked like an experiment with graduating greys; dark rocks like coal, shading through iron-oxide red and blue to a glittering silverfish grey, before finally fusing with a snow-white brother. Beyond the undulating landscape the frozen fjords led to melted rivers and ultimately into the shining blue distant ocean. The air was so sharp, so crystal clear that everything stood out in severe outline.

"Wow!" said Carrie, her voice coming out in a cloud, "what a view. Definitely worth the walk."

"The walk up maybe. But the walk down, my liberling, is always worse. There you'll find you slip in the heat of your feet and slide on the steepness of the ground. Tell me, has it ever occurred to you your husband might have had another wife?"

Carrie looked at him, momentarily shocked by this swift change of subject. "What? Don't be daft?" She shivered.

"Just a suggestion. I notice you seem to know very little about the antecedents of your beloved ones. Isn't that the case? What was the White Thai before he was number one husband?"

"I..you don't understand...leave it out Kieran! It was love." Carrie hugged herself and walked away from him. She didn't want to talk about her first husband. Nor, however, did Kieran. He followed her, apparently seriously concerned.

"What did your third husband do before you were married? Could he have been married previously? He was around forty...odd not to have married before don't you think? Especially such a good looking, such a physical, man! Not to mention your surprise in discovering he had been in Florida. Buying a plane even. Telling you nothing! Well! And not being properly insured, although you are..."

Carrie gasped, replying before thinking. "How do you know?"

Kieran smiled mysteriously. "With that kind of deception, who knows what your pilot husband might not have been up to! Why not another little expensive pilot-lover tucked away in The Everglades or the heavenly Winter Haven? Or another wife? Who's to say she hasn't met you? Made it her business to meet you? Knows you and is laughing at you. Hence the plane, not from Spain, but in Florida..the rain in Florida stays mainly in the Everglades." Kieran began to sing.

Carrie felt sick.

"He wasn't an airline pilot or a ferry pilot," she retaliated stoutly, "he was a helicopter pilot for various game parks around South Africa. That didn't exactly give him the opportunity for one in every port did it? And he'd only been to Florida once in his life; that's not enough for a wife. Come on let's go down, I'm getting cold."

"Ah, but you're thinking about it now, aren't you," breathed Kieran mischievously. "And you know I have a point: Ignatius the bigamist!"

Annoyed, Carrie flounced down the mountain. Kieran was right about that, though, it was harder down than up and she slid and slipped in the ruts of her feet. Tripping and floundering, she kept her balance by concentrating exclusively on the rocks and snow around her, and on the warmth awaiting back in the village.

"Shit!" Kieran yelled, slipping in her wake. "Damn dog shit!"

"Really Kieran it's not Milou merde but mela," said Carrie, referring to Tintin-related joke she used to have with her friends and knowing her Eurotrash nonsense would baffle him: a small revenge for forcing her to examine doubts in the deepest recesses of her mind.

That night, after some more Danish beers, Kieran asked Knut why he was out in Narssarssuaq. "Is there money to be made here? What made you come here?"

"What do you do with these stories, Kieran?" Knut asked. "Are you interested, or asking for a reason? A reason hé?"

"Mankind, the joy of all desiring. I just like to see the human condition undressed and vital before my eyes. Man unclothed and woman unhung. Tell me a story and I'll show you a reality. There are no imagined happenings. Everything we hear is only a truth or a variation on the truth of somebody, somewhere. There is no story you could tell me that I have not already heard."

"Of course! And yet in my case there is no story. I come here to work minerals, I meet Anna, love her and stay. That is all there is."

It was not until Easter Monday that the weather cleared up. While getting ready to leave and packing the cases into the Warrior, Carrie flicked on the radio. There were two planes transmitting alternately; one calling for start up, the other for landing. This time, though, there were no worries about the landing pilot's safety. The air was thin and blue and the sun was reflecting harshly off the hard, white ice. The mountain reached up to heaven without even scratching a cloud.

Her packing finished, Carrie watched the distant approaching plane. A black spot over the fjord, moving this way fast, like a large bluebottle aiming for a shut window. As she watched, leaning on the Warrior's wing, the other plane's cargo came out of the hangar; the dead man. His corpse, covered in a bed sheet, was wheeled across the apron on the best trolley Narssarssuaq could find: a slightly too short food-shuttle. The man's legs stuck inelegantly beyond the metal base, like a stick out of a termite's nest. Although the man was already dead, a blood sack hovered over the side of the trolley, held in place by a long pole. The attendant passed Carrie at speed, wheeling smoothly over the level ice, when suddenly the front tyre struck a broken stone pricked up through the snow. The shuttle stopped sharply and tipped forward. With slow, ponderous grace the blood sack broke away from its stand and looped across the frozen air, falling heavily with the sound of fat cheeks sucking air. At first Carrie thought the bag had not broken. Then a crimson crawl crept out onto the snow, huge blobs dissolving into thin rivulets and tentacles which edged brokenly through the ice crystals, until there was a huge bloodstain across the snow; as though a Red Widow had been squashed there on the Narssarssuaq apron. Carrie stared obsessed: shivering.

The first plane collected itself for landing; slowed and descended, aiming for the long, black runway ahead, just as the Warrior had done a few days before. Carrie watched him approach, flare and land, touching down early on the runway and taxiing in towards the miniature air traffic control. As he rolled in past the body-carrying food trolley the pilot gave a blast of power. The bed-sheet lifted violently in the wind like an exploding Sainsbury's bag and blew off the body. Carrie turned, compelled by curiosity and the stress of the growing blood pool. She gasped. It was Ignatius. Then the attendant pulled the cover over the corpse and the vision was gone. But Carrie couldn't let it go. She ran up to the trolley.

"Hello?" said the attendant, "I'm sorry if..."

He may have been about to apologise for scaring her, but Carrie wasn't listening. She grabbed an edge of the bed sheet and ripped it off the head. There lay a bearded man, dressed but vulnerably helpless, definitely dead and indisputably not Ignatius. Carrie gaped, gradually realising that she had been wrong. Impossible: of course. Ignatius was already dead, killed in a helicopter crash in Africa. He could not be here.

"I'm sorry" she said, backing away, blind with embarrassment; longing to hide. "I'm sorry, sorry. Really. Sorry." She ran, unaware of her movements.

The attendant shook his head, but he wasn't surprised. In many years of hotel duties he had come to realise that the benign image of a human being was irrelevant; the real thing tiresome, cantankerous and impossible to explain. He loaded his trolley plus body onto the plane.

Just an understandable mistake, Carrie told herself shivering. No problem. No problem. She hastily left the apron, forcing her mind determinedly onto the subject of her bills. No problem. Binding her thoughts, she felt the outline of her purse in her pocket and tried to convince herself that its bulge was the result of money inside, rather than, as was the truth, the fatness of many receipts.

Kieran was already in the office, leaning on the IKEA pine wood desk, having a strong, sweet coffee. "Want one?" He asked as she entered the room. "Strong and sweet like your men?"

"Please." She replied absentmindedly, her thoughts fighting elsewhere.

Kieran gestured to the Cheerful Chappie, who was doing the paperwork. "Mind if she makes herself a coffee."

"No, no," he replied busily, "help yourself love. There is one thing though." He looked at Carrie, not exactly smiling. "If you leave today I'll have to open the airfield specially and that means another $100."

"What!? But one plane's just landed, and another is loading!"

"That's exactly it...I had to charge him a special fee for landing, for you a special fee for taking off. The other, being an emergency plane, is free, but you wouldn't grudge a dead man that, would you?" He gave her a capricious look.

"Surely...." Carrie turned to Kieran for help, but he was looking out of the door, wondering who had just landed, and was indifferent. "Surely, I mean..what's the difference?"

"I can see you're green," said the Cheerful Chappie, now smiling larkily, "it's Transatlantic charges. I can be open for landing, or open for leaving, but if I'm landing and taking off there's another fee. And each pilot must pay his due."

Carrie didn't believe it, but couldn't see how to call him a liar. Last night she had counted her remaining cash and did have just enough to pay the landing fee and the hangarage, but this little extra clear-off fee meant she would have to go for credit.

"I suppose you take credit cards."

"Of course," said the Cheerful Chap, beaming, "but only American Express."

"I've only got Visa."

"Have to be cash then."

"How about a British cheque?"

"Are you gassing me babe?"

"Ah!"

And then she really wondered what to do.

"Can I owe you?"

He laughed sarcastically. "Babe...do you know how far away from anywhere we are? Look outside..is it crowded with gents 'eh? Now! How can I go giving credit? Do I look like a bank?"

"Yeah, sure, thanks," Carrie again looked hopefully at Kieran for help. However he was making coffee for the slim, elderly pilot of the recently landed King Air, and merely smiled vaguely in her direction, nodding without listening and saying nothing, engrossed as he apparently was in the richer man's conversation. Instead the elderly gentleman responded:

"can I help? Is there a problem?"

Carrie was about to demur, when the Cheerful Chappie said "well, sir, if you can lend our little lady here a couple of hundred smackeroos there's no problem at all."

The man smiled gently at Carrie. "Certainly, my dear," he said, "I'd be delighted. American Express OK. How much exactly?"

"Oh, wow," Carrie said overcome with surprise, "thank you so much. You must be my guardian angel. I'll pay you back immediately you send me the bill."

"I know you will," said the man calmly, taking a silver case out of his pocket. "Give me your address. Here's my card. Do you have one?"

Carrie took a card; Kieran immediately lent forward and took another. She meanwhile found a scrappy piece of paper in her pocket and wrote her name on it, plus her cousin's address, in capitals.

"Can you read it all right?" she asked.

The old man looked at the paper. "Carrie Nordsoot..Noodsoort...how do you pronounce that exactly?"

"Nordsuitlaan."

"Oh, I've heard that name before. Isn't there a pilot of that name?"

Carrie's stomach did a barrel roll. Did he have a copy of their wedding photo too? Drive a purple Peugeot? Know girls with names like flowers?

"Why yes, my husband. Was, I mean. He was killed last November in a flying accident."

The old man looked at her for a cool moment, then he said. "Oh, I am sorry. I never met him, but he lent me his mobile home in North Piri Piri airfield. Aviation is such a small world, isn't it."

"Yes," said Carrie, shaken but not allowing the man to know this was the first time she had heard of a mobile home. "It certainly is."

The man paid his own bill and told the Cheerful Chappie he was leaving for Goose Bay as soon as his plane was fuelled.

"I'm sorry you're not going my way," he said turning politely, to Carrie "we could fly together. Or at least," he added, realising the Warrior was hardly up to his King Air's speed, "we could meet at the other end and have a celebratory drink. Goodbye my dear, perhaps we will meet again in England. Goodbye Kieran. Goodbye Jo.. isn't it?"

The Cheerie Chap winked. "Sure is Mr Keenes, Jo King at your service."

Mr Keenes shook all their hands and left the office. Jo King followed him, while Kieran said quietly to Carrie, "do you know who that is?"

"A nice man," Carrie said with feeling. Kieran had been absolutely no help and probably had loads of credit cards or cash tucked away in his leathers.

"Maybe! Certainly in the way Goebels loved his children, but that little man of history is not one who needs to be worried you'll double-cross him. He runs the Essex Mafia you know. No chance you'll get away with cheating him. I imagine he'll break a few of your arms and legs if you run out of money....Funny him knowing your husband 'eh? North Piri Piri too! What a small world indeed." Kieran let the phrase hang in the air, expectantly.

"Thanks," Carrie said defiantly, refusing to let Kieran beat her down, "but don't worry, if I run out of money and can't pay him, I'll explain it was because you tried to increase your fee during the trip and he'll come and break your legs instead. I've heard men are sensitive to young women's legs." Kieran said nothing, but he never mentioned increasing his fees again.

Carrie went to change into her immersion suit.

It was a beautiful late morning by the time they left Narssarssuaq. Carrie was getting a bit anxious; the flight was due to take seven hours and she didn't want to risk landing in the dark.

"Actually," Kieran said, "Warriors prefer the dark. You hear it all the time, don't you. 'The Warriors left it until dark to go for their attack.' Bears fuck in the park, Warriors sack in the dark," Kieran sang.

"Haha."

"Spectacles, testicles, wallet and watch. Let's go get Daddy."

Leaving the airfield the Warrior climbed to 9,500 feet and, still climbing, turned towards the ocean. East of Narssarssuaq the mountains stretch to 9,000 feet, and since the Warrior had managed 11,000 feet in Canada Carrie judged it possible to cross over to the coast that way, thereby cutting off an hour's flying. At first their climb was enhanced by warming and rising air, lifting them up to 10,500 feet. Then, as they crossed a ridge, they were unceremoniously dumped. The Warrior began to sink, slowly at first then gathering momentum, their descent increased by the cold currents which dropped steadily towards the granite floor. With full power, best climbing angle and all human encouragement, they were sinking at 500 feet a minute, caught in a Katabatic downflow on the lee side of the ridge.

"This dog climbs like a pregnant lap licker," said Kieran. "I'm dropping it in the next piece of water and we're swimming."

"Sure you are!" Carrie no longer worried about his mouth.

The Warrior turned down the valley and Carrie once again watched the sides of the mountains getting closer as they slipped further and further into the depths of the fjord. There was nowhere to turn, no chance of returning to the airfield and the only way to go was out towards the sea. She hoped the wind would allow them to go around the tip of Greenland, rather than across the ice turrets, without running out of fuel. The only viable alternative made her think of Ditcher.

"OK, I'm trying this route out to the coast. No more heroics in this bow wow."

They plunged on down towards the coast, still sinking in the warm air, like a man caught in quicksand. Carrie watching the vertical speed indicator wind itself down. The altimeter read 8,500. 8,000. 7,500.

"Look at this piece of excrescence," barked Kieran. "Even a dog would not fly it."

Gradually their vertical speed descent decreased to 400 feet per minute, then 300, 200, 100. The Warrior finally stabilised at 7,000 feet, and its occupants, feeling sick and looking at the peaks of the ridges far above them, heaved a sigh of relief. What was her husband thinking of when he bought this, as Kieran would call it, little Barker? She shivered. Was he really dead? Or could he be still alive and waiting for an insurance payout? Then to return and stake his claim? She no longer knew what was feasible and what was ridiculous fantasy.

The fjord left Greenland at the sea and they followed the peaks and inlets around to Cap Favel, seldom going above 1,500 feet and always looking up at the land beside them. For a while they followed the coast north, but gradually getting further and further away from Greenland and angling east towards Iceland. Carrie felt a strangely sad desolation, as they left the large, inappropriately named, white country behind them and headed once again out into the North Atlantic Ocean. Sea and more sea; a constant reminder that we are but bits of water and chemicals, that will someday return to nothing more than fluid and dust.

At first the weather remained fine, but the next front was already catching up with them and Carrie could feel the cold air behind them, gradually suffusing the little Warrior in its misty wetness. This was Ditcher's downfall-area. She hated seeing the dark approaching with the damp. Fixing her eyes on the sea ahead, desperately hoping to see a volcanic outline, she reminded herself that they still had plenty of fuel, the wind was light and the instruments were working; mostly.

Four hours into the flight, Kieran suggested they use the HF radio to make a telephone call. "It's a speciality of Transatlantic flying! Want to ring your little cousin, the harbinger of sweetness and light, as opposed of course to being a harpy of sharpness and fight? Wouldn't it cheer the little cockles of your heart to hear her happy voice prattling away from Peckham? And wouldn't she, who is no doubt fretting about your safety, be lifted to hear your voice from out the blue of the Atlantic Ocean."

"OK," said Carrie, "it might be a laugh, let's try her."

Kieran called up on the HF radio, got the operator and gave him

Roberta's number. The operator dialled Roberta and there on the other end of the echoing radio was Carrie's cousin.

"Hello," said Carrie, conscious of the echo in the call and the lag before it reached the other end. Hello, Roberta it's me, Carrie."

"So I see," replied Roberta, "what do you want? Shit, that phone has a terrible echo..."

"Nothing particular," said Carrie, because of the lag cutting in before Roberta had finished. "I just thought it would be fun to call you from the Atlantic."

"Oh. Did you? Your half-witted lawyer seems to think it's fun to call me from South Africa too."

"Oh? What did he want?"

"Phrr. He said he had some answers for you and some questions. Git! Then I got some babble, did I know about your husband's background? I can tell you I gave him pretty short shrift on that. I wanted to know whose money he was wasting on this international phone call. Must be yours. Ever known a benevolent lawyer? Then he said he'd put it all in a letter. In which case why did he waste my time, 'eh?"

"Oh, I'm sor..."

"And the Rozzers have been by again. Great heffalumps! Wasting my time with their nonsense. Apparently they are pretty certain who killed your friend Ben, although they weren't telling me. Gits! They seemed worried about your health. That's a laugh, I told them people like you outlive fiddles. Time wasters!"

"Oh, I'm sorr.."

"Was that all you wanted?"

"Yes...I..er..why.."

"Goodbye then."

Carrie heard the echoing click of the receiver being returned to its seat, slightly delayed by the lag. Her own "goodbye" being too late.

"Usual cheery self was she?" asked Kieran happily.

Carrie said nothing, looking out at the darkening damp, wondering what had excited the lawyer enough to ring her all the way from South Africa. What answers, which questions? Had he found the missing money? What did the detectives want? If they'd really thought she was in danger, Roberta would have taken it seriously, wouldn't she? The little Warrior swept on over the Atlantic waves.

Kieran tried to call Reykjavik on the radio. No response.

"Oh, no," said Carrie sarcastically, hearing the reverberating silence, "it's not Christmas now is it. Have we been asleep for half a year?"

"Very funny, my child,...." began Kieran, but he was interrupted by another call on the radio.

"N2122 this is Speedbird 41 do you receive?"

"Ah," said Kieran, "a passing British Airway's bird has come to the rescue. Let's hope he doesn't shit on us! Never shit on those below you in case one day they end up above you."

Carrie looked up into the sky, imagining she might see a British Airways carrier passing overhead, but could see nothing but mist. "How do they..."

Kieran silenced her with his hand. "Hello Speedbird, Warrior November22 very glad to hear you and hoping you can relay a message for us to Reykjavik."

"Sure can, good buddy," replied Speedbird cheerfully, "pass me your details."

The Speedbird relayed their first message, but then asked their distance from Keflavik on the DME 111.2. Kieran replied 70 miles and Speedbird, after repeating the information to Reykjavik reported back to them: "I'm told by Reykjavik that Keflavik are receiving you. Call Keflavik on 119.3"

"Thanks Speedbird, have a good one."

"Same to you Warrior. Bar's open in half an hour. Speedbird out!"

Kieran flicked the dials over to 119.3 and called Keflavik on the radio. They directed him to fly overhead, and were already telling him about the best approach when Carrie saw land. Burdened by her overwrought imagination she cheered.

As they drew nearer, the island became more detailed; the flattened volcano was decorated with brown tufts of chocolate icing whipped in a bowl. In the near distance twinkling lights flashed like beacons, while beyond was a compelling desolate expanse, a vacant, chocolate slab parking lot.

As they approached the spit of land holding the Keflavik military airfield the Warrior gave a leap of pride; Kieran broke his unusually thoughtful silence to say it was a gust. They passed over the closed airbase. Carrie noticed a little jeep driving amongst the airfield's darkly outlined runways and hangars, its pencil-light headlamps illuminating a man walking in the opposite direction. Then they flew on into the darkness down the coast.

For a while, after leaving the beams on military airfield, the return to the lightless night with the clamminess of the black sea below tempted Carrie to believe it had all been an illusion; there was no island, no spit of land, no airport; only a delusion brought on by misty hope. Then to their right, gradually shining out of the increasing dusk, appeared the coloured, corrugated iron roofs which made up downtown Reykjavik. At first there were just one or two, then a whole host popped out of the mist. Bright reds, blues, greens, yellows: they gave the countryside the colourful element that nature had left out; architects had reproduced the flow-ers that God forgot.

Flat, brown Iceland was so noticeably different from the white moun-tains of Greenland that it was amazing they were often referred to in one breath; twin brothers with totally opposing characters. Here they were no longer at the edge of the world but moving back into civilised society: Iceland has a famous opera house. And Bjork.

Reykjavik airport. An enormous airfield with six runways, but as busy as a vegetarian cafe in Argentina. It seemed they were the only people on the radio and the only plane landing. To the left of the airfield were air-port buildings, hangars and a large hotel, and in the distance a return to snow splattered, brown-grey lava leftovers.

They flew over the town and landed on runway 32. Kieran taxied in and parked on the tarmac, away from the larger jets but next to another Lear Jet 45.

"The Warrior must be getting rather used to Lears," Carrie said to Kieran, "everywhere she goes the ATC seem to put her next to them."

"Especially this one."

"Huh?"

"This is the same one she was next to in Teterboro, don't you recognise it. Look up at the registration, that's a hell of a give away my smart little Hawk-eye."

Carrie looked up and sure enough it was indeed the same Lear 45.

"Hey! Great! That means Mitch.."

"Yes, and your jolly ex-husband too. I'll unload the bags if you like, while you book us in at the hotel. Ask someone to come and get the things, I'm too pooped to carry them." Climbing out on the wing he lit a cigarette and scraped the other hand through his hair.

Sympathetically she realised he did look tired, and was once again hit by the fact that he was a smoker, over 40 and, although he carried his weight well, was not fit. Not someone you'd expect to do a long trip including three nights on a hard Greenland futon without some exhaus-tion setting in.

"Sure. I'll do that. I'm sure they can get the bags out of the plane too," Carrie suggested obligingly.

"Maybe. Off you go."

Carrie went, hurt that he so obviously wanted to get rid of her. As she reached the hotel door she looked back. Kieran was climbing the steps up into Lear Jet.

Surprised but assuming he'd been invited in, she walked into the hotel, looking for the reception. Compared to Wabush, Goose and Narssarssuaq this place was so sophisticated Carrie found herself suffering from culture shock, and had to remind herself she was a trendy from Cape Town. As she walked through the central sofas she saw Kees and Mitch relaxing silently on the hard, IKEA striped cushions.

"Hey! I thought you were out in the plane."

Mitch jumped up and spun around, her pearls side-slipping on her jumper.

"Hi ya Carrie, where've you been? We thought you'd be ahead of us. In England yonks ago."

"Nice idea. I don't think Kieran's in a hurry."

"No?" asked Kees. "You left New York pretty quickly, I thought there was a dog at your heels. What's the definition of slimy? An eel in a bowl of snot."

Mitch was nodding, tucking her pearls back into her shirt. "Absolutely. Talking of the old boy, where is Kieran anyway? I thought he was the one who always walked ahead."

"Very funny! To be honest, that's why I thought you were in your plane, I just saw him climbing in there."

Mitch jumped up. "You did?! I think I know what that is about, come on Kees. You were right!"

Before a Dutchman could have said another proverb, they chose the 'path of the hare' and were out of there. Bemused, Carrie went to the desk to register.

When she returned to the apron with the bell boy, the three pilots were standing in uneasy conversation next to the Warrior. Kieran smoking like a man on his last gasp, Mitch hopping around like a nervy embarrassed sparrow and Kees hunched up; the world's pain on his right shoulder obviously increasing.

"What's going on?" Carrie asked Kees, as Mitch, Kieran and the bell-hop strode ahead of them across the tarmac. He looked at her softly, noticing how the reflecting hotel lights gleamed on her fair hair, transforming it into a welcoming beacon in the dark. He shuddered suddenly, torn by conflicting emotions he didn't want to understand.

"What? Is it something I did? Something I said?" Carrie asked nervously; confused.

"Don't start jumping into conclusions," replied Kees. "I can't tell you such much. But so to say Kieran is not as he seems, schatje."

Having said, 'such little' he trotted off to join the others. Carrie remembered that was another tiresome habit of her husbands: all about as open as a Group Four lock-up. Perhaps something would slip out eventually.

The four of them had dinner in the hotel restaurant, a large room divided into quarters with wooden columns and fences between, rather as though animals had once been penned there. Kieran ordered four beers to start. "But none of your alcohol free muck, OK. Alcohol free is to the stomach what blood was to Robespierre."

"Only wine," said the tall waitress, looking at him as though she thought he was purposely trying to upset her, "we don't drink beer in the hotel at Easter or on Sundays. It's a mark of respect for the past."

"Ah ha! All part of the Colonialists committing liberticide against the poor indigenous innocents," said Kieran, "the Icelandics hated the Danes and wouldn't allow any beer into the country on holy days. There was a huge riot and thousands of Icelandics were massacred, there was blood on the streets....."

"Not true," corrected Kees, "it was always, not just holy days. No beer in Iceland stronger than 2.2% after independence already. That's why the people leaving Holland, you saw, bringing such much crates of beer on their shoulders to Iceland."

The waitress tapped her pad, bored of these history lessons. "You want wine or not?"

"Oh, yes, please," said Mitch. "Anything you can recommend?"

"I can't recommend anything until I know what you are eating," she remarked puristically.

"Then we'd better order fish," said Kieran, "fish should always be drunk with red wine, meat with white because it best brings out the taste of your food..."

Mitch sighed loudly. "For Goodness sake, shut off your rubbish! We'll have a bottle of the house red. And I'll have steak and chips." She gave Kieran a challenging look, .

Kieran shrugged and returned to arguing with Kees. Carrie's mind wandered. Kees loved trivial facts, Kieran loved a contest; she just wanted to get her plane home, sell it, find the missing money and start a new life. She wondered what the lawyer knew and whether it was worth the cost of an international call. Nine o'clock local, the same as the UK so, eleven o'clock in South Africa. No lawyer works that late, especially on Easter Monday. Easter Monday! She'd forgotten. When did he ring? If it was during the Easter Weekend it must be serious. And then there were the police...

"How was your flight, Carrie?" Asked Mitch, breaking in to her reverie. "How was the little Warrior over so much sea. One engine and two pilots. That's something I've never done. I prefer two engines and one pilot."

"Oh, you're so right," began Carrie, longing to discuss all the deep emotional feelings provoked by the flight. "It was strange. I don't know if you feel this way Mitch, but I felt as though there was no Iceland, no country ahead, only sea and sea and more sea, which would never end. I began to think the Warrior, Kieran and I were the only beings still left on a waterlogged planet; to wonder if we would ever see land again. Slightly surreal. I asked myself if anything really had consequences...a life-sized computer game going on, but never really happening at all. At one point I wanted to push the stick forward, to bury the little Warrior in the ocean.."

"I'm glad you didn't," said the practical pilot, "actually ferry pilots have to fight against those sorts of emotion! Personally I like to play a cheerful CD in my headsets to keep the gloom away."

"Oh!" Carrie felt deflated; a hysterical monster punctured by reason.

"You are very eccentric Mitch," Kieran interrupted roughly, "I would say even idiosyncratic. Not only do you fly in pearls, but a little birdie told me you were the last person to see a certain young man before his death..."

Mitch flared at him passionately, intellectual fists clenched. The complex anger of a wounded woman against a mercurial man.

"Actually I'd watch it if I were you. I think your position regarding me is a bit weak right now, wouldn't you say? If I were you I wouldn't go holding myself the Lord of the Universe unless you are interested in revelations that make the Bible look tame!"

Carrie perked up, hoping Mitch's angry challenge was going progress into disclosures, but Kieran shrugged and reverted to his discussion about beer.

Pilots' Pals

The next day the weather was appalling; low clouds zipped past the hotel windows, chased by driving, sleety rain, which lashed the Warrior and Lear stationed on the saturated tarmac, so their long noses seemed turned-in, bottoms rucked up like dejected hackney horses. Mitch watched the dripping dreadlocks and decided there was no way she was leaving Iceland this morning.

"I checked the Metars and the weather's on the ground in the Faeroes," she explained to Kees, "even if we could get out of here, I'm not sure we'd get in anywhere north of the UK actually, so we're better off staying and biding our time."

Kees said he was happy with the speed of the snail, while Kieran murmured hopefully that the Heavens were open to any who dared test their blue delights and wander far, far away.

"We're going to visit the hot springs, Carrie. Do you want to come?" asked Mitch as they ate breakfast. "They're not far and apparently they are well worth visiting."

Carrie was making a mound with her breakfast, piling the unwanted Parma ham on top of its melon, wondering why she hadn't stuck just to coffee. "Yeah, I'd be.."

"She can't!" cut in Kieran.

"Can't! Why not? What can't?" Carrie's knife hit the plate, so that her melon skidded onto the floor. She watched it thoughtlessly. "What's it got to do with you?"

"Gently my little one," sang Kieran, also watching the falling melon, "and rock him when he cries, the day may come when baby now, is director of the sighs. I've arranged for me and you to be interviewed by the editor of Flugette, the local flying rag. A flying rag is better than ragged flying. He was all gung ho about the idea of a girl from South Africa bringing a plane from Florida all the way to little old homestead in Cape Town. Especially after I told him your sad, romantic story."

Carrie picked up the melon, returning it to her plate. "Do I want to be interviewed by the editor of Flugette? Besides we're not going further than..."

"He doesn't know that. It might help you make some money! Think of the lecture tours, the books, the articles, the fame. There is mileage to be made here."

"Oh, I see. Maybe."

In spite of Mitch pointing out that ferry pilots brought planes across the pond constantly and Kees saying there was the chance of a massage at the springs, Carrie agreed to accompany Kieran. Money and potential striking a cord in her needy heart. However, they did arrange to all meet for dinner.

"Take care Carrie," said Kees, "I must nothing, so to say. But make careful. Kieran is a louse with a sore head."

The interview was supposed to be at 10 o'clock, but at 9.45 Kieran still hadn't arrived in the hotel lobby. Carrie cursed. She looked at her watch and wondered why some people were always late. Time moved on. 9.50. Carrie walked towards to the lifts, hoping wildly that Kieran would be coming out as she reached them. Still no Kieran. She went into the lift and pushed the button for the 15th floor.

In the lift was a plaque which read:

"Would be spare? Take the stair.

Rather be swift? Take the lift."

At the 15th floor there was still no Kieran. Snail-like she crawled towards his room. The door was ajar and she hesitated for a while outside. Finally she strode in boldly, calling his name.

"Kieran. Kieran. Are you there?"

Kieran was on the bed reading a magazine. He dropped it guiltily, but not before Carrie saw the front cover; a naked girl climbing a rope, half covered by a slithering snake, on her face a mask which left only her mouth exposed.

"My God!" She said frankly, "how disgusting! Where did that come from?"

"Oh, they come free with the room."

"Wow! They are liberal in Iceland! But I didn't get one in my room."

"Yes, indeed," Kieran muttered. "Am I late? Never apologise, never explain as Disraeli might have said, had he had the sex drive of Gladstone. OK, spectacles, testicles, wallet and watch...off we go.."

Flugette's office was a few blocks from the airfield. They walked there through the snow, Carrie bundled up in sheepskin boots and a duffel coat that Mitch had lent her, Kieran in elegant crocodile boots and a black leather jacket with matching hat.

"It feels like Christmas with all this snow," said Carrie lightly, "do you think the editor will have a white beard and give us presents?"

"Maybe," replied Kieran absently. "Look! The Phallogical Museum, there I shall donate my body parts for streams of women to ogle in delight."

"Ah," said Carrie blankly, uncertain whether her internet education covered that.

Kieran glanced at his watch, his long fingers simultaneously flicking his cigarette into a drift, while Carrie pushed through the double doors. Reinforced woollen draft absorbers with plastic rims, they sighed slightly as they scraped against the wooden jambs. Inside the poorly lit office Carrie blinked, hemeralopic after the outside glare. Fluggette's editorial workplace was more of a long passage than an office, and was heavily over heated, compensating for the paralysing cold outside. Carrie stopped dead in the confined area, staring at the walls. Kieran, for once not striding ahead, cannoned into her back.

"Opps, breaks on and mind out to lunch, was it knowledge or did she stop on a hunch? What's happened my poppet, the muscles seized after all this resting, the spirit was willing but the legs were weak?"

"Umm, I was expecting.... I mean.. this is a flying magazine isn't it?"

She moued at the walls covered in semi-clothed women posed on planes, some some sitting cross-legged on the wing or spread-eagled over the nose.

"Cop an eye-ful," said Kieran appreciatively. "Real class arse."

"I suppose I should have expected it," Carrie continued, "Iceland is so liberal ..."

"Not just Iceland, my little love," said a voice from the depth of the room. "Flugette is an International Magazine. I can tell you we have a circulation of more than one million through many countries of the world. 'Flugette, the flag of a million homes all over the globe' that's our motto! 'Popular in Palestine', 'Irreplaceable in Israel'. And not only men read our magazine. Surveys show we have a very distinctive female allegiance. Very! As you girls know, flight is for all!"

The voice materialised out of the gloom, appearing part by part like graphics on a website. First, black hair at medium height, then an extra chin. Sideboards followed, giving him the spooky appearance of an Elvis look-alike. There was something forcibly sleazy about him. "Elvis found in Iceland," thought Carrie and giggled.

Elvis rolled over with a lolliping dance. "Nicey spicey 'eh, foxy? All our gals are pilot's pals! Ready for their job's worth and more, I think you know what I mean. Marshallers, signalling ready for unmasting." His voice changed. "So, Kieran to business. Here you have brought me a very pretty girl but a very hot one! Let me help you take your clothes off. I like to talk to cool chicks." He winked at her.

"That's all right," Carrie said tartly, "now I know you give porn mags away in the hotel rooms, I realise Iceland is quite a different country. In fact I brought myself. And I'll keep my coat thanks."

The editor raised his eyebrows at Kieran, who shrugged. The editor pulled a male-bonding face. He looked at Carrie, who had just noticed a Leopard Club sticker on the wall and was staring at it perturbed.

"Smack my wrist," he said roguishly. "Now, my dear, are you South African? You sound British. Very British. Bullish Brit beats liberal SA chicks with batons!"

"That sticker..."

Elvis looked and nodded. "Oh, yes we get many presents from content-ed readers. Where was that from...oh Britain...you a member are you?"

"This is Mrs Nordsuitlaan," intervened Kieran. "So, where do we start? By the plane, or would you like to ask us some questions in here first. I expect you'll want to take some photographs."

"Although of course only Kieran will be naked," Carrie joked. For the second time Elvis's eyebrows shot up and Kieran shrugged.

Hope Springs Eternal

Mitch drove Kees and herself over to the hot springs, in silence. The roads were good but all the car headlights beamed challengingly, even though it was daylight. Outside the steamy windows the weather fell in buckets; inside it was worse, a slicing tension fracturing the air as though they had rowed and not made it up. In fact they never argued. Mitch seldom rowed at all, her major interest being flying, and Kees spoke little. Only with Carrie and Kieran did the conversation leave the level of instruction.

Mitch felt a little uneasy about Carrie. Carrie spoke four languages and while her flying skills were still green, she had a good feel for the machine. However, Mitch feared, she had too much imagination. In contrast, Mitch knew herself to be unidimensional. An intelligent woman with a quick grasp of technical issues, whom those outside flying considered dull, she found it hard to sympathise with people when they allowed their private lives to affect their flying. Particularly Kees, who, since re-meeting his ex-wife, had been fidgety and had stopped concentrating. Mitch would be glad when the trip was over.

"What's the matter Kees," she asked hoping to improve the atmosphere by talking. "Is it Kieran and Carrie?"

"Yes, I think we should tell her already. About...about...Kieran..."

"What for? The trip is almost over. It will only make her nervous, actually and he's not going to do anything. Not now we've warned him."

Kees wrinkled his face. "Maybe he make to seduce her and then you see what he likes doing already.." Kees was apparently too full of horror to continue.

Mitch glanced at him skeptically, amused. "I do believe you are jealous," she remarked bluntly.

"No of course not, she gave me the hard shoulder. But maybe I don't like that she is upset, so to say."

"She won't be hurt, Kees. I've met the Carrie type before actually; and they are much tougher than they seem. She appears sweet and passive, letting other people do what they want with her but underneath she is like a ...a... Chinook...."

"What!" Kees suddenly laughed. "You mean a weapons carrier with twin rotors! Nice simile! Carrie foresure!"

Aggravated Mitch shook her head and returned to the point. "A girl like Carrie will see out an old kink like Kieran any day."

"Humm. Why did he want to bring her to the editor of that dreadful magazine? It's a a...a Chinook eater!" Unable to express himself in English, Kees began to mutter in Dutch.

Mitch shrugged. The whys of Kieran's mind were a closed book she had no inclination to open. "Publicity perhaps? Or money. The circulation is large actually."

"Sure! I know so things. But why Carrie? Is she to stand naked on her plane? In the snow?"

"I shouldn't worry about it Kees, I don't think the interview has anything to do with Carrie at all. Actually I rather suspect old Kieran has a separate agenda. Perhaps he wants to be in the magazine himself. Or maybe he's stocking up on supplies. Whatever! Carrie's a big girl, she can look after herself."

Kees said nothing, sorry they had discussed it. He saw Mitch as an unimaginative, practical women whose reason held no grey areas. Obviously she had no understanding of the complicated woman in Carrie; the vulnerability. Not that he felt anything..that was finished, but...she did look good. He shook his head and tried to concentrate on the excitement of the approaching hot springs.

Queen of the Scene

When they met for dinner, in one of Reykjavik's finest restaurants, Kieran was full of the interview, telling tales of how amused and interested the editor had been by his adventures.

"I think he saw I was a pretty unusual chap. There may be a lot of ferry pilots around but he could see I was rather different; when the going gets tough, the tough go Warrioring...She was sorrier for the Warrior than I, when I bid my baby goodbye.."

"Absolutely," said Mitch, "but not necessarily in the way that would make interesting reading in a flying magazine, even such a grown-up one."

"What do you mean by that? Princess Mitch! If you are referring to the girls on the planes I consider them to be very tasteful. Where are you leading with this line in questions?"

Mitch bristled. "Leading with this line of questions? Is that a form of threat? "

"Princess Mitch, Queen of the scene. I tell you young woman, I've had girls like you gagging. I said GAGGING...begging me for it. I've had girls cleverer, prettier and richer than you...."

"Yeah," drawled Mitch, "then you can save it for them actually, don't bother me with your ego..."

Carrie yawned, bored by the Mitch and Kieran Show. She looked out of the iron-cut window. The tall wattle and daub building had once been the house of a botanist, and shadowed Reykjavik's large central lake. Around the lake antique gas lamps provided little clear circles of light at regular intervals. Ducks slid in and out of the lights, looking like tiny Atlantic ghosts gliding through the centre of town.

Carrie felt relaxed, but simultaneously nervous depression lapped, barely controlled, under the surface. She still hadn't yet completed the job. The plane still wasn't safely home and the missing money was unfound. Besides, although she preferred to avoid the thought: Ignatius's body was also still missing. Could Kieran be right? Could Ignatius have slipped off to another wife in Florida? Could the whole gamepark have been in on the conspiracy? Surely impossible. Pierre? An accomplice to murder? No! She had tried to ring Mr Barbar this afternoon, only to be told by his secretary that he was out of the office for a week. A week! A week before she could hear any answers. Meanwhile Mitch and Kieran wrangled remorselessly like an incompatible brother and sister forced to share a bedroom.

Kees turned spontaneously to Carrie. He was glad to see her. He was amazed how much he had looked forward to her arrival this evening, as though they were suddenly back at the zenith of their original passion. He watched her for a moment as she studied the ducks, without a clue that she was thinking about death and her third husband. He felt a strange physical pull towards her, and moved his chair a little closer to her, smiling gently into her eyes.

"How was your day Carrie? Did you right to the buff for the hungry photographer go?"

"Hardly! I'm far too bony and oddly shaped," she replied, still watching the ducks. "Those girls were much more...you know.." she shrugged and her eyes raised to his, before sliding quickly away, embarrassed by what she saw there.

He laughed indulgently, unaware of the withdrawal of her gaze. "Oh! So if you were fatter you'd strip?'

"No, of course not.." she cried incensed, her eyes flying back to his face, before realising he was teasing and looking down at the table again. "Oh, you're joking, Kees. I forgot that's your thing!"

Kees liked that, taking it as an acknowledgement of his underlying humanity, of her involvement with him as a person rather than as a source of information.

"Yes, but the magazine I saw. Not only aeroplanes, plenty of lekker wives for the bouwvakkers."

Lekker wives. Bow-fuckers. Funny language. Whereas Kieran would have called a woman a sexy bitch if he fancied her, Kees talked about lekker wives; tasty women! And Dutch food was so dreadful, only one step up from their bathrooms! Perhaps the women were tasty to compensate.

Bouwvakkers were builders in Dutch, something she'd always found funny, but went almost unnoticed by the Dutch themselves. Clearly Kees was trying to get her attention, to bolster her amusement. She understood and tried to be sympathetic, although in reality her nervous unease about the future decreased her concentration.

"Ah," she said. "Then he'll probably make it up. Kieran talked and talked, I hardly said a thing. He didn't ask me much either. In fact I left them for a while to go and brush the snow off the plane, and when I got back Kieran was still talking."

"Still talking, hoor? Amazing!"

This time Carrie realised he was making a joke and half smiled.

"Do you know, Carrie, from what the word pilot comes?" Kees asked enthusiastically.

"From pilot boats in the harbour isn't it?"

"Forsure. But before that?"

"No. Do you?" She asked, without much interest but glad to have him fill the silence which would otherwise ensue.

"Forsure. It's from the Dutch words 'peilen' to measure and 'lood' a lead. The pilots dropped a lead weight out of the boat to measure the depth...hence pilot. Good hoor."

"Really!"

"More: logbook. To measure their speed they threw a log on a string out back the boat and drawing it in showed how quickly they go, which is well registered in the logbook."

"Really.."

"The rope was tied with knots. Each space between the knots was a certain length hence.."

"..hence, sea speed and then airspeed, in knots. How interesting!"

Carrie watched the ducks while Kees smiled warmly, assured of her approbation.

"Will you come back to America, Carrie, when your trip it is over already?"

Carrie dwelt on this for a moment, wondering whether the 'come' arose from a linguistic mistake or reality. She decided to take his English at face value.

"Come? Have you left Holland then?"

"Yes."

"But I thought you loved Holland. You refused to move to South Africa..."

"I a fool was," said Kees, moving still closer to her, putting his arm on the table next to hers, so she could feel his hair on the skin of her hand. "I still had cheese in my blood, now apples."

His ex-wife laughed, smelling not cider but wine on his breath.

"Well, well," she said. "Well, well, what a surprise."

One of the major fallouts between them had been her dislike of living in Holland with its constant wet weather, dreadful bathrooms, herrings and cheese. Once you start on the road to divorce though, many more things join the original sins. But that had been the turning point: her desire to live anywhere with sun, running water and hills.

"I've bought a house .." Kees started.

"With my alimony I suppose," Carrie said, regretting it immediately but remembering sharply how much it had cost her to give up part of her White Tie's money to pay off her penniless second husband.

"Godverdomme no! I spent that money on learning to fly! No, Oom Jan died, remember him? The money I used buying a house in Idaho, good value. Since longtime you are welcome to come over." Kees smiled gently at Carrie, again feeling a memory of their love. "Often I remember," he said, "how we are visiting Venice in the spring..."

"So what are you two love-birds crooning about," broke in Kieran. "Enough of this mental masturbation, the armour of the bourgeoisie against the activity of the proletariat. Now my little sweet-cake, Lady

Mitch here has kindly offered to foot the whole bill. Won't that brighten your little bourgeois life a peek? Although I think we should refuse, it seems to me that the Queen of Mitch is getting far too grand for us mere mortals who worship at her feet...."

After dinner Carrie felt tired. She said goodbye to the others as they made their way towards the hotel bar. Kees stopped and gave her a good-night hug.

"Goodbye," he said, "is not the end but a call to the future, when you can say hello again. Goodbye means Hello!"

Mitch and Kieran just waved, walking towards the bar, arguing about something trivial that anyone else would have let go.

Carrie left them and took the lift to the second floor. As the lift door opened into the corridor the human sensitive lights started to flicker, then fluttered, suggesting they would eventually light fully, given time. Finally they burst into light, just before she closed her room door. Once inside, surrounded by floral wallpaper, she flopped onto the bed, turned on the TV, and flicked through the channels, looking for news.

CNN had a customer-call-in show with a previously disgraced Evangelical priest. He was explaining that really he'd never gone wrong, but that God had merely tested him and his followers and was planning a new route for him through the jail yard, when she heard a tap on the door.

"Hello?" Carrie said, across the space and through the wood, unwilling to be disturbed. "Who is it?"

There was a little silence and then Kees's voice whispered, "Carrie?" across the divide. "It's me. Can I enter?"

Goodbye, she thought, was never so short. "Kees, what do you want?"

"Can I in-come?"

For a moment Carrie thought about it. Thought about his little house in Idaho. Knew he wanted a return to the past. Knew the softness she had seen in his eyes had not been mere candlelight twinkling. Knew even that she still retained a flame of affection for him too. That that way would lead to a much easier life for her.

"No, sorry Kees, I'm tired, go away."

He did. But five minutes later there was another knocking on the door. Carrie was torn between anger and admiration; Kees never usually showed much spirit when things didn't go his way. Then she heard Kieran's voice speaking into the wood.

"Carrie, are you there? I just wanted to have a chat about the morning. Bit of flight planning. Tie up a few loose ends, don't you know. As the actress said to the reacting circus master, bring on your troop, troop on your bins..."

She looked at her watch. It was midnight. Before they had parted they had spoken briefly on the likelihood of bad weather tomorrow and decided to wait and see. She was pretty certain that it wasn't flight planning Kieran had in mind either. Bloody Hell, she thought, must be something in the fresh Icelandic air: or the free magazines.

"Sorry Kieran," she lied, "I've just put a face mask on and I wouldn't come out of my tomb wearing that."

He too went away and Carrie wondered what wicked crime Kieran had committed. She didn't think it would stop her sleeping. Indeed she slept so well and dreamt so deeply that by the time she got up in the morning the Lear Jet and its occupants had gone and Kieran was also ready to leave. Elvis the editor came to wave them goodbye.

"Goodbye Canoodling Carrie from the Cape," he said, kissing her hand. "I enjoyed our chat. If ever you want to be in the magazine again let me know. I do love the south, it's just such a pity about the snakes. Remember, being in Flugette means sharing in over a million homes all over the globe! Carrie in Cairo. Kieran in Kenya."

I Follow Roads

The last leg was seven and a half hours from Iceland to Prestwick. Carrie had decided she was doing all the flying from now on: things only went wrong when Kieran was at the controls. She took off on the southeast runway and turned left towards the south coast. The crystal clear air smelt fresh and slightly fishy through the storm window. A strong spring sun warmed the former volcano and the rock glistened with recent rain. The Warrior flew over the harsh brown, rutted earth to the coast. There was something so elevating about this volcanic remnant; appealing in the way an icy wind is compulsive in a hot, tropical climate.

Kieran pointed out a couple of pieces of volcanic rock in the sea just off the south coast of Iceland. One was small and unoccupied but the other had a dorp and even a landing site on it. "Look over there. That is the newest piece of rock in the world. The result of the shift in the Atlantic plate in the sixties. Great time the sixties, upheaval everywhere; not only in music and politics! Look at that little island. Been here for less than forty years and already full of trippers. Where do you go if you've nothing to do in Iceland? Not over the sea to Skye like us but, out to sea to see a volcano. Or as the actress said to the bishop, I love your eruptions!"

The sun warmed the Warrior, and Carrie couldn't quell her hopeful mood. They were nearly home. Nearly safe. Nearly onto the roller coaster of success. Carrie flew higher than Kieran, at 1,000 feet,.

"What difference does it make?" Kieran countered her unspoken question. "Even if you get the little rescue row-boat out you won't last long out here in March. We fall as hard from 150 feet as from 1050 feet, so take off your clothes and show off your plenty. Oh sweet Molly Malone, there was a girl who baked a good bone." Kieran sang.

Carrie said nothing and watched the sea and sky swell on and on and on to infinity. It was hard to envisage anything more insubstantial than this little Warrior 1000 feet above the Ocean, going on its journey, while the whole of the world in its vast variety continued with day to day life. She stared at the water mesmerised, hearing Elvis editor saying; "Flugette flown in a million homes. Indispensable in Iraq." She laughed. This was good; could she ever go back to real life again?

Just as they came in sight of the Scottish coast, a bank of cloud arose from nowhere to obscure the shore. A deep thick impenetrable cloud. Suddenly they could see nothing except dank, grey fog. There was no way of passing through; it was as high as a mountain and had emerged from the bottom of the sea. The little Warrior flew up and down, looking for a gap, trying to climb it or sink below it but there was simply no way around.

Carrie felt desperate. So close to Scotland and suddenly they couldn't see it any more. They'd gone too far from Iceland to go back, but now they were blocked from going on. She had done a few hours of instrument flying but was scared to risk going into cloud. She knew Kieran hated instrument flying, he'd said so. What could they do? Would they end up sinking into the sea only a few miles away from safety? Dying here on the shores of her own country.

Then suddenly Carrie saw a little gap. This was it!

She turned into the gap and was immediately swallowed into cloud. Biting her lower lip, her eyes glued to the artificial horizon, she held as steady a course as she could. Slowly she realised she could do this if she concentrated. On and on they flew until suddenly they broke cloud and were once again in cold, clear air and in sight of Scotland. Shaking, she flew on towards the coast and future sales.

Crossing into the Scottish Isles Carrie climbed to 2,000 feet and flew on over Stornaway. Kieran called the ATC on the radio to tell them cheerfully they were not landing, just passing through. They replied that they were closed anyway.

"Thank God!" Carrie thought, "we weren't planning to land there, or that would inevitably be yet another fine."

Her mood of trepidation changed at Prestwick. They really were almost home. Almost safe. Worst case, she could get a lorry and drive the plane home.

"We've done it!" she gasped, suddenly overpowered by the magnitude of what they had just achieved. "We've done it! Whoppe! Yippee! Waha! We have crossed the Atlantic in a tiny, weeney little plane! Wow. What will Roberta say now!?"

Ahead of her, she thought, was just a short flight on to the south of England, then a sale and loads of profit. Then wealth! Money! A new life.

"My God, they'll be piling up to see me. TV. Radio. I'm a star. An achiever. Look what I..we..have done. I expect there'll be a reception committee waiting for us at Biggin Hill."

"Um," said Kieran, "my little flibberty gibbet, enjoy the moment while you can. At least you still have that sense of satisfaction. Many pilots have forgotten all the beauty and magnificence of flight and think only of the financial gain. Not that there's much of that either in aviation."

"Oh," said Carrie still elated, but falling, "of course I'll have plenty of both."

Once again she was about to discover she had absolutely no idea.

The Warrior landed at Prestwick, after the longest leg and Carrie shot out of the plane and over to the loo. It was all right for Kieran with his pee-bottle, she thought, but she had had to bottle-it-up for seven hours and was desperate. She had bought a 'Jane's John' in the hope of being able to use it in the plane; but in the event was unable to contemplate the idea of Kieran leering lecherously next to her, hoping for a sneaky flash.

Inside the 'Ladies,' marked by a metal plate depicting an eighteenth century woman on the door, Carrie saw a face she recognised. Another long distance traveller preparing for her flight. The girl, in mirror image of Carrie, was struggling into her immersion suit. Not easy in the cramped conditions of a cloakroom, and hampered by the proximity of the basins.

"Hi, aren't you Hazel Brown?"

"I am. Carrie Nordsuitlaan isn't it? So you made it back with your plane!"

"Yup. We're staying here tonight, then tomorrow it's on to Biggin Hill. I'm thrilled to be nearly home. And you? What are you doing?"

"I'm ferrying a Mitsubishi to Botswana.."

"A Mitsubishi? A car?"

"No, they make planes as well, this is a twin engine, tip-tank type. If I wasn't about to go, I'd let you have a look. Another time. Whom did you choose as your pilot?"

"Kieran O'Toole."

"Indeed! I congratulate you on arriving safely home. I shall come out and say hello, but then I must fly. Perhaps we'll meet again later."

They shook hands, and Hazel, after a few words with Kieran, went to prepare her Mitsubishi for the long flight. "Break a spar!" yelled Kieran after her.

At the Custom's Office the official, shaking his head at the holes in the Warrior's interior but omitting to climb inside with a torch, wanted to be paid import duty. Carrie wanted to do anything rather than shell out more money.

"But I might take it on to South Africa or probably I'll sell it."

"Humm. If it stays in the country it needs a permit. If you're going through you can have a temporary one, but that'll need firming-up with the tax office."

"OK, give me a temporary one."

"All right, I will. But make sure you contact your local tax office or you'll be in violation! Big Fine! Big! Got that."

Carrie nodded her head meekly. They asked the customs man for a lift into town, but he shook his head. "Sorry, I'm not allowed to fraternise with clients," he explained, "besides the petrol costs more than my job's worth."

Carrie wondered if he was making a joke.

The Bed and Breakfast in Prestwick was a small house with a cafe where clients could have sandwiches. The beds were slim, second-hand army regulation. The rooms had pink fluffy carpets and green, sheer vyella curtains. Carrie spent the whole night dreaming she was under the sea and woke up just as Ditcher arrived to save her in his sinking seaplane. The last thing she noticed was that he was wearing Kieran's lizard skin boots, nicked from the plane checkers back in Moncton.

Before going to bed Carrie had had a beer with Kieran. "So, Kieran," she had asked suddenly, "you are so interested in everyone else's story, what's yours?"

"Oh, my little floo flish, here we are back on Alba's sweet shore and now you are all into the unveiling of the bomber; this you should have investigated weeks ago before it was too late. Oh, the saddest words in the English language, and so often used: too late, too little and too late. Although too much and too late is still the same. The truth behind the man. I have no story. No past. No present. But I will tell you a story for your amusement. Not mine but about your, and my, friend Hazel Brown."

"Hazel Brown!? Did she have time to tell you a story?"

"Not today, but on previous occasions we have shot the breeze together, blown hot and cold on flying, and I have levitated with laughter at her on-dits."

"Really? She seemed pretty straight to me."

"Straight as a die, honest as the unwary but once, just once, she got caught into the sweet trap of belief in others. Shall I begin? Begin the begin?"

"Fire away pompier," said Carrie, slipping into Kieran jargon.

"She was working for a freight company in California. I knew them myself, worked for them indeed, but in my way, with my difference. I was drawing pictures in the sky with a Pitts Special, she was drawing money for the boss for moving freight. My life is infinitely more romantic."

"Tell me your story then?"

"Ah, if only that was the option." He gave Carrie a long, inviting look but when she made no move, continued.

"She had a 3am start, beastly time of the morning but beggars can't be choosers and you must admit your Hazel has an unusual temperament; not everyone's cup of chocolate. Not unlike your cousin there, but I digress. She was dressed and ready to leave the house, when the telephone rang. It had to be work. How many of your friends ring at three in the morning? Only lovers. And Hazel, bless her reinforced cotton socks, had none. Again I digress. Forgive my wanderings."

Carrie remembered Greenland and wished Knut was here to make Kieran stick to the story, but he continued.

"So, she answered the telephone. It was the flight engineer. 'Hazel' he said, 'come over to the captain's house straight-away. He needs you to give him a lift.'

A lift my child! A lift is what one lover gives another; shirt lifters; the lift of love: but this, sadly was not a sexual story. I shall continue, for stories must never be splattered with interruptions.

Young Hazel tried to argue but there was no fighting and soon she was on her way to the captain's house on the other side of whatever small American town she worked in during those far off days. When she arrived the captain was drunk. Out cold. And I bet that you, like me, thought Americans were sissies who hardly touched a drop. But this was other days, past eras."

"Hardly, she's 40 something not 70."

"OK, OK, don't interrupt; story tellers so easily lose the thread of gold. So she and the flight engineer picked up the captain and carried him gently into her car. She drove to the airport. Up to the plane. They placed him in his Captain's seat and she flew the whole route with him out cold and sleeping. And when they landed at base..well..not to put too fine a point on it..he was dead."

"Dead!?"

"Yup as a jolly old doornail. And was there scandal? Was there? Your mother would have heard it from Canada, if you had had a mother in Canada. Young Hazel could never work in freight again. A sad and sorry story, wouldn't you say? But clearly one with a moral which you, young Carrie will immediately have spotted."

"Don't fly with drunks?"

"Ah, the sweet innocence of youth. Never, my little darling, never say yes in the morning, never lose control. If she had told the flight engineer to get off the phone and see her at the airport the whole commoodle would never have happened."

Slant Visibility

From Prestwick it was another hour and a half to Blackpool, where they were due to refuel. The day was again strabismically bright and sunny but the air was skin-pinchingly cold, surprisingly so for a spring day. They left Prestwick, without a hitch, just as it opened and flew happily along in the sunshine. When they called Blackpool Approach, though, there was a unexpected glitch in the celestial system.

"N2122 reading you fives. Temporarily closed due to fog. RVR 100, state your intention," replied Blackpool ATC.

Carrie and Kieran stared at each other, they were flying in perfect blue early morning sky without a cloud in sight. It didn't seem possible. Kieran called again.

"Blackpool Tower, five squared!" Kieran joked. " Confirm your RVR."

Blackpool came back, reiterating that they were in fog.

"Impossible," said Kieran, "all ATCs are incapable idiots or they would not have been put in the Tower in the first place. Ah my wit, it is too good for you pearl-less swine. How come Mitch with the pearls doesn't laugh and show her pearly whites you ask. We shall fly closer and examine their predicament."

As they flew towards Blackpool, Carrie could see that the ATC were right. Although they could see downward from the Warrior to the ground, there was indeed a patch of fog lying right over the runway, which must have completely obscured the vision of those inside it.

"Nonsense," said Kieran, "we can see quite well enough to go in. I'm not staying up here with this doggie any longer. I shall declare a low oil pressure; a hot doggie in fact. No! Better than that, I shall insist on making a VFR approach. Never ask; just tell; that way they cannot refuse. Blackpool Tower N2122, I am VFR and I shall be making a VFR approach to your main runway."

Blackpool tried to stop him, then, giving up, said it was at his discretion. Kieran lined up on the runway and made his approach. Until the very last minute they were in the clear, but at about 50 feet from the ground they suddenly dropped into obscuring fog. Kieran continued down, landing with a bump. The Warrior braked and came to a halt.

"Now, my child," he said, "we need that chap with the red flag your grandfather used to have walking in front of his car; although to my grandfather the red flag was the British bullies' oppression of his country! Let's hope the 'Follow Me' van does not crash into us in the fog. Oh the irony of landing safely but then having a car crash. Now that's a story I must remember to tell you, about a time when I had an engine failure in an Auster with no where to go but to land on the motorway...but for my skill Auster would have been Buster and Kieran cute jam..."

While Carrie refuelled the plane, Kieran went to talk to the tower. He returned saying they were a bunch of bozo's who couldn't have found their arse with both hands and a metal detector.

"Come, my child, lunch. My blood sugar level is sadly in need of topping up. Never make a pain of a pleasure as the actress told the bishop."

They walked into the sandwich bar, a strangely anachronistic wooden affair, entered from the apron down a couple of steps. Above the bar hanging planes swung in the human breezes, on the walls hung pictures of famous aviators, and over the fire-place a propeller converted into a clock. The air smelt of cooking onions.

"Any bar snacks?" Kieran asked a man standing behind the bar.

"Er.. yes, yes.. sure, must be, menu here. Drinks?" A stammering blond man handed Kieran the menu, while half smiling at Carrie. He looked at her in the manner of one who thinks he knows you but is afraid to make the contact.

"Do I know you?" Asked Carrie, smiling encouragingly at his restless fidgeting.

The nervous barman stuck out his hand in a straight line. "Absolutely Mam. Clive Somerset. Interviewed for ferry pilot job. Pleased to meet you again."

"Of course," she said disengaging her hand, "what are you doing here?"

"Oh, teaching aeros..er aerobatics at school. Just helping out in bar while barman at lunch. Done it before, Bigamy Hill, terminal bar."

"Barman out to lunch?" asked Kieran. "Clearly a case of lights on no-one at home, then. Hello Clive, I'm Kieran O'Toole, young Carrie's pilot. Now what type of plane are you teaching aeros on here...the pulsating Pitts, the energetic Extra, the awkward aerobat..."

"Hum" Carrie muttered, "they all sound expensive. "

"Oh, yes. Licence to print money," said Clive as sycophantic as a nervous man can be. "Aerobatic instructors, very rich. Not helpful. Taught myself, mostly."

"Well," said Kieran, "you know it's a case of how much a life is worth. I've taught enough aerobatics in my time to know there are those who suddenly become alive in a roll. Totally useless in straight and level, then bolt upright and interested when the going gets tough. When the going gets tough, the tough get rolling. Now...if I were to teach you well in the beginning, you'd survive a hundred accidents of self-taught men. As it is I happen to have a list of prices on me. There are two ways we can do this, on an hourly rate where I fit you into my schedule, or a daily rate where I am completely at your service..."

"er..but.." bleated Clive timidly, "already teach...er.. mean.."

In spite of constantly hopeful reports from the weather men the fog, far from clearing, got worse. Clive dropped them at a bed and breakfast with a promise to pick them up the following morning.

"I shan't be surprised," remarked Kieran guilelessly, "if he doesn't fetch us tomorrow. Very unreliable, pilots. All talk and no action. Maybe he can't even do aeros; I asked him questions that wouldn't baffle a baby and he gave me bullshit.. "

The Bed and Breakfast was on a main road. Once a private home in a backwater, times had changed and Blackpool had grown, leaving the attractive house sitting in a run-down suburb. The owner offered them dinner in his huge empty restaurant, "although usually it is only for breakfast. I'm doing this because I like pilots, but there's only eggs and bacon mind."

When they were sitting alone in Imperial State over scrambled eggs and bacon, Carrie asked: "That girl Charleen.."

"Who? These eggs are great with tomato ketchup, try some. Catch up with ketchup on..come on with aplomb..."

"Charleen, I mean, you called her Charlee."

"Don't you want your eggs? You've not touched them. I'll eat them if you like; never waste food, it looks rude and shows you've never been hung..."

"Charlee the girl in Florida..." Carrie continued, refusing to be side-tracked even though Kieran was now spooning the egg off her plate onto his own.

"In the Florida swamps, the piggie-bird dumps, finest lumps of mango, cheese and brownies..."

"..she was my husband's other wife wasn't she?" Carrie broke in loudly, determined to prevent his side-tracking by drowning out his voice.

"What?!" Kieran stopped spooning the egg and stared at her. "You're barmy!"

"She was, wasn't she? She suddenly appeared, then she said she wanted to meet me. You knew her before. You didn't want her to talk to me alone, so you stopped us flying together..."

"That plane was a heap of pants!"

"..she said she only learnt to fly because of another pilot.."

"She said her father," Kieran pointed out, returning to his spooning.

"..she worked at North Piri Piri and my husband had a mobile home there..and Rhum said he met my husband with someone who had a name like a fruit or a flower.. Charlee sounds a bit like cherry! Especially if you're a linguist."

She stopped. Aware that the conclusion sounded a bit weak.

Kieran took all the egg off her plate and began to eat noisily.

"A spurious connection, as the purist said to the sow; and that was a connection to make lights shine. I wonder if you remember how large

North Piri Piri is, how many pilots?" He burped, his mouth gungey. "What are the chances of them meeting at all, let alone getting married?"

Carrie refused to give up. "It was you who suggested the wife in Florida. It all fits."

Kieran laughed melodramatically. "If the cap fits, wear it! You really do have the most innovative imagination. Most unusual. I don't think any of my previous clients have ever..."

"She is, though, isn't she...I kept thinking about why she looked so familiar and of whom she reminded me. Then it came in a flash: I must have seen a photo...probably Ignatius left one lying around..."

Her voice dying, Carrie saw a flaw in her premise; she winced.

"So clever! And so completely wrong. Well, my little hoo haa. Some of your observations are spot on but your conclusion is spot off and in the boondocks! No, the truth is she is my sister."

"Your sister!" Now Carrie was dumbfounded. "She's your sister! You mean my husband was married to your sister?"

Kieran sighed. "No! My sister is not married. My sister is a spinster, the poor man cried, she'd never had much fun since father died! Stop thinking about Ignatius. I never met him and I doubt my sister did either."

"Oh," said Carrie, trying to digest this change in the picture she'd been dwelling on for so many days. "Oh. Are you sure?"

Kieran leant back on his seat. Looking older. For a moment Carrie wished she hadn't spoken; feeling a soft stab of sympathy. She was about to put her hand out when he stretched his arms up towards the sky, interlacing his fingers before bringing them down onto his head. For a long while he was silent then he said. "Yes, my nosy little house-frau, she really is my sister."

"So that's why I thought I recognised her; she looked like you. Your sister? But then why..why didn't you.."

"Why didn't I introduce her? It's a complicated story."

Kieran was silent again. Low cloud menacing his thoughts. Eventually he said "all right I'll tell you, but don't go navel gazing! Don't go mistaking this for revelations: those will come to God alone. It's not a particularly hard story. Merely that when I was born my parents were just out of school, or not even. They couldn't cope. They left me with the Jesuits, an orphanage, not in Ireland but in London. I was brought up thinking my parents were dead. They weren't. They had fled to America, and much later had another child, a girl. One day I was ferrying through America...this young, blond babe came over. I lit her cigarette. She smoked one of mine. Usual thing. From fag to shag!

In the morning she told me she was my sister. Of course I didn't believe her but she told me things...about our parents; our shared mother and father. She knew what my parents had done to me and she said she was giving herself to me in recompense. You won't understand that, with your husbands and your ego, but some women care..they are different! Softer. Kinder. Anyway, she continues to do so...and lifts in cars too, as you'll have noticed. Now our father's dead she wants me to tell everyone she's my sister. But I don't know. I'm not sure that I want to acknowledge that that man ever was my father. He was an aerobatic pilot too. Really. Sickening that a man like that should have been allowed at the controls of an aeroplane."

"What happened to him?"

"He walked of course. The last she heard he'd died, but by then he was married to someone else anyway. He's your bigamist if you want one!"

"Oh! What about your mother..?"

"I don't know. She didn't stand up for me, so now I shall not stand out for her, but this is trivial talking and enough of a dull subject."

"I see. I'm sorry...I thought.."

"I see" said Kieran, "as the deaf ferret said to the traffic lights. I hear as the mute actress said to the megaphone. We see and hear so much and we understand so little. So, my liberchern, what next? A fight, a flight or a bit of the old brilliantine. Will we talk again? In thunder, lightning or in rain. So many things in the hurly burly are still unknown....pass me my 'tit fer' I will away. Goodnight."

He took his hat from her and put it on his head before turning to the door. Carrie watched him through the glass pane, climbing up the creaking, wooden staircase to his room. She'd really got it wrong there. And it had led to an unexpected revelation. She wondered if amongst the bullshit there was something she ought to understand. Would Kieran have been the same person with a different upbringing? Better? Worse? Amazing how one event can sometimes cause generations of devastation.

Flying is a computer game with humans.

A Computer Game with Humans

The next day the Warrior took off, heading south through the low-level route under Manchester's flight paths, keeping clear of the jet-lanes. "Some of those airliners," thought Carrie quivering, "are doing today what I spent the last month doing. Atlantic Fighting. Flying the good fight."

While Carrie flew Kieran sang and chatted as usual, but his mind was not with them and a couple of times the Manchester Radar Controller chided him for missing radio calls. An hour and a half out of Blackpool Kieran called Biggin Hill.

"Bigamy Hill this is N2122, a Warrior inbound to you from Fort Lauderdale Florida...."

As Biggin replied, Carrie realised she was back where it had all started, laden with her golden egg, but still full of unanswered questions. She did the final landing, holding the plane off the runway until they made the last gentle plop onto the tarmac.

"Hey," she breathed, "how was that for a landing! What a way to end the flight! We are home. Home and dry. Where are the crowds?"

"Not bad," said Kieran, "bit long. Personally I always like to test myself, to go for the shortest possible landing. Always aim for perfection!"

Carrie dropped Kieran off at Colin Larfman's office and taxied the plane around to John's hangar. He had agreed to allow her to leave the Warrior there for a couple of days. For a price, of course.

"Hello," said John, as she climbed out on the wing. "Sold it yet?"

"No, do you want to buy it?"

"Get real! I'd sell the ones I've got if anyone would have them. Incidentally have you got a pound coin? I need it for the coffee machine."

Upstairs Janie asked her if she'd heard Ben had probably been killed by some big time gangster he was attempting to blackmail. When Carrie said, no, she'd been away, flying across the Atlantic, Janie nodded absently and went back to counting her points. Carrie noticed she'd added a chin stud to her beauty.

Deflated, Carrie joined Kieran in the cafe, where he demanded his money.

"What! We've only just landed! You, of all people, must know I haven't a penny."

"Ah, but you know what we ferry pilots are, here there, gone tomorrow, worse than the wickedest bigamist. And I need the dosh."

"Maybe, however, I need to sell the plane before I have any money for details."

"Details?! You call the way I saved your life over and over again a detail? You'd better take a loan out and pay me."

"Legally I've got a month after the month in which the work was done," Carrie said suavely, although she wasn't entirely sure she was right; all she knew for certain was that she hadn't got the money right now. As it was, she was going to have to extend her credit. Much to her relief he either believed her or simply couldn't be bothered to push an already dead horse.

"Oh, all right. I'm off on another job tomorrow so you'll have to send it to me."

"Tomorrow! That's pretty quick."

He gave a ghost of a smile. "I never disappoint Colin. Go, go, go that's me and having said that I must go off to see the little wife, before I dismay her with the news I shall be wending away again. Thanks. I was fun. I'll look forward to the cheque. Spectacles, testicles, wallet and watch."

Away went the boots and the hat in a final Kieranic sweep. Carrie felt an enormous anticlimax. Here she was back in England, safely, with her plane ready to sell, and there was no one to celebrate with. Instead of the adoring crowds of Lindbergh lifting her high in triumph she had requests for money. She might have been across the Atlantic but people here were more interested in car parking and congestion, coffee machines and landing fees. For a moment she even wished for the return of Kees. Instead she got Colin.

"Hello, hello, my darling girl. Here she is! How was it? How was the trip and what have you done to poor Kieran?"

"Hi. It was fine. The trip was eventful and expensive and it's more what Kieran has done to me than the other way around."

"Ah, you say that, but he was in my office begging for another job at once. You'd think that the angels of vengeance were at his heels the way he asked me to let him leave as soon as possible. And normally I'm the one begging him to take a job."

"Gosh! I don't know, he made it sound as though you were forcing him to go."

"Very odd. Now how about a bottle of champagne and you tell me the whole story. I love a good ferry trip by proxy!"

By the time Carrie got back to her cousin's house it was late. Roberta had gone to bed but had left a note, balanced on a pile of letters, mostly credit card bills.

The note, in Roberta's harsh hand, said:

"The Heffalumps came again!!!! They want you to ring them URGENT! So do it. I don't want them around again with their flat-feet and guilty consciences."

Carrie left the bills unopened, but seeing Mr Barbar's stamp ripped open the letter. As usual it was partly incomprehensible. However one thing was clear: Ignatius had indeed gone to Florida for a week. He had travelled first class; and had paid for two return tickets. The airline, while verifying that Ignatius had travelled, would neither confirm nor deny that he had a companion. Perhaps, thought Carrie, he bought two tickets because he thought I would go with him, then, when I couldn't because of my father's funeral, he went alone and forgot to tell me. Somehow she had more difficulty believing that now than she had had in Mr Footsie's Florida office.

He had also purchased a mobile home in North Florida. Mr Barbar had been sent the title deeds by the vendor's solicitor and wished to know whether Carrie would like him to effect a resale or if she wanted to preserve the purchase. (The good news?)

Finally the lawyer, who, thought Carrie, was no doubt charging heavily for this time spent on her behalf, wrote that he had recently been contacted by some individuals over a 'matter of discretion'. He would let her know the outcome of this insidious matter when he had discovered the true facts of the perniciousness himself. And in the meantime, did she know anything about her husband's past? And don't spend all the money yet.

"Ha, ha," thought Carrie, "what money?"

What was the 'matter of discretion?' Ignatius's other wife?

Remembering her Prestwick promise Carrie rang the local the tax office.
"Hello. I want some advice on importing a plane."

"Oh? You probably want some other department."

"This is the number I got from Directory Inquiries. I just want some advice."

"This is the switchboard," said the boy. "Shall I transfer you to somebody?"

"Thank you," replied Carrie, too amazed even to grind her teeth.

Mr Somebody asked for her reference number.

"I don't have one. I just want some advice on importing a plane."

"A plain what?" Asked the baffled tax official.

"A plane. Plane, you know, a plane.. for flying."

"Do you mean an aircraft?"

"Yes. A four seat Piper Warrior."

"Oh. And you don't have a reference number?"

Carrie thought they were going backwards. "No."

"Honestly, I don't think this is the right office to ask, I think you'll need to contact our Heathrow branch. Where is the plane exactly?" Carrie could tell from his voice that he was reaching his limits.

"Near Maidenhead."

"Ah, that will be our Reading branch. You'll need to ring them. Don't ring me again, I'm moving," he said and put down the phone.

Carrie rang the Reading branch of the tax office.

"What's your customer number?" Asked this Somebody.

Carrie took a gulp of coffee and began again.

"Why did you ring here?" He interrupted her.

Carrie explained: "..the other office told me to. They don't know any-thing."

"We don't either," the tax official concurred phlegmatically. She could hear him clicking his computer mouse while he talked to her. Playing games perhaps? "You'll have to ring them again." He too put the phone down, and Carrie meditated on the realisation that computer games did no good in the long run.

She wrote to the Southwark office, explaining her problem and sending a copy of the temporary import certificate. She got a reply from an office in Prestwick, with forms for her to fill in and mail on to the Reading office. A few months later she received a letter, from the Southwark office, say-ing she now had imported the plane. To her surprise no further money changed hands.

A week later Carrie flew to White Waltham, where the Warrior was to be leased. The sun was shining and she waved at the Biggin school where all her adventures had begun. No one waved back. Inside John was busy sending her a bill for three days hangarage and Janie was weighing her chin-stud.

Carrie flew south of London, talked to Farnborough Radar, then turned north to fly up the west side of London: across the M4 junction with its melee of competing cars and past the sturdy Reading gasometers, before turning right and following the railway line to White Waltham.

"Amazing," she thought as she flew over a stationary train, "only a short time ago I didn't know a Warrior from a Cessna, and now here I am con-trolling one, in charge and at the helm. Polling my ship up to Heaven or at any rate beating public transport."

The thought cheered her slightly after the disappointment of coming home and finding everything exactly the same. No one appeared to have missed her. Even her cousin had been more interested in Big Brother's winner than in her absence.

She called White Waltham on the radio. No reply. The railway line zoomed far into the distance, leading, she hoped, to the White Waltham circuit. Squinting along the iron track she hoped to see the airfield before she reached Heathrow, was arrested for over-flying Windsor Castle or hit a circuiting aircraft. After a couple of false hopes she saw a large grass air-field with a long, wooden-slatted club house. On a gently sloping runway near a fluttering windsock a Tiger Moth was landing, the sun glinting on it's silver wings. Watching its stately progress to the ground, Carrie's smile dilated. White Waltham was known as an old-fashioned, romantic airfield, full of vintage aircraft and tea and cakes on the lawn. As different from bustling, commercial Biggin Hill as an airship from Concorde.

"Will I, after tea and cakes and ices, have the strength to force the sale to its crisis?" misquoted Carrie awkwardly.

She was shutting down the engine, listening to its modern 'ting' and comparing it with the heavy throb on the gypsy engine beside her, when she heard a tap tap on the far window. Mitch was standing on the Warrior's wing.

"Hey," Carrie said, leaning over, opening the door so fast she hit her former instructor mid-thigh, "you must be following me around!"

Mitch laughed, rubbing her thigh automatically. "So you made it then, back from Iceland. How was the trip? What are you doing here?"

"I'm leasing my plane to the school. You? Of course, you teach here, don't you?"

"Occasionally. I am glad to see you. In spite of everything I couldn't help worrying that Kieran might try and ditch the plane and do a runner."

Carrie climbed out, shut the door and tried to lock it. The key ground around in the barrel; it still hadn't been fixed in spite of doing time in the engineering lock-up. They walked over to the office, where Carrie gave the keys to a couple of boys. She followed Mitch into the long, plane-decorated bar. Mitch bought some coffees, while Carrie flopped into a creaking wicker chair, left over, no doubt, from the days when 'men were men...'

"Tell me!" said Carrie.

"Tell you what?" Asked Mitch sitting down, getting out her next student's notes.

"What was going on in Iceland? With Kieran I mean. All that secrecy and warnings from Kees...it was bizarre."

"Oh, that." Mitch dropped a bunch of student notes on the table. "So, Kieran isn't a very nice person actually. If there's something bad happening he did it!"

Carrie laughed. "Rather extreme isn't it? He was a bit kinky but he was OK in his way. Selfish. He's had a hard life you know."

"Spare me! I've heard about his orphanage. And the rest. Look, I didn't want to tell you at the time but he was importing porn mags." Mitch shut her eyes as she talked, as though unable to bear visualising such sordid horrors.

Carrie giggled; she'd been expecting something much worse. "Phut! Why would he bother to do that? You can get them here. Anyway how do you know? I never saw any. Or..in fact I did see one..a girl tied with belts and things, but Kieran said it came free with the room in that Icelandic hotel. Did you get one too, I didn't?"

Mitch snorted. "Free with the room indeed! People pay heavy money for those bound-up babes. Actually, you didn't see them because he hid them in the Lear Jet. He knew he couldn't carry them in his case, because everything would be taken out for the cross-Atlantic check. I reckon he was planning to hide them in the Warrior's upholstery."

"What!?" exclaimed Carrie, "you don't think he cut those holes himself?"

Mitch shrugged. "Could be! But when the engineers kept pointing them out, he must have thought you'd notice the mags. Lucky for you really. If the Special Customs's Lady had found them it would have been hellishly embarrassing, actually. So the Lear got 'em. Transferred in Teterborough, fetching his hat, actually."

"But, it doesn't make any sense. Porn mags aren't illegal."

"These might be, but actually I think his real concern was that you might sack him."

"Oh." Carrie was more likely to sack him for financial reasons.

"It was disgusting stuff." Mitch, clearly outraged, fiddled absently with her students' note. "Animals. Bondage. Domination. That kind of rubbish. I threw them all into the Atlantic, actually."

Carrie gave up trying to lighten Mitch's ire. "So that was why he shot into the Lear when we landed at Reykjavik."

"Yup. Going to retrieve his magazines, only by then they were fish food. I threatened to expose him, but I didn't want you to suffer; tricky if your pilot ditches mid-stream. Now he's scarpered off again."

"So Kees imagined Kieran might lead me into wicked ways by reading porn to me!" Carrie smiled.

"Oh, Kees! Male jealousy! Your ex-husband still has a tender spot for you, actually."

Carrie nodded. She didn't want to think about that. "Were you going to report Kieran to the police? The CAA?" She grinned.

Mitch was serious. "I don't think they'd be interested. No, actually I thought if I told Colin I could stop him getting work that way, but Colin said it wasn't his business."

"What do you expect. He's short of pilots. Money talks. Besides he's a man, he probably doesn't think it's so bad."

"Even so," said Mitch. "Even so. Actually I think he should be more professional."

Carrie said nothing, but when she got home she made an appointment to see DIs Kundera and Jones.

Major Overhaul

"So," asked Kundera, "did your husband use the internet?"

Carrie frowned. Odd question. "No, he didn't. He was computer illiterate, wouldn't even try. Why?"

The detectives exchanged glances. Jones nodded. "It was rather what we thought," she said, "you used it, I suppose, being younger?"

"Yes, all the time. But why?"

Jones pursed her lips, as though she thought what she was going to say might shock or surprise the listener. "Well, your husband had met Ben." "The murdered man," put in Kundera. "In fact, it seems Ben did a courier job for him. They were identified meeting in the first class lounge at Heathrow." "Ben went there to pick something up," added Kundera, while Jones continued, stretching out her arm as though to check her watch. "Your husband gave him a $100 note and a package. One of the reception girls remembers them."

Carrie said nothing. Heathrow. First Class. Courier jobs. $100. Why?

"We think," said DI Kundera, "your husband may have given your wedding photo to Ben. Of course if he'd been a computer user he could just have scanned it and sent it on the internet."

"Did Ben have a computer?" asked Carrie amazed. Small, useful fallout shelter with full mod cons, electricity and accompanying airport.

"He had access, he knew how to use them. We think Ben's murder may be a local issue, something to do with his counterfeit sales. Yardies. The two things may not be connected at all."

"But they might?" suggested Carrie.

"Yes."

"Why would Ben need a picture of me?"

The two detectives exchanged glances again. "We're not entirely certain," said DI Jones, so casually that Carrie felt she was hiding something.

Carrie's plane stayed at White Waltham for the summer, but nobody wanted to buy it. Carrie was astounded. The blithe way the lawyer had told her about the plane shortage in the UK, she imagined it would be snapped up the moment she plopped down on the Biggin runway. She had a few inquiries, but when people discovered it was on the American register no one was interested.

Worse still, by now Carrie was deeply in debt.

She was receiving some income from leasing the Warrior to White Waltham for training but not a lot. Meanwhile she was aware that she was making the plane even less desirable to a possible purchaser, decreasing the number of hours left on the airframe and engine before a major overhaul would be needed.

Furthermore, she still hadn't paid Kieran or Colin or the man from the

Essex Mafia. Her credit cards were full and interest was everywhere increasing daily. She knew that if someone didn't buy the plane soon she was going to be in big trouble. In the back of her mind Kieran's Mafia thugs lurked, blighting her dreams.

To increase her chances of selling the plane, she decided to convert it to the British register. It would increase her loan slightly but at least she could sell it for more money. Colin recommended a firm in Sighing Well, whom, he said, were fast, efficient and cheap.

"No problem, Madam," the engineer said ingratiatingly, "we'll start on it right away. Subject to CAA permits and my 'hangar rats' working patterns, we'll be done shortly. No problem. We are real workers, not like some scum I could mention."

British Banana Republic

Carrie was in the bath when the phone rang. She knew Roberta was out because her cousin had shouted up the stairs before she left: "I'm going out for about an hour but I'm expecting an important call...don't muck it up for me, all right!"

Carrie listened to the phone ringing and wondered whether she would 'muck it up' more by answering the call, or by leaving it alone. Eventually, as the phone kept on ringing, she pulled a towel around her lean body and went into Roberta's bedroom.

"Hello."

"Ah, hello," said an exasperated voice. "I thought you'd never answer the phone! Very busy?"

"Eerr.." said Carrie, wishing Roberta had given her some more information about this call. "Umm."

The man clearly thought this unhelpful. "Look, who is this? You are selling planes there aren't you?"

"What!" said Carrie dropping the towel. "Why, yes, yes absolutely..I'm sorry there was a little confusion..yes...absolutely..."

The man was calling from Birmingham. He had seen the advert for the Warrior in Flight International and was interested. He wanted to see the plane immediately.

"Purr, no problem," said Carrie excitedly, scrabbling with her towel. "Tomorrow? It's at Sighing Wells. At the engineers. It's being transferred onto the British register."

"Fine. I'll be there. Twelve o'clock suit you?"

"Absolutely no problem," replied Carrie.

She put the phone down hugging herself in excitement. At last. At last.

When Roberta came in Carrie asked if she could borrow her car. Roberta looked at her in amazement. "You are joking aren't you?"

"..err.."

"First it's the house, then the telephone, now the car...what would madam like next? Perhaps you would prefer my bedroom with its nicer view or would you like me to bring you your meals in bed...or maybe..."

"It's fine," said Carrie hastily, "it's fine. I'll look up the train times. Thanks!"

Next morning Carrie walked through Camberwell to Denmark Hill Station, accompanying Roberta on her way to work. This was a cosmopolitan area, where FitzRightly Carpets abutted on Wok on Buy, and Thai me Tonite jostled the Mixed Blessings Bakery. Here men, whose faces suggested they had been fish in a previous life, sat staunchly preventing the pub from going bust. Carrie and Roberta crunched over the partially-recycled bottles and kicked aside smouldering tyres and leaded bags of rubbish. Posters warned that carrying knives led to prison or to the funeral parlour, their dramatic graphics supported by the minimum of text in an area clearly considered largely illiterate. Roberta gestured towards the children playing dare across the railway line.

"Short life here. The only choice you get is the way you die."

They passed on into the cleaner Camberwell Grove, where Georgian 'safe' houses dwarfed the memories of Victorian streets, and long hidden gardens mocked the less discreet patios of the newer streets. Here the local council could collect parking fines, instead of ignoring burnt-out or merely dumped cars.

The station at Denmark Hill had been recently renovated and smelt of paint. Tall Victorian poles gleamed metallic blue and airline orange. Sacks of sand, cement and forgotten tools sat unwanted in a corner. Roberta spat.

"Looks like they're putting in turnstiles. Money grabbers!"

"Why do you care?" Asked Carrie surprised. "You have a season ticket."

"I resent the implication that we're all thieves. Which is fine coming from this government of leeches. Take, take, take and what come-back do we have? None. We work and work and half of it goes in fucking taxes, so the ministers can have bigger cars and more bodyguards. Not that anyone would bother to shoot those no-hopers. You know," Roberta continued mysteriously, "sometimes I wish I was invisible."

Carrie paid for her ticket at the blue painted window. "I'd say you were patently visible!"

"Do you mean I'm fat?!"

"No. No. Of course not!" Carrie muttered. "I just meant...." her voice petered out. Impossible to explain. "I think it was a joke," she added hopefully.

"Good! It's lucky I have a sense of humour."

"Yes, absolutely," replied Carrie, starting the descent down to Platform One.

"Don't go down there!"

"Why not? It says Platform One for the Victoria train."

Roberta snorted. "May say it, but won't happen. You've left America now and you're back in the British Banana Republic. The train can come in at any platform and they won't let you know until it involves a long run to the other side."

"Oh. What do we do, then?"

"Stand here in the middle, between the platforms. We're not alone. See! The wise ones know."

"But why?"

"Why is there rubbish," replied Roberta obliquely. "Government!"

Five people were already standing on the bridge between the stairs. All had thin black cords in their ears like film directors. Talking to tiny phones, shielded by the world of distance, not one watcher acknowledged the others. Ten eyes scanned the four rail lines beneath.

Ten minutes late, the Victoria train came in on Platform Four, accompanied by a tannoy announcement. Carrie and Roberta were caught in the fevered flow as punters dashed across the station, accompanied by the music of mobiles and the perfume of hot bodies. They were crushed into the first carriage, the door clamping behind them leaving an old man outside. He shook his stick, cursing like a cartoon character.

"Silly old fool," said Roberta unsympathetically, "should know better at his age. It's always a lottery on this station."

From Victoria Carrie took a tube over to Euston and from there got the train to Northampton. It had taken her over an hour just to get to the station. She thought nostalgically of her hired car.

The Northampton train left on time, chugging happily along at the speed of a sedan chair. Then it stopped. Stuttered through another 100 yards. And stopped again. Carrie stared out of the scarred windows seeing the green countryside through deep graffiti-gouges, hoping fervently that this was just a short stay. But the time lengthened and the rolling stock remained still. Mobile phones began to ring. "I'm on the train but..."

After a long silence broken only by one-sided cellular conversations, an overhead voice wheedled into the atmosphere. At first the announcer spoke so fast that no one could understand; and all sat twiddling with their phones, uncertain what was happening. Carrie stared at the junk cluttered carriage, watching the slow fall of a corrugated coffee cup onto the floor. Behind her a South African talked about poundage per blade and grinding. Then the mechanical voice returned, this time speaking more slowly, laden with apologies: the tracks; the wind; the leaves. Finally it admitted that the train had broken down. Mobiles began bleeping with added anxiety.

By the time the iron-horses finally limped into Northampton it was dark. Carrie had missed her appointment with the longed-for buyer and she could do nothing but return, plus prospective complimentary train tickets, to London.

As Carrie walked into her cousin's house, Roberta yelled at her through the open sitting room door. "I had a very angry man on the phone. He doesn't think much of your manners, or your plane come to that. I agreed with him, I told him you arrived last year to stay for a month and were still here. By the end we were getting along famously. He wants you to ring him back. I'd chat him up if I were you, he sounds single to me."

Roberta was sitting on the sofa, her feet curled under her, her elbow on the telephone table holding the VCR control, her head resting back on the cushions. She looked, to Carrie, like an advert for comfortable garden gnomes.

"How do you sound single? No clicking of wedding rings?"

"Don't be stupid. Here's his number. Don't spend too long on the phone, you haven't paid me for the last lot of calls yet. I'm not made of money."

"I know and as soon..."

"Save it! We'll drink the champagne when that darn plane is sold. I always knew that Afrikaaner would be no good, it's the Dutch blood in them. You only have to look at that Kees to see what a useless lump of cheese they are. Not that the first one was any better really but at least he left more than a heap of tin in a foreign country."

Carrie looked at her watch. "Do you think it's too late to ring.." she looked at the note, "..Tom now?"

"No, he sounded to me like the sort of man that stays up all night watching TV."

"How does..oh never mind."

She rang Tom and he was indeed affronted. When Carrie explained about the train he forgave her that side of the problem, but there was worse to come.

"Your plane was full of water! You can't expect me to buy something in that condition."

"Full of water? How? I don't understand. Isn't it stripped down in the hangar?"

"Huh, if that's what they told you, I'd take it away from them. It's sitting outside without any kind of cover, the door bent. I opened the door and water cascaded out over me. I nearly sent you a bill for my suit. It stinks too. Mouldy."

When he rang off he was mollified, but no way was he buying. Carrie felt like crying. Worse she had no money, no home, no husband, a useless, decrepit plane that no one wanted, huge debts and no hope; she hadn't been in this situation since she was nineteen and it was always harder to be broke as you got older. She couldn't see a single silver lining ahead. Where was the optimistically drifting Sainsbury's bag now?

The next day she rang the engineer at Sighing Wells.

"Oh, Mrs Norseland, yes your plane is getting on nicely."

"I believe a prospective client came to visit it yesterday.

"Indeed yes, charming young man. Will he be buying?"

"He told me the plane was outside and full of water."

"Ah! Well, you could say it is outside, but that is owing to the CAA's slowness at producing the import permit. They seem to think we have nothing to do but wait on them. And the new rules they are bringing out for us every day…I mean Mrs Norsebrand it's enough to make you give up aviation….do you know they now want us to mark any door which opens with EXIT stickers. I mean, that might be all right on a 747 but in your little Warrior there only is one door, so unless people are planning to jump through the roof that is plainly ridiculous, scuse my pun!"

"He said the plane was full of water."

"Oh, Mrs Norsey what are they like, those people? They hate to just say they don't like something and that's it. There is always an excuse…"

"He sounded pretty trustworthy to me. I thought.."

"They always do! Mark my words! Many come and look, but so few buy. Time wasters. You and I with so little time on our hands are always amazed by these guys. But some people just love to waste other folk's time. Shocking really."

"I see. When will you be starting work?"

"Oh, we have your Warrior in the hangar already. We are only waiting for the CAA inspection and then we can begin…but you know the CAA…"

"All right. Let me know as soon as it's ready. I want it earning money again."

"Of course we will, Mrs Norsebrands, of course we will. We are completely on your side you know. Completely on your side."

Paling's Policy

"You don't seem to be finding out much," Carrie said testily to the two detectives in front of her. "I come back after a month, and all you can tell me is my husband met Ben. Now, six weeks later, you can only add that my husband had a beautiful, young companion with him at Heathrow."

The detectives, who had asked for another meeting hoping Carrie could identify the girl, looking guiltily at each other. It seemed to Carrie that without moving they had jelled into one being, as invincible as a wall of customs officers to a drug smuggler.

"I know it seems that way," began Jones, her voice resonant with sympathy, "but the problem is priorities." "Resources," put in Kundera. "You see," Jones went on, "while the case is of paramount importance to you," "and us," added Kundera. "It isn't the only one we're dealing with."

"The problem is," Kundera took over, "it isn't a high profile case. It has not been on the TV at all, and only a small patch in some newspapers." "Low-life," put in Jones. "Probably Ben was a great guy, but no pulling power." "Poor people," pointed out Kundera, "get stabbed everyday. He was a petty criminal who sold counterfeit and drugs, and did underworld errands. He may even have been a snitch." "Police informer," explained Jones.

"But isn't his death part of a bigger case?" Carrie remonstrated. "A man was murdered, wasn't he? And you are looking for reasons, aren't you? And there may be a wider...a world-wide connection...with.. with Ignatius..." her voice fell away. She felt like a child who was insisting to intransigent adults, sympathetic but uninvolved, that her lost toy was important. "Supposing I was murdered too?"

"Ah," said Kundera thoughtfully, "well that would, of course, make it a much higher profile case."

Six weeks later the engineers finally finished the Warrior, obtained CAA clearance for the British registration, and invited Carrie to come and pay the bill. Using her complimentary-train-tickets-thanks-to-the-people's-charter she went up to The Sighing Wells. The engineer-in-chief, Mr Paling, was a round grey man with a small head and an insinuating manner. Carrie was delighted, 'paling' means eel in Dutch.

"Hello Mrs Noodi-slant," he crooned at her, "it is so nice to see you again. I am very fond of South Africans you know. Not nearly enough of them around. Shame it's all gone wrong down there."

"Has it? I thought things were pretty optimistic myself, especially compared to the mess you've got here!"

"Aww, well we'll just have to hope you're right, won't we, but personally I think it was a pity the British ever left the place. Give me back colonialism. You know we went there and saved them savages and look what gratitude we got! Personally..."

"Really! How is my plane?"

"Aww, such a lot of work it was too. Such a lot. Terrible condition it was in. I really hadn't the heart to charge for all the work my men did, so much overtime too, with you being in such a hurry. Such a shame that nice young man didn't buy the plane. Such a shame you missed him."

"How much is the bill?"

"£6,000, and I'm cheating myself at that. If I charged for all the labour we did it would be nearer twice the price. I thank God I'm such an honest man that I'd never take advantage of a young girl on her own."

"£6,000! You quoted me £2,000." Carrie was shocked. She'd never heard of such an escalation.

"Ah yes, but that was before I knew what a lot of work it was going to be. I think you'll be pleased with how good we've made it. Such a lot of work it was. If I charged you for all the hours we spent on the plane...well now that would be a BILL! Really I'm cheating myself. I didn't make a penny from it, in spite of all the hassle we had from the CAA. They didn't like the holes in the fabric and asked me to do drug tests on the machine. Drug tests! I ask you. I've never been into anything illegal in my whole life."

Carrie didn't know what to do. She knew he must be cheating her but she felt loathe to go into another fight. Most of all she knew she couldn't pay him.

"OK," she said, "well I've a cheque here for £2,000 since that was the original agreed price, but I can't just give you more without talking to the bank. I'll need a full breakdown of expenses. You can't just go tripling the price without telling me. You should have rung me first."

Mr Paling ignored that. "Oh, I don't usually let people take the goods away without full payment, you know. Still I suppose since it's you I can. I know I can trust a nice lady from South Africa like you, don't I?"

He smiled at her insincerely.

Carrie 'checked out' the plane as Mitch had taught her. Nothing appeared to have been changed; certainly nothing to justify charging £6,000. She found there was only a small amount of oil in the sump.

"I've hardly got any oil," she told the engineer.

"Oh, no problem. I've got some good stuff fairly cheap. I'll add it to the bill." He smiled happily. He'd always liked female pilots; they were so intelligent, so gentle.

After refuelling her plane Carrie got ready to leave. "You will send me a break down of your charges, Mr Paling, won't you?"

"Yes, yes. Don't worry about a thing. You just have a nice flight home."

After flying back to White Waltham, Carrie took the train up to

London. She rang the bank. They refused to let her have any more money. So she rang the engineer, reminded him she had asked for a full breakdown of his costs and waited; the ball was in his court now.

Roberta came home keen to talk about the future. "When you sell your plane, supposing you do, what then?"

"What, what?"

"I'm just wondering if I should order your coffin when I get fitted up for mine! I like living alone; in case you thought I needed a companion."

"Oh, absolutely," said Carrie, wishing she had Kieran's gift of the gab, "and I do appreciate what you are..."

"Cut the crap! When can I hope to see you gone?"

"Would you like to go flying, now the plane is back in working condition? I think you'd enjoy ..."

"Yeah, sure. You've got another month and then you can look to someone else to house and feed you; this Mama is losing the call. And now I'm going to bed. Goodnight."

Carrie told herself Roberta didn't really mean it. She rang the lawyer but he had gone home for the night. The answer machine cheerfully took her call instead. The next day, while Roberta was out at work, she rang again. His secretary said he had 'gone bush for a week of r and r' and couldn't be contacted.

"Ah," said Carrie thoughtfully, while the secretary replied wittily. "No, r and r, rest and relaxation!"

"Again! He's always on holiday."

"Oh, this isn't a holiday. This is family time."

"Sure," said Carrie, "tell him to ring me urgently when he unbushes or whatever!"

A week later she got a call, not from the lawyer but from White Waltham.

"Carrie," said Mitch, "have you been down to see your plane recently?"

"No, why?"

"It's got no instruments in it!"

"What?"

"Yup, someone's taken the lot. We can't use it like this. I'm really sorry but we do need at least the basics. Everything has gone, even the cigarette lighter! They weren't forced out either, they were taken out scientifically."

Carrie groaned. Could this be related to Ben's death? Was it a warning to her? First your instruments, then you? She was silent; frightened.

"..er..." said Mitch tentatively, "..er Carrie, it merely.. that is... I just wondered?"

"Yeah?" Carrie's voice reflected her depression. Would the next thing be finding smashed instruments on the door-step or in her bed?

"I..er..that is.. I wondered," said Mitch, "if you'd paid Kieran? It could be him. Or perhaps, since I don't think his engineering expertise is up to that pretty excellent work, ...have you ..er..paid the engineers?"

Mitch, like many people who have inherited wealth, found talking about money far more embarrassing than using it.

"No. Not yet." Carrie was lost. What had engineers to do with Ben's death?

"Then probably it's Paling. In lieu of payment; a hostage!"

"Paling?! Good God! Isn't anyone in flying honest?" Carrie asked in angry dismay, put out that something she thought so life-threatening turned out to be mere trivia.

"I am."

"You're unique, Mitch!" said Carrie, wondering irrelevantly if Mitch could really have had an affair with Ben.

"Carrie, look, the boys here say they'd be happy to go and beat the day-lights out of the engineer. No charge. He isn't well liked."

Carrie was surprised at law-abiding Mitch suggesting such a thing; for a moment she considered it, then she remembered the police. "No, it's OK, Mitch. I'll deal with it."

She rang the engineer.

"Right Paling," she said, "I know you've got my instruments. If you don't return them immediately I'm going to the police. I shall be at White Waltham tomorrow and if my plane is not fully instrumented I will see you and your slimy outfit in court."

The next day the instruments were back, but the bill was still out-standing. In the second post Carrie got a nice, polite letter from Mr Essex-Mafia. He invited her to tea, looked forward to seeing her again and asked for payment of his bill, which had now come up on his American Express card and must be paid by the end of the month. When she got home in the evening her cousin told her Kieran had called.

"He said he wanted to know why his bill hadn't been paid, was it an oversight? I said oversight be damned, you hadn't a pot to piss in and if it wasn't for me you'd be living in the fucking plane. That's what."

"Great. Thanks. So now he'll be round to beat the Hell out of me."

"Probably. He looked like a lout to me last time he was here."

Carrie sat down in despair. What? Where? How? Money. It all came down to money. She couldn't see any alternative but to kill herself. Strangely her cousin came to the rescue in her normal brusque manner.

"Want a cup of tea?"

"Please."

"Good, make me one while you're up."

"Thanks," Carrie got up, while Roberta made herself more comfortable on the sofa, tucking her short legs under her long, black skirt.

"Oh, and you had a letter, it's in the kitchen."

"Was it a lottery win?"

"Ha! No wonder you've got no money if you're wasting it on that faint hope. Anyway it's from South Africa so I doubt it."

The letter was from the lawyer, dated before he went bush. He had been disposing of her furniture, which Carrie had pretty well forgotten about, and had news. They hadn't owned anything of value so she hadn't hoped for a massive check and she didn't get one, but he had been able to raise £250.

"Furthermore," he added, "in my research through the furniture I discovered some aeroplane tickets. You may, of course, already have cognition of these, but it seems that you and Sissy (your sister-in-law) were to travel to London on 6th June for two weeks. I checked with the airline whether the tickets, clearly now valueless, could be refunded and was told emphatically not; such cheap tickets are totally un-refundable, even in the case of death, which is anyway not applicable here since you are both alive."

Just for a second Carrie reflected that, had Ignatius been alive, she would anyway have been in London. What a lovely surprise! But, more important for Carrie, the lawyer wanted to know who to make the cheque out to. She had a brain wave. She took her cousin her tea and a biscuit.

"Oh! Biscuit is it?" said Roberta immediately alert. "What do you want? You know I haven't enough money to lend you any."

"Yes, I know but if the lawyer in South Africa makes the cheque out to you can you advance me the £250?"

"Oh? And avoid the bank 'eh. I suppose your husbands taught you those kinds of tricks. Well, all right. I'm only doing it because you're blood mind. And it doesn't mean I think any better of any of your idiot husbands or of your playing around with planes when you haven't got a pot of your own to piss in."

"Thanks. Now I've only got to decide which creditor to pay first."

"I'd pay the prospective leg-breaker myself. He might be a nice man but I don't suppose his thugs are. Besides my little lovey £250, nice though it is, isn't going to do much for your £13,000 deficit, is it?"

"Do you think that was legit.? The English-Mafia thing? Not just Kieran being Kieran. He didn't look like ...."

"They never do. Pay him. That slimy engineer you can deal with. Even Kieran isn't really a threat. At least you can blackmail him, now you know about his habits. Pornographic magazines indeed. That Mitch is a fool too, for throwing them away. If he could sell them for money so could you. Still, blackmail will probably be more fun."

"Great. I don't think…"

"Goodie two-shoes. Get me another biscuit."

Only later did Carrie wonder why Ignatius had bought a ticket for his sister. A nice surprise for his wife, giving her a ticket to travel to the UK. Probably he thought he would be too busy to accompany her. But with Sissy? Sissy who hated her! And who hated to leave her children. Had Sissy agreed to that? Why?

It's lucky he's dead, thought Carrie, for the first time; and then felt guilty.

Hangar Rats

The next day Carrie sent the English-Mafia man her cousin's cheque, then she went down to White Waltham to check that her plane was earning again. The club was week-day quiet. Carrie went for a quick flight around Henley and low-level up the river, marvelling as she did so at the freedom that owning a small plane gives you. She returned revived. As she was landing she heard a familiar voice on the radio.

"White Waltham, home of the brave, this is Golf Bravo Bravo Foxtrot Oscar a Pitts Special inbound to, and spellbound by, you from North America. Just jassing, from North Weald, request landing and joining instructions post haste."

No one replied.

Carrie was out of her plane and in the office by the time Kieran reached the airfield. She and the hangar rats watched through the large glass window as Kieran came flying in. He arrived overhead, did a steep spiralling turn, and in one swift movement cut straight in towards the runway from a close-in down-wind leg, slicing ahead of the Chief Pilot, who was on long finals. He ended with a dashing side-slip to the ground, rounding out flamboyantly at the last minute just before he hit the deck.

"Oh, ho," said Rudy, a slight lad in his early twenties. "Big Bertie isn't going to like that! I forecast a heavy wind blowing over young Kieran."

"Ah," giggled Piggy, a stockier, darker lad of the same age, excitedly, "is that the aging playboy then?"

A few moments later the Chief Pilot walked into the office, in the stiff way of angry men. A tall but well-built man, with greying sides to his dark hair, he had an air of orders given and respect received. He didn't bang his books onto the counter, but the intense rigidity with which he placed them there testified to his fury.

"Rudolph! Who was flying that Pitts Special?"

"Kieran O'Toole, sir."

"I see. As soon as he gets in, send him in to my office. You boys, and you too young lady," he bowed his head in Carrie's direction to show he thought no less of her for being a woman, "I hope you learn from that appalling piece of airmanship! That is not the way we behaved when I was a young man in the airforce."

"Old hypocrite," said Piggy, when he was well out of earshot, "he was once disciplined for flying so low over Chichester he nearly hit the cathedral. Talk about poacher turned game-keeper."

"Yeah," said Rudy wisely, "but of course Kieran's still the boy he would have liked to be if he wasn't pushing 50."

Kieran waltzed into the office, followed by an admiring young man.

"Pay the bill here, Charles, me dear. Hello girls, how's jolly old Wanky Waltham these days. I haven't been here for a while and I must say you've

[259]

let the grass grow, it was almost too long for my perfect side-slip and last minute roll-out to be seen. Oh, hello Mrs Northslag, I didn't see you there hanging around by the till. How's the wee Warrior. I hear it nearly had to play in an orchestra without its trumpet: no instruments 'eh. We can't go around enjoying ourselves and not paying the bills now, can we?"

"Kieran, the big white chief wants a word," said Rudy, "you cut him up on the approach something rotten. He's a mite teased about it."

"Why the little honey! He probably wants to know the secret of my skill. I shall go and teach him, where is his hiding hole? Before I depart, young Mrs North, I would like a word, if you could spare me a second of your precious."

Carrie was sitting in the bar, examining the painted silhouettes of planes, trying to identify them, when Kieran swept in, aroused by his encounter with the Chief Pilot.

"Well," he said, sitting down heavily, "did that boy need to learn a thing or two. Thanks I'll have a coffee, sweet one," he ordered the girl behind the bar, who looked at him for a moment and then decided it was less hassle to serve him than to argue about it. "He was lucky it was me and not a violent man he was talking to. The trouble is you can take the man out of the military, but you can't take the military out of the man. Once they've been corrupted it's all discipline and obedience, no thought, just blind canon-fodder. Shame how it ruins a good man..but you don't want to stretch your little ears with my problems, when you have so many of your own. Do you perhaps have a cheque for me in one of your dinky little pockets?"

"Nope."

"Well my good girl, why not? It was the best and safest trip of your life, was it not? And it would seem a shame to ruin it now, after all our great times together. Now I would like to help you, so what I will do is I will buy something from you..."

"Like what?"

"Well I can't buy your virginity, alas, you gave that away and no doubt to a much lesser man. But I could buy some of the instruments from your plane, although I must say I'd be a fool to do so considering what a dog's breakfast the whole thing is..."

"OK you can buy the plane's second VOR for £200."

"£200? £200! My little darling. I'd be cheating myself and leading you astray, allowing you to think that others would follow my generous and self-defeating paths. I'll give you £150 for the whole instrument panel."

"Ha ha."

"Now my little sugar, I think you would agree that..."

"Forget it Kieran. This isn't going to work.."

"Spoken with your usually subtlety! Well my little love there is another option. Princess Mitch has some of my property and if you could get it back from her I might consider allowing you a percentage of the profits..."

"Even if she has, she isn't likely to give it to me, is she?"

"So negative! So negative when I am trying so hard to give you a helping hand in this cruel sea of life. Looks like we are getting to the option where I send the boys in doesn't it? Or you could try a loan from the bank, it might be softer."

"Look Kieran, it's advertised. I'm doing my best. That's all."

Kieran finished his coffee and stood up. "You've got a week," he said. "Thanks for the coffee." And putting on his hat he swept out of the bar.

Carrie, realising Kieran had slid off without paying, asked the girl to put the coffee on her tab.

"Forget it," she said, "no more credit. Sor-ry."

"Look you're using my plane here..."

"Yeah, and you haven't paid its keep either."

"We're only talking two coffees."

"Sor-ry, I'm afraid not. I've got a business to run."

Carrie wrote her a cheque for four pounds and hoped it would bounce.

"Any chance of someone giving me a lift to the station?"

One of the donglers, White Waltham-speak for plane pushers, drove her to the station. He had a suggestion. "Look Mrs Northless," he said, "sorry if I'm speaking out of turn and all that, but seems to me you could do worse than ask Mitch for a loan, if you're really in trouble. I mean," he said, getting a bit embarrassed, "only till you've sold your plane and that, but she's got the wander. Well wedged up, she is."

"Thanks. When's she due back?"

"Dunno, but she's never away long. She loves it here. Can't stay away."

At Roberta's house there was a letter from the bank asking Carrie to make an appointment to see them as soon as convenient.

"That's a laugh," said Roberta, snuggling down on her sofa, safe in the knowledge that her house was paid for and she was earning well, "as soon as convenient. At your earliest convenience. Well it's never convenient to be asked to give the money back, now is it! What they really mean but are too chicken to say is; give that money back or we'll move in, take the plane and where will you be then!"

"Humm."

"Another guy left a message. He saw the advert in Pilot. Here's his number."

She passed over a scrumpled piece of paper, where her stabbing hand had scrawled a name and number.

"Oh? Did this one sound single too?"

"Aren't you the comic. Might be, he certainly shallied around, 'shall I call back or shall I leave my number.' All sorts of time wasting. I said just give me the fucking number or get off my blower. I've got better things to do than be my cousin's secretary all day. And then he started apologising and getting right on my tits."

"Oh, sorry."

"Don't you start."

Carrie rang the nervous young man and the first thing he asked was. "Who is that woman you live with?" Followed by the nervous laugh that accompanied most of his speech.

"Say again? I thought you were interested in buying the plane?"

Nervous laugh. "Oh, yes. I am.. sorry..it's just..I mean she was so strong in the head.. that is.. I mean you oh she.. you see.. yes.. yes.. I am.. could I.. that is I'd like to come.. I mean.."

"Would you like to come and see the plane?" Carrie asked hopefully.

"Oh, yes, yes splendid. Thank you. er.. when would suit you?"

"Tomorrow."

"Tomorrow.. er.. yes.. er.. tomorrow," nervous laughter. "I might.. that is or.. perhaps I could ring.."

"Any day you like is fine with me, would you prefer the day after?"

"Why, why yes, that would be better. Thanks." Little laugh.

Eventually, after three changes of date, two of time and several phone calls, Mr Twifle came down to White Waltham. He was a surprisingly tall ageless man, slim but with big bone structure and a way of dropping his head forward on his neck to make himself seem smaller. He wore gold rimmed glasses, which gave him an erroneously inquisitive air, and had a nervous way of moving his face, which made Carrie think he might be wearing ill-fitting false teeth. He apparently liked the plane.

"Oh, it is pretty," he said laughing, "such a nice colour. I mean I suppose it was painted when you bought it.. that is.. What a lovely shape. Although I suppose it would be, that shape, that is, being a Warrior."

"Would you like to go for a flight?" Carrie asked, hoping to direct his nervousness.

"Oh yes! That is.. I mean, should I pay you to fly me? I don't want to assume." He laughed lightly.

"Nice idea, but no, just enjoy it and decide whether to buy it," said Carrie, starting her walk round.

Desperate for money though she was, Carrie didn't think she could start charging for a few minutes in the air. Besides, one thing she did remember from her lessons with the Steves and Daves was that that was illegal. Both Steve and Dave loved to talk about 'dodgy charters'; flights for which they were paid cash, when really it should have been for free.

"We've enough fuel for an hour, how long will you need to make up your mind?" Carrie asked, so bluntly that Mr Twifle blushed and laughed.

"Er.. that is.. how long would you I mean.. I don't want to look a gift horse.." His voice petered out.

It was a warm, sunny day with a straggling of light, flimsy cumulus clouds and a spider's web of cirrus above. Carrie took off and flew out down the railway, past Henley-on-Thames and up the river, so low on the water that their shadow danced in and out of reflected trees like a ghost plane. She pulled up to display some steep turns.

"Heavenly," she said feeling happily relaxed, "this is great isn't it. Isn't this what we fly for? Look at the way the sunlight drifts in and out of the clouds.. how can you feel bad when the world is so beautiful?"

She let Mr Twifle have control and he flew a few minutes, did some accurate flat turns and gave the controls back. "Nice," he said, "very nice.. Lovely."

She flew them back to the airfield but Twifle spoke no more and Carrie sadly realised he wasn't really serious. She landed gently, once again rather pleased with herself. Unfortunately Twifle didn't notice. She taxied in and shut down outside the club house. As they climbed out of the Warrior, Twifle was already keen to be away.

"I'll ring you," he said, almost running towards his car.

"Great." She wasn't surprised. Perhaps her husband would have been better at selling planes than she was. Clearly it was not a straightforward business. Her success so far had been negligible. Twifle stopped and shouted across the distance.

"..er.. when's the best time to get you.. I mean.. Ringing... that woman.." Inevitably laughter followed his speech.

"My cousin?"

"Oh, is she? What does she do?"

"She's a PA. Don't call her a secretary she doesn't like it."

"No, no, no. No, no, no. I wouldn't. Absolutely not. So if I rang during the day I'd get you? I mean not that I.. that is.." He laughed.

"Yup. I'll be there."

"Nice," and he leapt off again. He stopped once more. "Thanks. For the flight that is. Thanks." He giggled once again. "It was nice."

Carrie cleaned a small patch of oil off the Warrior and tied it to the long, metal wires that White Waltham string through the grass to protect small planes from hurricanes in the night. She looked at the shiny strength of its skin and wondered what its life had been like.

"If you could talk," she said stroking the hard sheen on the wings with her hand, "I bet you'd be able to explain why my husband bought you in Florida without a moment's pause, and why no one here seems to want you in spite of beautiful, lyrical, romantic flights in the evening sunlight."

The Warrior revealed no secrets. Carrie turned sadly away and with one last look back at her faithful steed, padded across the springy grass to return the keys to the flight office.

For several days Carrie heard nothing from Mr Twifle and there were no other buyers hotly demanding to see the Warrior. Then, out of the blue, Mr Twifle amazed her; he rang. "Hello.. it's er.. it's er Marco Twifle here. Is that Carrie Nordsuchland?"

"Yes, hello, how are you?"

"Eer.. er.. well.. yes.I'm well.. er thank you for asking. How are you?"

"Well thanks."

"Good, good."

"Good."

There was long pause, then Twifle began again.

"The thing is.. er.. it's like this.. er.."

Carrie wondered if he'd left something in the plane and was calling to ask if she'd found it. She didn't remember seeing anything unusual, but who knows.

"Er.. the thing is.. er.. I wondered if.. that is.. subject to an engineering check I rather think I'd like to buy it.. er.. the plane that is.. if that's OK."

Carrie gulped, wondered if she'd misunderstood, and nearly asked him if he was sure. She revived her business instincts just in time and asked for a deposit.

"Of course," he said, "er.. how much would you like? That is.. Would 10% be sufficient?"

"Yes, indeed. Fine."

Carrie put the phone down and stared into the air. She done it! She'd absolutely bloody well done it! Alone. Unaided. And judging from the bank manager's restlessness, just in time.

"Yippee," Carrie screamed, dancing around the room, "yippee!"

"You haven't sold it yet," said her cousin, when she suggested champagne. "I should wait before you start cheering, until the whole things bound and gagged."

"No, no this is a done deed. He's even taking me to dinner to hand over the deposit."

"Out to dinner, is it? You be careful, going out to dinner with a stranger. Remember Ben!"

"I married a stranger."

"You married three and look what good that did. Jesus wept, talk about learning nothing from life. I'd better come as your escort."

Carrie laughed and nearly agreed, but the thought of Mr Twifle backing out of buying the plane just because of Roberta stopped her. "I'll be all right. Don't worry."

"I'm not. I just don't like the responsibility. I just don't like the idea of having to go and face all those policemen when I identify your body. It might even be the same heffalumps. Think of Suzy Lamplugh, and others. Strangers in the night, pah!"

Completely discouraged now, Carrie promised not to get into his car, not to walk down any dark streets with him and to always remain in public places with plenty of people. Even so Roberta continued to look at her cousin as though she thought she might never see her again. Every now and then, particularly while showering, Carrie could hear her muttering, 'young fool,' and sighing deeply.

The Warrior's Conquest

Dinner with Mr Twifle was in fact more scary for him than for Carrie. He jumped up when she arrived in the restaurant and seemed unwilling to sit down again, dancing on his toes for many minutes before finally poising back in his chair.

"Hello, nice of you to come. Ha ha."

"Not at all, thank you for inviting me."

There was a silence where Twifle laughed a little without speaking and fiddled with his cutlery. Carrie broke the frost. "So you want my little Warrior?"

Twifle laughed. "Yes, yes, indeed. Nice plane. Er.. nice."

Carrie tried to think of something to say, something that did not involve 'how soon can I have the money, do you have it on you now?' She felt certain she ought to make small talk, to give him some banalities for his 10% deposit, but couldn't think of anything to say except: "Where is it? Is the cheque in your pocket?"

"Have you been flying long?" she asked in desperation.

"Yes.. er.. and no.. really.." replied Twifle laughing nervously.

Carrie decided to talk about herself, attempting to fill the increasingly tense vacuum between them. To avoid talking about her plane, she talked about Africa. After a few minutes of inspired conversation on Ignatius and the darting season, during which Twifle said absolutely nothing, she tried to bring him into the conversation.

"Have you ever been to Africa?" she asked.

"No. I mean, that is, I'd like to. I mean you make it sound very.. very interesting." He laughed nervously.

"Oh, good. Where were you thinking of going?"

"Oh, er.. where do you recommend?" More laughter.

At that moment, much to Carrie's relief, the blond Australian waitress bounced over with the menus. She reeled off a string of specials, repeated them again when Twifle couldn't understand her accent, checked that they got them all right, and departed saying she'd give them a few minutes to make up their minds. Twifle couldn't decide what to eat and Carrie chose for him, Dover sole, reminding herself of the Baroness de Vocov. She also chose the wine.

"Would you like red or white?"

Twifle laughed. "Oh, you choose.. I'm.. er.. I'm eating.. oh well you know of course.. haha.. well actually I can eat anything with any colour really.. you choose."

"I'm having fish too," said Carrie, "so I thought about a Chilean Sauvignon Blanc. Would that suit you?"

"Eer.. yes.. absolutely.. great choice.. I don't really know why Chardonnay is so popular.."

He gave a disarming laugh, just in case she preferred Chardonnay.

Carrie was confused, unused to this limitless self-deprecation.

"Would you prefer Chardonnay? There is a quite nice Ryman's Chardonnay which isn't too expensive?"

"No, no, no.. that is whatever you think best."

Carrie sighed internally and thought about the 10%. Never mind the conversation, feel the consequences. She stuck with the Sauvignon Blanc.

"Oh, look here," said Twifle, "I almost forgot.. er.. this is for you.. I hope it's enough I mean we did agree.. that is.."

He shuffled the cheque, disguised in a brown envelop, over to her; as embarrassed as if it was pornographic material. Carrie opened it, and saw her 10% written in ink with pure delight. "Absolutely fine," she crowed. "Absolutely fine."

She got down to eating her roasted pepper salad.

By the end of the meal, listening to Twifle start a story, wonder if she would rather speak instead, or should he continue, and then laughing nervously, Carrie was exhausted. So when he offered to give her a lift home she nearly accepted, despite her promise to her cousin. However, then she considered what sort of driving such a nervous man must have and ordered a cab. Twifle insisted on waiting for her taxi to arrive, when it did he lent into the front cab and gave the driver a tenner.

"Hope you don't mind," he said staring at the stars above, "only I rather thought I should." He giggled.

"Thanks," she said unhassled, leaning back against the cushions in the luxury of a sale found and a meal finished with for ever.

When Carrie got home her cousin was still up, pottering around the garden in the moist night, looking for snails to teach to fly.

"Oh, you are still alive then?" She said, coming back into the house as the front door slammed on the taxi.

"Guess so."

"Here." She forced a tenner into Carrie's hand. "But don't think I'll be there for you every time you go gadding around with strange men."

"Thanks, that's really kind." Carrie felt strangely touched. Rather like a millionaire who has just been given a fiver by a pauper.

"Yeah, well don't go bleating about it or I may change my mind. Pah. Nights out with strangers! How was he anyway?"

"Nervous."

"Ha, I wouldn't have needed dinner with him to tell you that. Got the money?"

"Yup."

"Hum. Well, don't get overexcited. There's many a slip twixt cup and lip, you know. Don't say I didn't warn you."

"I know," said Carrie, dutifully hiding her extreme excitement. "Sure, I know."

Carrie couldn't stop smiling as she made her way to bed. "This is OK. I might even go and use the money to buy some more planes and bring them back and sell them. This is an OK way of life. Perhaps I'll become a ferry pilot myself."

She went to bed in bliss that night and dreamt of opening futures; new planes; great sales and heavy winnings. Carrie was happy.

Graffiti Gouged Glass

Carrie used Mr Twifle's deposit to pay half the engineer's invoice and half of Kieran's bill. She made an appointment with the bank, but only to tell them that the plane had probably been bought and there would soon be some money. The bank manager reminded her that soon was not a word he liked.

"Mrs Naughtyland, I really prefer the word now," he said. "Soon is rather a vague term. When exactly will the plane be sold?"

"Well, the buyer is having an engineer's check next week. So then."

"Exactly when next week? Which day?"

Carrie guessed. "Friday."

"Very well. You have until Friday but after that we are going to have to think of some other way for you to pay off these loans. We are not a charity Mrs Noddyland."

On Tuesday Twifle rang, already laughing nervously when she picked up the phone he nearly had apoplexy when he heard her voice. The engineer at White Waltham couldn't do the check and he'd rather have his own engineer in Luton do it, ".. if she didn't mind. Would it be all right?"

"Yes indeed. I can fly it up for you if you like."

"If that's OK. Very kind. He's very reputable." Twifle said between laughs. "There shouldn't be any problem."

The flight to Luton was lyrical, the air clear, with little white clouds passing her like tiny puffs of dandelion dust. Leaving the plane she took the train back to London; noting to her surprise that the Luton coaches were cleaner and more comfortable than the others, although the windows were still decorated with graffiti-gouged glass and the view outside still ornamented with 'Shar luvs Ted' and 'Fuck Phaggots'.

Arriving back in Peckham Carrie was so excited she danced gleefully around the tiny hall, hitting the pictures with her shoulders. "Yippee, yippee, I could burst, I can sing, tralala Twifle the king! He's ringing me on Thursday and, I tell you what Roberta, when I get the money I'm going to buy you a present. Then I'm going to pay off my debts, and finally I'm going to invest in the future. I may even do a Commercial Pilot's Licence like Kees."

"Ha," said her cousin, watching her from the kitchen, stuffing cold pizza into her mouth. She shut the fridge aggressively. "I shouldn't jump around like that! Ever heard of putting the cart before the horse. Remember the story about the spilt milk?"

"Oh yes, but this plane has already been checked to death by engineers. It can't fail. There cannot be a thing wrong with it, now can there."

"Ha. I expect you thought that about your husbands too! And they were certainly well checked; although not all well chequed!"

Carrie went for a walk.

All through Wednesday night Carrie tossed and turned, disturbed by the street noise; cats on night duty, wind-blown papers along the gutters, someone whistling, a train halting: how could you sleep with all that going on. At 5.30 she got up, prepared Roberta's breakfast, and began to tidy the house. Every few minutes she glanced at her watch. At seven o'clock the post arrived. There was nothing for Carrie. Just a couple of bills for Roberta. Carrie put them on a tray and took it to Roberta in bed.

"Hello, you awake?"

"No."

"I brought you some breakfast."

Roberta sat up jerkily, her still sleepy face as red as her nightgown.

"What do you want? You know I haven't any money. I should never have given you that tenner; now you think I'm easy."

Carrie left the tray and fled.

On Thursday afternoon the phone rang. Carrie answered and heard the elegant, nervous voice of Twifle. She imagined his face twitching away with smiles.

"Hi, Marco, how was it, everything OK?"

There was a slight pause. Then he said, "look.. er.. Carrie.. I like you. I don't know anything about engineering myself. You see I'm not an expert. Look I .. er.. I have to believe what they tell me.. you do understand that, don't you. I mean I'd like us to stay friends." He laughed nervously.

Carrie felt a chilling ice in her soul. She recognised this feeling from the lawyer's office in Cape Town. Only here there were no engraved, wooden lions to give her courage.

"What? What? What do you mean?"

"Look, I'm really sorry. Really I am. I like you. If there was any way. If it was only something small.."

"Just tell me what's the matter?"

"Corrosion! Corrosion. The whole plane is full of corrosion. It must have been sitting out in Florida for so long. Look I'm really sorry but the engineer said it would be more than his licence was worth to give it a clean bill of health. I am sorry, but I'll have to ask for my deposit back."

"What?"

"Eer.. I'm terribly sorry, really."

"I told you so," said her cousin, when she came in from work. "Always happens, just when you think things are going well. It's always best to expect the worst, then you don't get so disappointed."

Carrie went for another walk.

The next day she travelled up to Luton to fetch the plane. She took a train, disgusted at the filthy way they kept their carriages, mortified that the government couldn't keep vandals from massacring the windows.

The engineer was out on the tarmac examining a Piper Seneca. He climbed out from under the plane and walked over to her, as she walked towards the Warrior.

"Hello! You Mrs Snodland?"

"I'm Mrs Nordsuitlaan."

"Yeah, that's what I said. Here's your dog lead," he said, reaching into his pocket and giving her the keys. He laid his hand on the Warrior's wing, smiling sorrowfully at Carrie.

"That's the trouble with amateurs. If you'd asked me to give it a check before it left Florida I could have saved you a lot of money."

Carrie felt instantly annoyed. Who was this man with his patronising attitude?

"Why would you have been in Florida?"

"I go there all the time. I import these things professionally, in a box that is; I wouldn't trust a ferry pilot further than I could throw one. If you'd asked my advice, I'd have told you never fly with a pilot. Especially not one like that Killem O'Balls-up; he's got a reputation you know. I couldn't begin to tell you all the planes he's grave-yarded. You should have asked me before you went."

"Thanks. I'll call on you next time shall I!" She gave him one of her bull-dozer smiles, started up the plane and turned the Warrior in a whiplash movement, hoping to catch him with a wing. Unfortunately he was standing well clear.

"Goodbye, Mr Engineer." She said angrily. "Have a nice life!"

Carrie flew the plane back to White Waltham furiously. The weather had changed and she had to avoid dark clouds and rain showers. Thunder rumbled in the distance. The only silver lining was a flash of lightning ahead. Full of corrosion! Her plane was full of corrosion! Even Carrie knew that 'corrosion' meant falling to pieces bit by rusty and untreated bit.

"That bloody husband of mine," thought Carrie, watching the strafing rain on the brown fields beneath her. "If he wasn't dead already, I would have killed him."

She called White Waltham on the radio. No reply. But the landing was brilliant. 'Smooth and sensuous as butter' in Kieran-speak. No one was watching.

Taxiing in she saw the sloping-right-shoulder shape of Kees waving. Even before Carrie had shut down, Kees was on the wing and fumbling with the door clasp.

"How is things, schatje?" He shouted to her, over the zing of slowing gyros.

"Dreadful! I can't tell you how bad. What are you doing here?"

"I've got a job with Maybinot Airlines. As a First Officer. I'm on long haul. It's such great. So good routes! Such much money already."

Funny how when your life is on the downhill slope everyone else seems to be doing so well.

She jumped out of the plane, attempted to lock the door, forgetting it was still broken in spite of a host of engineers. The key ground round in the socket. They walked together over the White Waltham grass to the office, where she gave Rudy and Piggy the keys. The boys realised there had been no sale and looked sympathetic.

Kees bought her a coffee in the bar. "Carrie," he said, as they sat down in the creaking wicker chairs, "will you have dinner with me this night? I'm only here for tonight." When she hesitated he added. "I'm paying."

Great, Carrie thought, that's the sort of woman I've become. You have to tell her in advance it's OK she won't have to pick up the tab. Then she smiled, realising this was the first time she'd minded being paid for; learning independence perhaps.

"Sure. Thanks Kees. I'd enjoy it. Are we dressing up or shall I come as I am?"

"Oh, you're fine. Beautiful already."

"Of course," said Carrie remembering Holland. The Dutch are expert down-dressers; wearing jeans for a wedding or a mini skirt for a funeral was not considered unusual or disrespectful in the Netherlands.

Cooked Cheese

Kees took her to a converted Jacobean house outside Reading. Paths wound down to the river through a wisteria arch and into an ornamental garden; the elegant creation of some long-term enthusiast. The air was soft, with altocirrus clouds and still evening lightness. A couple of swallows flew above them, doing sensuous aerobatics in the dusk that Kieran would have been hard pushed to imitate in his Pitts Special. Carrie noticed a light scent of honeysuckle. She knew her mood should be lightened by such exquisite natural beauty, but only found herself regretting her lost house in Cape Town. Kees took her hand.

"Champagne, schatje? Tonight we are celebrating."

"Or commiserating. Thanks Kees."

Vintage Bollinger surrounded by flowers sat waiting for them on a wooden table, as though left there by fairies. Down a paved stairway swans slid on the green river. Carrie sat down on the upper step and watched their stately passage. She drank deeply while Kees, unusually chatty, told her about his airline job, how much he enjoyed it, what fun everyone was, what opportunities he got, how sexy the aircraft was, which lines he flew.

"I never thought I could have so a life," he said, "the stews.. sorry stewardesses all love my humour. The call me Cheesie, I think it's because my smile."

Carrie laughed, realising he was being kind, trying to take her mind off the tragedy that was her future. When the waiter brought out the menus, she remembered how the White Tie liked to order for her; it was one of his charming tricks, that and walking on the outside of the pavement; presumably to protect her from pollution. With her next two husbands she had made it clear she could do these things for herself.

Dinner was first class. The wine, Kees reminded her, 'felt like an angel had pissed on your tongue'. She tried to eat, drink and be enthusiastic about Kees's job, but her mind wandered. Her problems were too heavy for beauty and good food to suppress. At least no one had sent in heavies yet, but that might still come.

"I went last week to a dinner party," said Kees, "I talking to a policeman and his wife was, they asked me, 'why you learn to fly'? I said I had a lot of money to burn.."

"My money," Carrie pointed out dryly. Still, she thought, so what! Would it have saved her? Probably not. If she had had more money her third husband would probably simply have bought a bigger plane, or more of them. For a moment she balked at the idea of two or more planes to bring back from America.

"You sound like them," said Kees annoyed. "It was a joke! Instead of laughing they look serious, they ask why I have such much money. I embarrassed was, they are thinking I showing off am."

He looked at his ex-wife and wondered at her sadness. He was used to her light hearted optimism and this was only one sale lost; there'd be another. He wanted to tell her more jokes, to hear her laugh; but she was on another wavelength. Kees didn't know that life got harder as you got older; for him it had got easier, more pleasurable.

"Americans?"

"What?" asked Kees, "what Americans? Are you concentrated Carrie?" Carrie ignored the mistake, he wasn't her husband any more.

"I mean were they Americans, those people, the ones you talked about? Their humour is often different.."

"Ah, humour forsure! Only the British understand the British humour. You explain me why it is funny that Hitler called the Dutch 'Cheese Heads.' Only every time you say that to a British person they laugh."

Carrie laughed too, but dutifully, knowing she owed Kees thanks.

After dinner they went out to the river again for coffee and brandy. Kees was drinking heavily. She remembered him as abstemious. Besides, he had an early start next morning. Looked like he was becoming a pilot through and through. Next stop oxygen to clear the hangover.

"Eight hours throttle to bottle" Kees told her, "is a myth like the Lochness Monster." He moved a little closer to her smiling. "Cassie," he said. "Cassie, look I know I a joker and a fool am. I know we have our bad times had, but.. things have changed now. I've changed. I a proper job and a house have. We don't have to live in Idaho."

"Castles in Idaho?"

"Serious," said Kees putting his hand on her arm, "..look Cassie, there's never been anyone else for me quite like you. I know we, me as well as you, bad things said when we parted but I didn't mean it. For me you was always special, such special.."

"So special you had your lawyer complain I made myself a gin and tonic without offering you one?" she asked unable to stop herself.

"That's lawyers," came back Kees robustly. "It was you that gave me the hard-shoulder. You complain I cut my cheese too thick."

Carrie laughed. It wasn't true. She had complained that he left his socks on the floor as though he had a maid, but not about the thickness of the cheese. Some of the things on their divorce petition, however, should have been in the trivia court.

She remembered the flat in Amsterdam. The rail carriage bathroom, one man wide with the loo at the far end. To prevent the water flooding the house after a shower, since the sewage system was unaltered since the fifties, there was a plastic brush to move the water around the floor until the drain could be persuaded to take it down to the cesspit beneath. The place held the fetid smell of embedded dirt. When Carrie had arrived, full of romance after their frost encrusted honeymoon, it was mid-winter. Ice water trickled grudgingly out of the shower head in spasms. Then she discovered there was no heating in the house at all.

"Cold shoulder," she mentioned, "not hard."

He hadn't liked it when she corrected his English. He complained she was a teacher and said that since he was a communicator the occasional mistake was acceptable.

Kees realised that they were going down a one way street in the wrong direction and tried to get the conversation back into a soft sentimental mood. This was not the way he had planned the evening in his dreams.

"Darling, remember when we took the gondolier in Venice. We got in, then the man gets in. I take the pole laughingly and the man he say. 'OK let's go'. We are out in Grand Canal, when I say to man, 'No! Too fast for me, you take it back.' And he say. 'What! I never used pole before, I thought you was Gondolier.' And there we stuck in middle of canal are, with no poleman on board. Remember?"

"I remember." She smiled. It was one of the funny times. They had had their first wedding anniversary in Venice. Things were good then. They'd left the memories of Dutch bathrooms and constant rain behind, invested in the culture and beauty of Italy. But for Carrie it only strengthened the longing to get out of Holland. The desire to be elsewhere in the world.

"I was worried then you thought I was an airbrush."

"Air head. Airbrush is for hair." She knew she was being hard, controversial but that was the way she felt at this moment. Not silky.

"Best time of my life," said Kees gently, stroking her cheek with his finger; seeing only silk. "You too, baby? My only love."

Carrie smelt the champagne on his breath and knew now what was coming. She thought about it. It was a way out of her problems, and God knows she'd married men for less in the past. It would solve everything. She could leave the plane earning money here, go and live in America. Kees loved her, and she retained a lot of affection for him. Looking back she wondered if she had been exactly potty over any of her husbands; well, the White Tie, but he hadn't really lived long enough to disappoint her. And her Afrikaana pilot; but he had flirted away her love and now it seemed he had been making plans to live a life without her: possibly still was. So now Kees again. Perhaps, she thought, she should have babies. Now that Kees was an airline pilot they could afford it. All she had to do was say yes.

"..what do you say Carrie? Shall we again try? Since longtime I think only of you. We could do such much this time?"

He was very close now, his lips almost touching hers. Carrie could smell the cheese behind the champagne. It would be very easy just to give in, to say 'yes,' to let him take all the burdens now. After all, she thought, he owes me for the alimony I gave him, which allowed him to learn to fly in the first place.

"What do you say Carrie? Will you marry me once again?"

She looked at the swans. Two were rubbing their necks together. Kees looked too.

"They marry for life," said Kees lovingly, "perhaps we should try a life of remarrying."

She laughed and kissed him gently on the cheek.

"Actually it's a myth Kees. Some swans have two or three partners, especially if the early ones die. Sadly there are some mistakes you cannot mend with 'I'm sorry'."

Kees looked away and a slight sigh trembled through his slim body. His right shoulder dropped a little lower. "Oh, well," he said heavily, "I guess it's just back to the admiration of the Maybinot stews then."

When Carrie got home it was very late and there was a message from her cousin. The note, written in black, in Roberta's heavy angular hand-writing, said: 'That Twifle rang, git! Wanted to know when you'd be back. I told him you were pretty unreliable, and after all the pain he'd caused you'd probably committed suicide. He was SO worried! Said you could call him any time day or night. Wet rag!'

Carrie went to bed; the last person she wanted to talk to now was Twifle.

In the morning she heard the phone ringing with the urgency that it gains in the early hours. She hoped desperately it was someone for her cousin. A few moments later she heard Roberta's heel-first walk slam-ming down the corridor. Roberta's face came around the door curiously disembodied, like a head out of a turtle shell.

"It's that Twifle. I told him you were still alive and he wants a word. I told the silly git you were still in bed after drowning your sorrows all night and were hardly in the mood for chit chat, but he was going on and on 'til I thought I'd have to go round to his house and disconnect his 'phone."

Carrie heaved herself out of bed, feeling the memory of last night's over-champagning, and put her bathrobe on. "Did anyone ever tell you you're a character, Roberta?" she asked.

"Yes, and I understood what they meant, but if anyone had ever told me you'd be living here rent free for over a year I wouldn't have believed them."

Carrie picked up the phone and there was Twifle twifling about 'oh so sorry' and 'he really didn't mean to get her out of bed. So worried. So upset.' And when he finally got to the nub of it he wondered if they could have dinner and she would return his money.

"I'm a bit busy this week," Carrie improvised, "a friend in Suffolk's having a baby and she's asked me to help...next week...well, tell you what, I'll ring as soon as I'm back. Yup. Yup. Fantastic. Absolutely. Look forward to it too. Great. Bye."

"Friend in Suffolk is it?" said Roberta. "If you had any friends anywhere they'd have seen you by now. Still I guess you bamboozled that Twifle. Now what?"

What indeed?

"Can you ring the bank, and tell them I've got flu and tell them I'll make another appointment as soon as I can." Carrie asked, her eyes begging her cousin to sympathise.

"Lies, lies and more lies. This'll do you no good in the end. All right I will, but might I suggest you join the rest of us human beings and try to get a job?"

"Doing what?"

"Well you could be an internet stripper! Businesses that never go bust."

"Ha, ha," murmured Carrie, feeling sick.

"Yeah," said the short, tubby Roberta, "but you probably haven't the figure anyway. However, you can be my cleaner. Mine's quit. I'll pay you £30. I'm robbing myself, but at least it's a start."

After Roberta left, Carrie, wearing a tee-shirt and a hangover, began cleaning. It wasn't difficult work. Roberta's former cleaner had been thorough and efficient and Carrie was only dusting shiny surfaces. After a while it occurred to her that Roberta might not notice she'd cleaned at all. So she started moving things: scent to the other side of the dressing table. Books into a tidy pile. Adjusting pictures. By the end of the day she felt she had done a good job; she looked forward to Roberta getting home.

When Roberta walked in the door, however, she wasn't alone.

"Look what jolly little friends I found on the doorstep," she said sarcastically, stopping to straighten a picture. "It's your friendly local bobbies again. Please do use my front room, but watch for piles of things in the wrong place; it's recently been cleaned." And she flounced off to the kitchen, slamming the door so hard the pictures bounced back into their original positions.

"I'm afraid she doesn't like us," said DI Kundera. "We won't be long," added Jones. "But we wanted to ask her a question too."

Carrie nodded and followed Roberta, opening the door carefully in case it was booby-trapped.

In the kitchen Roberta said, "it's the last time you clean my house, you maniac. You've moved everything. I don't know, you do a kindness to someone and..."

"The police want to talk to you?"

"Me? Why? Until you came here I lived a blameless life. Now I'm mixed up with criminals, murders, insurance fraud.. you name it.. well bring them in then. I haven't all day to wait for police questions."

"It's only routine," began Kundera sympathetically, his thin face full of worried alarm. "Just a short query," added Jones more robustly.

"OK, OK, don't hang about. They always say that in detective novels. What's the question?"

"Do you know Dennis Keenes?"

"Never heard of him. Who is he?"

"You wrote him a cheque. A personal cheque."

"I did? Aren't I the kind one. Did he sell me some soap, perhaps, or a chicken? Forgive me but although I already know we live in a police state, I think I am free to write cheques to anyone, or anything, I please without having to explain it to you. Or have I suddenly been transported to Zimbabwe?"

The detectives exchanged glances. "Perhaps we'd better explain," said Kundera gently, embarrassed, while Jones seemed to grow in size to protect him. "Don't want any upset." "It's about the murder of Ben."

"Oh," said Roberta giving Carrie a hard glance. "I knew you'd be at the bottom of it. So this guy murdered Ben, I sent him a cheque and you think I'm paying him to murder Carrie too. I can tell you I'm tempted. Often. But why pay for something you can so easily do yourself; for free."

Everyone except Roberta laughed. "Actually," said Kundera apologetically, "it's not quite like that. But he is an underworld figure, who appears to be implicated in the murder of Ben and who owed Ignatius a favour, so we wondered why you wrote him a cheque."

"I think," said Carrie, "it was me, not Roberta, who gave him money. You see I owed him some Greenland dollars." She laughed. "Flying is such a small world."

Life Enhancing Curve

Carrie took the train to White Waltham. She had a proposition she wanted to suggest to Mitch. She hadn't forgotten the dongler's words about Mitch's untapped sources of wealth and she was hoping there might be an untapped reservoir of generosity too. Mitch wasn't there. Rudy said she was on a Boeing training course.

"She's being upgraded from '73s to 74s," he explained, "lucky devil. Means more money and better routes. One day, one day," he continued wistfully. "One day I'll be doing the same; I've nearly finished my private you know."

Carrie smiled. She had become aware there was a whole pre-airline-pilot industry around airfields. Young people, mostly boys, washing planes and dongling, scrimping to get enough money to train to be pilots. Some made it all the way to the airlines. Here people easily fell into debt; she was not alone. Sponsorship was rare and the only fully paid way to make it to the airlines was through the military. Even there the numbers of pilots were being cut. And yet, with the increasingly travelling public, the need was growing. Normal bureaucratic lack of foresight. Flying was a computer game with bureaucracy.

On the Monday of the following week the assistant bank manager called. "Ah Mrs Norseland, your flu is better it seems. When will it be convenient for you to visit us? I am free today."

Reluctantly Carrie agreed to go and see him. On the tube she read an article explaining that today's bank managers dress according to the level of their clients. She stroked her smart silk funeral outfit; it at least was eminently suitable.

Arriving at the square concrete building she told the bored bank clerk she had come to see the manager's assistant. The young man immediately said he was not there.

Carrie felt ill-used. "I made an appointment," she said crossly, although she'd have been glad to go away without seeing him.

"Oh, OK. You'd better wait, I'll check."

Eventually Mr Anthony Lower appeared, from an open plan office where he could be one with his staff, wearing jeans. He ushered her into a small room. In line with the bank's current friendliness policy there was no large imposing office for Carrie to shiver in, instead they talked in a small, bland box room, with cheap, modern, furniture chosen to make clients feel at home. A glass fronted wooden bookcase demonstrated a selection of books about mortgages. A computer on the pine table was surrounded by pine chairs. Luckily Mr Lower was able to undermine the modern informality of his office and dress by his delicately patronising manner.

"So, Mrs Norseland.."

"Nordsuitlaan, it's Afrikaans. It means North South Lane. I suppose you could look on it as an oxymoron!"

"Oh, I'm so sorry Mrs Norserland, do forgive me. How very interesting. I've always admired our African cousins. "Now to business. As I understand it you have outstanding loans of £13,276. 86."

He clicked at the computer which stood on the table. Punched in his password, tutted a few times, squeezing his lips onto his teeth. Finally he brought up a screen full of minuses: her account. The number £13,276.86 shone out in bold. She restrained the desire to say that she had the pence in her pocket and could return them immediately.

"Well now, to be simple, let's say almost £14,000 including the interest. Interest which appears to be accumulating rather than being being paid back. Your plane, on the other hand, is on the market for..how much did you say...?"

"£30,000."

"£30,000. Splendid as far as our little debt goes. If you sell it. If you paid it off today that would leave you £16,000 in the clear. And supposing you do manage to sell it before the interest payments overtake the projected sales target, what then?"

"I'm planning to import and export planes."

"Oh, thanks to the success of this venture?" There was just a suggestion of raised eyebrows in his voice, while his face continued to observe her with heart-warming interest in her welfare.

"Absolutely so. All life is a learning curve, wouldn't you agree?"

"Naturally I would, but in this case, my dear Mrs N., our interests need to coincide with your life-enhancing curve, don't they?"

After half an hour they agreed on a payback regime of £117.27 a month, to start from following week. Carrie was baffled by how he got to that amount, assuming from the speed of his explanation that he was late for lunch. She wondered if she could persuade her cousin to let her do two days of cleaning a week, until she sold the plane. After that? Well, she preferred not to think too far ahead.

Roberta was not over-excited when Carrie suggested her proposition.

"Are you taking this debt seriously."

"What do you mean?"

"Professional cleaners don't just do one job a week and spend the rest of the time loafing. They do lots of jobs and so can you. Get yourself out to an agency. Since you weren't born with money, lovey, and marrying it clearly didn't work, you'll have to make it yourself. Or you could marry Twifle, I had him wittering away on the phone again this morning. He doesn't seem such a bad guy when you get over the nervousness and he is definitely single. No surprise there. Apparently he wants his money back. Honestly! What a vulgarian. So uncouth!"

Carrie went to White Waltham. When she left Peckham, Roberta, who was having an unscheduled day off, was on the phone to Twifle. He appeared to be telling her his life history, as she could hear her cousin interjecting punchy remarks like; "..well good God! What can you expect if you do something so foolish.." Glad to escape Twifle, Carrie scooted out of the house.

Mitch was at White Waltham. When Carrie arrived she'd just finished teaching a middle aged accountant and was drinking coffee in the Waltham wicker chairs. As Carrie came over the accountant got up to leave. Mitch introduced them and he gave Carrie a speculative look, clearly wondering if she might become a client.

"Am I glad to see you!" said Mitch, watching his well-covered bottom fade out of sight. "Actually he was in the process of trying to sell me a pension fund. Last week it was licence protection insurance, now a pension fund. I don't know why he can't just relax and enjoy the flying. Anyway, enough of that. I am glad to see you. I've been meaning to ring you, actually. Rudy said you came looking for me while I was in Seattle. That was fun! I can tell you. And I learnt a lot actually. When you're flying regularly you take a lot for granted, so it's good to be on a new type and get reminded of how little you really know. Any luck with the plane yet?"

Carrie made a face and swirled her coffee with the spoon. It spilled over into the saucer and made little brown rivers across the grooves of the china. If Kees had been present he would have laughed at the 'foot bath' she had created.

"No. Disaster! I'll never sell it. The engineer at Luton said it was riddled with corrosion. That's it I guess. I'm doomed."

Mitch frowned a little, drawing her eyebrows together thoughtfully. "Have you asked the engineer here to have a look?"

"No.. I thought.." Carrie picked up a napkin and began to angrily blot the coffee foot bath.

"Never take one opinion only," Mitch said. "That guy at Luton flies regularly out to Florida to buy planes for clients. He doesn't want someone like you queering his pitch. I'll get Jo to give it the once over. He's an honest man and, as you've noticed, they are unusual. Rare, as Kieran would say, as rocking horse shit."

"Thanks. You're a problem solver."

"Absolutely. But, you know, you have to have an exchange of thoughts sometimes. It's amazing, actually, how other people can often scotch your worries simply because they are not involved in them."

Carrie wondered if anything could upset Mitch, she always looked untroubled and efficient. Carrie imagined Mitch would meet each obstacle as a challenge to be overcome; clapping her hands with delight at another mountain to scale.

"All right then, solve the rest. Why did my husband buy the plane in the first place? Why did he sell the house? Where's the rest of the money?"

Mitch took a sip of her coffee and returned it to the saucer without spilling a drop. "Are you asking me?"

"I thought you might have some ideas."

"I have, but I'm surprised you don't.. Hey wait a moment." Mitch leant forward and lowered her voice. "Look! See that pilot just going out of the door."

Carrie looked. A middle aged man with short dark hair and jeans was leaving the bar. It crossed Carrie's mind that there was nothing even slightly remarkable about him and she'd be lucky to recognise him a second time.

"See him?" asked Mitch. "I'll bet you think he's just one of those hangers-on normally found loafing around airfields."

Carrie nodded, more interested in her own problems than Mitch's pilot.

"He's Lord Lucan's pilot," said Mitch excitedly, sitting back in her chair in triumph at this mind-blowing revelation.

Carrie smiled gallantly. "Isn't he dead? Lucan I mean, not the pilot."

"Apparently not! Actually, they say that every three months that guy flies out to Sierra Leone to take cigars out to Lord Lucan."

Carrie didn't believe it and was surprised Mitch did; it was a bit too romantic. Wasn't Lord Lucan a bankrupt? Perhaps straightforward women like Mitch accepted things rejected by their more divergent cousins. And Sierra Leone?

"Oh, really," she said. "Anyway, what were your ideas...about Ig I mean."

Disappointed by Carrie's lack of interest, Mitch returned to Ignatius. "Politics! South Africa, or Africa generally for that matter, isn't exactly the place to have property or a business at the moment. He probably thought you'd need money in another country. America was the safest. That's most likely it, don't you think so?"

"No. Ignatius was a risk taker, not a long term planner.. I don't think.."

"Maybe so, but have you noticed the descent of the Rand?"

"Yes, but.." Carrie was looking for a much more complicated, more exciting reason. She tried to drink her coffee but her hand shook and more brown foot baths appeared in the white saucer. "So no drugs? No flights to Cuba? You don't think he was involved in some petty or large criminal schemes. What about the photograph?"

"Cuba?" asked Mitch, looking seriously surprised. "Cuba?"

"Smuggling people."

"Get real! In a Warrior?" Mitch laughed. "But seriously Carrie," she went on, "you need to think about this. When I have a problem I can't solve, I imagine I am building an engine without a manual. I get all the pieces and lay them out in front of me, and slowly I work out what goes where and why."

Carrie said nothing, listening intently.

"So, what are our parts? We have a dead husband who was uninsured; an insurance policy where the wrong person was insured for most; a photograph brought to the UK by Ignatius and an unknown young woman; a dead courier; a house sold and money spent; a plane bought in Florida and a mobile home in North Piri Piri..."

"And the tickets," Carrie broke in, "Ig had arranged for Sissy and me to come to London for a week."

Mitch looked interested. "Tickets too. You hated Sissy right?"

Carrie nodded, "right."

Mitch was thoughtful for a moment then she said rather too directly. "I think we are missing a step. Carrie did you ever have a drugs problem?"

Carrie said nothing, she was over this, it had gone. She wasn't going to let anyone in her new life know. It was over. What was this sudden gratuitous curiosity?

Mitch watched her carefully, even feeling she might understand. Previously Mitch had scorned weakness, not even been able to understand its grasp. But then her affection for Ben, followed by his fall, had opened her mind to the concept of good people doing bad things. And, although she could never quite forgive, there was an element of creeping understanding.

Gently she said, "actually it's relevant Carrie. You know how Ben died?"

Carrie shook her head, realising that she'd never cared enough to find out.

"He ODed, but the police know it wasn't self-induced, because the killer was kind enough to clean up afterwards! It's always the little thing people forget." She didn't laugh, although she was amused, because she thought Carrie might misunderstand.

Slow awakening dawned on Carrie: perhaps Mitch wasn't just judging her. "You think.. you think that that might have been my intended end? That Ignatius and Sissy.. no.. no they couldn't have hated me so much." She shook her head, unconsciously hugging herself, drawing back into her chair. "No, surely not. I was his wife."

"Each man kills the thing he loves," said Mitch, surprising her former student who had imagined Mitch's education had stopped at spanners.

"Maybe," replied Carrie close to tears, "but remember where Oscar was when he said that. I can't quite believe it. I think Ignatius hated me."

Mitch said nothing, but her compassion-learning-curve got steeper. Carrie went on, talking almost to herself now.

"Sissy was going to make sure I met Ben, and struck up a relationship, a friendship.. and then.. oh my God! That is what you think; that they were going to have me OD too. Everyone would say it was just a repeat of my past. They wouldn't believe I hadn't touched drugs since I was 18. He and Sissy would say I had made their lives Hell with my drug taking. What a joke!" she shuddered, horrified.

No one would have doubted her relapse, not with her background. They'd all have believed the squeaky clean Sissy and brother.

"And, of course, no odour of suspicion could fall on Ignatius because he wasn't even in the country. So he would collect the insurance, and .." But Carrie's self-devastation wasn't quite over. "Wait, supposing he isn't dead? Wasn't killed but escaped to America with the lekker wife, won't he come back? I'm still insured."

Mitch frowned. "Forget it. If he is alive he's gone for good; he'd have too much explaining to do to reappear. But I doubt he's alive, it's not easy to hide living people," she said, rather ironically considering her tale about Lord Lucan's pilot, "much easier to hide dead bodies. Besides wouldn't he want to keep the plane, actually?"

"Double bluff? Perhaps he never intended to leave Africa. Maybe all the rest of the money is stashed elsewhere."

Mitch shook her head, this was getting surreal. "Perhaps, but I think you should always look for the simplest solution first, otherwise you may build your engine upside-down!"

"But he knew the Essex Mafia guy," said Carrie. "Perhaps he spirited him.."

"The guy borrowed his mobile home, he hadn't even met him, and the guy told you about it."

"Kieran thought he was getting set up to do a contract on me."

Mitch spat. "Kieran! Do you really believe what Kieran says?"

Carrie thought about it. "So, you don't think there was another wife he bought the plane for? A lekker wife he would kill for!"

"This wife again? Which wife would this be? A Cuban wife? Or the girl on the first class ticket.. that she had a ticket is no indication he was committing bigamy!"

"Maybe," said Carrie, "but.. I mean.. I know it does happen, I read an article in the paper about an airline pilot with two wives only recently."

Mitch had another sip of coffee. "Was that another Kieran suggestion?"

"Well, yes it was.." muttered Carrie feeling a bit wet.

"Manipulator!" Mitch banged her cup down so the coffee jumped into mountains and ripples, threatening the rim with overflow. "That man is a manipulator. He saw your weakness and moved in." In a calmer voice she added. "It is funny how people who use others actually have an uncanny sense for the nerve endings."

"..maybe, but I've been having all sorts of correspondence with the lawyer.."

"What sort of correspondence?"

"A confusing one, to tell the truth. His letters refer to my husband's past.."

"Has he actually mentioned bigamy?"

"Well, no.."

"Or suggested a second wife?"

"Well, no.."

"Then I think it's pretty unlikely. Actually it isn't that easy to run two families. Not unless you're loaded.. Oh! You think that's where the money went?"

"So you don't think he's alive and involved in Ben's death? No fake crash? No.."

Mitch shook her head. She hoped Carrie's imagination wouldn't get in the way of her becoming a good pilot. "If he is alive, how come you got the deeds of the mobile home back?" she asked logically.

"Ah. I hadn't thought of that."

They both drank coffee, embarrassed.

Carrie began to lose herself in memories but Mitch wanted to stick doggedly to the point. Somehow bigamy didn't strike her reasonable soul as the logical outcome of this money loss.

"Actually," she said, "the easiest thing is to ask the lawyer what he meant."

"Good point." Carrie fiddled with her nails, picking dead-skin off one side. She was beginning to feel a bit of an idiot. Mitch was so reasonable. Carrie's imagination was crushed beneath the weight of her good sense. Amazing, thought Carrie, that Mitch, who was so willing to believe that Lord Lucan was alive, could totally discount any idea of a bigamist husband with mafia connections, being involved in the murder of someone he had only met once in a different country. Amazing.

"Humm. OK. Next problem. Now, tell me how to make a fortune out of flying, or indeed any money."

"Absolutely. That would be genius. Actually, they say that the only way to make a small fortune in aviation is to start with a large one."

"It's true," said Carrie sadly. "It's true."

There were noises around them. Bottles clinked; the bar was opening up. Mitch looked around. "Actually Carrie, are you flying or would you like a drink? A real drink I mean, I've finished for the day and I fancy a glass of red wine. You too?"

"You bet," said Carrie. If it hadn't been for Mitch's presence she'd have had several whiskies by now.

Mitch bought Carrie a drink and they settled themselves on the wicker chairs in the bar. She gave Carrie a couple of napkins, having noticed her propensity to spill things.

"What are you going to do now? I mean long term? Even if you sell the plane?" Mitch passed her a peanut.

"I thought I might marry Kieran," Carrie joked. "Create bigamy!"

"Anything else?" Mitch didn't laugh.

Carrie looked at Mitch and knew that this was the moment to ask for a loan, a loan large enough to pay off her debts and start up a business. She faltered.

"Any ideas?" asked Mitch. "You must have some dream or vision? You haven't passed your train-by-date yet."

"Look, Mitch, you won't laugh, will you? John says you mock us normal types."

"Does he indeed! I never laugh at people's dreams. On the contrary I hardly judge people at all. Tell me."

"I thought.. um.. well, I thought I might start an agency like Colin's. There's clearly a need. I could advise people on ferrying planes back from America, find them companies to ship the plane, if they want to do it that way. Or get them pilots if they want the plane to fly. I know I've still got a lot to learn, but at least I've done it once and I have a basis to rely on. What do you think?"

Mitch was silent for a moment. Torn. Carrie's good side was her languages and her travelling, but it was offset by a wacky imagination. Could she make a good pilot? A few months ago Mitch would have let Carrie take her chances like the rest of the world, but the events of the last few weeks had mellowed her. She wanted to help.

"Look Carrie, why don't you train as a commercial pilot. Then you can decide whether you prefer ferrying or airline flying. You weren't a bad student. It isn't hard; you're bright enough. There's far more money in airline flying and, actually, as you know, airlines are short of pilots."

"How could I afford to pay for that? I've got loans and debts coming out of my ears as it is." It's all very well for Mitch, thought Carrie, she's never been on this knife edge of moneylessness.

"I know. But I have a suggestion. I will buy your plane from you. I like the idea of having something small actually and I'll keep it leased out here at White Waltham. If you are prepared to try and become a commercial pilot, I'll help you through the bad times, but only if you are trying to help yourself. There are aviation loan houses but you might do better with me if you want a loan. I'll charge you interest too but far less than the banks, then we both gain. What do you say, deal?"

Carrie laughed. Suddenly it was all so simple. All that wasted effort to sell the plane and Mitch coolly decides to buy it sitting in the bar. She even mentioned the purchase as an aside; an after thought. Oh for such wealth! When she pointed that out to Mitch, the girl said: "Most flying business is done in the bar! That's the place to go when you want a job. Where do you think Kees met me?"

"Well, Hell! But I haven't got enough hours to be a commercial pilot."

"That's not a problem, you can quickly run them up flying the Lear with me, and I'll have a word with my boss about finding you some payment for that. Come to that Carrie, you might look him over as a potential next husband, he's single having just divorced number four, or was it five! And he can't be more than 60 or so! Failing that, you'll get a job more easily with lots of jet hours than you would if you had loads of single engine piston hours like most of the hopeful-airline-pilots in waiting."

"Another problem solved in the bar," Carrie said, "we ought to have a psychotherapist's couch here! OK I'll try it, but on the understanding that if it doesn't work out, you help me start up the ferry business instead. Do we have a deal on that?"

Mitch grinned. She noticed Carrie hadn't spilt a drop of wine.

"Absolutely," said Mitch thoughtfully, "subject to contract, I think we can agree something. Now, as the Lear man's over here in the UK at the moment, you may as well start by meeting him."

Carrie raised her glass. "To a successful venture," she said, suddenly her hopes revived. "Wow! Mitch this could be fun!"

As they climbed into Mitch's Mercedes sport's car Carrie murmured, "Ben?"

"Ben," said Mitch her voice sad, "was a popular instructor. One day he was pushing a plane out of the hangar and he crashed it into the metal door. Unfortunately he had forgotten to get his licence stamped up-to-date and so the insurance refused to pay! Silly Bugger," said Mitch. "He had had a great career ahead of him."

Air-Mail Letters

When Carrie got home late that night there were two letters waiting for her, one was from the lawyer.

> **Barbar, Beard and Barbar,**
> **Lower Kloof Lane,**
> **The Kloof,**
> **Cape Town**
> **South Africa**

Dear Mrs Nordsuitlaan,

Firstly, your husband's body has finally been found, in a poor state of decomposition, quite a distance from the lake where the helicopter went down. It is possible he was thrown out of the machine as it span out of control, or otherwise that he had started walking to get help, and unfortunately met his death from one or several animals.

Secondly, I have traced Ignatius's companion on the trip to Florida. Her name is Rosa and she is a pilot. In a very frank and open discussion she admitted to being Ignatius's lover. However, she claimed she had not seen him since the trip to Florida. I think that there is no reason to suppose she is not telling the complete truth.

Thirdly, as you will have gathered from my previous letters, I have been in deep discussion with the South African Tax Office. They were unhappy about the manner in which your husband had managed to evade tax for so many years. It appears since marrying you and starting his business he has not paid tax. He owed the Revenue Service for five years plus interest. However, after I brought to their attention the fact your husband deceased without any assets in this country, they have decided, given the International nature of the case, and some difficulty in collection, not to press for the sale of the Warrior and the mobile home leading to the repayment of the unpaid back taxes on your husband's account. You are therefore free of any additional expense in that matter.

I, therefore, enclose my bill for your attention.

I remain, as ever, respectfully yours, Kevin Barbar.

"Was that it?" Thought Carrie, "tax evasion!"

All the secrecy, photos, insurance, dead couriers, holes, anything, everything, down simply to tax evasion. No bigamy? No falsification of death? Just tax evasion. Perhaps Roberta was right; governments should butt out, leave citizens alone. Or perhaps Mitch was right: the simple answer is usually the right one.

Carrie didn't look at the bill or dwell on companion Rosa. Her mind touched on the possibility that Ignatius might have purposely crashed the helicopter for his own ends: then put it aside. It didn't really matter now, did it. She looked at the other letter.

Originally from Florida, it had come via the Fluggett Office in Iceland. Written in a round, childish hand, the signature was Hulda Hodottir; an unknown.

> **Far Fields,**
> **1 Hangar Walk,**
> **North Piri Piri Airfield,**
> **Florida**

Dear Mrs Nordsuitlaan, (um, thought Carrie, correct spelling!)
I hope you don't mind me writing to you but I saw the article about your trip in Flugette. When I read about the sad death of your husband and your trip from Florida I recognised the name, and after checking my records, I saw that my suspicions were correct. So I felt I should inform you about what I knew.

This is to say that your husband (now sadly deceased) purchased an airfield hangar lot number 2386 by mail on our airfield in North Florida on 3rd September last year. This is currently sitting empty but we would be very happy to resell it for you, minus our small commission, if you would give instructions.....

Carrie stopped reading and laughed. She felt a pulse of happiness and wondered what else her husband might have bought which would come to light over the next few years: another helicopter, acres of land, horses, cars? Perhaps soon the lawyer would discover he had applied for residency in America. It didn't really matter now. Selling the hangar and mobile home would give her some money. Even if he had intended to make money from her death it was no longer important; he was dead and she was alive and starting on a new career. Whatever the past, the future looked good. She was looking forward to her reinvention.

As she climbed the stairs, wondering if Mitch would pay the lawyer's bill as a gesture of good faith, Carrie heard noises from her cousin's room. Noises that a veteran of three marriages identified as signifying someone not alone. She crept amazedly past. Roberta, with a tongue that could have burnt paint off the Warrior, let alone a man. What kind of tough cookie could be in there with her?

In the morning Carrie went down to breakfast full of curiosity. And nearly had a heart attack. Sitting at breakfast, humming away to himself was Twifle.

"Marco! My goodness."

"Ho," said her cousin, appearing like a spirit from behind the fridge door, a piece of pizza in her hand. "You think you're the only one who can have a man. Not at all. My little Twifle's moving in."

Twifle bleated something and she gave him an affectionate cuff. "That's my boy. He came round to look for you last night and then one thing led to another."

"..awfully good.." muttered Twifle, before making a dash for the door. "See.. er.. see you tonight.. dear-ling.."

Roberta grinned. "He'll be back," she said. "We were great. Now, about my, well Marco's and my, money.."

She was stopped by the phone ringing. For a moment they both stared at it, uncertain who could have dared to interrupt such an important conversation, then Carrie took charge and answered it. "Hello?"

"Carrie?" asked Mitch's voice.

Carrie felt relieved, it was only Mitch checking up on her.

"Oh, hi Mitch, OK?"

"Fine, fine. Look, bit of an oddity here. I've had the old man on the phone. He's had to fly over to the States. He wants to be picked up and brought home Saturday week. Unfortunately the Lear is in for engineering. That leaves the King Air, but I'm back on duty. What do you say? Can you go over to the states and pick him up?"

Carrie's heart leapt more than it had on each proposal of marriage. Was Mitch really asking her to cross the Atlantic, alone? Was she? Could she really do this? No, she couldn't possibly. She was still a beginner; only just had a licence. She wasn't good enough. On the other hand she'd made this crossing before; knew the way and definitely knew the pitfalls. The Warrior was one thing but this was something else. The old man needed to be picked up. He needed her help. She couldn't say no! This would really be a challenge.

"Carrie? Carrie?" asked Mitch, surprised by the silence. "Are you still there?"

"I'm here." Carrie replied. "It's just.. Is it legal? I'm not rated on the King Air."

"That's OK," said Mitch, "you can do it as a private flight. For the rating we've got more than a week. It's only five hours. Come to Biggin, later we'll slip up to the CAA and get your paper rating. I've told the old man about your inexperience and he's happy to chance it if you are.. He does not even mind weather delays. What do you say?"

Carrie's spirits suddenly swelled: in some ways she'd been looking for a challenge like this all her life.

"OK, Mitch," she said, "I'm on! If he's happy to risk me flying his plane across the Atlantic, then I'm definitely happy to risk flying out to fetch him."

"Good girl," said Mitch, "so..can you be at Biggin in two hours? Bring your kit and your passport! Oh, and your driving licence!"

"Yes," said Carrie, "yes I can. Indeed I can." She put the phone down.

Carrie turned to Roberta smiling, her heart beating.

"Well," she said, "it looks like I'll be away for a while. We'll have to talk again when I return."

Suddenly she leant over and kissed her cousin. "But thanks Roberta. Without you and Mitch I'd never have got so far. Not even close. Thanks. Really. You were a star."

Roberta blushed and for a moment a smile flashed over her face. Then she shook her head. "Don't try and sweet talk me! Hell, but some people will do anything to get out of a debt!"

The Wisdom of the Pilot

As she taxied the King Air towards the runway Carrie was conscious of a sense of elation. Of the feeling that all the hard work of the past lay behind her and she was about to embark on a life of adventure. She shuddered, her legs shaking all the way down to the rudder pedals. She heard the flip flop of the controls as her nervous knees jolted over them.

The past few days, learning to fly the considerably more sophisticated King Air, had been very hard and Mitch had not given an inch. She had said, 'actually, if you're going to learn at all, you must learn properly," and pushed her pupil to her limits.

Mitch taught her all about the plane's systems, the hydraulics and mechanics that Carrie had hardly touched on in her first licence and had mostly forgotten since. More, Mitch had played with possible scenarios: 'what would happen if this disaster occurred, how would you get out of it; would you survive?'

She forced Carrie to respond to 'incidents' which might arise from all the possible vagaries of the machine, not only its propellers and engines but what would happen if a tyre burst; if you lost all the hydraulics; if an aileron stuck or if a flap failed to come down; if you hit an eagle in flight. There was hardly any scenario that Mitch and Carrie had not recreated in the last few days.

"And," thought Carrie, "I believed Mitch had no imagination!"

Carrie flew fourteen hours and studied day and night on 'ground school'. By the end it was hard for Carrie to look at a nut without examining its potential for disaster. This kind of intensive learning had taken a toll on Carrie's normally easy going character and after the fourth day she told Mitch to stuff her job and herself.

"I'm not going to do it," Carrie said suddenly, as they were landing after a particularly gruelling session. "Fuck you! This is no life for me. I'm the marrying kind. Leave me alone and stuff your bloody careers."

She jumped off the wing of the plane as they stopped and ran away leaving the door wide open and her unimaginative instructor staring after her in amazement.

Carrie got into her car and drove out out of the oppressive Biggin Hills towards London and freedom. Bars and fun. A few trips around her favourite bars found acquaintances she knew and soon she was drinking for England. With each drink she found a handsomer man and yet each drink made her more sober, less willing to entertain their advances. She tottered and drank more, but stayed solo.

Mitch found her, plastered and hardly able to speak, at 4 o'clock the following morning. How she knew where to find her Carrie never knew, but some instinct drove her to the club where Carrie sat incapable, leaning against the swaying wall. Mitch put the wobbling girl into her car and drove her home. She never spoke of it again.

It was early afternoon before Carrie staggered down to breakfast, her stomach queasy, her head toxic and her energy levels at zero. She felt depressed. She wanted to die, to get free of this tiresome demanding life. What was the point of living anyway? There was nothing for her, only endless days of working for money to keep herself alive. All the men she had loved were dead, even her father. Why bother?

"Hello," said Mitch, looking up from her newspaper as Carrie entered the kitchen, "want a tomato juice."

Carrie looked at her, wondering depressedly why Mitch was still there, still wanting to give her another chance. And still wearing that stupid short sleeved shirt with pearls. She flopped down at the table, her ago-nised heart pumping like an engine at altitude.

"Mitch.."

"Um?"

"I don't think I can fly today."

Mitch gave a laughing snort. "No, no I don't think you should. You look awful!"

"Thanks."

Mitch poured herself some more coffee and turned a page of the paper.

"Mitch?"

"Um?"

"Why do you still care.. I mean.." Shit her head ached. It used to be harder than this; lack of recent boozing had made her fragile, turned her into a techie, unable to take her liquor. "I fucked up, why are you still here?"

"We all make mistakes," said Mitch ponderously, "even me. We all need a safe environment in which to rebel.."

"Oh, yeah." Carrie couldn't believe it, Mitch the grasshopper-armed, ultra-efficient, pearl-wearing superhero, what could she have ever done wrong? "What did you do then? Kill someone?"

Even as she said it, she shuddered. Did Mitch kill Ben? But Mitch was smiling: Carrie's thought patterns not even crossing her innocent mind.

"Hardly!"

"What then? I don't believe you've ever done anything worse than..than a.. a.. speeding ticket?"

"It depends on the ticket. I slept with Kieran actually," said Mitch, in the same voice she used for describing principles of flight.

"What! Jesus Christ! Why? When?"

"In Iceland."

"Jesus Christ!" said Carrie her voice full of excited amusement, "wow! That is bad. Blimey it makes me look like a pathetic saint. Well, well and

Bloody Hell, who'd have thought it! In Iceland..."

There was a strangely triumphant look on Mitch's face; the good girl who has just qualified for the devil's gang. "I know. I realise it was adultery but I'd never slept with anyone except my husband, and Kieran was clearly available but wouldn't stay around. It was a sort of experiment, actually. I guess I used him, but then.. well, wasn't that apt! The adultery I justified on the grounds that Kieran had misbehaved elsewhere and with me it was only a one night stand, so no threat to his wife's future."

"Wow!" Thought Carrie, "how rational! Mitch and I think in very different ways!" She started to feel substantially better as all the implications percolated through her numb brain. "Well well well!" She giggled a bit.

Mitch ignored her and concentrated on the obituaries. Then she stopped and looked up at Carrie with unwanted insight.

"I guess your last husband wasn't much fun, actually?"

Carrie squashed her nose, looking thoughtful. "No! You're wrong. Sometimes it was as much fun as living with a leaking valve. He kissed with angry lips, as we say in Holland. But other times were great, lively sparky. I certainly didn't think he felt murderous.. all my marriages had been a combination of good and bad.. it's just the bad got out of hand. Perhaps all marriages are like that; about as relaxing as an Australian bush fire."

Mitch sighed. Wished she'd stayed with the superficial and put her hand on the girl's shoulder. "I'm sorry. My marriage was much more straightforward, but he died." She dropped her eyes to the paper, began reading.

"Mitch."

"Yes?" This time Carrie thought Mitch sounded testy, perhaps wishing all these secrets had been kept as just that. "What?"

"Have we still got time.. I mean can I still have.. I mean..! Oh shit! Have I blown it?"

Mitch didn't allow the relief she felt to make it to her face. She'd always believed that Carrie was made of tougher stuff than the paper bag drifter her father saw; it seemed she was right. Instead she smiled, looking up at her protegee. "No! Forget it. We've time. When you recover we'll do a practice session, a couple more single engine go-arounds, a couple of emergencies and then .. the test."

"The test! Pants." Carrie rested her head on her hands. Finally, when she was completely distraught and feeling she could hardly fly at all, let alone take a comparatively sophisticated plane across the Atlantic, Mitch announced that she had put her in for a test. What a joker that girl was. A test. Carrie stood up and went back to bed. Still, knowing Mitch had slept with Kieran made up for most things.

The next afternoon Carrie flew through her test, remarking afterwards that the examiner was a breeze compared with Mitch. "He was kind," she said. "A gentleman!"

"Maybe so," replied Mitch, unapologetic for her harsh training, "but actually he's still wondering if he'd let you fly with his daughters whereas I know you are ready to fly my father!"

"Oh," said Carrie, wondering if Mitch had a father.

But now all that was over. The training was done, and she had waved Mitch goodbye yesterday morning.

Last night had been a turning point for Carrie. She'd passed the test and she was ready, but the solo flight across the Atlantic still stood out there as an awful, beckoning nightmare or adventure; she wasn't sure which. She fell asleep thinking she might decide to chicken out after all. She could tell Mitch there was something wrong with the plane, or she could go and disappear again, this time not to return. But then she dreamt. And in her dreams she was flying, not in a King Air, not in a Warrior, not in a plane at all. She was flying alone. Without wings. She could fly. She jumped. She soared into the air, she looped, she floated, she achieved. Suddenly she knew that this was right. That this was not just a flight alone across the Atlantic, leading to a job in flying: this was her life, her chance of freedom from the chardonnay and cappuccino castle she had built around herself. The hope that she could use flying to help her look outside herself, instead of always inwards. And she was ready for it.

Only a circle, thought Carrie, changes her into hero. Ferry pilots constantly fly all around the world. So far she'd only touched the circle, but in time she could go on and complete the full circumnavigation of the globe; for money. The full heroic, and paid, circle.

Since then Carrie had flown the comparatively easy legs up north from Biggin Hill. Now she was taxying out towards the Prestwick runway alone, with the Atlantic beckoning ahead. Her stomach heaved with a mixture of excitement and fear; this was it. Her solo debut across the pond.

Carrie laughed as the taxyway passed beneath her wheels. Here she was on the edge of her big life change.

She lined up on the runway and checked her instruments. Looked at the empty seat beside her and marvelled. She really was alone. No Kieran; no Mitch; no boss. She breathed deeply. This was it; no one but herself to blame. She checked her instruments again. Working fine. Then gently she pushed forward the throttles, watching the gauges.

The engines gave a little purr as they crept from basic life at idle into ready-to-fly mode. Then slowly the machine started to rumble forward. The King Air trundled down the long, tarmac mile towards lift off. Carrie stiffened as the end of the runway grew closer; as the control wheel in her hands ceased bumping and became lighter. She felt joy as gently, very gently, the little craft nudged off the runway and into the diaphanous air.

She let the King Air climb at its own speed for a while before bringing up the wheels, remembering all that extra fuel on board and that she should not overload the engine. She found herself sighing involuntarily. This was OK. More than OK: Kieran would have been jealous of that neat take-off. Good omen.

She climbed straight ahead up to a thousand feet and adjusted her direction, wound her instrument needles a little, then looked out through the window. She was planning to fly due north for a few miles, before veering north-west towards the west coast and beyond that the edge of the Atlantic.

"Goodbye Prestwick," she said into the radio, "King Air 997, changing frequency to Shannon en-route...see you on our return."

"Goodbye Carrie," said the controller, "have a nice trip! See you in the bar in a couple of weeks."

She smiled again and bleeped the transmit button a couple of times before changing frequency. She couldn't help a shudder of pride as she watching the nearing seascape ahead. This, it seemed, she had been waiting for all her life, this adventure alone into the partially known and mainly uncertain.

As she crossed the coast and headed out to sea she watched the land disappearing behind her, and knew that around her was nothing but water, sea, sea and more water: engulfing oceans, volatile seas, and unreliable weather. Ahead there was only Iceland, Greenland, America and adventure. Carrie smiled. Bless my husbands, she said aloud, none of them would ever have thought that this would happen to me, especially not the last one, the instigator: not in his wildest dreams.

The King Air flew on into the morning haze.

Glossary

ADF: Automatic Direction Finder. A plane based radio receptor which can pick up ground signals from NDBs (non directional beacon) including, in the past, Radio Caroline. Problems include distortion at night and coastal effect.

Ailerons: movable surfaces on the trailing edge (back) of the wings at the outer edge, which turn the plane left and right.

ATA: Actual Time of Arrival. (Late in Kieran's world).

Carburettor heat: by pulling a lever, heat from the engine is allowed to enter the carburettor and melt any ice which may have formed. Sometimes giving a graunching noise and rpm drop.

Circuit: a way of practising taking off and landing at at airfield, which involves following an approved pattern around the field.
(See also Pattern).

Collective: helicopter lever for increasing pitch and giving lift.

Cyclic: helicopter stick in front of the pilot used for directional control and for changes in attitude.

DME: Distance Measuring Equipment, usually calibrated in nautical miles. Pilots sometimes talk about eg 3 DME instead of 3 miles.

ETA: Estimated Time of Arrival.

Finals: on the approach to land.

Flaps: next to the ailerons on the wing. The flaps drop down to increase lift (one stage only) and drag. Used for landing and taking off.

GPS: Global Positioning System: a navigational aid using satellites. The Warrior's GPS included a moving map.

Go-around: don't land but return to the circuit.

IFR: Instrument Flight Rules. Flight regulated by ATC, radar, airways and flight plans.

IMC: Instrument Meteorological Conditions; i.e. cloud.

Katabatic: downflow of winds from the mountains.

Mela: Italian for apple. Used as a swear-phrase by Carrie to Kieran 'Not Milou merda but mela' literally means not dog shit but apple, but for Carrie is simply a way of using her languages to get one-up over Kieran.

Metars: weather forecast.

Pattern: US for Circuit (see above).

Pitot: a tube measuring dynamic pressure, which when contrasted with the static source within the instrument gives air speed on the indicator. If it gets blocked the airspeed does not register on the dial.

QDM: Q code Direction Magnetic. Shows an air traffic controller monitoring the equipment which direction the pilot is calling from, and the pilot the direction he should steer to get to the airport. The opposite is **QDR,** which shows the reciprocal direction.

QFE: Q code Field Elevation: the pressure setting that when set on your altimeter will give you the height above the airfield.

QNH: Q code Nautical Height: the pressure setting that when set on your altimeter will give you the height above sea-level.

RPM: Revolutions Per Minute e.g. of the engine or of the rotor blades in a helicopter.

RVR: Runway Visual Range ie how far you can see into the fog.

Robot: South African for traffic lights.

Step: the take-off run for a seaplane.

TBO: Terminal Base Operator, i.e. somewhere you can park your private plane and get fuel and customs clearances and general TLC.

TLC: Tender Loving Care.

VFR: Visual Flight Rules i.e. regulations that stipulate what is VMC.

VMC: Visual Meteorological Conditions i.e. good weather.

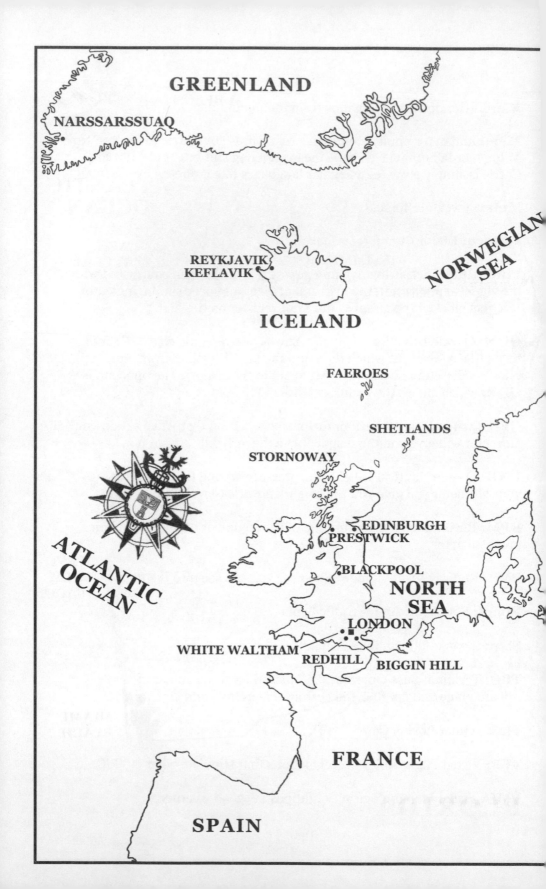

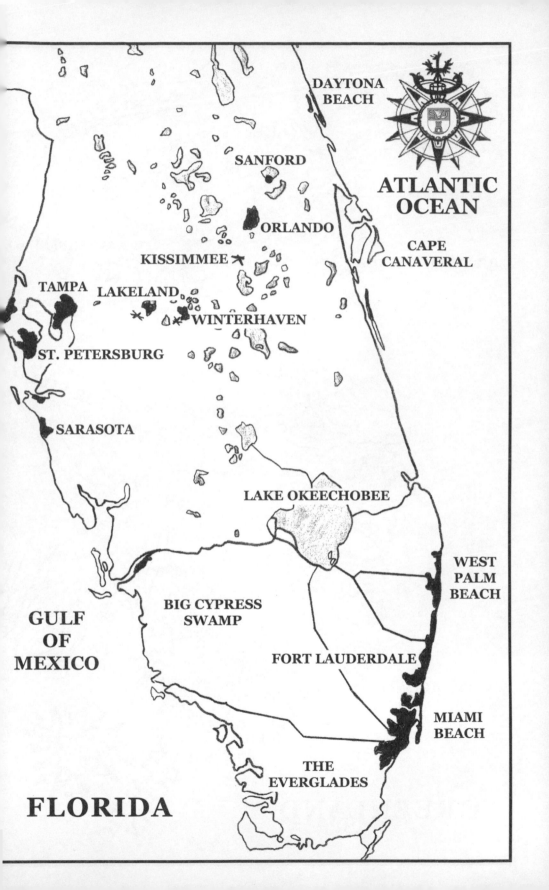

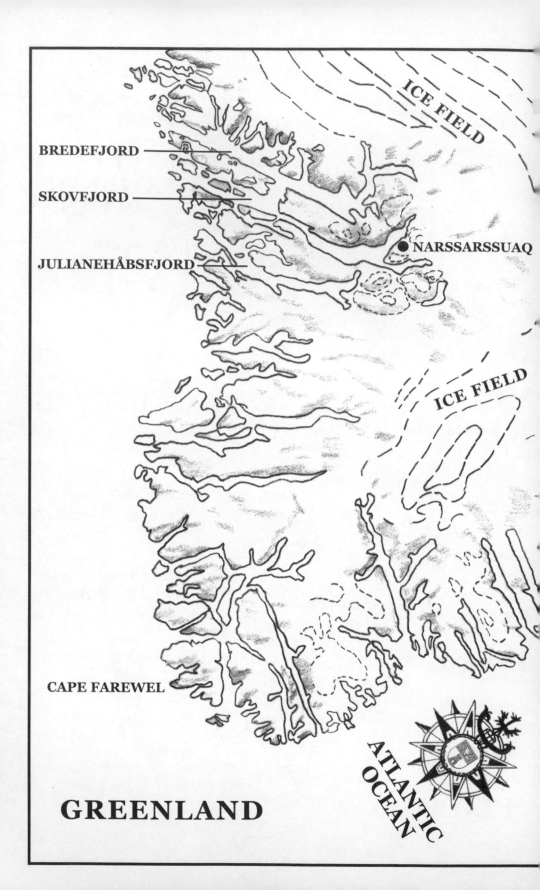